PRAISE FOR

Unlikely Heroes: Searching for Home in America

In this novel, the character is struggling with the fact that he is a man and not a slave. This story follows the mental, physical, and emotional turmoil, heartbreak, and tragedy, of a man and his family trapped in a system that says they are less than human, yet it focuses on the determination, perseverance, and the morals that each person held within them to obtain their goals, to find their place in this society.

The novel tells the story of a people's struggle from slave to free persons. It shows early on the value of education, no matter the length of time it takes to get it.

The author is descriptive of the times, places, and attitudes of the period.

The novel will cause the reader to look through a "different pair of glasses" before he/she dares judge the next person.

This novel was exciting and suspenseful.

Richard Wilder
President
Buffalo Soldiers Florida, Inc.
August 9, 2023

BY CHARLES B. WARREN

FOR ADULTS

From Slavery to Community Builder:
The Story of Lawrence B. Brown: nonfiction

Unlikely Heroes: Searching for Home in America: a novel

FOR MIDDLE GRADE

Address Unknown: a novel

UNLIKELY HEROES

SEARCHING FOR HOME IN AMERICA

UNLIKELY HEROES

SEARCHING FOR HOME
IN AMERICA

A novel

CHARLES B. WARREN

BEACH HOUSE PRESS
FLORIDA

Grateful acknowledgement is given for permission to reprint quotes from *Voices from Slavery: 100 Authentic Slave Narratives*. Editor Norman R. Yetman, Dover Publications, 1999, Mineola, New York

Library of Congress Control Number: 2024901712

ISBN: 979-8-218-36441-0 (Paperback Edition)
ISBN: 979-8-218-42906-5 (Ebook Edition)

Printed in the United States of America
www.charleswarrentheauthor.com
First Edition

Book Design by Stephanee Killen of Integrative Ink

Cover photo courtesy Library of Congress, Prints and Photographs Division, LC-DIG-cwpb-01005.
Cumberland Landing, VA. Group of "contrabands" at Foller's House

For

My wife, Bernie

Always Supportive

Always Encouraging

AND

Janet Durden,
Friend Extraordinaire
Giving countless hours
Of talent and skill

Even in our sleep, pain that does not forget
falls drop by drop upon the heart,
and in our despair, against our will,
comes wisdom to us by the awful grace of God.

Aeschylus

Slaves have been stripped naked and lashed, often to death. Dey would be left strapped after from twenty-five to fifty lashes every two or three hours to stand dere all night. De next day, de overseer would be back with a heavy paddle full of holes dat had been dipped in boiling water and beat until de whole body was full of blisters. Den he'd take a cat-and-nine-tails dipped in hot salt water to draw out de bruised blood and would open every one of dem blisters with dat. If de slave did not die from dat torture, he would be unfastened from de whipping post, and made to go to de field just as he was. Oftentimes he would die shortly after. Dey did de women de same.

—Henry Johnson, age 90+ (*Voices from Slavery*, p. 182)

Prologue

South Carolina, 1841

She was on a dead run, splashing swamp water as branches whipped and scratched her face and arms. Her left hand gripped her boy's hand. He struggled to keep up. His fear pushed him, fear of the vicious dogs and the angry white men.

He tried not to glance back but couldn't help himself. The snarling dogs, the blazing torches, and the enraged men were closing in.

His momma breathed hard and fast, refusing to give up, determination chiseled into her face.

Suddenly, hooting men carrying torches astride snorting beasts broke through the swamp in front of them, cutting off their escape.

One of the men shouted, "We got 'em, Mr. Delaney. We got 'em."

The woman grabbed her boy and clung to him. She whispered frantically in his ear, "Freedom, William. Gots to have freedom to live." She held his face to look into his eyes. "Hear me, boy!"

"Yes, Momma."

She held him tight, felt his heart pounding in his chest.

Then, quick as a bird, she said in hushed tones, "This way." She pulled her boy to the right, and they went into the deep swamp. Here the earth was soft. Her feet sank in oozy mud, slowing her.

But the narrow hooves of the horses sank deeply into the muck and could go no farther. The horses struggled and shrieked in panic.

"Dismount and get 'em," shouted one of the men.

"Forget it," ordered the man in charge. "We need to get our horses out of this muck before they break a leg. That's the deep swamp, full of gators, an' snakes. There's pluff mud all over the place. That stuff will suck you down so fast there ain't nuthin' you can do. Those two'll never come out alive."

The men and dogs chasing them from the rear caught up.

"Where's my slaves? I thought you said you had 'em."

"We did, Mr. Delaney, but she took off into the deep swamp. Ain't no way the horses could go in there."

"Okay, let's spread out along here and watch for her to come out. She's not going to escape through the swamp. They'll die in there."

"I got a better idea, Mr. Delaney. See that big Cypress over there? A man could easily hide behind it...

Kaziah stopped and looked back. No one chased them. She made out the torches, now far back and not getting closer. The men were quiet, though the dogs yapped and whined.

"Oh." Kaziah moaned, clutching her chest, grimacing in pain.

"You okay, Momma?"

She forced a smile. "I be good. All that running got me tired out. I be jus' fine."

She went to move forward when she spotted a pair of menacing eyes. She pulled William close and whispered, "Don' move. Keep quiet."

William wanted to run. He had seen dogs attack a man. That man had screamed, kicking and punching helplessly at the relentless dog. William would never forget the bloody scene. But he trusted his mother and remembered her stories of overcoming fear. Though he trembled, he remained still.

Kaziah kept watch on the eyes. She thought it was a wolf or a coyote. In the darkness, she could only see its grim silhouette and hear its guttural growl. Her muscles ached. Insects swarmed and bit her and William, buzzed in their eyes and ears, crawled over them, tormented them. But they did not move. The animal blinked, turned, and moved on.

Kaziah breathed deeply, relieved that one danger had passed. Her attention returned to the men. They seemed to be leaving. *Perhaps they ain't willing to pursue into the deep swamp. Too many dangers. It could be a trap. We'll see. We not going back out there until I be sure they gone.*

"What we gonna do, Momma?" whispered William.

"I think it best we waits here a while, see what them mens do."

She studied the area where the men were but didn't see any torch lights or other sign the men were still there. She couldn't be sure with only the sliver of a moon for light.

"Best we waits here 'til day. Then we see if those white devils gone. If they not gone, we go deeper into swamp an' try find a way out."

"Can't we jus' go into the swamp now an' get away from those men an' their dogs?"

"Not at night. Wild animals might attack us. An' we can't see the mud that sucks you down. Bes' we stays here for now so long as them mens don' come after us."

William clung to his mother. It was just yesterday when everything happened. The massa told Kaziah she had been sold to a man down in Georgia, but her son was staying. Kaziah begged him to let her take William with her, but he refused. Her new massa was coming first thing in the morning. That night, Kaziah took William and fled.

"Lissen, William. We meant to be free, like when I was in my land. Don' forget the stories. Be careful, but don' give up on freedom."

"Okay, Momma. I won't. But…but we still gonna be together, ain't we, Momma? You still gonna tell me stories, and…"

"William, don't know how this might go. You knows I loves you more than my own life. I wants you to have freedom, to know how it feel to be a free man."

"Some day I will, Momma. I promise."

"Good. That's good. Now I'm gonna rest leaning on that tupelo there. And I'm gonna hold you tight. We'll spend the night here. Then, when day come, we decide."

Morning light came to the swamp, and in a few minutes the sun peeked over the trees. Kaziah and William stretched their cramping muscles; the cool, damp air sent a chill through them. Their feet had lost feeling after being in the dank swamp water all night.

William looked towards where they'd entered the deep swamp. No sign of Delaney and his men. He looked up at his mother. Her eyes were closed.

"Momma? You okay?"

She nodded but didn't open her eyes. "Jus' needs to rest a bit more. Let's wait a bit longer, William. Then we decide."

An hour passed with no sign of the men.

"Now, Momma, should we go now?"

"You gonna have to hep me. Somethin' bad wrong. Can't move good." She put her arm over William's shoulder, and they moved out slowly.

Halfway to the edge of the deep swamp, Kaziah collapsed.

"Momma," shouted William.

"Shhhh." She put her hand to his mouth.

But it was too late. One of Delaney's men peeked out from behind a Cypress and, seeing Kaziah on the ground with William tending to her, rushed to them. He pointed his rifle at William. "Get away from her."

William looked up at the man. "Something's wrong with my momma."

The man kicked William in the chest, sending him sprawling on the ground. "Do like I say." Then he fired his rifle into the air.

Delaney and his men rode in quickly. They left their horses on more solid ground and rushed to where William and his mother lay.

Delaney said, "Well, Kaziah, looks like you led us on quite a chase, but we got you and your kid now. Get up, you damn nigger."

When she didn't move, the man with the rifle said, "I think she might be dead."

William crawled to his mother and shook her gently. "Momma, wake up."

Kaziah turned her head to face William. She patted William's hand and then closed her eyes again.

"Damn you, Kaziah. You ain't gonna leave this world until I'm done with you. Carl, bring that buckboard around and put her in. We'll get her back and show 'em all what we do to runaways."

Later, at Delaney's Plantation

"Pull the buckboard over to the quarters and stake her to the ground. When we get through with her, ain't nobody ever want to run from here."

"Looks like we got a problem here, Mr. Delaney."

Delaney cursed his bad luck. But in the end, he decided her death would serve as a lesson.

"Get a couple of men and bury her."

"What happens with the kid, Mr. Delaney?"

"Have to sell him. His damn mother put running in his head. Can't keep no angry kid that's already run. Nothin' but trouble. He's gone, first chance I get."

The evening of the day Kaziah was buried, William went to his mother's grave. She was buried in a parcel of land set aside for the enslaved. The graves were not marked and were overgrown with weeds—all except for Kaziah's, which was covered in freshly dug soil.

A memory came to William: Some time ago, a group of men came to her for advice. The massa did not give those with large families enough food. They came asking her opinion on what they should do. His mother told them to speak with the massa and convince him that it would help him to give them more food. He would have stronger people to work, and they would get more done. But the men were afraid to approach the massa. Kaziah stood and said she would do it.

She was a shrewd and persuasive negotiator. She convinced Delaney to let the families have their own gardens and some small animals. William felt great pride in his mother.

William sat very still next to her grave. This mound of dirt was all he had left of her. He wondered what would happen to him without her. William remembered going past cemeteries where white people were buried. Their graves had white stones on them and were well cared for. William gathered stones and arranged them on her grave in a circle with one stone in the center.

He knelt beside her grave and spoke to her. "I'm never going to forget your stories. Someday, I'm gonna be free like you was before. I'm gonna make you proud of me." He stayed a bit longer before walking back.

Two months later, a slave auction was held in the town of Hopewell located in Williamsburg County, several counties to the east. William was put on the auction block and sold to Nathan Ramsey.

Ramsey had a small farm with five enslaved workers. He had twelve-year-old William live with a woman, Gina, and her eight-year-old son, Lucas, in their one-room shack. Life was more settled here, though the trauma of losing his mother so suddenly left him resentful for years. Gina's kindness and comfort helped William to become less bitter over time, but his hostility towards white men festered like a raw wound.

William did not forget his mother. He treasured her stories of life in Africa and never lost sight of her love of freedom. He told and retold her stories to himself. He heard her voice in his head and, in her voice, the love she had for her homeland.

One day he decided he should tell his mother's stories to others. It seemed like a good way to keep her memory alive. And so, on a hot Sunday afternoon when Gina and Lucas were resting in the shade, he said, "I could tell you a story if you want."

Gina perked up and smiled. "Sure, William. What story you gonna tell us?"

Lucas sat up. "I wanna hear a story."

William's favorite story was how his mother overcame fear. But on this day, he decided to tell a different story.

"I can still hear my momma's voice like she be tellin' this story."

I was the second girl in my family. My mother have five girls an' not one boy. My father not happy 'bout that 'cause he not have boy children he can brag on when they go huntin' or win a race. Girls not do those things.

My father love us, but I know he disappointed.

One day I out playing with other children an' we gets a little too far from our village. One of the childrens shout we gots to go back, so everyone run back to village. But I hears someone crying. So, I look for who crying an' find a small child, younger than me who is lost. She from other village.

That village close to us, but we not good friends. Sometimes fightin' happen with the two villages. But what I gonna do? Little girl lost. Can't jus' leave her there.

So, I takes her hand an' walks back to her village. It long walk and getting dark when I gets there. People run up to her an' hugs her. Her momma and papa happy to see her. They worried.

The girl's momma and papa thank me and others in the village thank me. I begins to go back to my village when the chief say for me to wait. He say it too dark for me to go alone. He tell two of his mens to take me back.

When we gets back, my momma and papa run to me and hug me. They thank the mens for bringing me home.

This start our village to talk about making friends with that other village because they see that they got good people.

Next day, some mens from both villages have long talk. After many long talks, the villages decide to have peace and work together.

My papa proud of me. He say I bring peace to villages when no one else can.

"My momma said from this, she learn to always do what is right.

Gina and Lucas clapped and thanked William. William was encouraged by their response to the story. Telling his mother's stories made him feel that she was still with him, so he decided to continue telling them every chance he had.

South Carolina, 1844

Three years later, Ramsey fell on hard times and decided to sell the workers he had purchased over the years. He took them to a slave auction in Darlington County, north of where he lived.

William stood with the others waiting their turn to be led to the platform. He looked out at the white faces in the small crowd. On the platform stood a young girl about his age. He saw the men point to her and make disgusting remarks.

I knows what those men be thinking. They just see her as a way to satisfy they wants. They jus' wants to use her. His breathing became heavy and deep, his hands fists, his eyes narrow and glaring. *They think they own us. That they can buy and sell us like we not human, like we they animal. I'll show them. I'll get—*

William was jerked forward, his thoughts interrupted, as the burly man yanked the chain attached to William's iron collar. "Let's go. Your time."

Standing on the platform, William looked down on the men. He wanted to spit in their faces. He'd jump into the crowd and pummel them until his fists were sore from breaking their bones and spilling their blood. Instead, he stood enraged while men vied to buy him. *Why can't they see*, he wondered, *that I am a person?*

The auctioneer began. "What's the bid for this strong specimen? He's a good worker." He spun William around. "Look at his back— no lash marks. He'll work hard for you. A good buy. Do I hear two hundred?"

Someone shouted two hundred dollars.

The bid worked up to eight hundred.

"Do I hear nine hundred?"

The crowd looked around to see who might go higher. No one.

"Eight hundred going once…"

William sold for eight hundred dollars.

"What is your name, sir?"

"Higgins, John Higgins."

John Higgins, from Florence County, farther to the east, took William home. A few years later, he matched William up with Harriet, and so began William's life as a husband and later, a father.

CHAPTER 1

John Higgins

South Carolina, 1859

John bolted upright, gasping for breath. His eyes darted around the still, dark room searching for anything familiar. He shook his head to wake his cloudy brain. *Another dream? Damn!* He pushed his hand through his thinning hair. *Underwater. Couldn't breathe. Eyes bulging like they were coming out of my head. Arms flailing. That nigger woman laughing, nodding her head like she knew something, wanting me dead. And something else…*

He squeezed his eyes shut to force out the grim image, but the horror stayed, hooked into his mind, needle-sharp visions dug into soft brain tissue, clinging, refusing to release him.

He turned and rested his hand on Martha's hip, hoping the familiar intimacy of touching her would dissolve the fear. But his demon stayed. Leaves, shimmering in the moonlight, caught his eye, the old imposing oak standing guard outside his window. He caught the outline of his dresser, and in the worn, red chair, his weathered hat. He knew these things to be real, though barely perceptible in the darkness. He wondered then about his dream, barely perceived in the darkness of his mind…how real could it be? The nocturnal air ruffled his damp nightshirt, sending a sobering chill through him.

Got to shake this.

The dreams came more often recently. Always the same two characters—a young slave woman and some unseen evil, hidden from view but deeply disturbing nonetheless.

Is this some kind of punishment? If so, for what?

John swung his legs onto the floor—the cold wood solid beneath his feet. *This is real.*

Fully awake now, he stood at the front door, mulling over his visions, scrutinizing the night. Nearby stood the old barn his daddy had built and beyond, the slaves' shacks.

He ambled to the kitchen where he reached up high on the top shelf and felt around for his whiskey. Bottle in hand, he eased out the front door onto the porch. His first swallow of the clear liquid burned his throat and sat like a hot poker in his belly, but brought no succor. Near the barn, eerie unseen scuffles caught his attention. High-pitched screeches of a night-animal, overpowered by a predator, pulled the nightmare back into his mind. The hunted and the hunter. His eyes widened, his breathing rapid, fear pulled at him to retreat into his house.

Those screams. Her staring at me through the dark, her eyes so piercing. Like she was hunting me, coming for me.

John pushed on his temples, hoping to squeeze the disturbing thoughts from his head. The tension, as always, lodged in his neck, tightened his muscles and gave him an intense headache. He reached back, massaging his neck. He knocked back another swig, this one a bit longer. The whiskey caused him to cough lightly as the liquid assailed his body. He turned his ear toward the open door listening for any sign he had awakened Martha or the children. The house remained quiet.

A memory stirred. He walked to the far side of the porch. Inside the nearest slave quarters, forty yards from the house, slept a young African slave with her family. A pleasurable urge arose in John that pushed away his grim reflections.

He had taken Dee before; the memory emboldened him. It happened a few months ago when she helped clear palmettos. She bent over in front of him; her thin dress clung to her curves, revealing the details of her young body. He remembered wanting her right then. And why not? She belonged to him.

"Dee, leave that and come with me. I got a special job for you," he had said. She followed him for a good way, and he had her right there in broad daylight. After, he gave her his handkerchief to clean herself, wipe off the blood. She had cried. He treated her kindly, he thought, by giving her a few minutes to calm herself before going back to work.

He raised the bottle and guzzled more whiskey. The damp air forgotten, the demons replaced, his mind focused only on the young girl. Cool night air filled his lungs, and the anticipation of pleasure flooded his body, easing his pain.

He set the bottle on the railing and went inside, picked up his rifle, checked to see it was loaded, pulled on his pants, and slipped out. Danger teased his resolve. But the whiskey had done its work by dulling his anxiety, and the rifle helped to manage it. At five foot nine, John measured shorter than all his adult male slaves—his slim body not as muscular as theirs. Despite the slaves' physical advantage, John kept a tight rein—they must have no doubt who is in charge. Never give them reason to think otherwise. Never let them see your fear. Never.

Pushing the door to the shanty open, he demanded in a hushed tone, "Dee, get out here."

Aroused from their sleep, the family sat staring at John. They noticed his rifle and smelled the whiskey. Silas and Katie looked at Dee at the same time and then back at their massa.

"What you want with my Dee, Massa? Why don't you jus' go back home an' be with your wife. Dee jus' a young—"

"Shut up." He pointed his rifle at Silas. "I'm the only one giving orders here." He glared at Dee, who had scooted over to her ma, clinging to her and her ma clinging back.

"You best come now, Dee, or your family going to suffer for it."

"Please, Massa John, don't take our Dee. She just a young'un." Her mother embraced her hard.

John eased his rifle over to point at her younger brother, Freddie. "Come on now, Dee, or something bad's gonna happen."

Freddie glanced at his sister, then back at the barrel of the rifle.

Dee pulled from her mother and stood. Dee, a young woman at fifteen, standing in her thin night shirt, aroused John—her bare legs inviting him to have her. Defeated, she walked out with John. Her mother cried, "Not my baby, she just a baby."

In the next room, William and his family, awakened by the turmoil, sat quietly on their sand floor listening. In the doorway, a hanging cloth separated the two families. When William made to get up, Harriet's strong hand grabbed his wrist.

"Don't go in there," she whispered.

"Ain't goin' inside. Jus' goin' to see what's happenin'," he whispered back.

"You heard the massa. He in a bad way. Don't go in there an' get shot."

"Jus' gonna peek through the cloth is all," he said, pulling away.

Their children, Hector and Margaret, awakened from their sleep by the ruckus, watched and listened. Margaret scooted over to snuggle against her mother.

William saw that the massa had gone and taken Dee with him. Katie cried softly. Their two small children held her tight. Silas beat his hand against the log wall, cursing in low, harsh tones. Freddie, their oldest boy, dazed, watched his father's bloody hand smack against the wall.

William entered the room followed by Harriet. He hurried to Silas and grabbed his arm. "Ain't gonna help Dee none for you to bust your hand."

Harriet embraced Katie. "I'm sorry."

William whispered in Silas' ear, "Someday, I gonna kill that massa." At times, he had a mind to. Standing a head taller than John, it wouldn't be hard. What if John came for Margaret or Harriet? Rifle or no rifle, William knew he would charge him and strangle the life out of him. There was danger in that, though. What then? White men would hunt him down and torture him to his death. What would happen to his family if he were gone?

"He no good," said Silas. "What kinda man take a young girl like my Dee?"

"He don't deserve to live," said William.

Harriet rushed to William, slapping her hand over his mouth. "Don't talk like that. If someone hears you, you be hanging from a tree. Then what good is all your talkin'?" She hugged him tightly. William wrapped his arms around her and said no more. But an emptiness gnawed inside him, for what good is a man if he can't protect those he loves.

John pushed the barn door open just enough for the two to slip through. Dee stopped at the entrance, head down, muttering softly, her arms crossed in front, clutching herself. John put his hand on the small of her back and shoved her inside to the stench of hay and horses and leather.

He slipped off her shabby night dress, ran his hands over her soft breasts. He grabbed a horse blanket and tossed it at her. She whimpered when the coarseness of it hit against her bare skin but made no effort to catch it.

"Spread that out and lay yourself down."

Dee stood shivering, trying to cover herself with her hands, but made no move to spread the blanket. John tightened his jaw and raised his rifle as though to hit her with the stock. Dee knew not to challenge him. She kneeled and, taking one corner of the blanket, stretched it out in slow motion, wanting to delay forever the massa's imminent assault. *If I had a knife, I would kill him,* she thought, *no matter what they would do to me after.* But as she lay down, she knew he owned her body and could do as he pleased with her. She wanted to hurt him, to make him feel pain so great he would die.

But he had all the power. He could hurt her worse than she could ever hurt him. And what about her family?

John set his rifle against a post and grabbed her ankles to spread her legs apart. He lowered his trousers and lay on top of her.

Dee covered her face with her hands. "Please don't, please don't."

"Stop your goddamn fussin'."

She let out a scream as he forced himself into her. As he moved, he panted, digging his fingers into her breasts.

Dee squeezed her eyes shut trying with all her strength to believe this was not happening—but his whiskey breath, his rough skin, his crushing weight, his sounds, all kept her shackled to this cursed moment.

He grunted low guttural sounds and was done. He rolled off her.

"You'll get used to it. Hell, you might even learn to like it."

She sat, willing herself not to cry, not to show weakness despite the throbbing pain between her legs. She noticed his rifle leaning against a post and wondered if she could reach it before he could stop her.

"Go on. Get the hell out of here with your damn sniffling."

She snatched up her dress, slipped it on, and ran out. She went to the pump and tried to wash him off her, his smell and feel, all of him. Then she crumbled to the ground sobbing and wishing he had killed her.

His desire satiated, the nightmare was all but forgotten.

John put his bottle back in the kitchen. He eased into bed, slid next to Martha, and placed his arm around her waist. Her body, rising and falling in a quiet rhythm, filled him with comfort even as he still felt the softness of the young black woman's naked body against him. It was good to have someone like Martha, someone you could depend on. Even so, he lay for a long time waiting for sleep, the woman and the evil lingering…

CHAPTER 2
William

The Daily Chronicle

October 1859

Abolitionist John Brown captured a federal arsenal in Virginia with the intention of starting a slave uprising. President Buchanan sent a contingent of Marines under the direction of Colonel Robert E. Lee to retake the arsenal. The Marines killed ten of his followers and forced Brown to surrender.

Slave is a throwaway. That's all. And I ain't no throwaway. William lay awake next to Harriet, thinking, planning, worrying. *The massa could come for Margaret in a year or so. Even Harriet. What would I do then? Kill him? Then get hung for killing a white man.*

He rolled off his mat and sat with his back to a wall staring into the blackness of their shanty. Harriet sensed he was not next to her. She found him in the dark and sat close, putting her head on his chest. "You okay?"

"I jus' be thinking. You go on back to sleep. I'll come soon."

"What you be thinkin' about?"

He rested his head back on the wall and closed his eyes. "Thinkin' 'bout my momma. She was right, you know. These white mens thinks they owns us, but they don't. Not really. Sure, they make us work for them, they tell us what we got to do, they even kill us an' nothin' happen to them. But they can't make us think like they think. They can't make us want what they want. My momma, she show me that. She want freedom an' the only way they could take that away from her was to kill her. These white mens not smart. Some day, we gonna rise up…"

Harriet put her finger to William's mouth. "Shhhh. Don't say no more."

"You knows I be right."

"You be thinking too much. Come and rest. Tomorrow another long day." She touched his cheek and looked into his eyes. Did she see worry or anger? She couldn't be sure. She returned to their mat and lay puzzling over William. *Got to find a way to help him. Freedom done got ahold of his mind, an' it won't let go. If he ain't careful, it gonna take him away. I ain't brave like him. I think maybe he too brave sometimes. Not careful enough.*

She saw the shadow outline of him, his back to the wall. She wanted to feel his muscular arms around her, the rise and fall of his chest against her. She desired to go to him, take his hands in hers, tell him everything would be all right. To stay here. But she didn't. How could she? She remembered Dee, the beatings, the broken bodies, and broken lives she had seen pass through. No one protected them. Their dreams, what little they might have had, whipped from them, or decayed with their bodies swaying in the cool evening breeze.

William studied his family. His resolve grew even stronger. *We needs to run away. We needs to get up North where we can be free. Get away from ole massa John before he take Harriet or Margaret. But how we gonna do that? Man down the road got caught runnin', an' they hung him. Left him hanging for days. Can't get caught, not with my family. Got to have a plan. Got to know where to go. Can't go on like this. Jus' can't.*

Morning came, relentless in its consistency. The wake-up bell caught William still in the corner where he slept awkwardly and fitfully. He stretched, working out the kinks—another day of back-breaking work until dark. On the way outside, each family member grabbed a hoecake from the pot resting by the door. They dreary-walked to the barn with the others, where they received their sacks to fill with cotton. Roscoe, the "head nigger," as John called him, handed out the sacks and verified that all reported for work.

Margaret, on her way to work at the massa's house, stopped for her mother's hug.

"See you tonight," said Harriet, holding Margaret close as though this might be the last time she would ever see her.

"All right, Momma."

"You be careful, little one," said William, patting her on the back. She took several steps towards the big house then spun around, hands on hips.

"I ain't so little, Papa," she said, with a playful smile.

"Yeah, I reckon that's right." *That's why you needs to be careful.*

Hector waved goodbye. More pensive than Margaret, he took after his father.

Harriet left William's side as she scurried to catch up with Katie and Dee. Though Dee kept her chin up, stepping out with resolve, her swollen red eyes told a different story. Harriet wrapped her arm around her shoulder as they approached the fields.

"Don't know what we gonna do," said Katie.

But the time for talking had ended—time to pick cotton.

"Let's go, walk faster," demanded the youngest massa, as he rode up behind them. They cringed when they heard Sam, John's seven-year-old boy, barking his commands. Sam whacked old Sarah on the back of her head with his whip. She stumbled and, but for William reaching out, would have fallen. Sam laughed grandly at this.

As they entered the cotton fields, Harriet lowered her voice. "William, why you lookin' so worried?"

"I don't like Margaret working at the massa house. You know what he done to Dee. What if he decide he want Margaret, too?"

"Oh, Lord. I can't think 'bout that."

William didn't want to say what else he thought—John might take Harriet if he wished, and William knew he couldn't let that happen without trying to kill him.

John's older son, Adam, galloped towards them, causing all talking to stop and the task of picking cotton to begin in earnest.

"Hector and Freddie," Adam called out, "get to the house right now." Seeing others stop to look at the two boys, he shouted, "This ain't no time to dawdle. Get to picking."

A stab of fear struck William on hearing Hector's name called out. Having to go to the big house could mean anything, but never anything good. Harriet's hands continued to move from the cotton plant to her bag, but she deposited no cotton. Her chest pounded with fear. She kept her eye on Hector jogging along, kicking up dust in his path. She repeated to herself, "Don't do nothing to hurt my Hector. Please don't do nothing. Don't do nothing…"

William looked towards the house. His jaw clenched with the scene before him. A buckboard stood in front of the house where a neighbor talked with John. Silas worked his way over to William. Keeping with his picking, he whispered, "He gonna sell our boys, William."

"Just stay calm an' keep on pickin'," said William.

Sam heard the men talking and started beating them with his whip. "Stop talking, you're going too slow." His whip went wide, hitting a cotton plant and breaking several stalks. "Now look what you made me do, you stupid old slave. That's twenty-five lashes apiece." He whipped them about the back and shoulders, his young face tense and red.

Adam rode to Sam and grabbed his arm. "Hold on. You broke that stalk yourself."

"Yeah, well they made me."

"You've hit 'em enough. Go get me some water."

"What do you care, they're just dumb niggers."

"You still gotta be fair, Sam."

"No, I don't." He kicked his horse. "Not if I don't want to." Adam watched Sam ride off; he wished Sam would listen to his advice but realized that wish would likely never come true.

William plucked faster and faster. If he kept his arms moving, kept focused on his task, perhaps he wouldn't throw down his sack and run to rescue Hector. Perhaps he could be patient, see what might happen. But he wasn't giving up Hector without a fight—no perhaps about that.

As best they could, the four parents kept one eye on their boys and one on the cotton. After an agonizing half-hour, the buckboard left with Freddie sitting in the back, eyes glued to the cotton fields to catch one final glimpse of his family. William saw the look of despair on Silas' face but could do nothing. When Hector returned, William calmed and then followed Harriet's gaze over to Katie, whose agitated demeanor promised trouble. Her face streaked with tears, she rubbed her arms and shivered, shaking her head violently. Adam gave particular attention to Silas and Katie so Harriet couldn't stop her picking to comfort her.

Suddenly, Katie bolted for the road shouting for Freddie. Adam spurred his horse and overtook her, blocking her way. He cracked the whip just a few inches from her face. "Get back to work, Katie. You gonna make it worse for yourself and your family."

Silas ran to her and held her trembling body.

Katie said fiercely, "Freddie a good boy. I loves him an' I'll never forget him."

Silas gently walked her back to where she was picking, keeping an eye on Adam. "Freddie a good boy, an' smart, too. He gonna be okay. Come on now, let's just get our pickin' done, Katie."

When Adam moved on, William worked his way over to Silas and grabbed him by the shoulder. "You gots to be strong for the rest of your children." He looked over at Katie and placed some cotton into her bag. "Freddie going be all right. You don't got to worry none 'bout him."

Adam rode up, sending a hard lash onto William's back. "Enough talkin'," he said.

William flinched at the cut of the whip. The pain sharpened his mind. His hands moved along the cotton bushes, filling his bag, but his thoughts focused elsewhere. *There's my wife pickin' cotton. If she don't get enough in that bag, she get a beatin'. Ain't nobody want to see their wife get a beatin'. And Hector pickin' fast as he can. Might get beat, too. He not much more than a boy. One time I glad Margaret not in the field with us. Don't like her being around the massa no more. He likely to take to her. Then what? Got to get us out of here. Got to hold onto my family. Got to go soon before I lose my family or my life.*

At mid-morning, John rode to his fields. Sitting astride his horse he felt invincible—a master of men. He passed down each row. As he moved by a slave, he placed the end of his whip on their back and let it drag across their body. *Give 'em a taste, keep 'em in line.* It pleased him when a slave twitched with the touch of his whip.

When all had been sufficiently intimidated, he shouted, "I seen you this morning running and talking like you didn't have nothing to do. Well, you better do some fast picking the rest of the day, 'cause whoever don't meet his quota is gonna get lashes as well as Sunday work. So, you better pick twice as fast." He observed the effect his speech had on them and felt gratified. He looked over the group of his Africans, picking his cotton. He grinned. *Must be what God feels like.*

John left to inspect his fields that had already been picked. He walked among the plants, examining the leaves and stalks, noticing their small size. He crouched, picked up a handful of dry, gray dirt, pinched it, and let it slip through his fingers.

Dirt. It all comes down to dirt.

He frowned, watching the dry sand fall to the earth.

This soil's not rich and black like it was years ago. Just dust, blown away by the wind. It don't feed the crops like it used to. Getting harder to make a living.

He sniffed the dirt, searching for the smells of his childhood, of the black, fertile earth, when just he and his father worked the land.

Those were good times with just my daddy and me working this land. Felt good working up a sweat, then seeing the crops grow. Can't do that no more, not if you want to get ahead.

He recalled years later going to the slave market with his father where they had bought two slaves.

I drove the buckboard back with them two niggers in the back. I didn't like it. Me and Pa could do it ourselves. What we need them for? Then we got more land. Made more money. Couldn't do without 'em now.

Looking back at his house, John shifted uneasily.

It's not a mansion, but it's been home to me all my life.

He surveyed the rest of his plantation—the weathered wooden barn, the cleared fields, and the slaves' quarters.

Memories flooded his mind of the place north of the house where his father had died. The picture in his mind as clear as if it happened yesterday: the slaves yelling as they ran to him, frantically waving their arms. As the meaning of their cries became clear, he rushed to where they had been clearing trees. Even now, the sense of horror returned. There lay his father's white hat, crushed and dirty under a branch, and his father's battered body, partially hidden by the fallen tree that had broken his neck, his head turned at an impossible angle. Filled with the dread of knowing yet not wanting to know, John struggled to remove the tree. The voices around him became inaudible and time, surreal. The scene lived in his bones, as did his absurd wish that his father would stand up, brush himself off, and say that he was fine. They would all have a good laugh, and it would be the talk for years. John stood transfixed at that place of loss, which changed his life forever.

He slipped out of the memory and gazed back at the house. He would miss the porch where he loved to sit in the evenings with Martha or one of the children. He removed his hat, wiping his brow.

I'm becoming a sentimental old fool.

He called Adam over. "Come on down here, boy, I want to show you something." He bent over to scoop up a handful of soil. "The land's givin' out. Don't feed the crops like it did once. Them slaves can barely make their quotas, even when we work 'em longer days. We'll talk some more with your ma tonight, but I 'spect we'll be headin' to Florida before long."

The long shadows and fading light brought that bitter-sweet time of day for the enslaved. As the sun dropped below the horizon, the house bell clanged in the distance, calling them in from the fields. Picking now done after a long day. Working the bags onto their heads, or dragging them behind, they plodded wearily on stiff legs to the barn, where their day's work would be weighed and judged sufficient or not.

John stood tall, a satisfied grin on his lips as he watched his exhausted slaves trudge past.

Like herding work animals. There they go, carrying my cotton on their backs like a bunch of mules.

He intended to teach Adam to manage slaves—all this would be his in the future. He leaned forward, hands on the porch railing. "These slaves will be yours someday. Don't forget you got to be firm with them, harsh when you need be. They ain't good for nothing unless you keep on 'em. Can't be trusted." He straightened again, facing his son. "And don't you ever forget that."

"Yessir," said Adam, whose eyes moved from his father to the distance, his gaze carrying him far away, dreaming of life past the plantation, out beyond the horizon.

The slaves plodded forward, dropping their eyes as they approached the massa. John raised himself to his full height; a sense of power puffed him up. Standing above them, watching them pass by, heads down because he owned them, was intoxicating.

His smile faded when William walked past and turned his face away. He couldn't see William's expression, but he knew without a doubt this arrogant slave hadn't bowed to him. He slammed his hand on the railing.

Someday, you're gonna regret your disrespect.

John and Adam walked to the barn, where they weighed the cotton. The men had quotas of up to two hundred pounds; the women and younger slaves had varying amounts according to their abilities. Three didn't make their quota. William met his quota, and he made sure Harriet and Hector had met theirs as well.

John considered William. *I'm gonna find out just what your limit is. I seen you giving your pickings away, and you still made your quota. Let's just see how fast you can be.*

"William, I'm upping you to two hundred and ten pounds. You three that didn't make your quota get outside. I'll teach you that you're here to work."

Roscoe tied the three to posts set up for this purpose. As promised, John gave each two lashes.

As they neared the house, John said to Adam, "William may be over his quota, but he can't be trusted." John spat on the ground. "Keep your eye on him."

The Higgins family sat around the dining room table while Margaret served them.

"Your mother and I," said John, "will be discussing Florida again. We need to make a decision soon."

"But, Papa..." said Sally.

"Now don't you say anything, young lady. Your mother and I will decide, and what we say will be final."

Sally enjoyed adventure; she just wanted it to take place where she currently lived. She handled a horse as well as most boys and often raced against them, her straw-colored hair tucked into her hat, leaning in to urge her horse on, focused on one thing—winning.

"I, for one, hope we go," said Adam. "Think of it—a journey to a wild land. I hear the alligators are the size of two men laid one on top of the other, and plenty of game, and a growing season all year round. Don't worry, Sally, there might even be a boy down there who can handle you." Adam and Sam laughed when Sally slammed her fork down.

"I wanna go, too," said Sam. "I wanna see the alligators."

"If we go," said John, "there will be plenty of excitement for us all. Even you, Sally."

Sarah, the oldest slave, and Dee set about making dinner for the others who were busy removing seeds with the cotton gin, spinning cotton into yarn, and finishing other assigned chores. When Sarah called them to eat, they sat outside the barn talking, sometimes in whispered voices, hurrying through the meal so they could finish their work and return to their quarters. Tomorrow would arrive all too soon.

Night after night, the same drudgery. They were animals. Nothing more. They couldn't survive without their white masters to feed, clothe, and tell them what to do. And they existed only to serve their owner, no different from an overworked mule. Or so they had been told. But each of them knew they were equal to these white people who believed they owned their black bodies. But their masters didn't own their dreams. Or their spirits.

Walking to their shack after the work had been completed, Harriet peered into William's face. "I seen you outta the corner of my eye. You didn't look down when we passed ol' man Higgins. An' givin' cotton you picked to Katie was brave, but you scares me, William. I respects you for what you believe, but I don't want to lose you. I don't want to be without you. An' your children, they loves you. What they do without you? Please don't go an' do nothing to give Higgins a reason to whip you or sell you." She grabbed his arm, squeezing it and pulling it close to her. But the strength of his arm in her calloused hands wasn't enough to reassure her.

"Don't you worry none." He put his arm around her shoulders. "I be careful." Then, a frightening premonition shot through her bones with the words he said next. He leaned close to her ear. "We gots to talk."

The warm summer evening blew a light, fragrant breeze across the land, and a few pinkish-gray clouds colored the darkening evening sky. The beauty went unnoticed by Harriet. She reached out, putting her arm around Hector's shoulders and, with her other hand, clung hard to William. It seemed to her a storm was coming.

CHAPTER 3
John

When he'd first read the letter a week ago, he'd crumpled it in his fist and threw it against the wall. "Damn you, Billy," he shouted.

John pulled his shirt off as he sorted through his jumbled thoughts.

"You're awfully quiet tonight. Are you thinking about your brother's letter again?" Martha asked, as they prepared for bed.

"It's not just that. Yeah, sure, the letter bothers me. I want to see Billy again after all these years. Got a million questions to ask him. I'd like to know why he shot that boy, if he did. But leaving our home…that's not easy. I'm thinking we need to move on anyway, Billy or no Billy. Our land is giving out. Hell, in a few years this land won't be much good at all. But traveling from here to Florida is a long trip. Dangerous, too. Goin' to a place we never been." Martha would go along with the move if he wanted, that much he was sure of. But he had misgivings. "Part of me wants to go; another part doesn't want to leave."

He sat on the edge of the bed next to Martha. "Sometimes I feel younger when I think about going. It's exciting to think about going somewhere far away." He reached out and touched her hand, forcing a smile.

Worry settled in Martha's eyes. Her mouth started a smile but didn't finish it. She was forty-two, two years younger than John, but she looked older. Her hair had started to gray several years ago. She worked hard, and it showed.

"We need to do what's best for the family, John. We've been through tough times before. Traveling to Florida won't be the hardest thing we've ever done. But still…we have so many memories here."

He squeezed her hand. She was always the strong one, the sensible one.

"I sold a boy today. That'll give us some money to help with the traveling and one less mouth to feed on the road." He wondered how Martha would react, but she didn't as far as he could tell. "If we go, that is."

"Speaking of selling slaves," said Martha, "I want you to sell that Dee girl."

John felt the blood rush to his neck. Her voice, hard and tight, hit him a solid blow.

"Why would I sell one of my best slaves?" he asked, peering at her from the corner of his eye.

Martha's answer came tense and firm. "I want her gone."

"Honey, she's one of the best pickers we got. Now I ain't selling her, and that's final. Just stop worrying about her."

"I can't, John."

"Well, you're gonna have to. Now let's stop talking about her and get back to deciding what we're gonna do."

Martha turned away, her chin held high, teeth grinding.

John went to the dresser and opened the top drawer, removing the crinkled letter. *Damn, Billy. All the heartache you put our folks through. Why didn't you write before our parents died? They were never the same after you left.*

John remembered his own heartache when his big brother, the person he looked up to even more than his father, had run off after being out drinking, celebrating his sixteenth birthday. The boy he had been with found shot dead. Billy gone. Until now. Billy had taught John how to ride a horse, to shoot a rifle, track wild animals through the woods, so many things.

After Billy's disappearance, John became the forgotten child. His parents mourned Billy's loss. John tried to remember a time when his folks enjoyed life after Billy vanished. He couldn't remember even one. For months after he left, his parents frequently looked to the road expecting to see Billy ride up, jump off his horse, and give them a big hug. Eventually they stopped looking and lost interest in living.

John opened the letter, smoothed it with his hand, and read it again.

Dear John,

I know you will be surprised to hear from me after all these years. You may have thought me dead many years ago, and perhaps you wished me to be so, for the pain I am sure to have caused you and our parents. I pray to God that we can sit down some day and discuss what happened that night I left so you can understand my side of the matter and perhaps have mercy on me.

I suppose that our mother and father have now gone to their reward, and I can cause them no more grief. May their souls rest in peace.

I am writing you from the land called Florida and have me a nice ranch of about 600 acres. I raise cattle and a few crops and make a good enough living off the land.

I don't know even if you are alive, if you are married and have any family, or what your life is made of. I am getting old and have no one to leave this ranch to. It seems that war is on its way soon, and what that holds for us no one can say. If you have a mind to, I would like for you to join me in Florida, and we could run this ranch together. When I am gone, the place would be yours. I fear I don't have much more time to live, and I would like to see what's left of my family before I die. I have drawed a map on the other side of this paper so you can find me if you decide to come.

Your brother, Billy

When John calmed down, he became curious about Billy, wondering about the details of his disappearance and of his life. Lars, the boy who had been drinking with Billy, was found shot through the chest, his horse gone. And Billy disappeared. Everyone wondered: had Billy been the killer, or had he also been killed?

John and Martha had talked of little else after having received the letter. The decision to leave encompassed more than Billy—concern of the approaching war for one. There was heightened tension with the North with their not wanting to allow slavery in the new territories out west, and now some fool tried to instigate a slave uprising. Damn Yankees. If it did come to war, no doubt South Carolina would be in the thick of it. With Adam nearly old enough to be a soldier, Martha remained firm.

"If there's going to be a war, I don't want Adam going off to be killed before his time. I don't aim to bury him."

"I don't want him killed neither, but a man's got to do his duty," replied John. He heard the uncompromising strength in her voice and knew he best not push too hard.

"Thank God for Sally," Martha had said. "At least I have one child that'll never go off to war."

John looked at Martha lying quietly in bed. She was done talking with him for the night. He knew this. He also knew that Florida called—the new frontier with a long growing season and ideal climate, plenty of land, room to expand. Become rich, be a pioneer, have a new beginning. It pulled at a man like a warm fire after a day battered by wind and cold. John knew he was going; in the bottom of his heart, he knew. He just hadn't convinced himself yet.

CHAPTER 4

Margaret

Margaret stood at the kitchen door, her eyes focused on the floor, her mind a jumble of nerves. She must stay alert, ready to serve the moment any of the family members required service. No mistakes. Fumbling at her dress, she couldn't help but replay that night to herself. Dee had returned sobbing, muttering to herself, calm one minute, then breaking down unexpectedly. And then Freddie, gone. Her father's warning. Too much had happened. Too much. Her life coming apart like her frayed dress. Was she only a rag, to be thrown away some day?

She cleared the table and washed the dishes in a pan of water on the rough wood table out back before hurrying off to join her family and the others in a meal of hoecakes, dried beef, and corn cooked over an outside fire. The flames died and the logs burned to hot, red coals. Evening was done. Each in turn rose, sauntering to their shanty eager for a night of rest.

Margaret and Hector placed their sleeping mats onto the dirt floor. "Papa, will you tell us the story of Grandma and the day she was no longer afraid?" said Margaret.

"That's your favorite story, I do believe," said Harriet. "She must ask for that story more than any other."

"Well, that sure's a good one," said William. "All right, I'll tell it if Hector wants it, too."

"That be fine with me. I like that story," said Hector.

The children sat cross-legged, anticipating their papa's story.

William gave a fleeting look at Harriet who, he believed, enjoyed his stories as much as the children. He eased his tired body down facing the children and started. "It happen like this: a long time ago, when my momma, your grandma, Kaziah, lived in Africa. You remember what I told you 'bout Africa?"

"I do." Margaret glanced at Hector. "It's far, far away. And everyone is dark-skinned like us."

"And they're all free," added Hector.

"That right. Kaziah was still a little girl, 'bout like you, Margaret. In her village, the people had to walk to the river to get water, an' it was a long ways. They had to pass through some dangerous woods with animals that would eat a man if they caught one out by hisself. That's why the people always go to the river in groups. One hot day, Kaziah was very thirsty. She look in the water jug, but it empty. Nobody else around, so she decide she must go by herself. She got to the river jus' fine and fill the water jug. On her way back, she heard a leopard roar not far from her. She got afraid and began walking faster. She scoot along fast as she can with that big water jug, when suddenly this leopard come out the bushes in front of her. He look at her like he gonna eat her up and then roared. That when she see his big teeth." William scrunched his face up, moved close to Margaret, their noses almost touching, and growled.

Margaret's eyes got big, and she jerked back. "Papa, you're scarin' me."

Hector clamped his hand over his mouth to keep from laughing. Harriet chuckled.

William continued. "Kaziah never be so scared in all her life. She know this animal could eat her quick. She also know there be no way she able to escape, 'cause that big animal could easy out run her. Do you know what she did?"

"You tell us, Papa," pleaded Margaret, her hands covering her mouth, though she had heard this story many times.

William leaned back, filled with pure contentment. He shut his eyes, illustrating the next part of the story. "She close her eyes tight and decide she not goin' to be scared. She calm herself. She stand for long time in darkness, not seeing nothin', tellin' herself to be brave, being still as a tree on a day with no wind. The animal growled an' got closer an' closer an' soon she feel hot breath on her skin as he move in real close and sniff her. But she didn't move not one bit. She want to cry out, but she know if she do, she get eat for sure. Then she think of her family. She forget about the scary leopard. She remember how she feel warm and loved when her momma or papa hold her. She begin feel safe. The sniffin' stop. Then she not hear him anymore. She keep her eyes closed a few more minutes. Then she open them real slow like. She look all around. But he nowhere around. He gone. She felt all good inside. And ever since that time, she never been afraid."

"Thanks, Papa." Margaret jumped up and hugged his neck, then dashed to her mother and hugged and kissed her. "If I ever see a big, scary animal, I hope I can be that brave."

"You my brave girl," said William.

Hector kissed his parents goodnight and lay down beside Margaret. "That must be nice," he said.

"What's that?" asked Harriet.

"To never be afraid."

William placed his hand on Hector's shoulder. "Being scared is all right. Most folks get scared one time or another. Doing the right thing even when you is scared can be hard. An' I'll tell you both somethin' else. It good to be scared of the massa, 'cause he can do what he wants with you, just like he done with Freddie."

"But I seen you stop pickin' to go help Miss Katie, and they didn't do nothin' to you."

"Hector," he said, "it ain't always easy to think what to do. Maybe I shouldn't a done that. Anyways, don't you go do nothin' that foolish. Freddie and his folks never gonna see each other again. We don't want that to happen to us. We a family. We got to do everything we can to stay together."

"That's the truth," said Harriet. "Your papa could of gotten whipped or sold for that. I know poor Miss Katie need some help, but it ain't gonna help her none if you is sold."

Hector said in a low voice, "I thought I was gonna be sold today."

"I know," said Harriet. "I ain't never been so scared. An' poor Freddie." Harriet shuddered at the thought. "Katie not takin' it well."

William's voice sounded heavy with worry. "How the massa been treatin' you lately, Margaret?"

"He treat me just like always. Why you ask, Papa?"

"Never mind. You just be careful 'round that man. If'n he do somethin' to you that you don't like, you tell me."

"Sure, Papa. But you ain't got to worry none. The massa's wife be good to me, too."

William grasped Margaret's arm. "Lissen to what I says, an' don't never forget it. That white woman up there only like you long as you does what she say. First time you messes up, she have you sold off or beat with a whip. She don't care nothin' 'bout you."

"But what about Sally?" said Margaret. "I think she like us."

"Sally is nice," said Hector.

"Now listen, both of you. I ain't never seen a white man, or woman neither, gonna stick up for no slave."

Margaret shrugged her shoulders. "Sure, Papa."

Though Hector admired his father, he didn't understand his father's warning about Sally. *We played together as children. If not for Masa Higgins, we would be best friends. She bring me treats from her momma's kitchen. I believe I can trust her.*

Margaret said, "Wish I could of met Grandma."

"If Grandma had met you, and you, Hector, she would of been real proud. She would a been the most proud Grandma in all the world. Now you two get to sleeping."

William thought about Silas and Katie with their children, three now with Freddie gone. *Silas and his family can't run, not yet. Children too small, two of them anyways.* He looked back at his children. *They old enough. They strong. But if they got caught...* He wouldn't allow them to be whipped. Not them or Harriet. He would die first.

CHAPTER 5

The Runaway Man

Looking out over his cottonfield the next morning, John considered the most important question of his life. Pack up and leave this plantation his father had built from nothing…or stay? He was never one for adventure—not like Billy, whose restless spirit compelled him to accept even the most dangerous challenge. Billy would pack up in a minute, and he'd be gone. But there were other considerations for John. Hell, he'd buried his parents here. Grew up here. Memories. Friends. Everything he'd ever known, everything he loved. Right here.

Then there was the other side of the coin. Florida had plenty of land. Good weather. And he had family there. Family. It seemed impossible to imagine, after all these years, to be with Billy again.

We could work together to build a future. Maybe Martha and the children would be better off down there. Stop being such a chickenshit and make the goddam move.

He gulped down a big breath and squeezed his eyes shut. When he opened his eyes, he held a half smile like he was mocking himself. He slapped his hands together, pivoted, and marched into the house. "Martha, Martha, where in thunder are you?"

The back door slammed. "I'm right here, John. What on earth's the matter?"

He stopped a few inches from her. "We've been talking long enough. Time for action. We're moving. Yep, I done decided. We're moving to Florida."

Martha's mouth fell open, and her body stiffened. "Are you sure that's what you want, John?"

John sensed Martha's resistance. "Well, yes. I…thought…"

"I am going to miss this place," said Martha, the sudden reality hitting her. Recovering, she said, "But it's probably for the best. If you're sure about it, then let's do it." She embraced him and pulled him close. "It'll be fine." But John didn't see her worried brow.

After dinner, the family gathered in the parlor for John's announcement. "But, Papa," complained Sally, "I don't want to leave here for some backwoods. My friends are all here, and they say there's nothing in Florida but mosquitoes and alligators."

"I don't want to hear any more complaining. The decision's been made."

"You can make friends with the bears," said Adam.

"Yes, and the raccoons," said Sam, pointing at Sally.

"That's enough, boys," said Martha.

John rode to the land acquisitions office a few days later to get the word out that his plantation was for sale. In just two months, Albert Burgess, a prominent landowner eager to expand, bought John's property. Burgess and Higgins signed the papers, and a date for Higgins to leave set at one month. John wrote Billy a letter and dispatched it the very next time he went into town. When he stepped out the door of the post office, he stopped in mid-thought; the weight of what he had done settled squarely on his shoulders. All the reasons for not going came roaring back like a thunderous river in the rainy season—the long and dangerous journey, living in an unknown undeveloped land, leaving his father's homestead… He shifted his body, willed himself to stand tall and strong. He adjusted his hat and stepped forward.

It's done now, he thought. *No backing out.* But lingering doubt stuck in his mind.

"I didn't expect everything to move so fast," said Martha.

"Me neither," said John. "But I wasn't about to turn down Burgess' offer."

John put all his time into preparing for the move: decisions made about what to take, how to safely pack the breakables, cages built to transport the hogs and chickens, and wagons procured to haul everything.

John clanged the bell on his front porch calling his enslaved workers to the house. When the last one arrived, he stepped to the edge of the porch and looked out at his people gathered before him. They came with feelings of fear mixed with curiosity, wondering what new demands would be put on them.

John puffed out his chest before speaking. "I have sold this land. We're all moving from here in two weeks. We're going to a place called Florida. It's a long trip. I want you ready to go, and anything you're taking with you packed up the night before. Bring only what you can carry 'cause I ain't gonna have room for your stuff on my wagons. We're going to get an early start. Roscoe will give you your jobs for the move. Now go finish your work. We got a busy day tomorrow."

As they returned to the barn, Jacob made his way next to William. "What you think of this move to Florida, William?" he asked in a low voice, his hands folded across his chest.

"Can't be nothin' good for us, that for sure."

"An' what about Sarah? She ain't fit to walk to no Florida," murmured Richard, who had come up alongside the two men. "I hear that's a long ways. A trip like that likely to kill her. She too old."

"Yeah, well you know old Massa John don' care nothin' about us," said William.

"Papa," said Hector, "why we leaving here?"

"'Cause the massa say so, that's why."

"Where be Florida?" Hector asked.

"A long ways from here, I reckon," said William.

"Naw," said Richard. "A long ways is walkin' to town. This Florida more than a long ways—you got to walk months to get there."

That night, William lay awake, soothed by the peaceful sounds of his sleeping family— their soft, rhythmic breathing, the rustling of a child turning in her sleep. These were voices calling him to protect them, make them free.

Running to the north would be impossible from Florida. Too far. Got to go now. But how? He remembered running with his momma and their getting caught. His momma dying. *I needs to have a better plan. Some plan that help us get far away before massa come lookin' for us. But how I'm gonna do that?*

"Look at this list, Martha." John held up the pages of items he aimed to take to Florida. "There's no way we can get all this into our two wagons. I'm going to see if Petersen will sell me the two old wagons he keeps behind his barn. Hell, he never uses them."

John burst out the front door and spotted Roscoe. "Roscoe, get over here."

"Yes, Massa."

"Send me someone to the barn that can handle a wagon."

"Yes, sir."

John hurried to the barn where he selected two horses. He placed a blanket on one and lifted a saddle when William entered. "What are you doing here?"

"Roscoe says you needs a driver."

John fumed that he would be spending the morning with William, but time constraints pushed the thought aside. "All right, I ain't got time to argue. Saddle that horse over there, and let's get going. You can saddle a horse, can't you?"

"Why yes, suh."

William's tone antagonized John. *Was there a hint of sarcasm in his "yes, suh?"*

They each pulled a reluctant mule behind, neither man saying much—neither wanting the company of the other.

John and Petersen struck a deal for the wagons. Peterson, realizing John needed them, held out for more than their worth. John had no choice but to pay Peterson's price.

John drove the lead wagon with William following close behind in another when a loud crack broke the silence. William pulled in the reins and shouted, "Whoa," as the rear of the wagon wobbled and then the right rear end shook. The left rear of William's wagon tilted, and a wheel lay on the ground. Reining in his mule, John jumped from his wagon to survey the damage and discovered an axle had broken.

"Stay with the wagon," he demanded. "That damn Peterson owes me an axle."

"Yes, sir, Massa."

John disappeared around the bend back to Peterson's house. William, taking advantage of the break, stepped into the woods to relieve himself. Three feet in he stopped, cocked his head, and listened. Rustling leaves caught his attention, but he didn't see any movement. *Just some animal.* When finished, he walked back towards the road when he heard dry leaves crunching behind him. He spun around and found himself face to face with a large black man, a head taller than himself, dressed in clothes befitting a white man.

"What you mean by pissing in my woods?" the man said. His eyes narrowed, legs spread wide, arms folded across his chest.

"These ain't your woods," said William, confused by his sudden appearance.

"Whose woods are they?"

"They ain't nobody's woods. They just woods is all."

"Well now, if they don't belong to anyone, then they belongs to everyone. Ain't that right?"

"What you talkin' about? You sure do talks different. More like a white man. Who are you? You ain't from aroun' here. Where you from?"

The big man broke into a wide grin. "None of that is really important." His eyes honed on William's, he walked towards him. "Tell me, friend, do you know any slaves who would like to be free?"

After Hector and Margaret had gone to bed, Harriet approached William. "You seem like your mind is way off. Ever since you got back from that trip with the massa, you been acting strange."

William put one finger to his lips. "Shhhh. Just wait a little," he whispered, motioning to the children. "We gots to talk."

Harriet frowned but didn't say a word. She did agonize about another late-night talk. They always caused her to lose sleep.

Hector, drowsy, but still awake, overheard his parents. Now he fought to stay awake to hear the secret his papa was about to tell. Margaret lay next to him, the rhythmic movement of her chest a sign she slept soundly. Occasionally, she turned or made a muffled cry, perhaps facing down a leopard in her dreams. The wind blew outside, whistling through cracks in the shanty walls. Hector closed his eyes and remained still, anticipating the secret.

William sat on his mat facing Harriet. Hector peeked through squinted eyelids, spying on his parents. His papa, excited like never before, took his momma's hands and held them tight. The muscles in William's neck trembled, his eyes wide with excitement. He leaned in close to Harriet and whispered, "Today I met a man in the woods who can help us get to freedom."

Harriet jerked a hand away and slapped it over her mouth. She froze for a second, glaring at William as though he were a mad man. "What you mean, William? Who is this man? How you know him?" She glanced at the door to be sure he wasn't overheard.

"I was in the woods by myself, waitin' for massa to come back with an axle an' this big Negro suddenly show up. He say he helps slaves escape up north where they be free. Where a man can work for money. Think of it, Harriett, away from white mens beatin' us an' makin' us work for *their* good. We does all the sweatin' an' hard labor. What we get? Nothin. Up North, we work our own land, be the boss of ourselves."

"But, William, who is he? How we know we can trust him? Maybe it be a trick, and they gonna hang you if you tries to run away."

"Ain't no trick. Least I don't think it be a trick. He seem like he can be trusted. But what you say is right. I needs to learn for sure. He wouldn't give his name or tell me where he from. He say he couldn't do that 'cause it put others in danger."

"I don't like it, William," she said, shaking her head. "It too risky."

"This may be our only chance. The trip to Florida will help us, give us time to get away. If we runs during the night, before massa leaves, he not going to stop his trip to look for us. Not long anyways. Not when he got all his belongings packed up on them wagons an' the livestock herded up an' ready to go."

"But if we get caught, the massa might kill you or sell us all, an' we never see each other again. What about Margaret and Hector, William? What about them?" she pleaded.

"This the best time for us to go. Once we leave here an' get to Florida, we be too far from freedom. They says Florida way far south of here. But what you say about trusting that man is true. I be meeting this 'Runaway Man' again tomorrow to make final plans. I'll find out more about him. I'll find out can he be trusted."

"I don't like it. I really don't."

Though wide awake, Hector lay silent, motionless…but his mind raced. *Freedom? Runaway? All the people I seen beat with a whip, they body tore up, the people I seen hanging after getting caught running. Are we going to run? Could we? Or might we all die?*

He remembered the stories of men and women he knew who had escaped—or were thought to have escaped. If someone ran away and disappeared, never heard from again, it was believed they made it to the North, and they told their story again and again in hushed voices. But frequently, runaways were captured and beaten severely in front of others—sometimes hung and left hanging for days.

Hector moaned, remembering their friend Ned hanging on the road to town. A group of white men stood below him, talking and laughing as though nothing of importance had happened, not caring that this good man had been tortured and killed. Hector remained haunted by this image and worked hard to rid himself of it. He blinked rapidly and touched his thumb to his fingers, each one in succession, until the image left. Only now, a new image emerged—his father, or himself, strung up. Hector blinked rapidly.

He knew the fear in his mother's voice. His parents held each other close, either from fear or from hope, he didn't know which.

The next night, William slipped out of the shanty. He traveled in the shadows, careful to keep a tree or a shack between him and the big house. His head throbbed with the anticipation of making plans with the Runaway Man for his family's escape and with the fear of being discovered. For once, he wished he were small, harder to see, as he dodged from tree to shadow, nervously inching to the wooded area where he would meet the big man. But on arriving at the agreed upon meeting place, a heavily wooded area with thick underbrush, he found himself alone.

Crouched in the dense bushes, he waited, vigilant. No one came. Doubts crept in. *Could be a trap. Maybe he just talk an' nuthin' more. Maybe he done been caught.* Defeated, William decided to return to Harriett. He took a few steps back towards his shanty.

"William."

The throaty voice startled him. He squinted in the darkness in the direction of the voice. The big man eased out from the cover of compact, low-hanging branches. Dressed in black, he had been perfectly hidden.

"Why you hiding from me? I been sitting here a long time waiting for you."

"I had to be sure you came alone. This is a dangerous business, and I won't take unnecessary risks."

"Speakin' of risk, my family and me taking big risk, too. How I know I can trust you?"

"That's a good question. You're wise to ask. I've learned you got to question everyone. Don't trust anyone completely first time you meet. You not gonna know if you can trust me 'til we begin traveling and you see for yourself. But if I wanted to trap you, wouldn't I have already done it? I could of had men hidden in the woods waitin' to grab you. But here we are, just you and me. Now, you ready to talk about plans?"

The stranger seemed calm, yet his eyes were intense. William knew he had no choice, really, not with the long trip to Florida looming in the next few days. If he was going to go, he had to do it now.

"All right," William said at last. "I gots some questions."

CHAPTER 6
William

The half-moon cast a weak, lusterless light as William snaked here and there, weaving from shadow to shadow. He struggled to keep his concentration on returning safely, but his mind spun with possibilities for the future. Freedom seemed within reach. So believed an elated William creeping back to his family. Living without fear had been a dream for so long. His children could learn to read and write. Harriett could live a safe, normal life. But he must be cautious. Be afraid. Always.

He arrived at the quarters, crouched, then darted silently from shanty to shanty, eager to tell Harriet the plan they had agreed upon. He eased the door to his cabin open, willing unsuccessfully for the rusty hinges to hush their squeaking.

He slipped past the sleeping Silas and Katie, and once inside his own room, saw their mat empty where he expected to find Harriet. His thoughts flashed to the massa and his taking of Dee nights before. Panic engulfed him as he considered what to do.

"William," she whispered from a corner.

He followed the sound of her voice and saw her dark silhouette outlined against the rough log wall. Relieved, he moved to her and held her close.

"What you doing over here?"

"I couldn't sleep. I was afraid. I thought you might not come back."

"What you mean? Why wouldn't I come back?"

"I feared you was going to a trap."

For a few moments, he held her without speaking. Then he held her at arm's length. "After tonight, I trust this man. I believes he can help us."

Harriet heard the intensity in William's voice. It made the running more real, which made her more afraid. Yes, life would be much better as a free person, but the consequences if caught would be horrible. Her family destroyed, William possibly killed, her children sold to some place far away.

"I be afraid, too, but this somethin' we gots to do, or we never be safe. This man I meet with, he got a good plan, and I trusts him. Lissen to the plan, an' tell me what you think. We all go the night before massa leave. He be packed up an' ready to go so not goin' to spend time lookin' for us. This Runaway Man lead us to safe place. He do this all the time. He know people can help us."

"William, I jus' don't know 'bout this. Seen too many left and didn't make it. We seen them beaten an' killed." She laid her head on his chest.

"Hey, you crying?" William held her and stroked her back. "It goin' to work just fine. You'll see. We get away from Massa John. He could sell our children any day, an' we never see them again. He could take you or Margaret, an' you carry his child. We needs to get away from all that. We could live with no fear of these things."

Hector lay listening to his parents. His body was tense. The wind blew uninvited through the walls. Could this be one of the last times the wind whispered him to sleep? His mind filled with the uncertainty of what lay ahead.

William led Harriet to their mat. After a few moments, Harriet broke the silence. "I know you right." A tear rolled off her cheek.

When Harriet was fifteen, her owner, a man named Tom Jacobs, came to her and said she was a woman now. He moved her from her parents to a cabin with Emmett, a man several years her senior. Over the course of five years, she had three children, Moses, Tyree, and Jamala. Moses and Tyree were competitive, yet protective of each other. They were the best of companions. But they loved their younger sister the best and would do anything for her. Harriet adored them all.

When the children were six, four, and three, Jacobs sold Harriet to John Higgins but kept her children. Harriet thought she would die from heartbreak. The babies she'd carried inside of her for so many months, given milk to from her body and raised with profound love, she would never see again. She often imagined what they must look like as the years went by and fantasized meeting them through some unlikely circumstance. She promised that if she had another family, she would never allow anyone to take them from her—a promise she knew she could not keep. She didn't know the opportunity for a new family would come a few years later.

William rested on his elbow, stroked Harriet's hair, then gently wrapped himself around her. In spite of their fears, they had to go. The contempt white people felt for him, and all his people, set a raging fire within. He was not sure he could contain it much longer. The hate in their eyes, the disgust in their voices, using black bodies like owned property, no more—they would go.

Can't walk down the road without puttin' your life in danger. Ain't nuthin' good 'bout livin' here. Soon, all that be different. Just five more days an' we be gone.

John rose before the sun and thrashed about the house making sure everyone woke with him. He told Martha to forget breakfast. He wanted to get started.

John clanged the bell, beginning the work day for the enslaved workers, and gave it another three short tolls to signal Roscoe to get to the house. There was a tornado of activity, seeming to be everywhere at once. John barked orders, made decisions, and directed the packing of belongings that would make the trip.

Roscoe had been with John for over twenty years. John trusted him more than he did the others and decided two years ago to make him "almost" an overseer. "Almost," because John didn't trust him enough to give him the full power and responsibility that such a position required.

Late Monday afternoon, Roscoe approached John. "Massa John, we 'bout done all the preparin' we can do for this trip. If we're not goin' to leave till Friday, I'll have to put everyone back to work in the fields. I know you don't want everyone just sittin' around."

John believed idle slaves become lazy and cause trouble. On the other hand, he hated the idea of his slaves working to benefit another man—in this case, Albert Burgess. After discussing the situation with Martha, it was decided they would move the departure date to Wednesday. No point in delaying it any longer.

Tuesday morning, John rang the bell five times, his signal for all slaves to come to the house. William and Harriet had just finished their hoecake breakfast.

"What that ol' massa want with us this morning?" said William.

"I don't know what he wants," said Harriet, looking towards the big house as she felt a shiver of apprehension pass through her. "It ain't nothin' good, you can be sure of that."

They hurried to the house, where John stood on the porch and Roscoe claimed his spot at the foot of the steps. Martha and the three children stood behind John. The chill in the morning air bit through the thin layer of clothing the slaves wore as they gathered around and looked up at the massa.

John stepped forward. "Well, we gonna have to leave tomorrow for Florida, so we got to start loading these wagons today. Be ready to leave first thing in the morning. I'll keep three of you here at the house to load everything except what we need today." He stopped to rub out the stiffness in the back of his neck. "Roscoe, you take the rest to get the livestock and tools ready.

William froze. Leave tomorrow? No. They would be gone long before the Runaway Man came for them on Thursday. His big hands trembled in desperation.

At first, the words could barely be heard. William was not sure where they came from.

"But, Massa."

If the sound had been the wind blowing through the leaves, or as it was, his own voice, William could not have stopped either. When the words rumbled louder, he became aware his own mouth gave them life, and they hung in the air, naked for all to hear. Nothing could take them back.

"Massa, we can't leave tomorrow."

John hardened when the words reached him. *Did a slave tell me what to do?* He saw Harriett grab hold of William's arm, her pleading with him.

"Please, William, just hush. What's done is done. Just be quiet."

Realizing William had openly defied him, John's hard eyes narrowed. His grim countenance frightened Harriet, who clung tighter to William.

"Listen here, you goddam nigger," John hissed through his clenched teeth as he scrambled down the steps. "You been needing to learn your place, and I'm goin' to teach you."

Harriet tugged on William's arm. "Please stop. Please don't," she begged.

But William ignored Harriet. He must convince his master to stay until Friday. He must. "Please, Massa, let's not leave tomorrow. We can't get ready in time."

William stepped towards John, reached out his pleading hand.

Immediately, Roscoe jumped him.

"Tie him to that oak over there, Roscoe. I'll show him who's in charge."

As Roscoe grabbed him by one arm and forced him to the tree, John threw him a coil of rope. William, though equal to Roscoe in stature, knew better than to resist—to resist meant death.

Roscoe whispered, "You crazy? You trying to get yourself killed?"

Harriet covered her face with her hands. Hector and Margaret watched, wide-eyed, as their father was tied to the oak tree. Margaret pressed herself to her mother. "What's happening, Momma? Why they hurting Papa?"

Hector, stoic, said nothing as enraged thoughts mushroomed inside him, seething in his young heart.

John stomped from the house brandishing his whip.

When he walked by Martha, she touched his arm but knew nothing could be done to stop him.

Roscoe said, "Massa John, why don't you let me take care of this here nigger? Then we can all get packed up for leaving tomorrow with no delays."

John snapped back, "Goddammit, I'll take care of him myself." He shouted at Roscoe, "You make sure everyone stays here and watches. I'll do the same to any of them that thinks to challenge me."

Sally ran to her father. "Papa, please don't do this. He's been your best worker, he—"

"Don't tell me what to do," he hissed. "Especially in front of these niggers."

"But, Papa..."

"Enough. You don't have to watch. But by God I'm going to teach him a lesson."

Harriet closed her eyes and whispered a prayer. "No, please, dear Lord, don't let this happen. Don't let this happen."

Katie moved to Harriet and held her. Then she saw Margaret staring intensely at her pappy. She grabbed her arm. "Harriet, you hang onto Margaret and don't let her run to her pappy. Don't want her to get in the way of that whip."

Silas put his hand on Hector's shoulder to steady him and to keep him from doing anything foolish. Margaret clung to her mother's dress and hid her face. Her muffled voice cried out, "What's happening, Momma? What's happening?" Others moved towards Harriet and her children, offering their support.

Roscoe had tied William's arms around the tree, hugging it. Bark dug into his flesh. The rope, tight around his wrists, cut off circulation to his hands. William strained against the rope. "I'll kill you someday, John Higgins," he whispered. If he could have broken the ropes, he would have jumped his master without caring about his fate.

John grabbed the top of William's shirt, ripping it off his back. "Don't you ever defy me! Don't you ever walk towards me like you are my equal. You are nothing, you hear me? Nothing." John drew back the whip and, with a snap, raised a red welt. The sting and pain of the strike surprised William, but he steeled himself, refusing to cry out.

Harriet's body shuddered each time the whip cut into William's back. Margaret, her face buried in her mother's dress, covered her ears in a futile attempt to shut out the mutilation of her father.

Harriet's worst fears played out before her eyes. She had witnessed men die from the whip. John seemed possessed by a demon—pummeling William with no mercy. She believed William would not survive the day. How could she and the children survive without him?

Hector, yearning to save his father, stood powerless. He closed his eyes, put his hands over his ears, and jerked his head back and forth, striving to block out the crack of each blow.

William's body tensed with each thwack. He struggled to suppress the screams that welled through him from deep inside. He focused on John. Warm blood flowed down his back. *I hate you.* Pain engulfed him. *You're stealing my freedom.* Though the lash stung unbearably, William did not yell out. He would not give John the satisfaction. Each hit intensified William's hate. *I will live to kill you. I will kill you. I will kill you.*

The thrashing shredded his flesh, yet John continued. William slumped, his head falling onto one shoulder. His body went still.

Unable to stand the brutality any longer, Sally ran to her father, shouting, "Stop. Stop before you kill him." He swung the whip, catching her on the neck. She screamed, holding her bleeding neck with both hands. He dropped the whip and rushed to her. Together, Martha and John held her by either side and led her inside, where they inspected the gash the whip had torn and applied bandages to stop the bleeding.

"You shouldn't a come running at me."

"Papa, you were too hard on him. You were killing him."

"He had it coming. And you need to stop sticking your nose in my business."

John went to the front door, where he shouted to Roscoe, "Get them to work, and leave that one on the tree."

Alone now, Sally lay on her bed, feeling the pain of her wound, but her mind dwelled on William's flogging and the tortured expressions of his family. She agonized for Hector especially. A forgotten memory came to her. She was six, and Hector had just turned six.

"Stop, Hector," she said, laughing. "I can't run anymore."

"You just want to catch me, but you know I'm too fast." He teased her by running close and then darting away.

"Come on, let's play something else."

Hector ran close to her again, but this time he tripped before he could run away. Sally came to life and pounced on him. They lay on the ground laughing when Sally reached over and kissed him on the cheek.

"Sally, go in the house," said her father, who had just walked up and witnessed the kiss.

That was the last day they were ever together. The next day, Hector worked in the fields.

She regretted the end of their friendship. Now, they were separated by a chasm of customs and beliefs so wide and so deep, it could never be crossed.

William showed no signs of life. No one was allowed near him. Katie and Silas each took an arm to help a tormented Harriet to her room. Blood covered William's torn back and dried, dark blood stains covered his trousers and the earth beneath him. Already flies had begun their frantic buzzing, encircling the bloody feast.

John returned to give further orders. He noticed Hector and called to him, "Hey, boy, come here."

Hector stopped, his fists clenched. He refused to move.

"Better get up here," said John, "unless you want to be sold and never see your family again."

Hector's fists softened but not his heart as he moved towards John slower than he might have on another day.

"Here, boy, take this note to the Simmons brothers and be quick about it. You get back here quick like. We got work to do. Now get."

Hector froze at the mention of the Simmons brothers. The frequent rumors he had heard flashed through his mind—the Simmons brothers beat a slave to death for the pleasure it gave them; the Simmons brothers killed a slave and ate his heart. Some scoffed at the tales, but everyone feared them.

Hector's hesitation ended when John issued a warning. "Didn't you hear me, boy? Get going right now, or do I have to beat you like I did your papa? Don't think I won't."

CHAPTER 7

Hector

Hector took off running, afraid of going to the Simmons' place, but, for now, more afraid of not going. He turned down the dusty road, the note held firmly in his trembling hand. His life had shattered in one unexpected moment. The safety and comfort found only in his father's strength—gone. The reliability found in a daily routine, turned upside down. Danger and insecurity invaded his life and took it over with brutal force.

A mile from John Higgins' place, Hector jumped when someone called to him from the woods.

"Hey, boy, come here."

Wide-eyed, Hector peered into the dark forest. His pounding heart urged him to flee, but his feet stuck to the dusty road. His mouth turned dry when he saw a man's face, his eyes fierce, staring back.

"You better get over here quick. You want the patrollers to get you? Get over here, NOW!" the man commanded.

Hector looked up and down the road for patrollers and, seeing none, edged timidly to the side of the road. Suddenly, the man grabbed him by the arm and carried him into the forest. The man stood taller than Hector's father. He seemed like a giant. Hector fought with all his strength, but he could do nothing.

The man set Hector down and motioned for him to be quiet. "No need to be frightened; I'm a friend," the man whispered. "What's your name?"

"Hector."

"Hector. Your papa told me about you."

Finding the courage to speak, Hector asked in a trembling voice, "You the Runaway Man?"

"Ha," he said, laughing softly. "Is that what your father calls me? Well, it doesn't matter, my friend. Right now, we must concentrate on saving your father. Tell me what happened back there. I saw Higgins beating your father. Why did he do that?"

Hector wondered if he could rely on the man sitting across from him. He remembered his father's nighttime conversations and that he trusted the Runaway Man. That was good enough for Hector. As they talked, Hector relaxed, secretly hoping this man could fix all that had gone wrong. He told the Runaway Man of the plan change and how his father had tried to get Higgins to stick with the original day.

"Let me see the note old Higgins gave you."

Hector gripped the note tighter and stuck it behind his back. "I can't give this to you. If I don't give it to the Simmons brothers, Massa Higgins will beat me, too."

"Don't worry none about that. He won't beat you. Just give me the note."

Hector shook his head.

Before Hector could move, the Runaway Man grabbed him and threw him to the ground. Hector started to yell, but the Runaway Man put his hand over Hector's mouth.

"Shush now, or we're both going to get beat," he whispered.

Then Hector saw the patrollers, and he knew to be quiet. Once they passed, the Runaway Man let go of Hector and said, "If you want to save your father, we need to come up with a plan. To do that, I need to know what's in that note." He put his hand on Hector's shoulder. "You've got to trust me."

The man could just take it if he wanted, but he didn't. This, too, gave Hector reason to trust him. Still, why would he want to see the note? Surely, he couldn't read it. But if showing him the note helped to come up with a plan to save his papa, then Hector would do it.

He brought it out from his back, and, after a brief hesitation, held it out. Hector watched in amazement as the Runaway Man appeared to read the note. Then he became curious when he noticed part of a finger missing from his hand.

When the Runaway Man looked up from the note, he asked, "Are you wondering about my finger? Haven't you ever seen an African with a finger cut off? This is what some folks do to an African if they catch him trying to learn to read or write. But I showed them." He tapped the note with his partial finger. "Their abuse can't stop a man who is determined. Now I can read and write better than most white men. And I talk better, too."

He returned to reading the note. He told Hector that Higgins' note offered to sell his father to the Simmons brothers, but they would need to come today to negotiate the agreement.

Hector's voice cracked as he said, "Why would he do that? My papa the best worker he got. He can pick a bunch more cotton than any of them. How you know you reading that note right?"

"He's doing it because he's scared. Your father challenged him today. Your master's afraid other slaves might rebel if he lets your father off too light. Before, Higgins could have sold your father for a lot of money, but in his beat-up condition he's not worth much, and he's in no shape to make a long trip."

"Why my papa go and do something crazy like that anyway? He knowed better. Now he going to the Simmons, and I'll never see him again."

"Listen, I have a plan, but for it to work you have to be brave. Listen to what I want you to do, and tell me if you can do it."

"What you want me to do?"

"You won't go to the Simmons place. We'll wait here together for about the amount of time it would take you to walk there and back. When you return to Higgins, tell him the Simmons brothers said if they are interested, they will come by sometime tonight to make a deal. You got that?"

"I think so."

"When they don't show up, he will suppose they aren't interested. He's going to have everything packed, so I doubt that he'll hang around for long. I figure he'll either take your father along or leave him behind. If he takes him, then your family will stay together. If he leaves him, I'll care for him. Either way, it will be better than being sold to the Simmons. Don't you agree?"

"I reckon so. Them Simmons bad people."

The Runaway Man tore the note into little pieces.

Hector took in a deep gulp of air. "Why you do that?"

"Because you don't need it, and we don't want to leave it around for someone to find."

The Runaway Man walked to a rock and sat. He motioned for Hector to join him.

"How come my papa did such a thing? If he hadn't said those things, everything would be all right now." Hector's head hung low.

"Your papa didn't have any choice about what he did. He had to challenge Higgins just as sure as a bird has to fly. Did you ever know a bird that was content to just walk on the ground?"

"No."

"Hector, we were never meant to be slaves. And your papa, he's determined to be free. Some folks allow life to take them down a notch, and eventually they forget who they really are and settle for less. But your papa can't forget who he is. His spirit cries out to be free. Your papa was living a life he couldn't accept.

"In Africa, the village where I come from, the spirits give a song to women to sing to their children when they are born. The song tells us who we are. That song is a gift to us from the Earth. Inside of your papa, there is a song that only he can hear. He heard his song, and it pulled him to freedom. I don't guess you understand what

I'm telling you. I hope someday you will. I hope someday you listen to your own song."

"Well, I reckon I kinda understands what you is saying, except about the song."

"Never mind that now," said the Runaway Man. "What are you going to say when you return?"

"I'll say that there wasn't anyone home, so I left the note on the porch." Hector waited to see if the man approved.

"Hmmm…maybe that's better than what I suggested. If you say you spoke with them, and they should show up at Higgins' place, then he would know you lied. The only problem is—they don't have a front porch." He thought about this and then said, "I've been by their place a few times, talked with their slaves. All too scared to escape. There is a chair out front near the door. Tell him you put the note on the chair with a stone on top. That'll save your skin should they happen by. If they should come visiting and claimed they never saw the note, tell them it must have blown away."

They practiced what Hector would say to John, and before his courage made him ready, Hector walked back to the Higgins plantation with the lie in his head. With each step, his self-doubts grew, as did his worry that he would say the wrong words and cause the death of himself and his father. But he also remembered the big man's words. *I gots to be brave.*

He turned off the road heading towards the massa's house. He stopped suddenly on seeing the Simmons brothers talking to John.

Had they just happened by? Did they somehow know of my lie? Their plan ruined. His world came crashing in on him. He wanted to hide.

But his master saw him. "It's about time, boy. Get up to the house and help the missus. Where's that note I gave you?"

Hector tried to appear calm while his insides shook with panic. From somewhere the lie came quick. "I left it at the house, Massa."

He rushed to the house in a hurry to get away from any more questions. As he passed by the men, one of the Simmons brothers sneered at him. "We'll be takin' your papa in the mornin'. Better say your goodbyes 'cause you won't be seein' him no more." The brothers laughed at their joke.

John shuffled his feet uncomfortably.

Hector paused as long as he dared to check out his beloved father. How could his father be saved now? No one could help.

CHAPTER 8

Harriet

John stared out from his porch at the bloodied, lacerated William. The flies found him almost the second the whip stopped. They buzzed wildly before landing to drink his blood. John finally called to Roscoe, "Cut William loose—and don't let a lot of carrying-on stop the work. Morning's almost gone."

John watched Roscoe cut the bonds, and then Silas help lay the unconscious William onto the ground. Remorse percolated inside John for a brief moment, but his dislike for William and his eagerness to dominate him stuffed the feeling into a remote part of his brain where it no longer burdened him. He returned to work, thinking no more of it.

Roscoe grabbed Richard to help, and with Silas, the three carried William into his shack. Harriet had spread out their worn sleeping mat where they laid him face-down. Harriet kneeled beside him, stroking his hair and whispering, "You get better." She gently kissed his head and ear, wanting him to know of her love, her presence, wanting him to wake up, to show some sign of life. She shooed the flies, disturbing their incessant buzzing for a brief moment. She laid his torn shirt over his back.

"All right, everybody get back to work," said Roscoe. "Harriet, you stay with William and do what you can for him. Don't go wanderin' around outside. If the massa sees you, he'll put you to work."

Roscoe then hurried to Sarah's cabin before John placed more demands on him. Too old to do any lifting or livestock work, Roscoe recruited her to use her herbal knowledge to help William.

When Sarah first saw William's back, she patted Harriet's arm and said, "Be strong. His back in bad shape, but I seen worse than this do well." She searched the wooded area behind the quarters, gathering horehound and slippery elm to make a paste for William's back and barks to make a healing tea.

When Sarah returned, she asked Harriet to get some water and to start a fire. For an instant, the two women held each other. Harriet whispered, "Please make him better, Sarah."

Sarah examined William again, then focused her small brown eyes on Harriet. "I gonna do all I can to hep him. Don' you worry none. We gonna take good care of him." Her wrinkled hand patted Harriet's arm.

William remained still, though at times his lips moved slightly, uttering barely audible, incoherent sounds. Sarah placed the horehound and slippery elm into the water when it started to bubble. Its pungent smell stung their noses as the mixture boiled into a thick paste, which she applied liberally to William's back. He twitched and groaned with each touch. She then made a tea from the bark to calm him.

"This gonna hep him to sleep, an' while he be sleepin', his back gonna start healin'," she said to Harriet.

Harriet helped turn him to one side, then held his head while Sarah poured her hot potion into his mouth. Some dribbled out onto his cheek and down his neck. He coughed as the dark liquid trickled into his throat. He lay still as death.

Harriet kept near him in spite of John's order for everyone to work. Caressing his arm, Harriet said, "We loves you, William." She clutched his arm against her bosom, swaying gently as she touched him.

As the day came to an end and darkness enshrouded the plantation, Hector and Margaret returned. Before entering their room, they stopped to view the solemn scene before them. Hector ventured in first and sat near his father. Hector was filled with rage at the massa for whipping his father and at himself for not stopping the beating.

Margaret ran to her mother and threw her arms around her. "Momma, is he dead? Is Papa dead?"

"No, child. Now hush, your daddy ain't dead. He hurt is all."

Hector's eyes met his mother's, and he said, "He hurt real bad, ain't he, Momma?"

"Well," she said, raising one hand to her mouth as if stopping the words from coming would somehow make him better. "I reckon he is that." Her voice cracked at the truth she spoke.

Silas, Katie, and Dee entered from their portion of the shanty. "How's William?" asked Silas.

"Sarah done some potions for him. She think he going to be all right."

"We brung you some food," said Katie. She handed a bowl to Hector. "You needs to keep your strength."

Harriet thanked them, and they left.

"Momma," said Margaret, "Massa John say we going to leave tomorrow for Florida. Papa going with us?"

Harriet's eyes teared. She could not respond.

"Papa's not going with us?" asked Margaret, her voice rising to a high pitch.

"Just be quiet," said Hector, his hands balled into fists.

Harriet and her children sat around William during much of the night, unable to sleep, worried about their future without this husband and father they loved so completely. As the night wore on, one by one each lay down. Their morning departure would come much too soon.

CHAPTER 9

Leaving

That night, John did not sleep well either. He, along with all his family, slept on quilts laid on the floor. But he didn't blame his interrupted sleep on the lack of a bed. He blamed, in part, anxiety about the move. He mostly blamed his nightmare. The dark figure returned to torment him so vividly that he thought he would die. Awake in the early morning hours, soaked with sweat, he succeeded in putting aside his dream and thought first about the impending move, going over in his mind what must be done, for the hundredth time. But his dream would not be denied. Vague in the beginning, detail by horrific detail came screaming back.

He lay in a coffin, the box tight against him. He heard his breath push against the lid. His cramped space closed in on him. He pounded frantically on the lid. He sensed something beside him and managed to turn his head. Even in the obscurity, he knew the same dark figure lay next to him. For the shortest moment, a memory of an attractive female slave flashed into his mind. He wondered about the connection—if one even existed. After a time, his vision faded, drowsiness overcame him, and he slept.

In spite of his interrupted sleep, John rose early, eager to begin his journey. With first light he rang the bell to summon everyone to the house. Fog hid the woods in clouds of wispy dampness.

The beauty of the earth belied the upheaval about to take place. Morning dew wet the grass and everything without a cover. The enslaved gathered their few belongings, careful not to take anything too heavy or awkward for their long trek. They all left for the big house—all except William's family.

Katie left the shanty with her family, but when she didn't see Harriet and her children, she became worried. She returned with Silas.

Katie called out, "Harriet?"

No response.

Katie and Silas entered the other room where they found Harriet, Hector, and Margaret sitting around William, unable to leave him.

The family knew they must say goodbye. They could not. Each hoped for a miracle. Maybe after a night's rest, he would be stronger and could go with them, or, perhaps, Higgins would change his mind. None of this happened.

Katie went to Harriet. "Come now, Harriet. You gots to get out now before Higgins get mad with you. Ain't no tellin' what that man'll do." She placed her hand on Harriet's shoulder. "Please."

"Can't leave him, Katie. Can't jus' walk out that door with him here like this."

"You gots to."

"No."

Silas got on the other side of Harriet and took her arm, trying to lift her. "Bring your children, Harriet."

She jerked her arm away. "Ain't right. Can't nobody make me go."

Suddenly, Sally entered the room. Looking very nervous, she said, "I'm so very sorry. How is William?"

Hector stood. "Thank you for coming, Miss Sally, and for what you did. We all hope he going to be all right."

"Well, I certainly hope so, too." She looked quickly over her shoulder. "I better go." She glanced at Hector as she made her way out.

Shortly after Sally left, Roscoe burst into the shanty bellowing out commands, but he quieted upon seeing the sorry scene before him. He said to Silas, "Take Hector and Margaret to the house."

Silas kneeled next to the children. "Say your goodbyes. We gots to go now."

Hector kissed his father on the cheek. "It seem wrong that I gots to leave you lying there. When I gets big, I'm gonna make you proud of me. When I gets big, I ain't gonna do nothin' that feels wrong." Fighting back tears, he stood and walked outside.

Margaret uttered a desperate cry. "Papa, wake up. Please wake up. You got to come with us. You our father."

Silas gently lifted Margaret. "Come with me, Margaret. We don't want no more trouble."

Roscoe, showing more compassion than Katie had ever seen from him, touched Harriet's shoulder. "Go with your children. They need you," he said. He motioned for her to help Harriet up.

Katie took Harriet's arm. "Roscoe's right. We all be aroun' to help you. We all family here."

Leaning heavily on Katie, Harriet rose and walked unsteadily towards the house, snatching a glimpse back every few steps, hoping for that miracle.

John barked out instructions for the last-minute packing, rounding up animals, and hitching wagons. Hector helped with gathering chickens and pigs and putting them in cages, his brooding mind never far from his papa. Harriet and Margaret, compelled to assist, unenthusiastically helped pack the last few household items.

Canvas, held in place by green willow branches bent and fastened to the sides, covered the four wagons. Two oxen pulled the heaviest wagon piled high with furniture and tools, while mules and horses pulled the others. Adam managed the first of the wagons; Silas another; Wiley, an older slave, managed a third; and the fourth, Richard. Old Sarah, too old to walk a long distance, rode in the wagon next to Wiley, as did Katie's younger children.

John scanned the road, searching impatiently for the Simmons brothers. "Well, the hell with them. I got my money. They can find William when they get here. We ain't waiting for them. Let's get movin'."

The small wagon convoy headed south with John leading the way and Roscoe in the rear. The cattle meandered along behind the wagons surrounded by slaves who kept them from straying. Martha, Sally, and Sam rode in the first wagon.

As they pulled away, Hector looked back one more time at their old shack.

What's gonna happen to Papa?

He wanted to feel the strong hand of his father on his shoulder, to listen to his stories. At every curve in the road, he stopped briefly, hoping to see his papa walking down the road, hurrying to catch up.

Harriet never looked back. *No need to go wishin' an' hopin' for somethin' that ain't gonna happen.* She remembered long ago when they took her from her parents and then took her from her children. Never saw them again. *Never gonna see William again neither. Might as well face it.*

Hector walked to his mother and took her hand. She managed a smile. "Hey, Momma," he said, feeling the heavy weight of his life, needing her strength.

Margaret walked alongside her mother, holding tight to her other hand.

"Hector, I been taken away from my family before and never seen them again after. Those was awful times. Never thought I'd live through it. But I did. This feel even worse. But we'll get through this." She squeezed Hector's hand.

Margaret listened to her mother's words. "When we goin' to see Papa again, Momma?" Her voice shook with emotion.

Harriet stopped and bent down to give Margret a hug and kiss her cheek. When they resumed walking, Margaret peered back over her shoulder. "Papa," she whispered, as tears filled her eyes.

As the wagons rounded a bend in the road, Roscoe rode to the front to talk with John. He pointed to the sky in the direction from which they had come. A thick stream of smoke rose some distance away, possibly from the area of the Simmons' farm. What the curl of smoke meant, no one could say. But Hector instinctively thought of the Runaway Man and, in the back of his mind, a secret grew that he couldn't share with anyone, a bit of hope that perhaps the Runaway Man could save his papa after all.

They traveled south on a trail that led them through the towns of Darlington and Barnwell. Gradually, the narrow trail became the only remaining sign of civilization. Rocks and tree stumps hampered their progress. Brush and small trees grew too close to the road, or sometimes, in the road. Their removal consumed valuable time.

They hadn't seen another person for three days. On the fourth day, traveling a low, flat, treeless stretch of terrain, John stopped his caravan. He had spotted a small group of travelers in the distance. Unable to tell if they posed a threat, he cautioned Adam and Roscoe to have their rifles ready and to stay alert. In these isolated regions, lawless groups of men roamed with impunity.

The travelers were a wandering family of Indians. They numbered eight in all, a man with a rifle and bow, a woman, and their six children. Two of the children looked to be in their teens and also carried bows.

The Indians stopped fifty yards from John's convoy. Each group studied the other, unsure of what to expect. The Indian leading them spoke to the others, then urged his horse forward; the others remained in place. The Indian raised his hand in peace as he approached.

John hadn't seen Indians around here for years. The man rode horseback, his muscular chest bare and his long, black hair flowing loosely over his shoulders. The woman wore clothing made of animal skins; her braided hair was adorned with colored beads.

A horse pulled their belongings, wrapped in skins and tied atop a travois. The Indian stopped his horse ten yards from John and said, "We have many fruits and other foods to trade for bullets."

John replied, "We don't have any bullets to trade." Following an awkward silence, the trade talks resumed, and eventually they settled on an exchange of a few chickens for a quantity of fruit and nuts.

The Indians passed by John's wagons in single file, for the narrow road bordered by sharp-edged palmettos allowed for nothing more. Hector watched as the Indians moved past him. The last Indian to pass, a young boy about Hector's age, stopped his horse and shouted something to Hector. Hector did not understand, but he waved at the Indian boy. The Indian raised his bow and shouted "Yip," as he kicked his horse and galloped away. Hector paused in wonder. *How great to be that free.*

CHAPTER 10

The Runaway Man

The Runaway Man remained hidden as he watched John and his unlikely procession travel down the road out of sight. He waited another few minutes, just to be safe, before approaching the building where William rested. He didn't expect the Simmons brothers to come anytime soon, he'd seen to that, but he wanted to work quickly nonetheless. No need to be in a hostile place any longer than necessary.

His first task—get William to a safe location. William looked to be unconscious or asleep, he couldn't tell which. "William. William," he said, in a subdued voice. He touched him on the arm, causing William to grimace and mumble unintelligibly.

I didn't want to do this, thought the Runaway Man. *But I have no choice.*

He brought William to a standing position by putting his hands under his shoulders and lifting. He guided William so he fell over his right shoulder, then carried him out. Cuts just beginning to scab ripped open, and blood trickled down his back once again. William pushed at the Runaway Man, grunting his displeasure. The Runaway Man, burdened with William's dead weight, struggled to get him to the travois he had prepared the day before. Once he placed William safely on the travois, he retraced his steps. Then he made his way back to William, erasing his tracks with a leafy branch.

As he pulled William, he stopped every few hundred feet to erase any trace of their passage. Their journey would be a dangerous one—two to three days travel, avoiding roads, struggling through wooded areas that didn't lend themselves to walking, much less pulling an injured person.

The Runaway Man reached to his side on occasion, checking his pistol. He hoped he could make it back without having to use it, but he wouldn't hesitate if anyone threatened their safety or freedom.

Hours after the Runaway Man left dragging William behind him, the Simmons brothers arrived. "Looks like ol' man Higgins couldn't wait."

"Yeah. He sure as hell better have left that big nigger for us."

"Let's look around in these shacks, see if we find him."

They dismounted and separated as they checked out each of the shanties.

"Jake, get over here."

"Did you find him?"

"No, but look here. This mat's got blood on it. Bet this is where he was. I don't think ol' man Higgins would've taken him. I bet he's hiding somewhere around here. Let's spread out and search around. We'll find him."

After a thorough search without finding William, Jake said, "Tell you what, I'll get the dogs. They'll sniff him out. You keep looking around."

"Good idea. They'll find him in no time."

The Runaway Man worried about his water supplies being low and William's condition, especially with the rocky, jarring terrain. He stopped to rest, leaning against a large oak tree. A few minutes later, he jerked upright. The unmistakable baying of hounds on the hunt electrified him. He jumped up and hustled along with William in tow.

He hoped to reach the river before the dogs reached him. It would be close—he knew the dogs and men travelled much faster than he. He calculated the river lay about a mile ahead.

The dogs sounded too close when he plunged into the river, pulling William with him. He knew the river here—he'd crossed it many times. The current wasn't impossibly fast, and the water, at its deepest, only about five feet deep. Still, he used the current to help him move downstream, floating William alongside him.

He came to a rocky area on the other side, where he left the river. He hid William in thick underbrush well off the path that ran alongside the river. He crouched among a thicket of trees fifty yards from where he had entered the water. He had a clear view of his hunters. He recognized them at once. *The Simmons brothers. Well, let's see what they'll do now.*

The dogs ran in circles sniffing the ground, howling like they'd gone mad. The men conversed briefly then split up, one crossing the river, the other taking the dogs downstream. Runaway Man focused on the one crossing the river. He recognized this one—they called him Lucky. Once he made it to shore, Lucky turned his horse and moved slowly in the direction of Runaway Man.

Well hidden, William would be safe from Lucky's view. Runaway Man quickly pulled one of the supports from the travois and hid along the path where Lucky likely would pass. Once he passed, Runaway Man stepped out and swung the support hard, connecting with Lucky's head. His hat flew off, and Lucky dropped like a rock. Just to be sure, he wacked him a second time. He used the rope coiled on Lucky's horse to tie him and stuffed a piece of Lucky's shirt in his mouth. Then he lugged Lucky into the thick brush. He struggled to hoist William onto the horse. Once William was seated, he jumped on behind and headed home.

CHAPTER 11
John

The hot, still air made walking and breathing a chore. The forest itself seemed to rest. No rustling of leaves, not a chirp was heard. The only noise was the creaking of wagon wheels and the footfalls of men, women, and beasts.

CRACK!

A rolling rumble broke the quiet; every head twisted upward in surprise. A huge cloud, so black it quickened pulses and stopped some in their tracks, drifted towards them, covering the sky. A sudden cool breeze invigorated people and animals alike. The cloud moved on their path, blocking the sun, turning afternoon to dusk. Trees came to life, their branches rustling in the wind, leaves and swaying bushes whipped into a frenzy. The sky rumbled loudly, far off at first, then closer. Water spattered leaves and pounded the earth with enormous drops, soaking the small caravan and those following behind. The downpour quickly became a torrential rain, drenching everything, scattering everyone to seek shelter.

"I never seen so much damn rain," shouted John, as he and his family squeezed into the loaded covered wagon as best they could.

The rocks came next. The hail pummeled everything in its path, shredding the tarps, striking the humans and animals with vicious force. John yelled at his family, "Get under the wagons!" They scrambled to get under the wagons, but they would all have welts and bruises when it ended. Hail, big as quarters, crashed around them. Everyone dashed to safety under a wagon. The cattle panicked, charging off in all directions. In the end, the landscape resembled a snow scene, except for the devastated foliage and shredded tarps. Over in a matter of minutes, much damage had been done.

John said, "Adam, you and Roscoe take some men and round up the cattle. Then clear some of this damn ice so we can set up camp. We'll be stuck here until this ice melts and the road's dry enough to travel. Hector, go check the livestock on the wagon, see how many survived the storm. Whatever was killed, we'll eat over the next few days."

"I'll go with you," said Sam, reaching for his whip. "You don't know how to count anyway," he said, laughing.

In three weeks' time, they came to the small town of Tebeauville, Georgia. Though small, it bustled with activity thanks to a railroad being built through its middle. John and his assemblage passed through the village and camped in a clearing on the other side.

"I'm going for supplies and taking Adam with me. We'll get cloth to cover the wagons and make repairs. Roscoe, get everything set up here. We'll spend whatever time it takes to make repairs and then move on."

"Yes, sir, Massa."

Before John could mount his horse, two men rode into camp. "Name's Burch. This here's my partner, Wilkes. Was looking over your niggers when you rode through town. We'd like to buy that big'un there." He pointed to Roscoe.

"He's not for sale," said John. "None of 'em are."

"You sure? I'll give you top dollar. Give you $900 for the big'un."

John searched for Hector. "How much you give me for that boy over there?" said John.

"He a problem?"

"No, he's a hard worker."

"Strong?"

"Reckon 'bout as strong as any boy his size."

"Three hunnerd."

Before John could answer, Sally ran up to him. "No. You can't sell Hector. I'll never speak to you again. Papa, don't do this."

"What's her problem?" asked Burch. He laughed. "Seems she likes that nigger a bit too much."

"What you mean by that?" asked John, his eyes drilling into the slave trader.

"Aw, I don't mean nothin'."

"I reckon it's time you men left," said John.

"All right then. Tomorrow afternoon we're selling some good, hard-working slaves. Come on by and see what we got."

"Not interested," said John.

After the men rode off, John turned to Sally. "Don't ever do that again or by God, I'll put you over my knee and paddle you in front of everybody."

"But, Papa…"

"Don't give me no back talk. That's the way it is." He mounted his horse. "Adam, let's go."

Sally watched him ride off, then said softly to herself, "Hector is my friend, and there's nothing you can do about it."

CHAPTER 12

William

William lay face down on a mattress in a darkened room, his consciousness coming and leaving, the fuzzy memories of his beating playing over and over in his head. Unrecognized, muffled voices leaked into his confused space.

Where am I? Who's that talking?

He opened his eyes, then struggled to turn his head, which caused screaming pain to stop him. His back throbbed.

Tiny streaks of light shot through cracks where the ceiling met the walls and from under the door, dimly lighting the room. Through blurred vision, he saw the outline of a small wooden table and two wooden chairs. He lay on a soft mattress. He tried to push himself up and recognized his mistake instantly. A painful surge wracked his body. He moaned.

The talk in the other room stopped. The door opened; the room brightened slightly. Someone stood over him and spoke. He struggled to focus on who spoke, what had been said, but the pain interfered. A hand gently touched his head. He blacked out.

Three hours passed before William woke again. The pain felt like a swarm of bees stabbing his back. The whipping rose to the surface of his mind, and one by one, the events of that fateful day returned.

What has Higgins done with Harriet and the children? Damn you, Higgins. I'll find you. I'll kill you. I'll find you, and I'll kill you with my two hands.

The next day, his vision cleared. He looked about the room as best he could. Nothing looked familiar.

Soft footsteps broke the silence. A door opened, offering more light. The person bent over so they were face to face, and the sight of her stunned him. She looked to be old and white. He shuddered, wondering what was in store for him.

"Hello, William. How are you feeling? For a while, I was afraid you might not make it. I want to assure you that you are perfectly safe here," said the elderly white woman.

William moaned. *Still in slavery. Don't know how I got from Higgins' place to here, but don't matter none. Still a damn slave. I done messed things up bad.*

The stale air freshened a bit with the door open. The scent of food cooking somewhere out of sight drifted into the room. Hunger pangs pricked him. He wanted to ask about his family. He mouthed the words but coughed instead. His throat was dry as cotton. His coughs jerked his body; pain stung his back. He tried to swallow, stop the coughing, but the dryness wouldn't let him. The words couldn't come. Again, he attempted to speak. Again, the words lodged behind his throat. Other footsteps, those of a man, came through the door. Runaway Man appeared beside the woman.

I've been betrayed! Runaway Man—a slave stealer, taking slaves to bring here to his master. William tried to shout his accusation at Runaway Man, but instead came a terrible dry coughing fit.

Runaway Man knelt beside William and held out a tin cup. "Hello, William. Here, drink this water. Help to stop your cough. Glad to see you're coming around. This here's Mrs. Stone. She and her husband help get slaves up North where they can be free. You're in their house now, and you're safe." He gently lifted William's head and trickled water into his mouth.

William drank eagerly, gratefully.

"And by the way, my name is Itch. That's what folks calls me anyway. Best not to call me Runaway Man." He chuckled. "Folks here might not like me helping slaves run away. Mrs. Stone will get you some food. When you're feeling stronger, we'll talk. For now, you need to get something in that stomach of yours."

Mrs. Stone brought in a tray of soup, bread, and another cup of water. Itch and Mrs. Stone helped William turn onto his side and fed him. He couldn't eat much, in spite of his hunger. His agony was too great to remain in this position for long. When she finished and had left, he laid his face back onto the mattress, now wet where water had run down his cheek.

Alone in the dark, he reminisced about his family and of his promise to his mother. He remembered the day when Harriet was first brought to him and told they were to be as man and wife.

When William and Harriet met for the first time in their room that evening after a long day working the fields, Harriet wanted to talk about her previous family and the children she left behind.

"William, I be afraid to have more children. Don't know if I could live through 'nother time of losin' my children. I loves them too much and misses them so much I think I want to die. I knows the massa wants us to make children, but I knows they could be taken any day from me, and I is scared."

William knew what it was like to be snatched from someone you love. He told about his mother and their failed attempt to escape. When they finally lay down to sleep, there had grown a bond between them that formed the beginning of their love for each other.

Rest and food served him well, for in the morning, William made modest gains. His mind cleared, and his appetite improved.

After breakfast, Itch entered the room and sat on the floor in front of William where he could be seen without William having to move.

"How you feeling today?"

"I'm gettin' along a bit better." He stopped to wet his throat. "Where am I, and how did I get here? Where's my family? What—"

"Whoa there, my friend, let's take one question at a time, shall we? How much do you remember from three days ago? You remember the whipping Higgins put on you?"

William's eyes narrowed. "Yeah, I remember that."

"Afterwards, you were unconscious. From a distance, I saw an old woman gathering herbs. She must have made the paste on your back when I found you. Higgins sold you to the Simmons brothers and took everyone south, your family included."

"Damn him, took my family from me. I got to go find them," said William, struggling to move.

"And then what? Get beat again, or hung, for being a runaway?"

Catherine Stone interrupted. "Now listen, you two, that's enough. Itch, William needs his rest. You can talk later." She shooed Itch from the room.

William wondered at the sight of this tiny woman chasing Itch, maybe three times her size, though this really didn't seem unusual. After all, white folks had been ordering around blacks his whole life. But this felt different—she chased him out in a kind, friendly manner. This struck him as peculiar, contrary to everything he'd experienced.

That evening, the door swung open, startling William, interrupting his sleep. Mrs. Stone led a man and woman with three small children, followed by Itch, into the room. The family had a darker complexion and sharper facial features than William. The man's eyes met William's. They nodded, but neither spoke.

"Now, you must all be very quiet until we come to get you. This may take a while, but we must be sure the men looking for you have moved on to look elsewhere. We'll bring you some food shortly. On the mattress over there is William," said Mrs. Stone.

Itch and Mrs. Stone slipped out, closing the door behind them. A solitary candle on the small table lit the room. The family turned to face William, their nervousness showing in their faces and in the rise and fall of their chests. The smallest child clung to his mother's neck, his arms wrapped tightly around her.

Lying in the presence of these strangers, William felt vulnerable; he feared they could cause him to be captured. The family whispered among themselves. William wished they would be quiet.

The troublesome sounds of horses and men penetrated from above. Angry voices invaded their hideaway. Mrs. Stone could be heard and then a man shouting. All faces in the little room stared upward, anxious of the outcome. The tension in the room melted away when the talking ended and the horses pounded off.

Mrs. Stone and a tall, slender man with a full head of white hair entered carrying a basket of fruit and bread. Setting the basket on the table, she said, "Please take what you want to eat for now and something for your journey." She then introduced the man. "This is my husband, Thomas. He's set up the escape plan for you. You will need to remain here for several more hours. We believe the search party has moved on to look for you south of here. My husband and Itch will take you to the next family on your way to Ohio and your freedom. You will need rest; it's a long and dangerous journey." She reached down and stroked the head of the oldest child, perhaps eight or nine, whose large brown eyes suggested her discomfort with all of this.

Thomas shook the hand of the Negro man and spoke softly to the family, encouraging them and assuring them that in a few days, they would be in free territory. He introduced himself to William, welcomed him, and said he expected him to make a complete recovery—though he would have scars on his back to the end of his life.

The family and William were soon left alone, a kerosene lamp their only means of light. William looked at the girl, who studied him. "I gots a girl 'bout same size as you. Her name Margaret. What's your name?"

The girl pushed up against her mother and lowered her head. Her lips moved, but her answer could not be heard. Her mother put her arm around her. "It's okay. Tell the man your name."

This time, a bit louder, "Mandisa."

Her father spoke up. "We go to Canada, where we be free. No more fear. No more slave."

William nodded in recognition of the risks involved and the good fortune the man had in having his family with him.

Shortly after the family left the room, William heard a wagon creak and rumble, and he realized the family was being carried away to safety.

Once again alone, he lay on the mattress with only his thoughts for company.

CHAPTER 13

John

By the end of the second month, the travelers longed for the journey to end. They came upon an abandoned plantation, where the fields had been cleared for planting but now contained overgrown weeds and a few trees. The charred remains of what looked to have been a beautiful home lay wasted among the fields. The partial remnants of a chimney and the ruins of a stone wall stood as testimony to what once had been here.

A short distance farther, they encountered a swamp that seemed at first to be a quiet body of shallow water dense with trees and bushes. But as they passed, the swamp came to life, giving birth to mosquitoes, flies, and tiny unseen insects, all swarming in great numbers. They invaded eyes, ears, and nose, attacking with great ferocity this welcome assortment of living creatures.

John spotted a clearing on the opposite side of the road from the swamp where, in spite of the bugs, he decided to make camp for the night. He had no choice—darkness would soon make travel impossible. The enslaved busied themselves gathering wood to build fires, hoping the heat and smoke would drive enough bugs away to make life bearable.

While dinner was being prepared, John noticed a stranger talking to Silas, who pointed John out to the stranger. Approaching John, the stranger stuck out his hand. "Name's Garner," he said.

"I'm Higgins, John Higgins."

"I'm heading north to Atlanta. Saw you folks making camp here. Where you headed?" he asked. He reached up and pushed his hat back, revealing a patch of skin that hadn't been tanned by the sun.

"Florida," said John. "'Bout how much farther before we get there?"

"Well," he said, his face taking on a serious look while he calculated his answer. "The way I figures it, with them wagons you got to pull an' all, I reckon you'll be rollin' in to Florida in two, maybe three days."

John stood. "That ain't so bad. Hey, Martha," he shouted. "We're just three days the most to Florida."

She said something John couldn't hear, then returned to repairing a blouse.

John invited Garner to stay for dinner. During the meal, he said, "Some folks say this part of that swamp over there is got ghosts in it an' they spook some folks that pass this way."

John raised his eyebrows. "You ever seen these so-called ghosts?"

"Nope. Never have. Now I ain't sayin' it's true," said Garner. He picked up a stick and broke it in two, then threw it into the fire. "I just know what folks say is all. The ghosts they talk of is all niggers." Garner dropped his voice. "The story goes that a long time ago, some coloreds was plannin' on killin' their white folks an' runnin' away. But one of them told his master, an' all them was caught right about here an' was hung on these trees aroun' here. All but one, that is. He escaped into the swamps an' never was seen again. Anyway, it's his ghost an' the others that live in the swamp." He looked at John, his eyes questioning whether John believed his story.

"That's crazy," said John, "There ain't no ghosts."

"Maybe not. I'm just telling you what people says is all."

During dinner, John asked Garner about Florida. They continued to chat as others moved about searching for a place to sleep. Eventually, John stood and said, "I'm tired. You're welcome to throw your blanket down anywhere you like. I'm turning in."

When the enslaved finished their chores, they also searched for a spot near a fire to sleep. Hector, his mother, and Margaret lay near each other in the grass, covering themselves with their blankets.

In Hector's dream, an African wearing a large, carved mask and carrying a wooden shaft came to him. He beckoned for Hector to follow. The African seemed friendly, and Hector did not fear him, so he followed. They stopped near a house, where the man motioned for Hector to continue. Hector floated toward an open window. He peeked inside. To his surprise, he saw his father talking with white men and black men. Then William saw Hector; his huge smile sent Hector encouragement and love. Hector's dream faded, and he woke up.

"Momma," he whispered. "Momma."

"What is it, child?"

"I saw Papa," he said excitedly.

Harriet's eyes opened wide. "What you talking 'bout, boy? Where?" she asked, sitting up.

"In a dream, Momma. I saw him in a dream, and he saw me."

Harriet closed her eyes and sighed. "Well, that's a nice dream, Hector, an' I wish it be true, but it just a dream."

"No, Momma, I think it really was him. I think he be all right."

"Hector, you talking foolish. That just wishing." She reached out her hand and touched his. "I knows you misses him, just like me. Now you best go back to sleep 'cause we gots lot more walking tomorrow." She reached over, hugging him close.

His mother hesitated, as though she wanted to say more. She smiled a cheerless smile and lay down.

Hector lay down as well, saddened by his mother's response. He felt Margaret touch his arm and heard her say, "Hector, I believes you."

Hector reached over to Margaret and put his hand on her shoulder.

John slept fitfully. He turned onto his side and pulled the blanket over his head. He saw himself outside of the wagon. The trees, nothing but dark outlines against the lighter moonlit sky, appeared odd. Thick vines hung from the tree branches. Wait. Not vines. Bodies. Limp, unmoving bodies in all the trees, dozens of them.

The swamp beckoned. Fear tried to hold him back, but the swamp's lure pulled too strong. He stopped at the edge of the water, sensing a presence beyond his vision in the murky darkness. A shadow moved. A familiar figure. "Who's there?" he called out.

Suddenly, a huge African man with wild hair and a long stick rushed him. John tried to step back, to run, but he couldn't move—stuck in a web. He struggled, but he could not get away from the terrifying man. The African grinned, his teeth white and sharp. He raised his stick, the end razor-edged. He brought it down on John's right shoulder, slicing through it. His arm fell to the ground and turned into an African female. She stood, scowling at John, staring with her piercing eyes before running into the swamp.

The African raised the sharp instrument to cut off John's head. As he swung it towards John—John sat up, gasping. He felt for his arm, just to be sure. It had all seemed so real.

Martha woke. "What is it, John? Are you okay?"

John's hands covered his face. "I'm fine," he said, "just a bad dream. Think I'll go for a walk. Maybe it'll help me get to sleep."

He climbed out of the wagon. A red glow from the coals of last night's fire provided some light. Everyone slept except Jacob, who kept watch. John didn't like giving the slaves a turn at watch, but it had become impossible for him, Adam, and Roscoe to stay up four-hour shifts every night.

John checked the trees—no hanging bodies. He walked towards the swamp. *Maybe I should walk somewhere else*, he thought. *But why should I? What am I afraid of? Surely not a ghost.* He shook his head at his foolishness. *And not a dream either.* His dread increased as he neared the swamp. He ignored it.

In the dark, the watery squish of his foot against the wet ground provided his first hint of the swamp's edge. He scanned the swamp. *What's out there? Just a bunch of insects and snakes. No damn ghosts.* He decided to go back, leave the swamp and his crazy thoughts. Someone pressed his shoulder. Startled, he spun.

"John! What on earth is wrong?" said Martha. "You look like you saw a ghost."

"No," he said. "No ghost." He held her tight. "Everything's all right, dear."

When they had taken a few steps towards the wagons, an eerie sound, almost a laugh with a human quality to it, came from the swamp. They stopped and turned to peer into the sinister marsh.

John took a deep breath. "What the hell was that?"

"Oh, just some swamp animal." She took his hand, giving him a gentle pull towards the camp. "Let's get some sleep, John."

He shuddered, standing transfixed for a few seconds longer, then ushered Martha towards the wagon, walking a bit faster than normal.

Martha said, "John, look how beautiful the sky is. It's so full of stars. There must be no end to them."

John grunted.

Back in the wagon he lay down, hoping for a quiet night's sleep. But his mind went to the woman in the swamp, the one who had sprang from his arm—she seemed familiar, but he couldn't place her. Someone from years ago, perhaps? The same woman in those damn nightmares? *How are they connected?* he wondered. *Why won't she leave me be?*

CHAPTER 14

William

William's strength returned a little each day. He stretched his arms until the pain became unbearable, then he rested before stretching again. He did not like depending on others. He focused on moving about, caring for himself.

After a week in the basement, he pushed onto his left side to feed himself, ignoring the pain. He sat upright for the first time—a thousand knives piercing his back. Over time, he was able to sit for longer periods, the effort becoming less agonizing—until finally, he stood. And then on to walking, a few steps at first, but gradually longer and longer strolls around the dismal basement.

The night finally came when Itch took him outside. William swallowed up the fresh night air until his lungs nearly burst. He placed his hand on Itch's shoulder. "Thank you. I feared I might never know fresh air again."

Itch showed him the boundaries where he could safely walk at night. "East—to where the road curves, but don't cross over. South—as far as you want, but don't get lost. West—stop at the fence that begins the neighbor's land. The road running in front of the house is north. Don't cross it. Take care you don't run into patrollers."

William walked every night, pushing himself to exhaustion. How he loved being under the infinite sky. Despite the risk of patrollers, he needed these walks.

William never knew when the next runners would join him in the basement. When they arrived, he had to remain inside with them—too many angry white men in the area. In the past few weeks, he'd witnessed four men, two women, and three families pass through on their way to freedom. Each time, the pattern repeated: They arrived with Itch, scared, hungry, and suspicious, with only the clothes on their backs. The Stones welcomed and fed them. When the slave owners came, the Stones sent them off in another direction or feigned ignorance. Later, Thomas Stone and Itch transported them to their next station.

"Glad to see you doing better," said Itch, approaching William on his nightly walk. "I been meaning to speak with you, but things been hectic 'round here, as you know. You must have a bunch of questions for me."

"Yeah, I got plenty of questions, that for sure. Mostly 'bout my family."

"I know Higgins took them south, I think to Florida, but I'm not sure."

"Florida? Yeah, that where Higgins say he was headed."

"It's a long way to Florida. It will be difficult to find your family. I'm sure you know this. When you get stronger, and the time is right, I'll do what I can to help. Meanwhile, I want to speak with you about something. When you're ready to return, come inside and let's talk."

The outdoors, with its forest and wildlife, reminded William of his mother. He loved the stories of her childhood and of her village. Her voice softened as she spoke of her remembered life. He would close his eyes and visualize her running free. A desire for such freedom welled up so great he thought he might fly apart.

Now he walked as a free man. Not totally free. The fear of being taken by the patrollers still existed. The color of his skin placed limits on him. But he tasted freedom—a small taste, like a swallow of water to a man with a parched throat. Walking at night with no one keeping tabs on him, no one telling him what to do, just him and the forest—these moments fueled his dreams.

William moved forward in the darkness, his mother's voice in his head. *They was shootin' guns at us an' we was runnin' to get away, runnin' to hide among de trees, jumpin' in de river, anywhere to get away from de white devils. An' dey had black peoples with dem to help catch us. Don' know why dem blacks would help de white devils. We was stacked into a dark room on a big boat for long time. Some dies an' men come to carry them away. We all sick. Didn't see no sun for long time. Jus dark an' more dark. Don't ever forget: Ain't nuthin' like freedom.*

He remembered her—tall, thin, determined. Physically stronger than she appeared. An ugly scar across her forehead marred her otherwise pretty face. And when he hugged her, the scars on her back endured as testimonials to her strong will.

Another half mile, and he had reached his limit—both his own physical limit and the land boundary where the road curved sharply to the right. He lay on his stomach to rest, allowing the earth to soothe him.

On William's return to the house, he found Itch at the kitchen table with the Stones. They waved William over to join them. Drawn curtains hid them from passersby.

Itch cleared his throat. "William, you know we help slaves escape to the North. We want to invite you to join us. I travel this area, sometimes twenty miles or more, to find slaves who want to escape. Dr. Stone travels in his work and gives me information that helps identify these slaves. I can't be effective in this area because people know me. But no one knows you. You could help local slaves escape, and no one could tie you to the Stones."

Dr. Stone added, "We'll be honest with you, William, this is very dangerous work." He shifted in his chair; an air of concern enveloped him. "You, of course, already know this. If you get caught, you will surely be tortured and killed. On the other hand, you will be doing very important work. You will be giving lives back to people and families who are living under a brutal system."

"Well, yes, sir, that's true, an' I did wish to escape. But now, I just wants to find my family."

"William, I know you want to be with your family, but right now that's impossible," said Itch. "There's no way a lone Negro could make it to Florida, even if you knew the way. The first time a white man saw you, you would be his slave, or they might hang you as a lesson to others. By helping us, you would actually have a better chance of returning to your family."

"How's that?"

"Because I would teach you everything I know about survival. Then, when you go to Florida, you wouldn't be caught by anyone, or, at least, it would be less likely. After a few years working with me, you would be better prepared to survive the trip and have a much better chance of finding your family."

William frowned. "A few years? That a very long time."

They talked deep into the night. When William finally went to bed, he mulled over their offer. He had decisions to make.

Having a conversation as equals with Dr. Stone and his wife seemed unreal. If white people were devils, where did Dr. Stone and his wife fit in? They treated William good now, but at any time, he knew they could change. What would it take for them to sell him, or beat him? Not much. After all, they were white.

With the morning's arrival, the questions from the night before came rushing back. His small basement room carried the odor of sweat and fear from all the runaways shuffled in and out. He waited in the dark for Itch to knock on the door, his signal that all was safe. His knock came soon enough.

Catherine Stone kept an immaculate kitchen. Breakfast graced the table. The small table had a clean, crisp tablecloth and silverware set out on a clean napkin. The inviting aromas of a bowl of hot, fresh cornbread, molasses, and ham pulled everyone to the kitchen.

Morning sunlight filtered in through the drawn curtains. Thomas blessed the food. William ate in silence, longing for his family to experience such comfort and plenty.

Shortly after the meal started, William set down his fork and looked at the three people around the table. "I been thinkin' about what you said last night." He picked up his fork, tapped it on the table, set it down. "I decided to stay for a short time and help you, and you teach me what you know to help me find my family. Don't know for sure how long I'll stay. Two years be a long time. Even one year be too long. But for now, I'll stay an' help you."

Itch nodded. "I'm happy to hear that, William. We won't go out together until you've regained more of your strength. For now, I'll teach you what I can. Perhaps, for starters, I can teach you to read and write."

Stunned, William looked at Itch. He hesitated, then found his voice. "Never thought I would read. I would like that…"

The next morning, Mrs. Stone welcomed William with, "Merry Christmas, William."

"I didn't know it was Christmas."

"We've been so busy we really haven't had much time to think about it. We thought today we would go to the town church to celebrate. Unfortunately, you will have to remain here to keep from being known by the town folks."

"That be fine. I can work on my letters." *And I can start thinkin' about finding my family and getting us all to Canada.*

CHAPTER 15

Itch

1860

William and Itch spent many nights together talking and planning for that first time they would go out together. Everything had to be precise—no mistakes, no unnecessary risks, follow Itch's orders to the letter.

One evening after a reading lesson, William asked Itch how he had gotten the name "Itch."

"I suppose I should start at the beginning. My real name is Intikuma." He breathed in deeply, closed his eyes, and allowed his story, with all its love and all its pain, to come to him. "I loved my village and the people in it. Such a wonderful place to grow up. I had been going through a ceremony to allow me to be trained by the healer of my village when a gang of slavers stole me. The thing I remember most about crossing the ocean on that horrible ship is a spiritual connection with my father. It got so bad that I wanted to die. My father spoke to me then and helped me survive those unbearable months in the bottom of the ship.

"Everyone calls me 'Itch' because Intikuma is too hard to say. Actually, as a slave, they called me Elijah. That's one of the ways they control us—take away our identity. I don't need to tell you that."

Itch opened his eyes and smiled as he glanced at William. "When I became free, I wanted to return to my own name. But one day, I got tangled up with some poison oak, and it drove me crazy. I scratched and complained all the time. So, after that, the name Itch kind of stuck. Answering to Itch took getting used to."

Now all the questions William had been wanting to ask came flooding back. "How you get me here from Higgins' place?"

"How much do you remember about that day Higgins beat you?" asked Itch. He plucked a weed to chew on.

"I remember Higgins called us to the big house to tell us he changing the date to move. And I recollects about the whipping. I don't remember nothing after that until I wakes up here."

"The day he called you to 'the big house,' I was watching from the woods. I saw you trying to say something to Higgins. Then he had you tied to a tree and started whipping you. He didn't stop until you were unconscious. During the time he was whipping you, I didn't hear you cry out one time. That was brave but also foolish. Higgins wanted to hurt you, and he might have stopped earlier if you had yelled out. You have a lot of pride in you, William. Don't let it get you killed."

"My Harriet tell me the same thing, but I wasn't going to give him any pleasure in whipping on me," said William, his voice hard.

"I know how you feel," said Itch. "After you blacked out, he sent your son with a note offering to sell you to the plantation next to yours. Only I stopped Hector, and he told me what happened." Itch laughed. "You should've seen the look on Hector's face when I called him. His eyes got big as saucers, an' he turned white as Higgins. Haw! He couldn't see me. He musta thought I was a ghost calling him."

"Hector, my boy, Hector—I would give anything to see him right now."

"Yeah, he a good boy. We made a plan to keep those ruthless brothers from getting you, but it didn't work because they showed up at Higgins' place. They were going to get you that morning before Higgins left. I distracted them to keep 'em away from you 'til Higgins left, so I could get you instead. They were with their slaves in the fields. It wasn't hard to get to the barn, so I figured a barn fire would keep them busy most of the morning. That allowed me to get you out."

"You set fire to Simmons' barn?"

"That's all I could think to do."

"That musta been somethin'," said William, a big grin on his face. "Sure do wish I coulda seen that!"

"Now look, William, we need to keep the barn-burning to ourselves. I don't want the Stones to get wind of it. Understand?"

"You think they wouldn't like you burning a barn, eh?" William said, with a twinkle in his eye.

"Well, I know they would be fine with the trade of a barn for your life, but they don't like any kind of violence. And I agree with them for the most part, but I'm willing to meet violence with violence when needed. They would say that God would show me a different way, and that I shouldn't have acted so rashly. And that may be true, but I sure couldn't think of anything else, and there wasn't much time."

"I sure is mighty grateful for what you did. Don't worry, I won't say nothing to Dr. Stone and his missus."

"Don't get me wrong, they're fine people and have been good to me. I just don't want to disappoint them."

"How come you talks like white folks? You sure don't talk like any black man I ever heard."

"Dr. Stone and his wife taught me to read, so I work to talk like a person with education. I guess I was just plain tired of hearing that we aren't as smart as whites."

The moon, now partially hidden by branches, eavesdropped on their conversation. "I know we as smart as them. When I get my family to freedom, my children goin' to get them an education an' learn to read an' write." William pointed to Itch's hand. "Does you mind my asking what happened to your finger?"

Itch shook his head slowly and said, "When I was a young man, I traveled north to the state of Ohio with my owner, who was buying horses. I was in town with him when I tried to read something on a package. Another slave I worked with on the plantation could read a little and taught me some. I was reading and going over the letters with my finger, learning how to make them. I didn't know my owner was standing behind me. My friend warned me many times, not to let a white person know I could read. But it was too late. He had seen me. I don't think I even knew what I read. He reached down, grabbed me by the hand, and said, 'This is what we do to blacks who try to read and write.' He pulled a knife and cut off this finger. But you know what? That was the best thing that ever happened to me."

"You sure don't make no sense sometimes. Why getting your finger cut off was the best thing ever happen to you?"

"When he cut off my finger, I got scared and took off running. I would never have run from him before, but I panicked and ran right into the town's young Dr. Stone. He grabbed me, and in his very gentle voice had me show him my bleeding stub. He opened his bag and began to take care of it. He calmed me. My owner demanded the doctor release me and stop attending to my wound. Dr. Stone stood between me and my owner. I still remember the rage on his face and the passion in his voice. He said something like, 'If you are the one who cut off this boy's finger, then you are not a man or a Christian. You have no claim to this boy. You have no right to maim an innocent child. Now get out of my sight.' I guess the man was surprised by the doctor's rebuke, because for a minute he just stood there. Then he drew his gun and told the doctor to give him his slave or he would show him what is done in the South to slave stealers and nigger lovers. I thought for sure he was going to kill Dr. Stone, and me, too.

"Just then the sheriff walked up and told him to put his gun away. If the sheriff had come five minutes later, the doctor and I would both have been shot. The sheriff said if he killed the only doctor in town, there was no telling what the people would do to him.

"My owner was furious, but there was nothing he could do. Dr. Stone insisted that I go with him to his office where he could tend to me properly. My owner had to wait outside. Then the doctor faked my escape."

"He helped you escape? With the owner outside the door? How he do that?"

Itch flashed a wide grin. "He opened a window at the back of his office and had me go outside to make footprints going away from the building. To come back in, he told me to walk backwards putting my feet down in the footprints I had already made. A closet in his office had a back wall with a small door. You wouldn't even know the door was there just by looking. I went through the door and hid in a very narrow space. He must have run out and told them I had escaped. He kept me in his office for a few days to make sure my owner had left town.

"Anyhow, after that, Dr. Stone and his wife sent me to Canada. The Stones are Mennonites and are strongly anti-slavery. Years after that, I rejoined them, and we came south to help free more slaves. They didn't want me to come because of the danger to me, but I insisted. And, as you can see, I won that argument.

"I'm sure folks around here talk plenty and don't like how good the Stones treat me, but he's the only doctor around, so they pretty much leave him alone."

"Dr. Stone an' his wife be good folks, but most white folks don't deserve to live," said William, an unexpected harshness to his voice. "Just want to get my family and leave this country. Never gonna be a place here for us black folks."

Itch recognized the feelings. He took the weed from his mouth, started to agree, then thought better of it. Their eyes met. Itch nodded his understanding. Then added, "Okay, William, let's get another reading lesson."

CHAPTER 16

John

John reached across, taking hold of Martha's hand. "Won't be long now. If this map is accurate, Billy's place should be up the road a piece." The wagons creaked along, pulled by tired four-legged animals and followed by equally tired two-legged humans.

"I can't wait for this journey to end," said Martha. "It's been unbearably long since we last set foot in a real house."

The rough, uneven road jostled the wagons and their passengers, but they had traveled worse. Martha sat straight and still, keeping her eye out for Billy's place. Tall, thin pines with an impenetrable undergrowth of palmetto bushes lined both sides of the road. Never had he seen land so flat—flat as a tabletop, he remarked. The road seemed sparsely traveled except for wildlife, judging by the tracks. In the first mile, he spotted prints of raccoons, deer, bear, and even some big cats. John took it all in and wondered if he had made the right decision. At the least, there would be no shortage of game.

On their left, the pine forest gave way to cultivated fields of corn, potatoes, and mostly tobacco. Two shirtless slaves worked the tobacco. Barely visible behind a line of pines, a corral with a handful of horses came into view, then one dilapidated shanty. Lastly, they came upon what appeared to be the main house—a roughly built cabin with a front porch. Set off the road about 200 feet, it appeared too small for his family and, by far, more rustic than the home they had left. Behind the cabin stood a barn, and off to one side, a substantial tree. Seeing the cabin, John's face went slack.

"Is that Billy's house? John, surely your brother wasn't inviting us to stay here?"

John shrugged. "Of course, Billy had no idea if I had a family. But even so, it don't look like much." He saw Martha's disillusionment and feared his shrinking heart might quit. "I'll go make sure we're in the right place." Then, to add some hope to her fading outlook, "And if it is, we can build us a house any size we want. Just look at all them trees."

John's stress increased with each step as he walked to within thirty feet of the cabin. He had hoped for a very different scene. No beautiful home, no Billy running down the steps to greet him, not like he thought it would be…wanted it to be. Not one bit. He hollered, "Hello, the house." No response. He hollered again, still no answer.

Hearing a clanking of metal against metal from behind the house, he walked to the back and then to the barn, taking in the sorry state of the house. The doors stood open. He peered inside, waiting for his sight to adjust to the dim light. His chest felt lighter now, as he anticipated seeing his long-absent brother. He wondered whether he would recognize him after so many years.

"Hello in there!" he shouted.

The clanking stopped.

"Hello," said someone in the shadows.

"Billy?" asked John, hopeful that any second Billy would reveal himself, making all the hardships of the journey worthwhile.

"Nope, name's Ed," said the tall man who stepped forward. John didn't like his squinty eyes. He walked with a swagger. John stiffened.

"There ain't no Billy around here. Don't know as I ever heard anyone called Billy in these parts."

"That's odd," said John. "My name is John Higgins." He put out his hand. Ed stood erect and didn't offer his hand. "My brother, Billy, wrote me a letter several months ago. I done moved my family and all our belongings all the way from South Carolina at his request to be with him. This place fits the directions he gave me. See, right here on the back of this letter."

John held out the crudely drawn map for Ed to see, but Ed didn't take it.

"Is there some other place in this area where Billy might live?"

"Just me and Dusty been living here for the past many years. We built this place. Dusty died a few months ago. He's buried out back. But Billy? Nope, don't know anyone what goes by that name. And there ain't another house around here for a good four, maybe five miles."

This doesn't make any sense, John thought.

"How about taking a look at this map and telling me where I made my mistake," said John, holding out the map again.

Ed took the map and stepped outside to have better light. After studying it for a few minutes, he said, "This appears to be where the map leads to all right, but it sure ain't no place that belongs to your brother. Seems as though somebody's playing a trick on you, Mister. Either that, or whoever drawed this map got it wrong."

John stood motionless, his mind reeling. *Come all this way and there ain't no Billy.* "Seems mighty strange," said John. He waited for Ed's reply.

"Not so strange, really. This here's new territory. Anyone drawing a map would have to know it pretty well. Easy to make a mistake."

"Maybe so. Maybe not. I'm going back to my family, but I might need to speak to you again."

"Anytime."

John started to leave when he realized Billy might have changed his name to hide from anyone pursuing him for the death of the young man back home.

"Where was Dusty from?"

"Says he was from Virginia. Folks died in a fire."

John scowled. "Virginia, eh?" He hesitated, wanting to ask more, but nothing came to him.

"Sorry to trouble you," he mumbled.

John left with a broken spirit. *Has all this journey been for nothing?* He advanced to the front of the house, wondering how Martha would take the news. There, lined up alongside the wagons and his livestock, stood his family and slaves, facing him, all anticipating, anxious, to hear their journey had ended. He made a direct line for Martha.

"John, there must be some logical explanation. Frankly, I'm not the least bit disappointed that we aren't going to move into that dreadful place." She hugged him, thinking he needed some reassurance. Her eyes met his. "We need to make a plan," she said.

"First, we need to find Billy. I know he's here somewhere. We followed his directions perfectly. Let's find a place to camp, then I'll take Adam with me. Roscoe can stay here and tend to things. We'll find Billy if we have to ride fifty miles in every direction. We'll find Billy and be in our new home soon."

As the wagons pulled away, John saw Ed watching them from the door. He didn't like Ed. John didn't trust him. Not one bit.

The caravan lumbered down the road a short way to a clearing of large, moss-filled oaks that provided relief from the intense midday sun. Nearby, a large lake would provide them with fresh water. John organized setting up camp, then left Roscoe in charge as he and Adam left to search for Billy.

Hours later, they returned to camp. An evening chill had set in. Martha knew from John's slumped shoulders that they hadn't found Billy.

"Damn, Martha. I don't know what to make of it. No one's ever heard of Billy. It's like he didn't exist. We learned there's a land office in Gainesville, about three hours ride from here. Tomorrow, I'm going to that land office an' see if they have any record of him."

"I'm sorry, John. I wish it was easier. I know how much you looked forward to seeing Billy." She put her arms around him and kissed him gently on the cheek. "And I've been thinking, John, we have money from selling our land, so we can always buy some land and start again…a fresh start."

"I been tossing that around, too. We'll see. I want you to be happy here—that we could have a better life."

"Our life in South Carolina wasn't so bad, but I'm sure we'll be happy here, too. Let's get some sleep. You've got a long ride ahead of you tomorrow."

"How about right here, Momma?" said Margaret.

"This looks just fine. What do you think, Hector?"

"This be a good place."

Margaret spread her blanket next to her mother's and stretched out. She reached out her left hand and touched her mother. Then she reached out her right hand but couldn't reach Hector.

"Hector, move your blanket in closer."

When Margaret woke up frightened, she wanted to be able to touch her family. Hector let out a sigh, but he moved in closer. Bracing himself on one elbow, he started to ask his mother for a story tonight when he saw Margaret already sleeping. He lay down, looked up at the sky filled with pin-point stars, and wondered about his father.

John rose early and woke Adam. The cool morning air, damp with idle patches of fog, lay like soft blankets spread here and there through the woods. He walked to the campfire and poured himself a cup of coffee. It was still dark, the time just before the sun rose over the horizon. Roscoe had the watch. He had made the coffee and saddled the horses, as John had commanded the night before. John didn't speak to Roscoe. He didn't need to or want to. His thinking focused solely on finding Billy and the long ride ahead. Even though

John and Adam began their trek to the land office at an early hour, the oppressive heat closed in way too early.

"Can't believe it's so damn hot. Back home, it'd be a good bit cooler."

"We made it, though," said Adam. "It was a long trip, but we finally got here."

"Yep," John replied.

"What was Uncle Billy like?"

"Don't know what he's like now. Back when I knew him, he was well-liked by about everyone. Friendly. He could ride and shoot about as good as anyone. Good looking. Don't think he was afraid of anything. Now, who knows what he's like."

"You never talked about him until that letter came. I didn't even know I had an uncle."

"After he disappeared…when he'd been gone for a few weeks, seems like we stopped talking about him. Like he was a bad memory. Now he's disappeared again. We come all this way."

"I think we'll find him. Can't be too far away. I know the trip's been hard on Ma, but we're done now, and I think we'll have a fine life here."

Here's my son trying to cheer me up. How'd he get so caring? Not from me, that's for sure.

They arrived in Gainesville several hours before midday. The town had one main road with wood buildings on either side. The Land Office made itself easy to find, with its big sign above the door.

"Hello, mister. What can I do fer ya?" said the man behind the counter.

He stood a few inches shorter than John, and his attempts to tame his sparse, gray hair did not succeed. Dressed in a suit and white shirt with a collar that pinched his neck, John wondered how the man could breathe with a collar tight as a hangman's noose.

John told him the situation. He ended by saying, "I'm hoping you can tell me where he lives."

"Can't say as I ever heard of Billy Higgins, and I know most folks around here 'cause they come here to lay claim to their land. Just where did his directions lead you?"

"A small cabin north of here. A fellow named Ed lives there. I believe he said his partner was named Dusty, and he died a few months ago."

John pulled out the letter and showed him Billy's map. The man took the map and studied it for a few seconds, gesturing in agreement that it did lead to Ed and Dusty's place.

"Yep, that's true enough what Ed told you. Dusty was quite famous around here. He and an old Spanish black man name of Santiago had their own private war. They finally killed each other a few months back. Hate that it happened. They sure added excitement to these parts and gave us a lot of stories to tell. Why, I remember once—"

"I ain't got time for stories. Are you sure there ain't been nobody here by the name of Billy?"

The man shifted uncomfortably. "Like I said, mister, ain't no Billy in these parts."

"That sure is strange. How about looking through your files just in case he was here and you forgot."

"I ain't fergot."

"Look, we rode half a day to get here. I would be much obliged."

The man rocked back on his heels. "Well, all right." He walked over to his filing cabinet. "Everything's in alphabet order. Shouldn't take long to look. Last name was Higgins?"

"Yes."

"Let's see." He pulled out a drawer. "Here's a Gillespie, Grant, Hampton, Horne, Houston, Jekyll. Nope, no Higgins." The man looked at John with a knowing smile.

After a pause, John said, "Well, guess that's that." He turned to leave, puzzled by there being no trace of Billy. A tremendous weight pressed down on him.

"Hey, mister, sometime when you're not in such a hurry, ask someone about Dusty and Santiago. We got some great stories around here 'bout them two."

"I ain't got time," said John.

"Hey, Pop, you think Billy could've changed his name to Dusty?"

John paused. The thought had occurred to him earlier. Billy on the run. Hiding who he was, what he had done.

"Just one more thing. Could you tell me when Dusty arrived in Gainesville?" asked John, a little hope creeping in.

"Oh, he was here long before I came to this town. I been here about fifteen years. When I got here, he an' Santiago were already going at each other. Stories I heard say that he bought Santiago's old place after Santiago killed the sheriff and a bunch of other men. Santiago swore no white man would ever live on his place, but that didn't scare Dusty. I heard he was a young man when he came here, but I couldn't put no age on him. If you'll hold on for one second," said the man, as he turned back to the file cabinet, "I'll tell you what year he laid claim to his land."

He opened a drawer and shuffled through the files. "Here it is. Let's see now," he said, adjusting his glasses. "It was in eighteen and twenty-six, yessir, that's when he claimed that land, eighteen and twenty-six."

1826. That's possible. Just a few years after Billy left.

"Thanks," said John. He stopped outside the office to consider his next move.

He reached back and kneaded his cramped neck. Tapping Adam on the arm, he said, "Let's get out of here."

More thinking out loud than talking, John said, "I wonder if Billy and Dusty are one and the same. That sure would explain a lot."

On the ride back to camp, John convinced himself that Billy had become Dusty to protect himself. It was the one explanation that made sense of all that had happened. Now came the hard part—deciding what to do next.

Arriving at camp, he hurried to speak with Martha. Martha listened as John explained his theory, and she grew worried as his voice became more intense with his final words. "If that is Billy's land, then I'm not letting some rascal like Ed take it from us."

"John, what you're saying makes sense. But you don't have any proof, and I'm sure Ed isn't going to give up his home and land without a fight."

"I know you're right. But I'm going to find out, one way or another."

CHAPTER 17
William

Itch packed a small bag with food for their journey and a special oil to hide their scent from dogs. "We're going to Chester to rescue a woman who wants to join her husband. He escaped a few months ago. Listen, William, do what I say, or we will both be in danger. No room for mistakes."

"I'll do what you says," said William, strumming his fingers on the table.

"Nervous?"

"A little."

"We leave in the evening. The moon is full tonight. We travel mostly at night. Might travel some in the day, but we have to be careful. Dr. Stone will get clothes for you. We wear only dark clothes to keep us less visible. Get some rest. When we get started, we move out fast."

When the time came, they met around the kitchen table, where their talk centered on strategy and timing. "If all goes well, we'll be back in four days. Then we'll take her to the next stop the following evening," said Itch.

"Itch," said Dr. Stone, "I'm concerned about this being so close in time to her husband leaving. There've been several runaways since then from Great Falls and Lancaster. I was seeing a patient in that area a few weeks ago, and they have the roads heavily patrolled. They're skittish. Don't take any chances."

"We'll be careful."

Heavily patrolled roads. They're skittish. William closed his eyes and took a few deep breaths. *Don't matter none. Ain't no backing out now.*

Just before dark, Dr. Stone stepped outside seeming to have no purpose in mind other than to relax and enjoy the night air. He observed the surrounding woods and the road running along the front of their property. The night seemed peaceful enough, with only the familiar sound of a nearby owl.

He returned. "It seems clear. Be careful. God be with you."

Itch and William left by the back door, slipping quietly away.

"Stay close," Itch warned.

William, his ears attuned to the slightest sound, his eyes to every movement, his heart pounding, felt a sense of purpose as he followed, hurrying along to keep up with Itch's fast pace. Drifting clouds muted the moon's light, giving them some cover. Now, at last, his actions had real meaning. He would learn all he could from his new friend, rescue his family, and escape to the North.

Itch slowed as they moved deeper into the woods. They encountered an occasional night predator, its eyes glowing at them before scampering off in search of smaller prey. He stopped at a fallen tree and cautiously surveyed the area. Close packed with large, spreading oaks and thick underbrush, it did not welcome the casual wanderer. Satisfied no one else was around, he removed some brush from the opening of a hollow place and reached inside. He pulled out an object wrapped in cloth and unwrapped it. William couldn't see what he had at first. He swallowed hard on seeing it was a gun.

"The Stones don't approve of guns and would never allow one in their house, so this has to be our secret." Itch checked the pistol. "I don't plan to ever be taken alive. I will never return to being a slave. I don't like killing another man, but I will if I have to. If you don't like the idea of having a gun with us, you can still turn back. No hard feelings. Just go back to the house and tell them you changed your mind."

William thought for a few moments before responding. "The way I figures it, you is the only chance I got to see my family again. I'm sticking with you."

"Good. Let's get moving. We shouldn't talk while we're walking at night. Never know who might hear us. We walk until dawn. Then we go over our plan."

After walking all night, they came to a resting place. William's back ached, and his legs felt heavy and tired. Itch had chosen a small rise away from water for their resting place. From the rise, they could see anyone approaching. A dense cover of trees and shrubs hid them from view.

Itch whispered, "Now we can talk, but keep it low. We stay here through the morning and afternoon. Take turns sleeping. If it's clear, we start late afternoon. We need to be at the plantation by dark. We're over halfway. The woman we'll be meeting is named Sandra. She will meet us at dusk by a clump of cedars on the edge of the woods."

William found a comfortable place to sit. Itch went to a rock and lifted it. Pulling out a leather jug of water hidden in a hole under the rock, he offered William a drink.

"Let me explain how Dr. Stone and I work together. When Dr. Stone goes to see a patient, he gets an idea of how the plantation is set up. How many buildings, where slaves live, things like that. Sometimes he asks to see a slave who is sick. He is kind to them, and they talk with him. He gets an idea of how the slaves are treated, and he is good at knowing people. When he comes back home, we talk. He draws a picture of the plantation and shows me where slaves live. I go out in two or three weeks, so no one suspects the doctor. I find the person the doctor helped, and we talk. Sometimes that person wants to go; sometimes they tell me of others who want to go. We make our plan, and here we are. With you, it was different. I was coming back from meeting someone when I saw you."

"So, you been to see Sandra before? And you had this place all picked out to stop here with the water and all?"

"That's right. We must have water, but we can't stop near water because others go there. We should rest now, but keep your ears open for anyone approaching."

Late afternoon, they prepared to leave on the final leg of their journey. "We have to be extra careful because we'll be traveling in daylight. There are plenty of patrols along the roads. When we get to the meeting place, we'll rub on this paste. It doesn't smell good, but it keeps the dogs off us. It throws off their sense of smell."

Itch pulled some cornbread and fat pork from the bag he had packed. "Here, eat this. It'll have to do until we stop again." After taking a bite, Itch continued. "The dogs they use have been trained to bite onto the man they're chasing and not let go. They can tear a man apart. Great sport for the white hunters, not pleasant for the poor Negro they catch."

They ate slowly, Itch telling William what he knew of the buildings and how they would approach the place where Sandra would be waiting. Before leaving, they scanned the area. William looked over to Itch. Itch looked back at William and raised his eyebrows, as if asking, "Well, what do you think?" They both nodded and cautiously left their hideaway to begin the last leg to rescue Sandra.

Caution slowed them. They travelled among the trees and underbrush, staying a good way from the road, dropping to their stomachs when a traveler approached. As darkness fell, cotton fields in the distance indicated they had arrived at their destination.

They stopped a hundred yards from the slave quarters, where they spied a young woman standing thirty yards from the quarters. Itch dropped low to the ground. William did the same. Itch put his finger to his lips. They waited for fifteen minutes...twenty minutes.... William's joints stiffened, and he puzzled over why they didn't move forward. Then he noticed something suspicious. Sandra remained very still and was facing the master's house. If expecting Itch, wouldn't she have been facing this way, trying to spot him?

Then he heard a noise. It was very faint but unmistakable. Voices. Somewhere over to the right and close to Sandra. Itch signaled to William that they should leave. Being careful to move quietly, they backed away. Suddenly a panting, sniffing dog sounded very close. The foul-smelling paste remained in its bag, useless.

The sudden savage howling of the dog alarmed them. The dog barreled after them.

Itch whispered, "Let's go." They dashed through the trees.

"There they go!" someone shouted. A bullet hammered into a tree near William's head and other bullets tore through leaves. The trees kept the men from having a clean shot, but they also prevented the two fleeing men from running fast. Even with their huge strides, Itch and William couldn't outrun the dog. Unsure where his strength and endurance came from, William sprinted faster than he thought possible. No matter—the dog snapped at his heels, growled, and bit into a piece of William's trouser, tearing it. The dog knocked William to the ground and went for his throat. William grabbed the dog's neck, struggling to hold him off. His claws scratched William's chest. Saliva from the snarling mouth spattered his face, their noses almost touching. William was close to being unable to hold the dog off any longer when a shot rang out. The dog let out a high-pitched yelp, then went limp.

"Let's go," said Itch, still aiming the gun at the dog as though he might attack again.

"Goddam!" The startled voice traveled through the darkness. "They got guns."

"My dog! My dog!" came another voice through the night. "Those black bastards better not have shot my dog!"

Itch and William sprinted fast as they dared in the evening light through unfamiliar forest. The voices of the two plantation men gradually became muffled as the distance increased. Then there was shouting and cursing when the men discovered their dead dog.

They fired in anger in the direction of Itch and William, who had now fled well out of their range.

Though exhausted, they ran until it seemed their sides would burst. They gradually eased up, believing their immediate danger had passed. They entered a stream and walked in the cold water for fifty yards when Itch spoke.

"We need a safe place before daylight. These woods won't be safe tomorrow. I know where we can go. Let's leave this stream. Rub this paste on your feet and legs. When we leave the stream, we'll cover our tracks."

The paste stung William's nose, and his eyes watered. "I understand why dogs don't like this stuff."

Occasionally, dogs bayed in the distance. Itch picked up the pace, the dogs' menacing howl spurring them on. Three hours later, they arrived at a stone house surrounded by a wooden fence. Itch hurried to the house and knocked on the door.

The door was opened by a man with a thick, red beard and unruly hair. He looked surprised but pleased to see Itch.

"Itch, how good to see you, and you've brought a friend. Come in quickly, 'though I don't believe anyone is on the road this time of night." He moved aside to let them in.

"Actually," said Itch, "there are men on the road this time of night, and they're looking for us."

"From the looks and smell of you, I doubt you're here on a social call."

"William, meet Alan Birdsong, a man who'll be your friend for life if you'll let him."

"And why shouldn't he let me? Do you know a finer man in these parts?" Alan said, laughing.

"Alan, this is William. Let me tell you quickly what happened and then you best hide us. And no, there isn't a finer man in these parts," said Itch, placing one hand on Alan's shoulder.

While Itch spoke to Alan, William took in the room. It was clean, sparsely furnished, but comfortable. A row of books lined a shelf along the far wall.

While listening to their story, Alan acted quickly to move a table and rug, revealing a trapdoor. William followed the two men down a ladder to a short passageway that led to a small room. Alan used his candle to light one of the four candles in the room. The room contained only a table, a chair, and a mattress. The candles and holder on the table would provide their light. The worn mattress had a clean sheet folded neatly on top. The stench of stale air was made worse by the foul-smelling paste on the men's clothing.

"I'll bring you some food and water, and then I'll need to close the door."

They entered the room. Itch sat cross-legged on the floor. William sat in the chair, though he would rather have stretched out on the mattress after a night of running.

Alan returned quickly with a basket of apples and a pitcher of water. "You'll be safe here." He returned to the passageway, climbed the ladder, closed the trap door, replaced the rug and table, and waited.

"We'll have plenty of time to talk now," said Itch. "An important lesson is to be learned from what happened back there. When you arrive to meet someone, always look around before moving too close. You never know if a trap may be waiting."

"How you think them mens find out we is coming tonight?"

"It's hard to know. Maybe someone overheard Sandra talking to another, or someone could have snitched in order to get a reward from the owner. Could be it was a trap from the beginning. Who knows? The point is, we have to be careful all the time. If something doesn't seem right, stop and figure out what isn't right and then decide if you should keep going or get out. We don't always know who our friends are."

"What make you think there be a trap tonight?"

"First, Sandra was standing where she could be seen easily. If she wanted to escape, it makes sense she would have been hiding so her master couldn't see her. Also, she didn't seem to be looking for us—she was looking towards her master's house."

Itch grew quiet when thudding horse hooves pounded above. Excited talk from two, maybe three men filtered into the basement hideaway, but the muffled voices could not be understood. Alan rapped on the door sometime later to announce, "It's safe to come up now. They've all gone."

They stayed with Alan for two days, hoping that would be enough time to quiet the furor they had started. They enjoyed quiet meals and discussions behind drawn curtains and on their second night, bid their host goodbye.

They moved silently, off well-traveled paths, always on the lookout for campfires. Travelling at night and part of the morning, they found a place to hide and rest during the day among several fallen trees—a dark area overgrown with brush and seedlings feeding on the rot. At the end of the next night, being close to home, they decided to continue in daylight in spite of the risks.

"How good to see you both, safe and sound," exclaimed Catherine Stone. "We were very worried. There were reports of trouble. Both of you sit here and rest while I prepare some hot food for you." She patted both men on the arm before hurrying into the kitchen.

As William sat at the table with his companions, his family came to mind. He heard their voices calling to him. He remembered their laugh, and he wished he could tell them a story. But after the aborted rescue attempt, he wondered whether he would live to see them again.

CHAPTER 18

John

John would call on Ed one more time. That's what he and Martha agreed on. But only after John promised he wouldn't do anything rash. John wanted to see Dusty's grave given the possibility that Dusty might be his brother. He also wanted to speak to Ed, hoping he would talk more about Dusty.

John rose early, ready to get started. The discussion with Ed could easily turn nasty.

Richard had built a fire and had a pot of coffee ready. He started to say good morning, but, seeing John's scowl, he saved his greeting for someone who would appreciate it.

John walked to the fire and poured himself a cup.

"Morning, Massa John," said Sarah in her low, raspy voice.

"Morning, Massa," echoed Wiley.

"Ain't nothing good about this morning," said John.

"No, sir," said Sarah and Wiley in unison, their eyes diverted to the ground.

Jacob worked by the wagons doing some repairs on one of them. John yelled, "Jacob, saddle my horse and bring him here."

"Yes, sir, Massa." He hurried off to do as told.

John watched Jacob enter the fog and slowly disappear into the white mist. The landscape appeared dreamlike, with shadowy figures waiting for the mist to clear so they could assume their daylight identities.

The damp air penetrated John's clothing, sending a chill through him. He appreciated the coolness but knew this would change as the day wore on. The sun would chase the fog, bringing rising temperatures and a brightness that seemed unlikely during these early morning hours.

Although John agreed not to do anything foolish, he became determined to find answers to his questions, no matter what it took. He pondered how to bring up the subject of Billy without Ed becoming defensive.

"Here's your horse, Massa," said Jacob, startling John out of his reflection. He took the horse's reins and mounted, pointing the horse towards Ed and the disputed land.

John dismounted fifty feet from the cabin and hollered, "Hello. Ed, you in there?" No response. He hollered louder. Still no response. He walked to the barn and stuck his head in. "Hello, anyone here?" No answer. Once his eyes adjusted to the diminished light, he surveyed the tools hanging from the walls, the worktable, noticing everything in sight, but he saw nothing that would tie Billy to this place.

He turned to leave when a saddle caught his eye. It was an old saddle, but it stirred a memory. John picked it up and placed it on the work bench. *This looks very familiar.* His parents had given Billy a saddle for his fifteenth birthday—one like this, sleek and lighter than a working saddle, to give Billy an edge when he raced. *Could he find proof this saddle belonged to Billy?* He searched for markings or a name that would identify it. Nothing, he could find nothing.

Afraid Ed might return any minute, John cut his snooping short.

I'll bet Ed knows Dusty is Billy. He's trying to keep me from finding out so he can keep this land. Well, Ed, you can't fool me. I'm going to get proof that Billy and Dusty are one and the same.

He studied the cleared land. What he saw quickened his pulse—a headstone. *Billy's grave?* The grave marker simply read, "Dusty—killed in battle with Santiago 1860." *Well, here it is, or is it?*

"'Lo there, Mr. Higgins."

Ed walked towards him.

"Hello, Ed. I looked for you but didn't see anyone. Saw this grave and thought I'd come over to take a look. We'll be leaving this morning, and I wanted to say goodbye."

"Wish you luck, Higgins. Where you off to?"

"Not sure yet. Going to head south. Need to find some place to settle down pretty quick, though. Can't put my family through much more of this traveling."

"I might suggest you head south for a week or so to Hillsborough County. It's a long ride, but I hear there's plenty of good land."

"Much obliged, Ed. Say, I hear this Dusty fella and someone by the name of Santiago had their own private war going on."

"That's about right. This was Santiago's land at one time, and he swore no white man would ever live here after they took it from him. He and Dusty were always tryin' to get the best of each other. Both knew all the tricks. Finally kilt each other. Least ways we reckon they did. Dusty's dead for sure. He claimed to have killed Santiago. Course we never found Santiago's body. Them injuns always takes their dead with them. Don't reckon it could of ended any other way."

"Fella at the land office says there's plenty of stories about Dusty's battles."

"Yeah, reckon so. Most of 'em was exaggerated. The more they was told, the better they got. But, I'll tell you what, ole Dusty could ride an' shoot, an' he could track anything in the woods as good as any Indian."

"He sounds just like my brother, Billy.

Ed's eyes turned hard; his body tensed. "Now look here, mister, I done told you all I know about him. Seems to me you're fishing for something to show Dusty to be your brother. But I'll tell you this, he never mentioned having a brother or any other family than what died in the fire." Ed narrowed his eyes and pointed a finger at John. "Now look, Higgins, I know you came here looking for your brother an' all, but he ain't here. Dusty was good to me. Me an' him was partners, an' he always treated me fair. Maybe Dusty did have a secret life before he came here. Maybe he had good reason to change his name an' his past. That's all gone now. If he even was your brother, he stopped being your brother a long time ago. This is my land now. Take your family an' move on."

"I'm not trying to take your land, but if Dusty is really my brother, then that's something else. It's strange his map showed this to be Billy's place, and he's not here—but here is Dusty who is dead. And then my brother also was good at riding and shooting." John spoke louder now, more forcefully, his intention to keep calm forgotten. "If Dusty is my brother, I have a right to know."

"We'll see about that." Ed turned and walked towards his cabin.

John stood in place, refusing to budge.

When Ed came out from his cabin, he carried a rifle. The rifle sat in the crook of his arm but pointed in John's direction. "You best be movin' on."

John tugged at his hat. "Guess there's no point in hanging around here," he mumbled to himself. But John had a scheme brewing. "Where'd you say that place was?" he asked. His eyes fixed on Dusty's grave and then moved slowly up to Ed.

"Hillsborough County? It's south of here about two days ride if it's just one man an' his horse. With them wagons you pullin', it'll be a lot more."

John held his gaze on Ed for a moment longer. No point in saying anything more. But underneath his calm demeanor, John's plot had mushroomed into a firm decision.

CHAPTER 19

William

Two days ago, a family had hidden with William in the basement. Their young daughter reminded William of Margaret. The girl spoke with William in a strong yet quiet voice, meeting his eye contact with her bright brown eyes. Her confidence and strength were so like Margaret that William's throat tightened, making it difficult for him to talk.

Days later, after the family had left and the turmoil swirling around their escape had calmed, William decided to go for a walk, hoping the night air might soothe him. He took a different path and spotted the silhouette of a lone figure seated and leaning against a large maple tree. He cautiously neared and quickly recognized Itch sitting very still, concentrating on something unseen. William changed direction to avoid disturbing him.

He continued walking until he came to a tree with fat, low branches. One limb ran parallel to the ground for several yards before shooting upwards. He sat on the branch mulling over his situation, considering his options. Having guns would make his revenge on Higgins much easier, but he questioned whether he had the ability to kill another man. He reached his arm around to his back and felt the scars. *Yes, I could kill John Higgins.* The thought sent a chill coursing through him.

William finished his walk and returned to the house. Itch had returned earlier and now sat by a candle reading a book. He spoke as William approached. "Want to talk?"

"What about?"

"You seem bothered these last few days," said Itch. "I thought maybe you'd want to discuss what's bothering you."

"Naw," said William, sitting in a chair opposite Itch. "I got nothin' to talk about."

Itch put his book down. "That's all right."

"What was you doing sitting out in the dark?"

"Do you believe there is a spirit world?"

"Why, sure. When peoples dies, they becomes a spirit."

Itch lowered his voice. "Do you believe we can communicate with those spirits?"

"I know there lots of folks says they can. I never paid it no mind."

"Remember I told you I was being prepared to be a leader of my village when kidnapped?"

William nodded.

"My grandfather was the Sangoma of our village. He was the spiritual leader. He taught me about the spirit world and how to communicate with them. Such things are laughed at by most. But the spirits communicate with us all the time; we just don't listen."

William interrupted him. "How does they do that? I don't never hear them say nothin'."

Itch leaned forward in his chair. "In different ways. Sometimes through dreams. Sometimes what we think is just a chance happening is them communicating."

"Oh. Yeah," said William. "So, what was you doin' out there in the woods?"

"I was communicating with my ancestors and my family in Africa." He waited for William's reaction.

William's eyebrows raised, and he let out a low whistle. "An' do they talk back with you?"

Itch laughed. "I don't always get an answer right away. Sometimes it comes later in a feeling, or something that happens. You have to be open to their response."

William shook his head. "I don't know 'bout that mumbo jumbo."

Itch leaned forward. "I used to worry about my mother. My father was killed before I was kidnapped, and I worried that my disappearance would be too much for her. I remembered the lessons my grandfather had taught me. So, I spent time every night trying to communicate, to see how she was and to let her know I had survived."

"You think she heard you?"

"It took a long time to get an answer. In a dream one night, she stood among a council of village elders, telling them of her great sorrow and her struggle to get beyond her grief. The elders sat in silence, listening intently, healing her with their listening. The dream then changed to my mother carrying me. She struggled greatly, her bare feet being cut on rocks as she struggled up a mountain, carrying my big, heavy body. At the top of the mountain, she cried out and raised me up. At that moment, I flew off. I looked back and saw a look of peacefulness on her face. In that moment, I knew my mother, too, was free. I believe she moved on with her life.

"To you, that story may sound foolish, but there is a thin curtain between us and the spirit world. It's a question of learning how to look beyond the curtain."

William sat silently for a few moments, wondering how this could be possible. He had known people who used spells and had the reputation for working magic. "I wish I could know how my family is. Can you find that out?"

"That's something you will have to do for yourself. I can teach you some things, but you will have to find what works for you. What I find most useful is being still and listening to the voices inside of me. Also, try to understand your dreams. They will tell you things you don't know."

"Sometimes I think to myself that I want to kill my old master, Higgins. Is that one of the voices I should listen to?"

"The voyage to this land, with all of its horrors, made me want to kill myself. I told you the story of my father coming to me in a vision. He told me that I must not do this. Sometimes, we listen to the wrong voice. As you learn to open your mind and heart, you will learn to listen to the right one."

"I don't know about different voices. The only voice I hear is that Higgins needs to feel the pain he made me an' my family feel." William stood and turned his back to Itch. Lifting his shirt, he said, "See these scars? Every time I move, every time I lie down, I remember the pain Higgins give me. Every day, every night, I wonder about my family, where they are, how they are. Higgins did this to me. When I see him, he's going to feel some pain, too. I will—" William stopped in mid-sentence, then said, "I needs to get some air."

Itch watched as William disappeared into the darkness.

CHAPTER 20

John

John told Martha his plan. She didn't like it.

"What if he sees you? He would be within his rights to shoot you. And then what? I don't like it, John. I just don't like it."

But John wouldn't budge. He hadn't come this far only to see his dream dashed by some low-life chiseler like Ed. Roscoe would be hidden outside to warn John if Ed left the cabin. Whatever it took, he was going back in the barn that night.

With the last bit of light disappearing from the sky, John and Roscoe mounted their horses. This night seemed darker than most. Storm clouds covered the waxing moon high in the sky. Lightning flashes introduced rumbling thunder, cutting across the sky in brilliant displays, briefly lighting the path for the two men—John defying fate with stubborn determination, Roscoe accepting fate with stoic patience. Each flash exposed their grim faces as they rode through the night.

They dismounted a good distance from Ed's cabin, continuing on foot. John carried four candles into the barn. Roscoe settled in behind a large tree fifty feet from the front of the barn that provided a good view of the cabin. Three short owl hoots would warn John to get out.

John lit a candle. He started under the workbench, brushing away old cobwebs and quietly pulling dusty boxes out to examine their contents. He quickly searched through each box for proof. He had never been so reckless. The candle flickered; the hot wax built to a soft glob on his hand. He explored the shelves, going through dirty forgotten containers, most of them empty or nearly so. He checked tools and the stalls, being careful not to disturb the horses. Finally, he lit his last candle.

The rain started slowly at first, with a few pings on the roof, then grew until the crashing of rain filled the barn. Impossible now to hear Roscoe's warning. But no matter. He checked the door for any sign of Ed coming, and then returned to his frantic work.

Where might Billy have left something from his past? He walked to the saddle he'd found earlier. He froze. The saddle rested on the floor. Had he replaced it? He couldn't remember. If Ed put it back, then he must be aware of John's snooping.

He knelt to do a more thorough search of the saddlebag. Reaching in a small side pocket, he felt something cold and hard. He pulled it out and held it close to the candlelight. Billy's buckle. John's heart leapt. He examined it closely. The initials BH were engraved in the metal. Now he had the proof he needed. He returned the buckle to the saddlebag. *I'll bring the sheriff out here and show him the buckle. That should be proof my brother was Dusty.*

His work completed, he poked his head out of the barn door. All clear. The rain had slowed to a drizzle. *Where's Roscoe?* He made his way out of the barn and into the wet night, noiselessly moving through puddles of water.

He neared the tree where Roscoe stood guard. *Where the hell is Roscoe?* A figure stepped out. "Everything clear on this end, Massa," Roscoe whispered.

When they reached their horses, both men relaxed. John stood by his horse for a moment wondering, *Will the buckle be enough to prove this is Billy's land? It's all I got. It'll have to do.*

When John and Roscoe returned, Martha ran to meet them. John told her of his findings. Now there was no doubt. John planned to go to Gainesville and get that thief Ed kicked off his land.

The next morning, John and Adam rose early. After another long ride to Gainesville, they located the sheriff's office in the middle of Main Street, just a few hundred feet from the land office.

"Sheriff," exclaimed John, barging in, "someone's stealing land that rightfully belongs to me, and I want you to arrest him."

"Hold on there, mister. Just exactly what are you talking about, and who are you?" The sheriff had a tough appearance, with a lined face and cold, piercing eyes. He might have been in his late thirties. His weathered face aged him. He was not the kind of man to back down. He stepped towards John and looked him firmly in the eye. John backed off.

"Have a seat, mister, an' tell me about what's got a burr under your saddle."

John sat as calmly as he could and told the sheriff his story.

"Mr. Higgins, you have sure come a long way, an' I can understand your being upset. But I got to level with you. I don't really know this Ed fellow except by name. But you got to have a lot more than a belt buckle and an old saddle before I can do anything. As I understand it, Ed has been on this land for close to forty years. I doubt any judge that comes to this town will force him to leave his home on such slim evidence. Now I'm sure any lawyer in town will be glad to take your money and fight your battle. But to be quite honest, I don't think you have a chance in hell of winning."

"But look here, Sheriff, Ed might have lived there forty years, but so did my brother. And he wanted me to come. He was going to give me the land. This map he drawed is exactly the land Ed is on. Even the fellow at the land office says so. And that belt buckle, how do you think it got there? Had to be Billy. Ain't no other explanation. Ed's poaching on my land. You got to do something about this. Can't let thieves like Ed just take other people's land."

The sheriff sighed and folded his arms across his chest. "Lemme tell you how it is, mister. There could be a number of explanations for those things. First of all, they won't mean a thing in a court of law. Why, you could of drawn that map yourself and put that buckle in that saddlebag. Hell, I don't know. I just know you ain't got a leg to stand on. A man's been on his land for forty years—now that's somethin' that'll stand up in court."

John's face reddened, and his eyes grew hard. "Ain't nobody got the right to take what's mine."

"Let me make one suggestion, Mr. Higgins." He took a step closer, looking down on John. "I wouldn't advise you taking this matter into your own hands. If I ride out to talk to Ed in a couple of days, and he's not looking very healthy, I will find you. Am I making myself clear?"

John's fists tightened. He stormed out, muttering under his breath something best the sheriff couldn't understand, slamming the door behind him. A second later, Adam sheepishly exited and hurried to catch up to his father. John looked for a judge, but the circuit judge wasn't due in town for months. Dejected and out of options, he and Adam left town.

On the way home, the matter weighed heavily on John, and he decided to confront Ed one more time. He sent Adam back to camp, away from danger—no telling what Ed would do when he saw John again.

John dismounted a good distance from Ed's cabin and walked his horse the rest of the way. He thought, or hoped, that walking would seem less threatening. At about a hundred paces from the cabin, Ed came out, rifle in hand.

"I thought you might be coming by today," said Ed. "I'm tired of you sneaking through my things and trying to take what's mine. I should shoot you and claim you was trespassing. Get off my property, Higgins. If you come back, I'll sure as hell shoot you."

"I just want to talk."

"I want you to leave now! We're done talking."

Two men came out of the barn carrying rifles. "I can't be responsible for what these men might do," said Ed. "Don't none of us around here like to have his land stolen. Next thing you might lay claim to someone else's property."

"That's right," said one of the men, as they raised their rifles.

"You'll rest in hell for this, you cowardly thief." But John knew he had reached the end of his options. He mounted his horse and returned to camp.

Arriving at camp, he gave instructions to get ready to move on. He told Martha what had taken place with the sheriff but decided it best to skip what happened with Ed.

John called everyone together to announce that they would leave in the morning. "Going to a place called Hillsborough County, just a few days' travel. Get everything ready to head out early."

In the morning they broke camp, beginning what everyone hoped would be the last leg of their search for a place to call home.

CHAPTER 21
William

The emaciated woman peered out from the forest at the house by the road. She prayed she had found the right place. If not, she would likely die. Whoever lived in the house might kill her or keep her as their slave. Not much difference, she thought.

In these wee hours of the morning, the road lay quiet. Yet that fifteen feet of open space could bring danger, even death, to a black woman in hiding. It was a hazard that must be crossed, a risk that must be taken. Stepping onto the vacant road meant exposing herself. She would be visible to patrollers who might be coming around the bend.

She gazed at the moon, then waited until a cloud blocked most of its light before moving towards the house. Mustering her last bit of strength, she managed to cross the road. She reached towards the door to knock. She held her bony fist in midair while she worked up her courage. *What have I got to lose? If this ain't it, I can't go no farther.*

An owl's hoot and a dog's howl in the distance muffled her soft, steady rapping. No one came to the door after her first knock. She knocked again. And again. And yet again.

Dr. Stone had become used to being awakened in the middle of his sleep, but this night he slept deeply after a late emergency several miles to the south. Her constant tapping finally woke him. He sat abruptly. Catherine continued sleeping soundly. His mind scrambled at first, he soon realized someone was at the door. He rushed to open his home to the nighttime caller.

He unlatched the door and opened it. The woman standing there was so thin her skin clung to her bones. She was covered in dirt and wearing rags that barely covered her. The worry in her eyes told a story of desperation.

He said, "Hello. Please come—" Before he could finish, she collapsed into his arms.

When she recovered, she had a difficult time making sense of the scene before her of an older white couple and two Negro men standing over her.

"Here, try to drink this broth. It will warm you and help you regain your strength," said Mrs. Stone.

The starved woman drank it too fast and choked, but she wouldn't let go of the bowl when Mrs. Stone tried to help her. "I be all right. Just let me get this down. Law, this is good. I ain't had nothin' so good in a long time." She drank the broth from the bowl, forsaking the spoon next to it.

Once the woman finished the broth, she took some time to study the people standing around her. The she said, "I come here hopin' you folks could hep me. But I be so tired. Been walkin' them woods all day to get here. 'Fraid to stop. Now I'm here, too tired to talk."

Dr. Stone said, "My wife will show you to our guest room and give you some clean clothes. You can tell us your story in the morning."

Her saga began one year ago. "My boy not be feelin' well one day, and I knowed he not goin' be able to pick enough cotton to satisfy the master. For this he would get a terrible whippin'. He not be a strong boy anyway. Such a whippin' just might do him in. That overseer we got, he like whipping young boy slaves. He beat them something fierce. So, I pick fast as I could. Try to pick for him and me, too. I give him enough so he not get the whip, but I fell short." She stopped, squeezed her eyes shut. A few seconds later, she continued. "That overseer shore put a good whippin' on me."

She shook her head and closed her eyes again as the events replayed in her mind. "That night I lay there thinkin' an' thinkin' about the whippin' I got—the whole time getting madder and madder. I decide it best for me to get away from these white mens that whip us black folks. So, I runs away. I planning on coming back for my children. I left on a Sunday after the preacher come and give his sermon. Figure that give me a whole day to be gone before the master puts the dogs out to find me. Oh Lord, was I nervous, but once I sets my mind to do something, I does it no matter.

"Lord, took me a long, long time, but I finally made it to Canady. Been living there now 'bout six months. Got me a job sewing dresses. I is good at stitching. Got me some good fingers and sharp eyes for needlework. You got something you want mended, just tell me and I'll take care of it.

"Got me a rented room and done saved some money to get a bigger place. Now I come back to take my childrens with me."

"How did you happen to come to our house?" asked Dr. Stone.

"Well, it's like this. Before I crossed over into Canady, I met me a man in Ohio that told me of a free black man living with a white couple, and they helped many a slave get free. He tell me how to find your house." She took a deep breath, as the frightening moments surfaced in her mind. "I walk here for a bunch of days. Finding what I could in the woods to eat. Oh Lord, was I scared when I finds this house. Didn't know if it was the right one, didn't know if them same peoples still live here. But couldn't go no farther. Had to take the chance."

"What's your friend's name?" asked Itch, partly out of curiosity and partly to verify her story. He didn't want to help her only to be led into a trap.

"His name be Abner Bailey," said the woman. "He lives in Ohio an' has his own business as a cobbler. He say he owes his life to you.

He say to remind you about the time you hid in a train water tower from the white men who was hunting him and you."

"Haw!" Itch said, laughing. "That was the best hiding place I ever found."

"Oh my!" exclaimed Mrs. Stone. "We don't even know your name. Please excuse our bad manners."

"I be Joan. The Edwards family help me when I lookin' for work in Canady. I just couldn't take the name of my master. They was such bad peoples. So, I took Edwards for a name."

"Well," said Dr. Stone, "that is quite a story. I have a patient to see this morning. When I return, we'll sit down and plan how to get Joan's children back to their mother."

That afternoon, Joan told more of her story. She had escaped from the Miller plantation fifteen miles to the west. The slave quarters were in back of the main house. "I just prays that my children are all still there and ain't been sold off."

"I have an idea," said Dr. Stone. "I know the Millers only slightly, but I was by there about six months ago to tend to an infected cut. Quite a nasty cut, actually. Suppose I stop there to inquire about the wound? I'll have to visit the slave quarters to do that, so I should be able to find out if Joan's children are still there. If I go on a Sunday afternoon, all of the slaves should be in or around their cabins. It won't be difficult to inquire without raising suspicions. If they are there, well then, we'll move forward from that point."

"Sounds like a good start," said Itch. The others nodded their agreement.

"Joan," said Dr. Stone, "you'll have to give me a description and the names of your children."

The following Sunday, Dr. Stone hitched up his carriage to make the trip west to the Miller plantation. When he arrived, he went straight to the main house. Before he reached the front door, Mrs. Miller, talkative and friendly as ever, sashayed out to greet him. "Why, hello, Dr. Stone. How nice to see you again. To what do we owe your visit?"

"Good afternoon, Mrs. Miller. Good to see you again. Is Mr. Miller available? I won't take much of his time."

"I'm sorry, but he's gone to Mount Falls to look at some horses. Please come in and have some tea. It's so hot outside, and you've had a long ride." She turned, looking into the house, and called out, "Benjamin, come here, boy." A handsome Negro boy, about twelve years old, came at once. "Go tell Auntie to fix us some tea. We have company. Then go to your room."

"Yes'm," he said, and he disappeared into the house.

Dr. Stone became hopeful when he heard the name "Benjamin." *That young man is likely Joan's oldest child.* He fit her description, though a bit taller now than what she remembered from a year ago. *Apparently lives in the house. Need to find out where.*

"We don't get company very often, so I want you to tell me all the local news while we drink our tea."

After chatting for what Dr. Stone thought a reasonable amount of time, he said, "Mrs. Miller, I'm considering adding a few rooms onto my house, and wherever I go, I ask to see the house, if it's a substantial one, to give me ideas for building my own. I don't believe I have ever seen a house quite like yours. It's laid out in a very interesting manner. Would it be an imposition for you to show me around?"

"Why, no, I'd be delighted, Doctor," said Mrs. Miller, smiling proudly.

After the house tour, Dr. Stone said, "You have a very lovely home with a well-thought-out design. Thank you for showing it. Mrs. Miller, about six months ago, your husband asked me to look at a slave who had a serious cut. I'd like to see him to check how he's doing."

"Oh, Doctor, you must be talking about Jesse. He healed up just fine. We sold him several months ago." She lowered her voice and said, "We had a slow year with that awful drought. Needed a little cash. You know how that is." She placed her hand on her heart. "Happens to us all."

He tried desperately to think of some way to get to the slaves' quarters to learn the whereabouts of the other two children, but he could think of nothing. He left with grave concerns. *Could they have sold the children as well?*

The five sat around the kitchen table devising a strategy. Timing was the biggest issue. They didn't want the escape tied to the doctor's visit. This meant they would have to wait a few days. But they didn't want to wait too long. When Mr. Miller returned, it would be more dangerous.

They threw out ideas, debated one after another, before finally deciding on a plan. "All right, let's go over this one more time," said Itch. "Dr. Stone will hide the buckboard off the road several hundred feet from the entrance to the Miller's place. William, you and I will go to the quarters to learn if Joan's two younger children are there and, if so, where. We'll take them to a spot that we'll determine later. Then you'll go to the house to get Benjamin. Dr. Stone will give us the layout of the house. You bring Benjamin to our meeting spot, and we'll head for the buckboard. We'll put the children in the false bottom, and Dr. Stone and I will ride back to the house. William will walk back to avoid suspicion in case Miller is home and comes chasing after his slaves. It's not unusual for Dr. Stone to be out at night, so hopefully we won't appear suspicious. Any questions?"

"I just prays that all my children be there and you gets back safe with them."

"We'll do the best we can," said Dr. Stone.

"In the cabin next to the end," said Joan, "there be a good friend. She named Clare. She could tell you where the children be. Probably any of them could tell you, but Clare be a good friend. Clare easy to know. She a bit taller than me, have real dark skin, and some marks on her face from the days in her village before she brought here."

"If Rufus and Manda are still there, we'll find them," said Itch.

Two days after Dr. Stone's visit to the Miller plantation, they put their quest to rescue Joan's children into motion. Darkness came half an hour before they arrived. Dr. Stone turned the buckboard off the road, stopping in a copse of trees where anyone passing by would not see him. They decided not to use the garlic compound, since Dr. Stone hadn't seen any dogs and William couldn't sneak into the house smelling of garlic.

At the edge of the woods, they stopped to survey the plantation. In order to get to the quarters unseen by someone in the main house, they needed to go through a small cornfield and then cross about 50 feet of open land to the shacks. They entered the cornfield, making their way to the stretch of open land, and again stopped to evaluate the surroundings. They continued across the open area to within thirty feet of the shacks, when they spotted a dog. At the same time, the dog spotted them. The dog sprang to life and ran to them. The men froze. The dog sniffed them, then wagged his tail. Itch patted the dog's head and whispered, "Nice to see a friendly dog for a change."

They eased their way to the second shack to find Clare. The dog followed close behind. Itch stuck his head in the window and called out softly, "Clare! Clare, you in there?"

A gruff female voice answered back, "Who the hell be outside my window wanting Clare? Speak up now 'cause I ain't got all the night to wait for your answer."

"I don't think that be Clare," whispered William.

"You better tell me who you is before I starts yellin'," said the voice.

"Let me talk with her," cautioned William, "'cause you don't sound like no black man."

Itch nodded his agreement.

"Listen, we needing Clare. You know where she is?" whispered William.

The woman in the shack peered suspiciously at the two men. A half-moon dimly lit the night. She hesitated, studying the two. "You men come 'round to the door and come in before someone sees you."

The woman eyed the two, hands on her hips, and said, "I'm Ann. Now you going to tell me what you wants with Clare before I says anymore."

"Joan asked us to get her children. She said Clare would know where they were."

Ann perked up. "Oh, my Lord, Joan is alive! Tell me how she is."

"She be fine," said William. "Right now, we gots to get her childrens so she can take them with her. No time for talking."

"Her two smaller ones three cabins down. The oldest, he stay up at the house."

"Thanks," said William.

When they left, the dog followed. Ann called out in a whisper, "Coon! Coon! You come here right now." Coon paused, looked first at Ann, then at Itch, then obediently went to Ann.

"William, you go to the house for Benjamin. I'll get the other two. We'll meet back at the first tree past the corn field then go to our meeting place."

William nodded, and then left for the main house. Itch made his way to the third shack. He slipped into the shack and, putting his hand over Clare's mouth, gently woke her.

"My name is Itch. Joan sent me to get her children."

Even in the darkness, Itch could see Clare's eyes well up with tears. Itch gave her a quick history of Joan's escape and return, then gathered up the children. At first frightened, they calmed when Clare assured them that this man would take them to be with their mother.

"What about Benjamin?" asked Clare.

"Someone's going to the house to get him," whispered Itch.

Clare turned towards the house. "I don't think he gonna make it out alive. Master Miller, he keep a gun beside his bed, and he use it mighty quick."

"But isn't he gone for a few days?" asked Itch.

"Naw, he come back yesterday and just as mean as ever."

Itch stepped to the doorway, but he didn't see William. He scooped up the children, and then ran through the cornfield to the first tree. He set the children down and, in a very stern voice, said, "Wait here for me. I'll be back for you. Don't talk or make any noise, understand?"

Both children trembled and clung to Itch's sleeve. Itch peeled their hands off. "You're going to be all right?" They could muster only a small shake of their heads. Itch took that as a yes. He ran to help William, but halfway there, he heard a shot, and then another, and then another.

"Oh my God," he said and sprinted towards the house.

While Itch told Clare about Joan, William arrived at the house. He found the front door unlocked. He reviewed Dr. Stone's information. He put his feet down gently, searching for a non-creaking board. If a board creaked, he would stop and step elsewhere—slow moving, but effective. Dr. Stone's memory proved exceptionally accurate. At the boy's room he went inside, put his hand over the boy's mouth, and woke him. "Your momma sent me to get you. We got to leave here real quiet. Don't be afraid."

Before Benjamin could speak, Mr. Miller called out, "Benjamin! That you walking around in there? What you doing, boy?"

William whispered in Benjamin's ear, "Don't be scared. Just talk real normal like."

"No, sir, I'm in my room, Massa."

"Don't you lie to me, boy. I know you up to something 'cause I hear you walking around in there."

William heard Miller get out of bed, his feet hitting the floor. Miller's bedroom slippers scraped along as he came towards Benjamin's room. William ducked behind the door.

The door opened, revealing Mr. Miller in his nightshirt, bleary-eyed, hair a mess, looking rough.

"Boy, I don't like no nigger lying to me. I knew it was a mistake letting you stay in my house. You belong out there with the rest of them darkies."

He raised his fist to teach the boy a lesson. He had done this a thousand times. It no longer bothered him. He knew how it would feel, the soft flesh against his fist. He believed it to be an act of justice, of the righteous teaching the damned, a Christian act. With his fist raised, he peered into Benjamin's eyes to see the fear. He must have fear—without fear, there would be no learning.

But this time, Benjamin seemed different. He wasn't looking at the fist or the massa's eyes. His eyes went past to something else. Miller hesitated, then turned his head to see what the boy stared at. He jumped back, startled by William's presence, but he quickly regained his composure. "Who the hell are you, and what you doing in my house? I'm going to show you what I do to niggers who steal from me."

When he took a step towards his room to get his gun, all of William's anger flowed into a punch to Miller's head that sent him reeling back against the wall. He fell unconscious to the floor.

"Let's go!" said William, as he grabbed Benjamin and ran out of the house, almost knocking over Mrs. Miller, who had just come out of the bedroom to see about all the fuss. Seeing her husband on the floor, she ran into the bedroom and grabbed her husband's gun. Though not an expert shot, she had learned to fire a pistol in case she ever needed to. This was a case of needing to.

She ran onto the front porch, pointing the pistol at William and Benjamin. She fired, then fired again and again. None of the shots came close to the fleeing man and boy, but the popping gunshots gave their legs power. They ran through the darkness, unconcerned about obstacles that might be in their path. They ran faster than they thought wise. They ran for their lives.

Itch had sprinted past the halfway point to the house when William and Benjamin ran by him. Itch took off after them. William and Benjamin arrived at the tree fifty feet ahead of Itch.

"What happened?" Itch said, panting.

"Let's get outta here. Talk later," responded William.

Itch, William, and the children hurried to where Dr. Stone waited. Itch said to the children, "Lie down in here and don't make a sound. We're going to take you to your mother, but you must be very quiet." The two younger ones nodded. Benjamin said, "Yes, sir." Itch and Dr. Stone headed for home in the buckboard. William cautiously made his way home through the woods.

The children arrived at the house, causing much joy, accompanied by kissing and hugging and stories to tell. Joan and her children remained in the basement hideaway for a few days. There would be much activity up and down the road once a revived Miller got the word out. When the excitement settled down, Dr. Stone would take Joan and her children on to the next stop on their journey to Canada.

The Daily Chronicle

November 1860

Republican Abraham Lincoln elected President of the United States. His election caused anger throughout the southern states. South Carolina threatened to secede from the Union.

CHAPTER 22

John

Florida, 1861

As they walked alongside the cattle, Harriet said, "Do you really think your papa be all right, Hector?"

Hector saw worry in his mother's eyes. "I think he might."

Harriet put her arm around Margaret's shoulders. "Sometimes I think he escaped from them mean Simmons an' he lookin' for us right now." She squeezed Margaret. "But mos' of the time, I don' think we goin' to see him again. What I do knows is we got to stick together. We can't let nothin' take us apart."

His mother's courage had returned, and Hector found hope for their future.

In late 1860, the caravan arrived in Hillsborough County in central Florida. Largely a wilderness area, this sparsely settled frontier had several good roads built by the U.S. Army during the Seminole Indian wars. Travelling these roads, they eventually came to a small town, Shallow Lake, where John asked around about land for sale. It didn't take long to find a good tract of land, which bordered on a lake and was only about fifteen miles from town. Tall, majestic pines grew everywhere—perfect for building. Tracks and scat indicated a variety of wild game in the area.

John made the long trek back to Gainesville, where he purchased 160 acres for \$1.25 per acre from the United States Government. With his return, he organized everyone to begin building their new home.

The Daily Chronicle

On January 10, Florida followed South Carolina and Mississippi, becoming the third state to leave the Union. Other southern states likely to follow.

They would camp on the land until the main house could be built. Pens to hold the animals would be the first task, and then would come the building of the main house. John marked off the area where he wanted his house and assigned everyone to the various tasks. They would begin in the early morning.

The men cut down trees and stripped limbs while women and children cleared the building site of debris and smaller brush. Everyone took part, including John's family.

The main house would have three bedrooms, a parlor, and dining area. Then would come a kitchen separate from the house. And last, the slave quarters and a barn. Roscoe's quarters were to be built before the others, to emphasize his importance. His cabin would be one hundred paces from the main house, and the other slave quarters were to be behind his.

Now actively engaged in building his new home, John no longer regretted the move. He thought of Billy now and then but resigned himself to accept that Billy was dead.

A rifle shot jolted John from his thoughts. A few minutes later, Adam rode in asking for a few men to help bring in the deer he had shot. John sent female slaves and children to gather dry wood for a fire. Tonight, they would eat well, thanks to Adam and this new-found paradise. In a short amount of time, everyone returned carrying armloads of firewood. Everyone except Harriet and Margaret.

Hector scanned the woods for his family but didn't see them. Alarmed, he went to Roscoe. "My momma and Margaret ain't come back yet. Maybe they can't find the way back."

Roscoe frowned. "We don't need no trouble." After a short pause, he said, "All right, you go find them, but hurry back. I don't want Higgins asking 'bout you."

His mother's scream pierced the air, sending a terrifying dread through Hector. He bolted towards her scream, hollering, "I'm coming, Momma, I'm coming!"

Others also dashed towards her scream.

Hector arrived at the scene first. "Momma! Momma! What's happened!"

Her words were incomprehensible. A small pile of wood lay beside her. There was no sign of Margaret.

John said, in a gruff voice, "Now listen, Harriet, stop this crying and tell us what's going on. You hear me?" He grabbed her by the shoulders, shaking her.

She sobbed softly. "My baby, they got my baby. We was right here getting wood jus' like you ask, when two men rode up…"

"Hey, nigger, where's your master?"

"He's over there building hisself a house, sir."

"Oh, he's back in them woods, eh? Tell you what I'm going to do." *He pulled his gun and pointed it at Harriet.*

Harriet's eyes grew wide with fear. Margaret hugged tight to her mother.

The man moved the barrel of his gun to Margaret's head. "You listen real close." He dismounted and gripped Margaret's arm. "We're going to take this girl of yours, and if you scream or warn anyone, we'll kill her. You got me?"

Harriet choked with fear. She pulled Margaret to her tight.

"I said do you understand me?" He pulled back the hammer on his gun.

"Yessir, I understands, please don't hurt my little girl. Please don't take her from me," Harriet pleaded.

But he forced Margaret from her mother and mounted his horse, holding onto her. "You yell or warn anyone, your girl is dead," said the other before they rode off.

Harriet sat terrified, unsure of what to do. When the men were out of sight, her anguish burst forth, and she screamed.

"C'mon, Adam, our horses. Hurry," shouted John. The two men had a good head start. Within minutes, the two galloped off in pursuit.

Hector, devastated, held tight to his mother. "It's goin' be all right. Massa John goin' find her," he whispered. Harriet held onto Hector and gently led him to the road. She stood waiting, staring off into the direction the men had gone.

When John and Adam returned several hours later, Harriet pressed her head with her arms in misery. They didn't have Margaret. John rode past Harriet and Hector without speaking, but Adam stopped. "I'm real sorry, Harriet. We couldn't find no trace of them."

Harriet fell to her knees and wailed.

The day went on forever and forever. The heat was oppressive. She would need all her strength to make it through to tomorrow. *Just breathe. Breathe,* she told herself. *Take one step, one step, and then, if you have the strength, take another. Breathe. Just keep breathing.*

John fumed. "Those damn slave stealers better not come anywhere near me 'cause I'll kill them."

"Poor Harriet and Margaret," said Sally.

"They're just common thieves. Ain't no man got a right to just come and take another man's property."

"But what about Harriet, Papa? Don't you feel bad for her? She lost her own child. I know if you and Momma lost one of us, you'd feel really bad."

"I ain't got time to worry about Harriet. She'll get over it soon enough."

Sally stuck her finger in her father's face. "But Papa, you should care about Harriet."

"Now hush, young'n. Go on and help your momma. I don't have time for your foolishness."

Over the next several months, they built the house, kitchen, barn, and slave quarters. They cleared acres, planting vegetables for their consumption and to sell or barter. They had abundant food and plenty of work—life moved along peacefully.

With the house built, John needed a house slave. He normally selected a young girl, as they didn't make good field hands. Sally intervened, convincing her father to choose Harriet. Harriet had more strength and experience than Katie's young daughter, she argued. Their rustic new house needed someone with her abilities. But Sally's real motive lived in her heart. Harriet needed and deserved a decent break.

With the arrival of March came the time to plant cotton on the acres they had cleared. Hector, now "nearly grown," as his mother often said, worked a mule to plow the beds upon which cotton seeds would be planted.

Life on John's homestead became settled and routine. Sally attended the one-room schoolhouse Dr. Daniel Waldron had opened at Peas Creek back in 1858. The five dollars per quarter seemed a good investment. Sally would become more desirable to an ambitious, wealthy young man. She had good looks, worked hard, and prided herself on having the skills a good homemaker needed. The boys didn't need school. Their mother taught them to read and count, and the farm taught them everything else. They toiled alongside their father, planting, tending the animals, and managing their slaves.

Their tranquil life would be short-lived.

The Daily Chronicle

WAR

On April 12, 1861, Confederate forces fired on Federal troops at Ft. Sumter, South Carolina, bringing the country at war with itself.

John traveled into town to gather supplies when he overheard two men passing by.

"I tell ya, them Yankees are in for it now. They dare set foot in Florida or any Southern state, and we'll knock 'em right back where they come from."

"Can't nobody fight like a man from the South," said the other.

"Excuse me," said John. "What's going on?"

"Didn't you hear? War done broke out. The Southern army captured a Yankee fort in South Carolina. We going to fight them Northern bastards."

"Humpf, ain't goin' ta be much of a fight. Be surprised if it last a week."

"You oughtta come on back into town tonight and bring your wife. Gonna be a big celebration."

John had seen newspaper reports describing the bickering in Washington with the slavery debate being the main issue. *The hell with Washington, Lincoln, and all them people. Ain't nobody taking my slaves or telling me what I can do.*

John and his family went to town that evening, leaving Roscoe in charge. In town, they found the celebration the two men had spoken of. A party atmosphere saturated the crowd. Bands played, politicians gave grand speeches extolling the inadequacies of the Yankee soldiers and the fierceness of the Southern army, how the need for cotton would rally the world to their side, and exhorting the citizens to support the war effort. Events planned to raise money included lotteries and a splendid ball. A feast was had. Preachers offered sermons and prayers, calling on their God to protect the glorious South.

War invaded even this frontier area, infectious and bloody, contaminating minds and poisoning hearts as it turned peace to animosity, pitted neighbor against neighbor, friend against friend, loved ones against loved ones. Farm families, who depended on slave labor, favored the Confederacy. Cattle ranchers generally favored keeping the union together.

John was busy saddling a horse in the barn when Adam approached him. "Can I talk with you, Pa?"

Adam's voice had been nervous. "Sure, son, what is it?"

"I want to join the army."

John shook his head. "Now, lis—"

"Wait, before you tell me I'm too young, listen to what I have to say."

John's eyes narrowed. "All right, just say it, but my answer ain't going to change none."

Adam took a deep breath. "Frederick Varn is only fifteen, and he joined. He rides as a dispatcher. Everybody's joining up, Pa."

"All right, Adam, now just you hold on. Sure, there's probably plenty of young boys like yourself out there in the army shooting and getting shot. But you're the oldest son we got, and we need you to take over this farm someday. I can't run this place by myself. I need you. Besides, it would kill your ma if you should get hurt. It won't be long you'll be eighteen, and then we'll talk again."

Adam walked off angry, but for now he would stay.

CHAPTER 23

William

William followed behind Itch. They moved deeper into the woods, pushing through thick underbrush until they came to two rotted, hollow logs—one on top of the other forming an "X."

"Here we are."

"So, this be where you hides your guns?"

"This is the place."

"You pick a good place. Nobody gonna come back in here."

"That was my thought, too. Before we start, I want to discuss something I worry about with you."

Itch sat on one of the logs and motioned for William to sit.

"Look, William, I know how you feel 'bout Higgins, and I understand you are thinking 'bout killing him if you ever find him."

"Yeah, I thought 'bout that. But I thought, too, 'bout what happen to me if I kill him. Be hunted like a dog an' killed, too. That not do my family any good."

"I'm glad you're thinking of your family because they have to be your main concern, not Higgins."

"I tries to keep it that way, but that man ruined my life. Sometimes I think he need to pay for what he did to me and plenty other Negroes."

"You have good reason to be bitter. He has treated you and others with great evil. What he and thousands like him have done is shameful and immoral. But be careful, don't give them reason to fear you."

"You right about that. I be careful, don't want nothing bad happening to me or my family. I know I gots to hide how I feels from white men."

"Men stole me and many others from our villages in Africa. Later, a white man cut off one of my fingers, and they have done many terrible things to me and others. Have I wished to get revenge on them? To be honest, at times, yes. Is it possible to forgive them? I don't know. I would like to get rid of this hate that builds up and makes life so miserable. There are times when I believe that it's possible. But there are other times when I know I have much work yet to do. I think forgiving something that is very hurtful is not easy and perhaps is never finished.

"If I saw Higgins now and had a gun in my hand, I might shoot him."

"I understand. Especially when I see the cruelty that is done. I am going to teach you how to use a handgun and a rifle because it will be a long time before you see Higgins again, and I'm hopeful that between now and then, you will mellow a bit and not try to kill him. But you might be in a dangerous situation and need to defend yourself. Of course, you should kill someone to stop them from killing you, but killing from hate or anger, I'm not sure that is a good idea. So, enough talk. Let's get started."

CHAPTER 24

John

"Hey, Sam, get out here, we got work to do," hollered John.

"That's odd," said Martha. "He's usually one of the first out of bed." She went to his room and called his name. When he didn't respond, she shook him gently and became alarmed at his high temperature. "John, John, get in here. Quick!"

Martha was seated next to Sam on his bed, her hand on his forehead. "He's very hot. I can't wake him."

Sam lay still, his face flushed, eyes closed.

Martha looked up at John. "Bring me a pan of cold water. I'll try to bring his fever down."

She placed cold, wet rags on his forehead, working tirelessly all morning. By early afternoon, Sam was still unresponsive, and his skin was feverish. Martha brushed his hair with her hand and leaned over to kiss his cheek. "We're going to get you better," she whispered.

She found Harriet in the kitchen. "Harriet, John is working in the garden today. Go tell him to come to the house at once."

John entered the house calling for Martha. Martha rushed to John. "Sam isn't any better." She wrapped John in a tight hug, then released him to look into his eyes. "He's still very hot. He doesn't talk to me or wake up. He needs the doctor."

John entered Sam's room and touched his forehead. "I'm on my way."

John arrived at Doctor Kaufmann's home, which also served as his office. His wife answered the door and ushered John in.

A plump woman, a little too self-important for John's taste, said, "My husband's out on another call. He's had three calls today already. He had plenty of calls yesterday and the day before that, too. Would you care for some tea, Mr. Higgins?" She raised her eyebrows and tilted her head to one side.

"No, thank you. Do you have any idea when he will return?"

"He went to Ralph Hall's house. So, I would guess that he will return in an hour or possibly two. Did you know, Mr. Higgins, that we're having a smallpox epidemic right here?"

The word "smallpox" jolted him. He had heard of the devastation and death smallpox caused in many towns. "What are its symptoms?" he asked.

"It's not pleasant, I assure you. First there is a high fever, and the person becomes very listless. Then a rash appears in the mouth and later all over the body."

"Do you have medicine for it?"

"Oh, goodness no." She turned abruptly and, opening a fan, fanned herself rapidly. "There is no cure, as you must surely know. Some lucky few souls survive it, but most die. We've lost three already in this small town. You can imagine how many a large city might lose."

"Our youngest child has a high fever and just lies in bed. He doesn't respond or talk. What can we do?"

"I'm very sorry to tell you, but there's nothing you can do. I've heard my husband tell others this very same thing. I hope your child is one of the lucky ones. You're welcome to wait here for him if you wish, but truthfully, he can't do anything to help your child."

"I have to go. I need to give this terrible news to my wife. Perhaps…maybe there's a chance that we…" He rushed out before she could say another word.

When John arrived home, Martha rushed to him.

"Where's the doctor?"

John took Martha's hand and guided her to a chair. "I have some bad news, my dear."

Martha squeezed his hand hard, her eyes worried and pleading. "Oh, no. What is it, John?"

John sat on the arm of the chair. He leaned in and kissed the top of her head. "Doctor Kaufmann can't help Sam. Sam has smallpox. There's an epidemic going on."

"Oh, my God, no. Please, no."

"Some do survive, so we need to do all we can to make sure Sam is one of those survivors."

Over the next days, John, Martha, and their children all had a turn trying desperately to keep Sam's fever down with cold, damp cloths, but nothing helped. Martha held a spoon of soup to his lips, but he sipped very little. After several days, a rash appeared around his mouth, and in a few more days, it covered his body. He died in two weeks.

Harriet was given the task of washing and dressing Sam's body. She believed this to be a virtuous duty and, as such, treated his body with respect. But as she washed and dressed him, she couldn't escape remembering Sam's cruel behavior towards her family and friends. She could still hear his laughter as he hit them with his whip and mocked them with his words. At one point, she stopped her work to look at his young face and felt deep regret that in his short life, he had known such hate.

Later, she prepared and served the feast for the family friends who came to pay their respects. Working in the house, she observed the pain and loss of the Higgins family. This was a new and unexpected experience for her, especially witnessing the massa. For she had only seen him as cold and cruel towards her people. She hadn't realized he was capable of sorrow or compassion.

The Higgins household grieved. John and Adam kept busy around the farm in a futile attempt to set aside their grief. Sally sought to comfort her mother, even though she herself was devastated. Harriet provided them with special meals and supported Sally and her mother in their grief by reminding them she had survived her losses and, though it seemed dark now, they, too, would survive.

Well, before the Higgins family learned to manage their grief, smallpox would strike again.

Late one evening, John walked to the front door and stepped outside. Harriet stood outside the shanty she shared with Silas and Katie and their children, talking with three others. A bit of light shone from Silas and Katie's shanty. Others walked up and hugged those already there.

What the hell's going on? John decided to find out. He barged in where he found Katie crying, caressing Dee's forehead. Silas and Hector sat beside her. Sarah held a wooden cup of herbal liquid to Dee's mouth, but she had no interest in drinking.

"What's going on here?" demanded John.

"It's Dee, Massa. She very sick," said Silas.

John touched her arm. Her hot skin reminded him of Sam. "That ain't gonna do her no good. Ain't nothin' you can do to save her."

John's words stuck in Katie's mind, but she was determined to save Dee. Each day, when she returned from work in the fields, she cared for Dee while Silas and the others tended to Katie's chores. In spite of Katie's efforts, Dee died in twelve days.

Katie and Silas begged John to let them wash her and wrap her in a white cloth, as their tradition called for, but John wasn't having anything disrupt the work schedules. He and Adam buried her on the grounds set aside for the enslaved.

Though not given time off to visit her grave, the enslaved paid their visit to Dee in the evening after they'd completed their chores.

They experienced death as relief from the agony of their enslavement and an opportunity to go "home" to their "mansion in the sky." At Dee's gravesite, they celebrated with jubilant singing and dancing. After the celebration, Dee's family uttered prayers for her spirit to travel safely home.

When Katie and Silas returned to their shanty after the gravesite celebration, Silas held Katie as she wept. After some minutes, she pulled herself together and looked into Silas' moist eyes. "Why that mass John not let us take care of our precious Dee? Why he gots to be so mean?"

"All he think about is hisself and his money. But we don' have no say. Try to say something to him an' he beat you like he done to William."

"What we gonna do without Dee, Silas? She such a good girl."

"We gonna miss her, that for sure. She in a better place now. No more worrying 'bout the massa an' his mean ways."

Silas and Katie, with their younger children, would visit Dee's grave many times over the next few months. During this time, Katie became despondent. She had difficulty keeping up with her picking quota, so others helped her by contributing to her bag. Although she gradually became herself again, she never could forgive John.

Sally lay in bed thinking about Sam being gone and then Dee also gone. Her thoughts soon turned to Hector and his losses. She imagined that perhaps Hector's losses were worse than hers because he had no knowledge of what befell his father or his sister.

She decided she would do something to help him. She considered several options when an idea began to take shape. She looked through her old school books and found her old speller.

She had to wait for the right moment to move forward with the next step. Her time came several days later during an evening her parents chatted peacefully on the back porch. Sally eased out of the house, making her way to the barn where Hector and the others worked on their evening chores.

Sally approached Hector. "I need to talk with you. Can you step out back with me for a minute?"

The others hushed, keeping their faces in their work, but they eavesdropped on their every word.

Outside, Hector asked, "What you want, Miss Sally?"

"I have a surprise for you."

Hector, frightened at what might happen if her father should discover them, only managed to stand rigid and wait for her to speak.

"Well, aren't you at least a little bit curious?"

"Yeah, I reckon so. But what you doing here anyway? You is likely to get yourself and all us in trouble—'specially me."

"Don't worry, no one saw me coming. Look what I brought for you." She reached forward and handed him her old speller.

Hector's eyes grew big. He held his hands up to fend off her dangerous offer.

"Don't worry, no one will know. And besides, once you learn to read, you'll be able to take care of yourself better, especially if the Union wins the war and you become free. C'mon, take it."

"You know what your father will do if he catches me with this book. I can't take it, Miss Sally, you know I can't."

"Hector, you're smart. You can do this. Just be careful, that's all. I could get in trouble just by being down here, but I'm here. Take it, I'll help you. You can't go around being afraid all the time."

"I ain't afraid all the time. I just know what's good for me, that's all."

"Your pa wasn't afraid."

"Yeah, and look what happen to him."

"Sorry, I shouldn't have brought that up." Then, excited again, she said, "This is your chance to get an education, Hector. Your father would be proud of you."

Hector paused. Then he reached out his hand and quickly stuffed the book under his shirt.

"You better go now, Miss Sally."

"Be careful, and it'll be fine."

"I don' know 'bout that."

"I know you'll do real well. I'll help when I can."

When she returned home, her father waited for her on the front porch.

"I been looking for you. What were you doing at the quarters?" he said in a rough tone.

"Nothing, Papa, I just wanted to see how Katie was doing."

She felt proud of herself for being so clever, but disappointed that she had been seen. She must be more careful, or her efforts would make life difficult for Hector.

With the day's work done, the enslaved lugged themselves to their shanties. Hector waited until his mother slept before he searched for a place to hide his book. The sparse shanty had few options. He didn't want his mother or Silas and Katie's family to know. The floor was nothing but dirt, the walls made from logs, the fireplace made with mud, sticks, and rocks. They had a table now and a chair—furniture the master's family no longer wanted and had given to Harriet. He decided on the mattress, nothing more than a threadbare cloth stuffed with moss. Parting several inches of the threads holding the seam on the side next to the wall, he made the opening just big enough to squeeze the book through, making sure the book lay against the floor, covered by the moss.

Two nights later, Hector mustered the courage to pull the book from its hiding place. A bright full moon provided him with light. Hector lay awake. He stood, careful not to wake his mother, and peered out of the opening that served as their window. Quiet. No lights at the big house. He reached under the mattress and felt the hardness of the book. He checked out the window one more time— not a sound except for buzzing mosquitoes and rustling nocturnal animals. He pulled the book out.

Sitting under the window, he opened it. He studied the confusing shapes and symbols, drew a deep breath, and closed it. Then he closed his eyes. His heart seemed about to rip out of his chest. He calmed himself and, after a moment, opened the book again. Then closed it.

He stared at the cover. The picture showed a woman with four children reading. Below the picture were all the strange symbols that he had seen on posters and newspapers. When he opened the cover, the first page showed these same shapes in columns. He turned page after page and found empty shapes, none of which he understood. He closed the book and sighed. Disappointed and discouraged, he returned it to its hiding place. How could he ever learn? Miss Sally had given him an impossible task.

But Sally was good to her word. Every chance encounter with Hector, even in passing for a few seconds, she would stop, write a letter in the dirt, and tell him how to pronounce it. Hector would repeat the sound Sally had taught, then scurry away.

That night, he would find the letter in his speller and repeat it over and over until he was sure he had learned it. After Hector had learned enough letters, Sally put together short words and pronounced them for him. And he would do the same that evening with his speller. She started with the words in the early lessons of the speller—"bag," "big," "bog," and so on through the speller. After doing this for several months, Hector became able to identify and pronounce words in later lessons on his own. His reading continued to improve without Sally's help, much to Hector's relief.

CHAPTER 25
William

William couldn't sleep for worrying about his family. How he longed to hold Harriet! Desperation fueled boldness and urgency. He threw his covers off and slipped out the back door needing to do *something*, even if only walking in the cool night air. The half-moon in a cloudless sky gave light enough to navigate the woods. He walked to his left, a different direction from his usual walks. He came to a fence. He remembered Itch's earlier instructions—don't go past the fence. He considered going back the way he had come, but he was sick of being fearful and dog-tired of others controlling his every move. He turned right and followed the fence.

He felt elated. His heart beat faster at making his own decisions, even if just deciding which direction to go. Small as it was, it tasted like freedom.

He picked his way through the dark woods. He had walked only a short distance when the fence ended and just ahead, the road. The ever-dangerous road. The tempting road. Not ready to give up his new found sense of freedom, he decided to walk along the side of the road. If he should see or hear anyone, he could jump into the woods.

He hadn't walked more than a few hundred feet when rustling broke the night's silence.

"Stop right there, or I'll shoot ye."

The next sound was of someone pulling back the hammer of a rifle. Footsteps approached William from behind. William felt a sharp pain on the back of his head, followed by darkness.

When William regained consciousness, he discovered his arms tied tightly behind his back and another rope around his neck with the end tied to a tree. He had an intense headache. He lifted his head and moaned.

"Awake, are ye?"

It was early morning. William realized he had been gone for several hours—hopefully Itch would miss him by now and come looking for him.

"I seen all them whip marks on yer back. Figure you're a real troublemaker. Thought maybe I oughtta just shoot ya. Nobody like runaways. But then I thought a good strong fella like you would make me quite a bit of money. So, I'm taking you into town. Might be a reward. Or better yet, might be someone will pay me good money. The way I figures it, you goin' ta bring me my first good meal in quite a while."

As the morning light progressed, William got his first good look at his captor. The old man's dirty white beard covered most of his face and grew down to his chest. His face was brown and cracked from the sun. Shorter than William, he nevertheless seemed strong. After breaking camp, he tied the neck rope to his saddle horn and rode towards town with William on foot struggling to keep up.

Hours later, an exhausted, thirsty William stumbled into town behind the grizzled old man. The man pulled up to the sheriff's office first to ask about any rewards for runaway slaves.

"None that I know of," said the sheriff. "But you might catch Wheeler over at the hardware store. I saw him there a few minutes ago. Carl Wheeler, short round man with a mustache. He's always looking for a strong nigger. Hardware store's just down a ways."

As the old man walked to the hardware store, he jerked the rope tied around William's neck and said in a low voice, "You better behave now, you hear. This man don't buy you, I might just have to shoot you right here in the street."

As they approached the hardware store, Wheeler came out carrying a bag of feed and dumped it into his buckboard. "Hey, mister, I hear you in need of a strong nigger. I got one right here."

Wheeler looked William over. "How much."

"A bargain for just eight hundred."

"Lift his shirt and have him turn around. I want to see his back."

Wheeler raised his eyebrows on seeing William's scars.

"I'll give you three hundred, not a penny more."

The old man opened his mouth to speak, but he decided not to. He had never seen three hundred dollars before and might not ever in his lifetime if he didn't jump on this offer. "Sold."

William rode in the back of the buckboard with sacks of flour and other supplies, his arms still tied behind him and his neck rope tied to the buckboard.

When they arrived at Wheeler's plantation, he took William into the barn. He shoved William against a pole. Then, he wrapped the neck rope around the pole, pulling it tight enough to choke William. William's eyes bulged as he gasped for breath.

"Now lissen here. You run from me, and I got two dogs'll track you down and tear you into little pieces. You got that?"

William nodded as best he could.

Wheeler unwound the rope from the pole and pulled William through the barn's back door. Immediately, two chained dogs leapt at William, their ferociousness leaving no doubt that they would indeed destroy him.

"You don't want to mess with these dogs. You understand me?"

"Yes, sir."

Wheeler shouted at a man he spotted walking by the barn. "Stan, get over here."

A white man, almost William's size but with a limp, hurried over. "Yes, sir, Mr. Wheeler."

"Got us a new nigger." Then, looking at William, "You ever work cotton, boy?"

"Yes, sir."

"Okay. Good. Get him going in the fields."

"Okay, Mr. Wheeler."

"Boy, this here is my second in command. He tell you to do something, you better do it cause it's the same as if I told you." Wheeler pulled the knife from its sheath on his belt. He put it to William's neck. "I could kill you right here." Then he laughed. He cut the rope from William's neck and his arms. "Get him working, Stan."

That night, William lay on a bunk in a small shanty with three others. He needed to get out of here and back to the Stones' house. But how? They would never find him here, if they were even looking for him.

William felt more hopeless with each day. Escape seemed impossible. Wheeler and his men kept a close watch, and the dogs always seemed eager to hunt and kill any runaways. It seemed impossible that he could make his way to Florida when just a short walk at night had led to his being enslaved again.

Six months after he became Wheeler's slave, a contingent of twelve Confederate soldiers rode onto Wheeler's property. They arrived with a buckboard and eight black men in the back, all chained together,

"Morning, Mr. Wheeler."

"Howdy, George. What brings you out this way?"

"You might of heard that the government has declared the army needs soldiers to do the fighting, and we need more Negroes to do the other work. We been told to round up one Negro from each of the plantations 'round here."

"So, you come to get one from me?"

"Yes, sir. Damn war's got so we all got to contribute something."

"What the hell is going on? Thought this war was just goin' to last a couple weeks."

"Doin' all we know how to do, Mr. Wheeler."

"God damn war, goin' to suck us all dry." Wheeler looked over the soldiers and the buckboard with the chained men in the back. He stood for a few moments considering who to give up. He thought first of William.

Only been here a few months but could be trouble down the road. Hell, I just paid three hundred damn dollars for him.

He spotted Stan coming out of the barn. "Hey, Stan, send that big nigger we got a few months ago to me."

When William arrived, Wheeler looked at George. "Here he is. You take him for now, but you boys better goddamn win this war."

George motioned for William to get into the buckboard. Two soldiers dismounted and chained him to the others.

"The Confederacy appreciates your donation, Mr. Wheeler."

"Yeah, I bet they do. That's three hundred dollars the government owes me. Now get the hell out of here and go find some Yankees to fight."

William bounced along the road with the others. He turned to the man on his right. "Where we going?"

"We goin' to help the secesh to fight the Yankees."

"You sure 'bout that?"

"That what they been saying."

William looked at the other eight chained men. He saw fear in some of their eyes. Others had empty, dark eyes—the result of a lifetime without hope. He glanced back at the soldiers riding behind them. They were his enemy. They were the secesh. They were fighting to keep him in chains.

William leaned back. He closed his eyes and took in a deep breath. *I ain't heping these mens fight nobody.*

William didn't know he and the eight men with him would very soon be engaged in the conflict.

De Yankees wasn't so bad. De most dey wanted was sumpin' to eat. Dey was all de time hungry, de first thing dey ask for when dey come was sumpin' to put in dey stomach. And chicken! I ain't never seed even a preacher eat chicken like dem Yankees. I believes to my soul dey ain't never seed no chicken 'twell dey come down here.

—Tempie Herndon, age 103 (*Voices from Slavery*, p. 165)

CHAPTER 26

John

The Southern states had cheered the war in the beginning and expected it to end in a victory for the South within a short time. But now the Union blockades were taking their toll, and necessities were hard to come by. Heads of families were often gone, as were the young men in families. Women and children were often left to the hard work of maintaining farms and households and keeping the struggling economy going. Times were difficult for people of the South.

Early morning dew wet the ground. Damp, misty fog hung in the woods and over the fields. John rode the buckboard into town for supplies. Halfway there, he encountered an acquaintance from Ft. Meade, Gene Struckerman, with other men he didn't know. They appeared agitated. John reined in the horses. "Something wrong?" he shouted.

"Damn Yankees come up from Ft. Myers, we figure, and burned Ft. Meade. Stole supplies, cattle, slaves. 'Bout wiped out our neighbor, Henry. Took every one of his slaves and killed his overseer. We got to do something about them coming in here like that."

Another man spoke up. "We're going to burn the home of every Union man in this county. They'll pay for this."

Another said, "Them Yankee sympathizers are spies. We need to get them traitors out of here."

Struckerman said, "We're getting up a group to go to Ft. Myers and blast them Yankees out of there. You with us?"

John paused, feeling trapped and not wanting to go. "Let me know when you're going. I'll do what I can."

Over the next few months, they developed a Regulator Unit to identify Union sympathizers, run them out of town, or kill them and burn their houses. To John's relief, an expedition to Ft. Myers never materialized.

War's getting too damn close to home. John considered how he might protect his family should Yankees raid his land. He needed to teach Sally and Martha to shoot. He did finally teach Sally to shoot a rifle, but he could never bring himself to teach Martha.

The Daily Chronicle

April 16, 1862

Confederate Congress passes Conscription Act

All white males between the ages of eighteen and thirty-five are subject to military service for a period of three years.

"Guess what I heard in town today, Martha," said John. "The Confederates done passed a law of conscription."

"What does that mean?"

"Every man from eighteen to thirty-five got to sign up to fight. They're even sending soldiers around to find those that don't sign up."

"Good Lord," said Martha. "Thank goodness you're too old and Adam is only seventeen. But that young man, what's his name?

Manny, I think. And his friend Arthur. They won't be so lucky." She put down the dress she was mending. "I'm afraid for some of our friends. So many have already lost husbands and sons."

"I know. Women are running half the plantations in the county."

The Daily Chronicle

September 27, 1862
Confederate Conscription Act
Today, the age limit was extended to forty-five years old. All white males between the ages of eighteen and forty-five years are subject to military service for three years.

On a stinking hot day in July, the air still and heavy, Adam worked the vegetable garden with Jacob as the sun beat down on them in mid-afternoon. Engrossed in their work, they didn't hear the six men ride up until they had turned off the road. When they saw the Confederate soldiers, they stopped their work and watched them approach.

The patrol came to a stop in front of the two men. The civilian asked, "How old are you, son?"

"Seventeen, sir."

"That's close enough," said the man. "Son, the Confederacy needs you, so by the power of the laws of these Confederate states, I demand you come with us. Where are your horses?"

Adam glanced at the house. "There are a few in the corral on the other side of the barn over there."

"What's your name?"

Adam shifted uneasily. "Adam Higgins, sir."

"Adam, go with these soldiers and saddle up two horses and bring the others."

As the three of them left to seize the horses, the man in charge said to Jacob, "You're now officially a helper in the Confederate army. You'll be coming with us."

Bewildered, Jacob hesitated, then, wishing he could refuse, mumbled, "Yes, sir."

When Adam and the soldiers returned, the civilian motioned for Jacob to get on the horse. Jacob, not an experienced rider, wanted to protest but didn't. He mounted the horse.

"Sir?" said Adam.

"What is it?"

"I would like to say goodbye to my mother and sister in the house just over there."

"Not today, son, we got to keep movin'. Let's go." He hurried back to the road. Adam hesitated, but when a soldier placed his hand on his revolver, Adam pointed his horse towards the road. Jacob slapped his horse to get him going, causing it to take off with a start. Jacob pulled on the reins, but the horse would not be slowed. He clung with one hand fast to the saddle horn and one hand pulled the reins. When his horse reached the road, it fell in line with the others and slowed to a more manageable pace, prompting Jacob to very briefly close his eyes and offer a prayer of thanks. Adam, though worried about his family's reaction, knew his dream to join the army had come true.

The civilian leader said to the officer, "No need getting involved with tearful mothers and emotional farewells. The army needs men and horses, and I'm going to see they get all I can find."

They led the conscripts several miles north of town to a meeting place where fifteen other young men stood around trying to look brave and unconcerned. From there, they would travel to Gainesville to be sworn in and trained. The four conscripted slaves would remain with their masters until needed by the army. Then they would be assigned physical labor to relieve the soldiers for combat duty.

When John returned from the sawmill with Richard, he noticed Adam and Jacob had abandoned their work and left tools on the ground. Annoyed, he made a mental note to tell Adam if he wanted to join the army, he'd have to learn to be more responsible.

John led the team of horses pulling the buckboard towards the barn. He spotted Martha running towards him, waving her arms, calling his name. "Whoa!" he shouted, pulling back on the reins. The wagon came to a slow stop. He hurried to Martha, shouting, "What's the matter?"

She stopped just short of John and screamed something about Adam.

"Hey, slow down, I can't understand you. What about Adam?

"They came and took him. They just took him!"

John's eyes grew hard. "Who took him? What are you talking about?"

"The army took him. A group of soldiers came and took him. He's not old enough. You've got to do something."

John moved in close and put his arms around her. "I'll get our boy back. Can't no one just come here and take our boy like that."

Richard took the wagon into the barn while John walked Martha to the house. He would raise hell until they gave him back.

While saddling a horse in the barn, John discovered they had taken three of his horses and Jacob. He believed he would find them in Gainesville, the closest location where recruits and conscripted men could be integrated into the regular army. Even if it took a week, he was going to get both his son and Jacob back.

"Hell," he said to Martha, "they can keep the horses, just consider that my contribution to the war. But Adam is only seventeen. We ain't giving him up yet."

Leaving Martha and Sally in charge for a few days concerned him, but women on other farms already proved they could manage. But still John wondered how the county could survive without enough men to run things. There were limits to what a family ought to be asked to do.

After two days of riding, he arrived in Gainesville and went directly to the military post. A soldier stopped him at the front gate.

"I want to see your commanding officer!" bellowed John.

"State your business, mister."

"I'll state my business to your superior."

"Then you might as well turn around an' go back where you come from. If you can't talk to me, you can't talk to the colonel."

John considered this, then said, "My son got conscripted, and he's not eighteen yet. I want him back."

The soldier shook his head. "Colonel can't help you, mister. So, you best be movin' on."

"What do you mean he can't help me? He's in command, ain't he?"

"Like I said, best be moving on," said the soldier. He moved his rifle in John's direction enough to send a message.

John checked around town. He wasn't giving up without a fight. He found the law offices of Smith, Winkle, and Markle on Main Street. They appeared to be a successful firm, if fancy leather furniture and an expensive looking office was any indication. Their receptionist ushered John into the office of Thomas Winkle. The two men talked for a long time. Finally, Winkle sighed. "I can't help you." John wasn't sure if they couldn't or wouldn't. John wasn't buying Winkle's offhand remark that "we all have to sacrifice for the war effort." John was willing to sacrifice just as much as anyone, but he wasn't sacrificing his underaged son. Nobody in their right mind would do that. It sounded to John like it just wasn't good for business.

To hell with these rich lawyers.

He spoke with the sheriff, who claimed he had no jurisdiction over the federal government.

He spoke to politicians, who refused to get involved—they had elections to win.

He spoke to business owners, but none were willing to help— they had customers to please.

He spoke to bartenders, who could only offer a drink.

No one offered hope. Not even a suggestion.

Some accused him of not supporting the Confederacy. "Why weren't you volunteering?" they would ask. John hated to admit defeat, but he had no options left. After five days, he mounted his horse and headed home. Defeat weighed heavily on him.

On the dreaded ride home, he rehearsed what to tell Martha. He decided it best to just tell her the truth. He would tell her who he had talked to and what they'd said to him. But when she saw him return without Adam, he didn't need to say a word. She met him at the door, looked for Adam, and burst into tears.

For days afterwards, she moped around the house. She often went into her room and closed the door. She thought of the boys and men who had returned from the war with missing limbs and ugly scars. She spent hours in prayer that her boy would survive unscathed. Over time, she improved, but never quite became her old self again. She lacked her old vitality and showed little interest in caring for her home. Even so, she always guarded Sally with ferocity—determined nothing would happen to her last child.

Months later, Sarah, the wise old slave, frequent doctor to John's family and all the workers, and mother to Jacob, died peacefully in her sleep. For several days before her death, she had seen visions of people from her distant past and had been actively teaching Louise, daughter to Silas and Katie, what she knew of herbs and curative potions. Some thought the heartbreak of missing her son contributed to her death.

Again, in the evening hours when all chores were complete, the enslaved congregated at Sarah's gravesite and celebrated her being free of slavery and moving on to her mansion in the sky.

Sally went to the quarters to pay her respects. She said, "Sarah was a fine person, and we shall miss her."

John watched from a distance as Sally moved amongst the enslaved. She moved slowly, speaking gently to each of them. He wondered why she would do that. He recalled there was a time when Sarah used her medicines to help his own family. But even so, that doesn't mean you should mix with them. It wasn't right to treat them like friends. *Oh well,* he decided. *She's just a foolish young girl who doesn't know you don't treat them with kindness. They're different from us. And always will be.*

CHAPTER 27

William

William and the other eight men rode in the buckboard for a day and a half before they reached an encampment of twenty Confederate soldiers. William noticed two rows of tents with one tent, larger than the others, separated by a short distance. Several soldiers in uniform milled about. An enslaved man stood at the larger tent entrance ready to do the bidding of the officer inside. Three others stood around a fire with pots hanging over it, tending to the evening meal.

The soldier pulled the wagon to a stop in front of the larger tent where the sergeant dismounted and went inside. Shortly, he returned, following a stout man who had an air of superiority about him.

The sergeant looked at one of his soldiers and nodded. That soldier dismounted, removed the shackles, and ordered the men out of the buckboard. Once they were on the ground, he told them to line-up side-by-side.

The officer in charge walked by the group, looking each man up and down as he went. After viewing them all, he stepped up to the first man and asked, "Do you know how to cook?"

"No, sir. Never cooked nothing before."

Finally, after asking four others the same question, he found one who had some experience. One of the soldiers led that man away to join the cooking crew.

When the officer asked one of the men if he knew how to care for horses, William was quick to speak. "I can do that, sir."

The officer slowly turned to face William, then turned back to the man he had first spoken with. "I asked you a question."

"No, sir. I ain't never worked with no horses."

The officer walked over to William. He stared at William for a bit, then slapped him hard. "Don't do that again. You understand?"

William hesitated for a split second before answering. "Yes, sir."

The officer stared at William in silence for what seemed to William like a long time. William recalled Harriett's words to him long ago: *Your anger get you killed someday.* He thought this could be that day.

"You're messing with the wrong man, nigger." The officer pulled his gun out of his holster and rammed it against William's forehead. "I got a bullet in this gun with your name on it. And if you ever mess with me again, I'm gonna give it to you. Understand?"

"Yes, sir."

"Sargeant, take this man to the barn. Find out can he handle horses."

William got the job of tending to the horses and, like the other men, also helped with the tasks of tending to the needs of the camp.

This small company of soldiers sent out patrols looking for Yankees. When found, they would set up an ambush. Because the Union soldiers did the same, the Confederate patrol moved their camp every few days. With each move, the enslaved men broke camp, loaded the equipment, and set it up again in the new location. This went on for several months.

"Don't know 'bout you, but I be ready to find me some Yankees and join up wid dem."

William looked around for soldiers and, seeing none, looked hard at Henry. "What you talkin' about, fool? Don't go running your mouth and get yourself in trouble with these secesh. They don't mind killing any one of us."

"I know, but think about it. We helpin' our enemies win this here war. I want to be killing these secesh, not helping them kill Yankees."

"You ain't tellin' me nothin' I don't know. But our day will come. I knows it. It will come."

Two weeks later, the soldiers returned from a just-completed ambush with two badly wounded comrades. The officer in charge ordered a soldier to use their buckboard to take them into the nearest town to find a doctor. He chose Henry and another enslaved man named Cal to accompany the soldier.

That evening, the soldiers sat around the campfire talking about their victory. Their spirits high, they bragged, and perhaps embellished a bit. The enslaved men sat in a group off to the side thirty feet from the soldiers. After a time, the stories died out, and the talk slowed to a crawl. The officer in charge stood, stretched his arms over his head, and announced he was going to turn in. Before he brought his arms down, a shot sounded and a bullet struck the officer in the middle of his back, knocking him to the ground. The black men hit the ground. The soldiers scrambled for their rifles too late, as a fusillade of shots showered the area. It seemed to William that hell itself had engulfed them. When the shooting stopped, only the stench of gun smoke remained. Silence. Slowly, the Yankees emerged from the woods, their rifles at the ready.

The enslaved lay still. They gradually lifted their heads to survey the area, not sure what to expect.

"You men can get up. The killing's over. Any more of these southern boys around?"

The enslaved men stood and dusted themselves off. William spoke first. "Not that I knows. Appears that you killed them all." The others nodded in agreement.

"Well then, I am Sargeant Roundtree, Fourth Battalion out of Maine. And you men are now free. You can thank your friend Henry here." Roundtree looked around and, not seeing Henry, called out for him. Henry and Cal emerged from the woods, still hiding. "We came across Henry and Cal a few miles from here helping take a couple of wounded men to the local doctor. Henry led us here. We been looking for these murdering bastards for a long, long time."

"What we suppose' do now? We in the middle of this war with no place to go."

"What's your name?" asked Roundtree.

"William, sir."

"Last name?"

"Don't got none yet."

"Well, Mr. William of no last name, how would you and your friends like to join the First Regiment of South Carolina Volunteers, among the first colored troops in the Union Army?"

"Does you mean we could fight the secesh?"

"That's exactly what I mean."

"Give me a gun, sir. I'm ready now."

And so were the others.

Roundtree and his troops escorted the men to the coast, where they would board a boat to carry them to Port Royal Island. It was late November of 1862. A new black regiment was being formed and trained to help in the fight against slavery and secession.

CHAPTER 28

Richard

The work crew looked to the road as a company of soldiers approached. They were surprised to see men wearing the dark blue of the Union army instead of Confederate gray.

Richard's immense grin could only mean one thing. Unable to contain himself, he dropped his hoe and bolted towards the soldiers, vigorously waving his arms. Roscoe shouted, "Richard, you fool, get back here!" But he could not be stopped. He reached the road and stood in the middle, facing the oncoming soldiers. The lieutenant ordered his company to stop.

For a few seconds, Richard and the young officer eyed each other. Then the soldier motioned to the buckboard and said, "Don't just stand there, get in."

"Yes, sir!" Richard ran to the buckboard and, with one smooth motion, jumped inside. He flaunted a huge grin at his friends and waved goodbye.

The young lieutenant moved his men out. Richard watched his friends grow smaller in the distance as he bumped down the road to his new life.

Roscoe stood watching Richard make his escape. He wondered whether he would live to regret not going with him.

The friends left behind were stunned by Richard's boldness. They couldn't take their eyes off the Union soldiers and Richard as they moved away. Then they all began talking at once. Some approved but others weren't so sure. And for many, it planted a bit of hope for what the future might hold.

"Damn, damn, damn!" said Roscoe, knowing he had to face John. He walked to his horse, his forehead furrowed, climbed into the saddle, and rode to find him.

Roscoe found John working in the corn fields. Faking a sense of urgency, he whipped his horse to a trot. "Massa, Massa! Them Yankees done got Richard! We was clearing that land up by the road when they come by and got him."

"Yankee soldiers?" John kicked at a clod of dirt. "Damn, this war is going to be the end of us all. Didn't know the Yankees was so close. Next time you hear soldiers coming down that road, get everybody away from the road as quick as you can. Don't want to lose any more."

When Roscoe returned to his crew, he said, "Don't none of the rest of you try doing such a dumb thing as Richard done." Then he broke into a grin.

The others, with smiles on their faces, didn't say a word.

CHAPTER 29

William

Beaufort, South Carolina, 1862

Beaufort, South Carolina is a city on Port Royal Island, one of South Carolina's coastal sea islands. It is also the site of Camp Saxton, the home of the new and controversial black regiment of the Union army.

William and his comrades stood at the boat's railing looking on enthusiastically as they approached their new home base for the duration of the war. They marveled at the large number of boats anchored in the area around the port—mostly schooners, a few gunboats, and steamers.

The white officers for this black regiment made their headquarters in an old rundown plantation house that at one time was the pride and joy of a wealthy plantation owner. Its owner had moved inland with his family and all of his enslaved persons, hoping to escape the Union army.

Just a short five-minute walk beyond the house stood row after row of white army tents that would house the regiment of formerly enslaved men. This regiment was the first made up entirely of freedmen, eight hundred strong, all volunteers, ready to fight for their freedom. Public opinion was against enlisting black men into the army, so this experiment was kept quiet.

After landing, William and the others joined a group of twenty-five new recruits assembled to hear General Saxton greet them.

General Saxton gave a warm welcoming speech. Then the commanding officer of the black regiment, Colonel Thomas Higginson, shook each man's hand and gave them his personal welcome. As he spoke to each man, he asked them for their last name. If they had none, he asked them to choose one, for they would need it in the army. William immediately decided on "Stone."

Though the black regiment was controversial, Colonel Higginson, previously of the Fifty-First Massachusetts, had always believed it was a good idea and wanted to be a part of it. He was aware that his regiment would be scrutinized carefully, and the slightest incident would end the experiment.

The first few days of the new regiment focused on turning the men into soldiers and making them a unified fighting force. They must get used to army rations, wearing uniforms according to regulations, carrying rifles and maintaining them, constant drilling, and learning their duties. They would have an unbroken training period of two months. Much of their daily routine was taken up with drilling, and drilling, and more drilling. They lived in tents, where the biggest problem was sand. It got into everything.

November 27, 1862—Thanksgiving Day. The constant sound of drumming filled the air, along with gunshots. The favorite celebration of the day was the shooting contest. William did well, thanks to Itch's instruction and practice those many months ago. But others who had never held a rifle previously often fired into the ground, kicking up a cloud of sand. This caused great merriment among the soldiers.

Captain Perkins, leader of William's company, read them instructions from the Secretary of War promising them full pay. The soldiers didn't believe it. When the soldiers were proved correct eighteen months later, Perkins and the other officers felt humiliated and angry. They believed these men deserved the same pay as white soldiers.

December 3, 1862, 7 pm. It was dark and mildly drizzling. William joined a small group of men around a fire discussing their lives when they were enslaved and how they had come to be in the army. William's mind wandered away from the discussion when he became aware of other groups throughout the camp singing, clapping, and laughing. His curiosity caused him to leave the group. He stood, took a few steps, closed his eyes, and breathed in the cool night air of freedom. He thrilled to the sounds of glee, and shouting, and a flute playing somewhere among the tents. Never had he felt so free.

William strolled among the camp and soon came to a fire enclosed in a little hut crammed with men singing at the tops of their voices, clapping and drumming their feet. William learned it was called a "shout." The excitement spread outside the hut as the men quivered and danced. William joined in, awkward at first, but becoming more adept as a circle formed around someone in the center. Some stooped and rose, others whirled, all kept steadily circling as spectators applauded. The circle enlarged, the singing grew louder, some shouted rousing encouragements, and the drumming and clapping continued in perfect cadence. Suddenly, the spell broke amid sighing and laughter. William had never seen such a spectacle.

Each night, William wandered through the camp, joining in activities when possible or watching and learning. He delighted in all that he witnessed. One evening, after watching a group work themselves into a frenzy singing and chanting, one of the soldiers jumped onto a barrel and began to speak.

William recognized him as Corporal Lambkin from Fernandina, a man who was known as a great orator. He spoke first about how the slaves in Florida were anxious to know about Mr. Lincoln's election and about how they refused to work on March 4th thinking they would be freed. Then he said, "Our masters, they have lived under the flag, they got their wealth under it, and everything beautiful for their children. Under it they have ground us up and put us in their pocket for money. But the first minute they think that old flag means freedom for we colored people, they pull it right down and run up the rag of their own. But we'll never desert the old flag, boys, never; we have lived under it for eighteen hundred sixty-two years, and we'll die for it now." To which William and the other men gave a rounding applause.

William was happy to be in a place where he so perfectly belonged. At times he was busy cleaning his gun, or he would stop to lend a hand when his experience proved helpful. Others smoked the tobacco they loved in silence, a habit William never picked up. The shout was always within hearing while others had quiet prayer meetings. Nearby, a woman spelled slow monosyllables out of a primer, an activity that always got the men's attention. William, eager to improve his reading skills, often joined her.

And thirty feet beyond, a stump orator perched on his barrel exhorted fidelity in war: "You don't know nothing about it, boys. You think you's brave enough. How you think if you stand clear in the open field—here you, an' there the secesh? You got to have the right thing inside of you. You got to harden it down inside of you, or it's nothin'. I mean to fight the war through and die a good soldier with the last kick."

December 25, 1862. Christmas was celebrated simply with not having "taps" but letting the men stay up having prayer meetings and shouts, and they were happy. The greatest excitement for Christmas day was target practice again.

The surgeon for the regiment arrived. A few days later, he and the chaplain converted an old gin-house into a ten-bed hospital with a number of straw pallets.

A battalion of black soldiers had never been seen on the Atlantic coast. They attracted a steady stream of visitors, but nothing like the number expected for New Year's Day. About five thousand guests were expected. There would be ten oxen roasted whole; for drink, simply molasses and water; and for dessert, hard bread with molasses.

About ten in the morning, people began arriving by land and water. Soon, all avenues of approach were crowded with throngs of guests. Most were black women with colorful handkerchiefs on their heads, and a sprinkling of men with that special respectable look they always have on Sundays. There were many white visitors also, including ladies on horseback and in carriages; superintendents and teachers; officers; and calvary men.

The companies were marched close to the platform. It was filled with dignitaries and the band of the Eighth Maine, which had volunteered for the occasion. Many of the dignitaries stood and applauded the arrival of the colored troops. The colored people filled up the space in the grove around, and beyond them were a cordon of mounted visitors. Above everyone, the great live oak branches waved in the breeze with their trailing moss, and beyond was a glimpse of the blue river.

The service began at 11:30 with a prayer by the chaplain. It was followed by the president's proclamation read by Dr. W. H. Brisbane. Dr. Brisbane was a South Carolinian who had grown up in these islands and had long ago emancipated his own slaves. A flag was presented to the colored regiment by the Rev. French, who had brought it from donors in New York.

Then something unforeseen happened. Just as the flag was waved for the first time, there arose an elderly but strong male voice, which was instantly joined by two women's voices. They sang, as if by an impulse that could no more be repressed than the morning song of a sparrow.

"My country, 'tis of thee,
Sweet land of liberty,
Of thee I sing!"

People looked at each other to see where the singing was coming from. The voices sang on, verse after verse. Other colored people joined in.

In the words of Colonel Higginson, "*Never had there been any-thing so electric; it made all other words cheap; it seemed the choked voice of a race at last unloosed. Just think of it—the first day they had ever had a country, the first flag they had ever had which promised their people anything; the life of the whole day was in those unknown people's song. Tears were everywhere.*"

A few days later, after the excitement of the New Year's celebration had died down, the men, growing impatient for action, sent a small representative group to speak with Colonel Higginson. "We ought to get to work, sir. Not right that we just sitting around eating up the provisions."

Little did they know, their desire for action would soon be realized.

CHAPTER 30

John

John pushed himself away from the table. "I'm going into town this morning. You need anything for the kitchen?"

"No," said Martha. "Be careful. Don't let them Yankees get you."

"Yankees wouldn't have any use for me."

He kissed Martha on the cheek. Her skin felt dry, and wrinkles lined her face. In two months, they would celebrate their thirtieth wedding anniversary. John planned to surprise her with a special gift from a store catalog.

"Roscoe'll take care of things 'til I get back."

Martha patted John on the arm.

The warm day had a slight breeze to it. The morning seemed peaceful enough. Though the war raged on, the pleasant day made it easy to forget. John concentrated on what he might buy for Martha, something that would please her—pretty and not practical. He had always been so practical. He wanted to surprise her with a different gift. She deserved it. But goods were becoming scarce, what with the damn Yankee blockades.

John's concentration on Martha's gift faded when he saw two men ahead blocking the road, their guns drawn.

"Where you headed, mister?"

John hesitated. He entertained telling them to mind their own business. But with two guns pointing his way, he thought better of it. "Just going to town. And I'm in a bit of a hurry."

"Well, sorry to trouble you, but would you mind getting down from your horse?"

"Look, I really need to—"

The other man brought his pistol up and cocked the hammer back, pointing it at John's face. "He wasn't asking, mister."

John reluctantly dismounted. The two men dismounted also. One walked around behind him.

For a split-second John felt a sharp pain on the back of his head…and then nothing.

When he regained consciousness, he tried to lift his head, but the pain proved too much.

He looked around as best he could, but his blurred vision didn't allow him to recognize anything in the room. He tried sitting, but the pain wouldn't allow it. He let out a cry. This brought two people to check on him.

"How you feelin'?"

"Where am I?"

"You in my house."

"And my house," said his wife, looking over at her husband.

"Our house," he corrected himself.

"My name is Otis, and this my wife, Olivia."

"Ask your master to come see me. I must get home."

Otis glanced at Olivia. "We don't have no master. We two free Negroes."

"What do you mean you're free?"

"Why yes, sir. We served Judge Holmes for many years while he was alive. He died a few years back, and before he died, he gave us our freedom. We been living here ever since."

"What happened to me? How did I get here?"

"Don't rightly know. Went out looking for firewood and found you on the side of the road just lying there. Thought you was dead. Lot's a blood by your head. When I saw you was still breathing, I dragged you here best I could. We put you in our bed and let you rest. Didn't know what else to do. Wasn't sure you was ever going to wake up."

"How long I been here?"

"Well, let's see now. Counting today, I brought you here day before yesterday.

"I got to get home. Martha's gonna be worried sick."

"You ain't had nothin' to eat an' just little to drink for last few days. Might be best to get some food in you and get some strength back before walking home."

"I got a horse."

"I didn't see no horse when I found you. An' I ain't got one neither. I know you wants to get home, and I'll help all I can, but first why don't you get some of my misses' soup in you and try getting strong again."

"I can do this." John inched one foot off the bed to the floor and tried to push himself up, but he was not able to. "Damn, damn, damn."

"Reckon we'll leave you alone then. Just let us know if you wants some soup. Olivia makes a mighty fine soup."

It wasn't long before Olivia had the soup warming over a fire. As the aroma filled the little one room house, John realized how hungry he was.

"I do believe the soup is ready. Would you care for some?"

"Yes, I'll have some."

Otis helped John sit up and let him rest against him so he could sit to eat. John lay afterwards dwelling on his deep resentment for having to rely on these free blacks for all his needs. But sitting and eating exhausted him, and he was soon fast asleep.

The next morning, John woke as night turned to light. He heard Otis and Olivia speaking in a low voice, and a third voice he didn't know spoke as well. The conversation seemed urgent. He attempted to turn to see the three, but his head hurt too much. He made a sound, causing the conversation to cease. He heard the scraping of a chair and the clomp, clomp of Otis' shoes, and soon enough he stood looking down at John.

"Sleep okay?"

"Better than I expected."

"Hungry?"

"I could use a bite to eat."

There was a softer, lighter sound of footsteps coming toward him. Into his sight came a young woman who stood next to Otis and put her arm around his waist. She glared at John but did not speak.

"This here's my daughter, Ellie. She stays with us. Say hello, Ellie."

But Ellie turned and walked away without speaking.

"She don't like my being here, does she?"

"You have to understand her. She had rough treatment from some white men."

"I ain't gonna hurt her."

"It's not just that. We been livin' here for a long time, and nobody ever bother us. She worries that you know where we live. Could be some whites don't like havin' free blacks around."

"Yeah. I'm sure that's true." He wanted to say more, tell them how he felt about free blacks, but he thought better of it. John hesitated before speaking again. "She looks like somebody."

"What you mean?"

"I'm not sure who. The minute I saw your daughter, I thought I knew her. From somewhere many years ago." He closed his eyes for a minute, then said, "Forget it. It's not important."

"I'll get you something to eat and then get to work. We all got plenty of work in the garden every morning."

Throughout the day, John improved bit by bit. By nightfall, he was able to walk on his own around the cabin and had the strength to venture outside for a few minutes.

During dinner, John frequently glanced at Ellie, trying to be inconspicuous while hoping to remember who she reminded him of. But when she caught him looking her way, she slammed her fork down and left the table.

After dinner, John proposed a plan to Otis. "I been thinking, Otis. I want to get home, and you want me gone. I'll give you a pass and directions to my home. You go there and bring Roscoe here with a buckboard and…"

"Now hold on just a minute. I would sure like to help you out, but it's just too dangerous for me to be walking the roads alone, even with a pass. You getting better fast. Likely day after tomorrow, you be able to leave here. Best we can do is share our food and home with you, an' we glad to do that, but can't take no chance goin' down the road."

John spent another half hour trying to convince Otis, but he wouldn't budge. John went to bed angry. He didn't like this. He didn't like living with colored people, sleeping in their bed, eating with them. It wasn't natural.

John couldn't sleep. His defenses down, he lay in a semi-conscious, half-asleep mode. He recalled a young female slave named Lindi. Her story came to him as clear and detailed as though it had happened yesterday. *He had gone to a slave market with his father where they bought Lindi and a male slave. He felt embarrassed for Lindi, having her naked body exposed to the crowd.*

His memory jumped to another day, much later.

At dusk the boy, John, walked to the quarters. "Hey, young master, come over here," called Lindi. "What you doing always hanging 'round here when you got that big, beautiful house? You like being with us slaves, eh?" she said, chiding him.

John felt self-conscious. He couldn't look her in the eye. "Just going for a walk," he said. Secretly happy she'd called him over, he worked up the courage to raise his eyes to meet hers. He put his hands in his pockets.

She studied him for a minute. "You want some cornbread? Just out the fire."

"Sure."

John heard footsteps and looked over to see String sauntering towards them, a big smile on his face. He sat down next to Lindi.

"Well, Master John, I declare we should builds you a shack out here. I think you out here much as we is."

John grinned. "Well, Lindi makes really good cornbread."

"Yeah, that she do, that she do."

"Hey, String," said John, "remember that story about monkeys stealing your food?"

String chuckled and shook his head. "Yes, sir, that was a funny one."

John's memory jumped ahead again, causing him to moan.

Twelve-year-old John crouched in the dark barn, his round, freckled face pushed up against the weathered pine wall. He peered through a crack at the young slave, Lindi, about to undress and step into the tub of cool bathwater. The full moon shone down, outlining the old slave shacks to the left and the tall, proud pines and broad oaks in the background. But above all, it shed light on Lindi's brown skin. John couldn't take his eyes off her. His heart pounded as he anticipated seeing her naked. The smell of horses and hay went unnoticed, the night sounds of crickets and nocturnal animals no longer heard. He was completely absorbed with the vision before him. Lindi pulled her dress over her head and prepared to step into the bath water. John yearned to reach out, to touch her, to touch her firm, pointed breasts.

Then came the sound of crunching pine needles. Footsteps. Someone was about to intrude on Lindi's bath. From the darkness between the two shanties, John's father emerged. John's desire for Lindi turned to fear that he had been discovered. Lindi grabbed her dress, covering herself. John gasped, resisting the urge to run away.

Lindi's expression changed from questioning the presence of her master to alarm when he approached her and ripped the dress from her grasp. John became horrified watching his father throw her to the ground and struggle with her. He reeled away from his crack in the wall. He held his hands tight to his ears, forcing away the sounds of Lindi's cries. He could not watch, did not want to believe his father was raping gentle Lindi.

After an unbearable length of time, the struggle ended. John, his eyes squeezed shut, face buried in the hay, pushed himself up and listened. He heard only the soft moaning of his devastated friend. His eyes red and stinging, his body weak and trembling, John peeked out through the crack. Lindi lay on the ground, her face buried in the crook of her arm, her body shaking.

John went to her. He gathered her dress and touched her shoulder, but she jerked away. She looked up at him, her face full of hate.

Seeing it wasn't her master, but his son, her face tightened and her eyes narrowed. "Ah, the little master come for me, too?"

"No, Lindi, I—"

"Well, Little Master, you have to kill me first." Her features contorted, she spit at him, snatched her dress, and hurried away.

John staggered home feeling confused and empty. He hated his father. He wanted to help her, but she had spit in his face.

The next day, John went to Lindi's shack, determined to set things straight. He stuck his head in her open door, but the dark room stood quiet. The lingering smell of ashes from a long dead fire and the hint of cornbread filled his senses. He softly called her name. No answer. He called louder—still no answer. The nervous, queasy sensation rising from his gut into his chest told him she had left for good.

He clenched his fist, glaring at her shack. Her desertion overwhelmed him. He picked up a rock, hurled it hard, and his cold, embittered heart felt appeased at the loud crack when it hit her wall.

He found another, hurled it, and then another. Each time, the sharp whack expressed his rage at the woman who had rejected him.

John gasped and sat up, his shirt soaked with sweat, his body trembling. He tried to calm his rapid breathing. Finally, he lay back on the bed and squeezed his eyes shut, trying to keep the rest of the memory from flooding back; but it would not be stopped.

Patrollers caught Lindi three days later. John's father tied her wrists and ankles to four stakes positioned in the ground. Then he forced John to watch as he beat her. Then, handing the whip to John, he said, "Now it's your turn."

"But Papa, I—"

"Listen, boy, you better give her as good as I gave her, or I'll thrash you. It's time you become a man. Now hit her, goddammit."

When John had finished, he wanted to kill himself.

Three days later, Lindi ran away again. The patrollers caught her again. They said she fought like a mad woman. They hanged her battered body on the road, where she remained for several days as an example to others.

The first time John saw her hanging body, he jumped out of the buggy and vomited in the road.

"You gotta be more of a man," his father said and laughed at him.

In the end, his pain pushed compassion into the dark subconscious of his mind. Hate rose to the surface and changed his life.

The next morning and all through the day, John could not look at Ellie. He focused all his energy on getting stronger. He would leave tomorrow, no matter how strong he felt.

On that night, when John didn't return from town, Martha sat on her front porch rocking fretfully and praying with her Bible clutched tightly in her hands. She wrote Roscoe a pass and sent him into town the next morning to inquire after her missing husband. She had been keeping a watchful eye on the road when Roscoe returned.

"Mrs. Higgins, them people at the store say they ain't seen Massa John. They don't know where he could be."

She had Roscoe hitch up the buckboard, and together they visited all the neighbors who lived on the road to town. They returned at dusk, a frantic Martha sitting alongside Roscoe.

Distraught almost to the point of panic, Martha considered all the possibilities: Abducted? Robbed and killed? Ran off on his own? Overtaken by sudden illness?

"Roscoe, what do you think has happened to him?"

Roscoe turned grim. "I don't know that I could say, Mrs. Higgins." Then he added, "He'll come back. He gets through his troubles."

She asked neighbors for their help in finding him. But with a war going on, most of the men had gone to fight the Yankees. A few of the men around, either very old or very young, did try to pick up his trail, but they could find no tracks or signs that anything had gone wrong. They all said it was probably "them damn Yankees." Tom Haverman, who lived five miles the other side of the Higgins' land, thought maybe he had been forced up North by the conscriptors to fight the Yankees. Anna Belle Simmons claimed to have seen him in one of her dreams traveling on a ship to Europe. But in the end, all Martha and Sally could do was to admit that John had disappeared, and they could only sit back waiting and wondering.

Martha did her best to keep the farm running. Harriet became indispensable in the house, and Roscoe managed the farm. Sally helped where needed, working both in the house and the farm. Every night before retiring, Martha touched John's face on the photograph of their wedding day.

The sun, about to drop below the horizon, made long shadows on the ground. The sky, filled with long, flat clouds, outlined an occasional bat doing acrobatics in the air. Martha sat on the front porch as she had every evening since John disappeared, hoping. She awoke from her musing when Silas came running to the house, shouting and waving his arms. She stepped towards the railing, gripping a post with both hands. A man walking down the road turned into their property. He waved and picked up his pace, and she knew John had returned. She held onto the railing repeating, "John, John."

John took the front steps two at a time. Taking her in with his eyes, he pulled her to him and held her. Sally came to see about all the fuss. She screamed and ran to him, almost knocking them both down. Reunited—the three of them, laughing, kissing, hugging. Martha pulled back from John. She touched his cheek, now with a short beard. "John, is it really you?"

John laughed. "It's really me."

Martha could not contain her joy and buried her face in his chest. John put his arms around his family and told them how much he had missed them and loved them. Seeing the commotion, many of the slaves congregated around the porch, some with grins, others more serious. Roscoe said, "Welcome back, Mr. Higgins. We all took you for dead."

John observed the black men and women standing around, staring at him. He became confused, his mind entangled from living with and being cared for by a black man and woman. Also, his memory of Lindi weighed heavily on his mind. "Thank you," was all he could manage to say. He took his family inside. *Let Roscoe deal with them.*

Harriet had been working in the house when John entered. "Welcome, Massa John."

"Thank you, Harriet. Did you think I would ever come back?"

"I didn't know for sure if you be coming home. I do know your family sure did miss you. I reckon about as much as I misses my man, William."

Her words stung John, and for the first time, he felt something close to regret for what he had done.

Once inside, Martha held tightly to John's arm and asked softly, "What happened to you, John?" Before he could speak, she asked Harriet to get them some tea and asked John if he was hungry.

"Starved," he replied.

His family had a hundred questions, but John decided to protect Otis' family, after all, they had saved his life. And there was their daughter. How could he possibly bring harm to her? His answers would be vague, never revealing who had cared for him.

"Any word from Adam?"

Tears filled Martha's eyes. "No letters. We haven't seen him since they took him away, and we haven't heard from him. We're very worried."

Harriet brought tea and a plate of cornbread and ham. The three spent the evening together, catching up.

Over the next several days, John inspected his land, buildings, fences, livestock, and crops, making mental notes of what he wanted done. He was pleased the farm had been managed efficiently.

Harriet had acquired a more significant position in the house. Though at times she made comments about William, which made for awkward moments, she appeared content with her role. She liked the ladies of the house, and they liked her. She had become more outspoken and tended to say what came to mind. This seemed to be fine with Sally and Martha, for they respected her opinion. She had a wisdom they both found refreshing. No longer the timid slave she once had been, she had become an important part of the household in John's short absence. She didn't plan to give up her new status just because he had returned.

Rain, no stranger to central Florida in the summer, had been falling from the dark sky since mid-morning. At times, it was a forceful hammering, then easing up, as if to rest before soaking the earth again. John and Hector had been working on fences when the rains came.

They worked in the rain for a while, but finally John said, "Let's get under that tree till this lets up."

Hector mounted the buckboard, maneuvering it to a spot where the tree protected it. They sat without talking. John thought of the work that needed to get done and was impatient for the rain to stop. As often happened these days, his thoughts drifted to Otis and his family. They had been kind to him and nursed him back to health, sharing what little they had. What did that mean, if anything, about having slaves and how they should be treated? The answer eluded John.

One look at the sky told John the rain was here to stay for a while. "Hector, go on back to the barn and get to work on those indoor repairs. This rain's not stopping anytime soon."

"Yessir, Massa."

John stayed out a bit longer, taking in the fresh smell of rain and grass. Growing weary of his thoughts, John rode to the barn. He brushed his horse, then sloshed through muddy terrain on his way to the house. Before he stepped inside, Harriet came to the door.

"Now, Massa John, I knows you ain't coming into this house with them dirty boots on your feets. Why don't you take them off right there so this floor don't get all muddy after I just been scrubbin' it."

John's old temper flared, but he pushed it down. He opened his mouth to tell her to step aside, when Martha came up behind Harriet and said, "John, please do as Harriet asks. The floor in here is clean, and we want it to stay that way."

John resented being challenged by his house slave and disturbed that his wife would side against him. But then he relented. *Hell, I don't live in a barn.* He took off his boots.

Over the next several months, John and Martha repeated the same conversation numerous times. "John," Martha would say, "what is it? You seem so distant."

"Oh, there's a lot to get done around here, that's all."

But he did have more on his mind. Living with a black family had complicated his life. The experience obscured the boundaries between black and white. He was no longer sure about right from wrong. Did he still have the stomach to whip a slave? If not, how would he control them? And Otis lived in his head. And then there was Lindi. He wanted desperately to get back to his old way of thinking.

"Roscoe, bring that wagon over here and get some help loading them branches. I want this land cleared by the end of today."

Roscoe drove the wagon to John. He stopped and pointed down the road. He shouted, "Well, look over there! That be Jacob coming down de road!" Everyone stopped their work to look, and, although still a good distance off, they recognized Jacob's long stride. He carried a bag.

John watched him and wondered why Adam wasn't with him.

Jacob walked to the group. The slaves greeted him, and he responded with a nod, yet kept a grave expression as he walked to John and handed him the bag.

"I is so sorry, Massa John. This here's the belongings of Massa Adam. I is sorry to tell you that he were killed in the fighting up there in Georgia."

John had tried to prepare himself for this possibility, yet hearing the news overwhelmed him. Instead of hugging his son returning from war, as he had so often imagined, he held only his belongings. "Tell me what happened."

"Well, sir, I was back at camp, waiting for Massa Adam to come back after a fight, like I always did, but this time the young massa didn't come back. So, I went out to the battlefield to find him. Oh, sir, it were terrible. They was dead soldiers everywhere. So, I commences looking for Massa Adam. Well, just before it get dark, I finds him. I borrows a shovel from one of the other soldiers and dig a grave to bury him and said a prayer for him. The officer in charge ask me to bring you his belongings. I been walking for a lot of days to get here. I'm real sorry, Massa."

John took Adam's belongings and walked to his horse. He rode halfway to his house before dismounting. Staggering to a fallen tree, he dropped onto a log and buried his face in his hands.

Damn war. Goddamn war. I shoulda tried harder to get him out. Both our boys—gone. What am I gonna tell Martha? Hell.

After some time, John found the strength to get back on his horse. Moving his horse at a slow pace, his own anguish overwhelming, he lamented the grief his news would bring. Adam had been their hope. He would be their heir to the farm. He was their future. This dream was now crushed—his boy dead and buried who knows where.

John arrived at the house long before he knew what to say. Entering the house, he looked for Martha. Just then, she came into the front room from their bedroom, smiled at John, and started to speak. But when she saw his face and the bag in his hands, her words would not come. She said, "Oh no, not Adam." John rushed to her.

John, Martha, and Sally supported each other and kept away from running the farm and the household. Roscoe ran the farm, and Harriet, the household, until the Higgins family had the strength to become involved in the affairs of daily life.

The morning John returned to work, he first paid a visit to the slave quarters and gathered the enslaved together. He said, "Thank you for… Well, just thank you for doing a good job in my absence." Everyone remained still. John looked each one in the eye. He felt uneasy. *What the hell am I doing?* "Okay, get to work."

Later that day, John said to Roscoe, "Keep everyone working, I'll be back shortly." Roscoe watched a subdued John ride off.

John found a secluded spot, dismounted, and sat on the ground. He leaned back onto a stately oak tree, the bright, cloudless sky as empty as he felt. A squirrel stopped its scampering down a tree, its tail flickering back and forth, checking on him.

John closed his eyes and tried to comprehend the twists and turns his life had taken. Sam and Adam gone, and now both Lindi and Otis lived in his mind. He had no peace.

The chattering squirrel interrupted his thoughts. It clung to the tree trunk, head facing the ground, tail up and still.

What's he squawking about? That squirrel's like me. He's running around going here and there, squawking about this and that, but he doesn't really know what he wants.

John stood, brushed off a few leaves, and walked to his horse. Full, white clouds now blew passively through the sky. A loud squawk broke the silence. The squirrel twitched, clamped in the claws of a hawk, as the last bit of life left its body. For a brief moment, John imagined he saw his own reflection in the squirrel's eye. He watched the lifeless creature be carried off, unaware that his hand moved to cover his throat. Death, it seemed, lurked everywhere. And close… always so close.

CHAPTER 31

William

Their First Expedition—Up the St. Mary's River

Corporal Robert Sutton was born into slavery in Northeast Florida and had been chiefly tasked with lumbering and piloting on the St. Mary's River, which divides Florida and Georgia. He constantly implored Colonel Higginson to allow him to lead an expedition up this river. He, like others, had grown impatient with drilling and guard duty and craved some real action.

Sutton was an intellectual, thus he and William had become fast friends. They would often sit around a fire in the evening with a few other soldiers discussing the day's events, which invariably would turn to their dreams of life as freedmen after the war.

Lumber was in short supply these days, especially after flooring all the tents. The Union army had to send north for it at great expense; however, it had been reported that there was plenty of lumber in the enemy's territory. A number of expeditions of white troops had travelled up the St. Mary's in search of lumber, but all had returned empty handed. Now it was the colored troops' turn. Although the returning troops had reported that all the mills had been burned to the ground, Corporal Sutton promised to lead an expedition that would find more lumber than they could transport.

On January 23, at last, the men's wishes came true. Colonel Higginson was to take three steamers with 462 men and officers down the coast in search of lumber. The men boarded the vessels with high spirits. The three vessels left at different times to avoid publicity, with orders to rendezvous at St. Simons Island on the coast of Georgia. The "flagship" was the *Ben de Ford*, as it was the largest of the three and carried most of the men. The other ships included the *John Adams*, an army gunboat, and the *Planter*, a side-wheel steamer. William's company, of which Corporal Sutton was a member, was on board the *Ben de Ford*.

The *Ben de Ford* arrived at St. Simons first. As it was delayed waiting for the others, Colonel Higginson decided to put the time to good use. They had heard rumors of a quantity of railroad iron hidden in the abandoned rebel forts on St. Simon's and Jekyll Islands. The iron had provided an impenetrable roof for their batteries. Some in the black regiment had worked on the batteries of these forts and were able to lead the expedition to the iron. While searching, they found a large flatboat that enabled them to transport the iron more easily. The soldiers regarded the iron as their first trophy in the war, which put them in a festive mood.

The other boats still had not arrived on the second day, which enabled the men to continue foraging iron as well as horses, cattle, agricultural instruments, and to move the few remaining colored families to Fernandina. The next morning, with all boats present, they left for Ft. Clinch, arriving there during the afternoon.

Colonel Higginson decided to make a side trip to Township Landing, about fifteen miles to the south, to surprise the rebel Captain Clark and his company of calvary, which had been reported to be in that vicinity. This also seemed to be a good use of his men. He wanted to get them under fire as soon as possible to give them some success and to teach them to apply what they had learned in camp.

Higginson had ascertained that the calvary's camp was about 5 miles from the landing. One of the roads to the camp had been built with the help of Corporal Sutton, so Sutton could lead them.

They planned to go at night, surround the house and Negro cabins to prevent an alarm from being given, and then take the road to the camp.

Just below the township, they landed a small force to surround the cabins silently. When the ship pulled into the landing, Corporal Sutton related that one of the colored men had just come from the camp and could give them updated information. They set off after midnight with about 100 men, with a small advance guard and a few flankers. They plunged into pine woods with its resinous smell, the only sounds croaking frogs from a nearby swamp and an occasional barking dog. Sutton marched with his captured Negro guide, who at first was fearful and sullen, but became more secure with a copy of the president's Proclamation in his possession. Governor Andrew had sent Higginson a large supply of the Proclamation, for even though many of the Negroes could not read it, they all seemed more secure with a copy in their hands.

The men had marched about two miles when suddenly they heard horses' hooves on the road ahead and then shots fired. The men dropped down and returned the fire, though the darkness made it difficult to see anything.

The enemy fire ceased after a time, and it was difficult for Colonel Higginson to get his soldiers to stop firing, the smell of gunpowder being so intoxicating. Finally, all firing stopped, leaving them in peaceful possession of the field. The men behaved very honorably, this being their first encounter with danger. Some of the men wanted to pursue the enemy, but Higginson decided not to, as this was a complete victory—and he felt it important to make the first encounter a complete victory. He felt the fortunes of the black race rested on his shoulders, and only a complete victory would satisfy public sentiment as to their competency.

They attended to the wounded and made stretchers to carry the dead and wounded to the landing. They now were in command of an enemy compound.

The surgeon's report stated the following:

One man killed instantly by ball through the heart, and seven wounded, one of whom will die. Braver men never lived. One man with two bullet holes through the large muscles of the shoulders and neck brought from the scene of action, two miles distant, and not a murmur has escaped his lips. Another, Robert Sutton, with three wounds, one of which, being on the skull, may cost him his life—would not report himself until compelled to do so by his officers. While I dressed his wounds, he quietly talked of what they had done, and of what they yet could do. The surgeon had the colonel order Sutton to obey him for fear he would not follow the care needed to recover. He is perfectly quiet and cool, but takes this whole affair with the religious bearing of a man who realizes that freedom is sweeter than life. Yet another soldier did not report himself at all, but remained all night on guard, and possibly I should not have known of his having had a buck-shot in his shoulder, if some duty requiring a sound shoulder had not been required of him today. He had a comrade to dig out the buck-shot, for fear of being ordered on the sick-list.

Since all hope of a surprise attack was gone, they returned to the cabins, not sure what to expect. Would there be other calvary charges? There were none. Colonel Higginson later reported that his men performed bravely, and he was pleased with their first encounter with the enemy.

With the morning came another problem. For the first time, they found themselves in the possession of an enemy abode. Though there was little temptation to plunder, Higginson drew the line that there should be no indiscriminate pilfering or destruction, and he allowed nothing to be taken or destroyed without proper authorization.

Most of the furniture had already been taken from the plantation house. The only thing of any value left was a piano and outside was a packing box for the piano. The only value the house had was to be used as a picket station. The commanding officer was instructed to burn all picket stations and all villages from which he could be covertly attacked. Since the house was to be burned, it seemed with the packing box readily available, providence was inviting him to save the piano. This was the only property he ever took or allowed to be taken from enemy territory. The piano was then given to the school for colored children in Fernandina.

The ruined town of St. Mary's had a bad reputation among military men. It was situated just north of Fernandina on the Georgia side and was occasionally visited by Union gunboats. According to information received, three older women who lived there as spies were the only inhabitants of the town. On the approach of Union boats, they would wave their white handkerchiefs. They would receive the Union men with hospitality, profess profound loyalty, display a portrait of Washington, and assure them no Confederate soldiers had been there for many weeks. But those Union men who had been there before warned Higginson that in the yard they would find many fresh horse tracks and would be fired upon by guerillas the minute they left the wharf. If this should happen, Higginson assured his men that they would burn the town to prevent other Union forces from being attacked.

Colonel Higginson had planned to stop at this town to acquire some valuable lumber that had been seen on the wharf. As they approached the town, just as the stories predicted, three old women came out waving their handkerchiefs. Higginson and his men took possession of the town, much of which had been destroyed by previous gunboats. They set up lookouts along exposed areas of the town and put a detail of men at work loading the lumber. After completing the work, Higginson withdrew the men, who boarded their boats to leave.

Just as their boat left the wharf and swung out into the stream, there came a sudden burst of gunfire, a regular hailstorm of bullets into the open end of the boat, driving every gunner in an instant from his post. The shock lasted only a second, and though the bullets sounded like hail hitting the boat, no one was hurt. Promptly, order was restored, and the Union boat's shells flew into the woods, focused on the origins of the attack. Once again, the Union boats steamed toward the wharf, just as promised.

Higginson dispatched a company of men in search of the assailants, who were soon silenced. The three old ladies came out with great theatrics, waving their handkerchiefs in wild motions. Col. Higginson told them he was to burn the town due to the attacks but would spare their house. The treacherous old women, grateful for their house being spared, surrounded the colonel and increased their courtesy and melodramatics. The colonel had some difficulty extricating himself from the three, much to the amusement of the men.

They went farther south to Fernandina, where they were given additional assignments. Colonel Hawley showed a letter from the War Department requesting him to ascertain the possibility of obtaining a supply of bricks from the brickyard at Fort Clinch, which had furnished the original bricks. Another request came from Lieutenant Hughes for the admiral regarding a rebel steamer, the *Berosa*, said to be lying somewhere upriver and waiting her chance to run the blockade. Both the *Berosa* and the brickyard were near Woodstock, the former home of Corporal Sutton, and he was eager to pilot them up the river.

The moon would be perfect that evening, and the *Ben de Ford* was the perfect boat to make the expedition. Due to its size, it could easily navigate the swift current and sharp turns. At seven o'clock on the evening of January 29, beneath a lovely moon, they steamed up the river.

As they continued, the banks grew steeper, the current swifter, the channel more tortuous and more encumbered with projecting branches and drifting wood. William moved to the bow, hoping to spot floating debris, but it was almost impossible. Only Corporal Sutton, with his excellent piloting skills, could have been successful in moving them safely through these dangers. The tide was with them, which made steering more difficult, and with the sharp angles of the river, there was often no recourse but to run the bow on shore, let the stern swing around and then reverse motion. This involved moments of anxiety—especially once, when they were aground for half an hour. At last, they came to the little town of Woodstock an hour before daybreak. They arrived so quietly not a person knew of their arrival.

Colonel Higginson ordered Captain Perkins' company and one other to board, as quietly as possible, the flatboat they'd brought from St. Simons with instructions to quietly surround the town. Their orders were to not allow anyone to leave, molest no one, and to hold as temporary prisoners every man they found.

William and Nathan were assigned to stand guard at a house situated in the middle of town. When they ascertained that a man and his wife lived there, Nathan accompanied the man to the prisoners' area while William kept watch on his wife at the house. The wife, not one to be easily controlled, berated him, demanding that her husband be returned and that she be allowed to leave her home if she desired. Having had enough, William got nose to nose with her and said, "Ma'am, we are at war, and you is our prisoner. Now you best get quiet and get in the house if you knows what's best for you."

"And what you gonna do if I don't?"

"I think I jus' might take you down to the river an' throw you in, madam."

The woman gave William her meanest look, but he stared her down until she finally gave a final "hmmpf," spun around, marched into the house, and slammed the door.

When daylight came, the main boat landed. The colonel was happy to find two men guarding every house and a small group of prisoners looking very forlorn. The commander later commented how pleased he was to find his men with good demeanor towards these white folks—including the more tumultuous women.

There was plenty of lumber, enough for five steamboats. On examining the wharves and buildings, they found building after building was stuffed with expensive furniture, pianos, china, pictures, and mahogany. And here were the men whose labor had allowed the owners to purchase such luxuries. And yet the soldiers submitted scarcely without a murmur to their orders, even knowing their own wives and children slept on floors. Bed and bedding they were allowed to take from the storeroom, as directed by the surgeon for the hospitals, but nothing more. It was a struggle for some, whose wives were destitute, but their pride was very easily touched, and they performed their duty with honor.

Later in the day, Higginson called on the lady who owned the wharves, the mill, and the enslaved who worked them. With him was Corporal Robert Sutton. He said to her, "I believe you have been previously acquainted with our Corporal Sutton?"

She drew herself up and spoke as if her words were nitric acid. "Ah, we called him Bob."

She had tried to reverse the whole drama of the war in an instant. But the tall, well-dressed, imposing, and philosophic corporal was too dignified in his nature to be moved by words. He simply turned from the lady, touched his hat to the colonel, and asked if he wished to see her slave jail, as he had the keys in his possession.

When the door of the jail was opened before Colonel Higginson, he was glad he had spoken to its proprietor before seeing it. It was a small building. In the middle of the door was a large staple with a rusty chain for fastening a victim down. Also found were three stocks with holes for feet of various sizes for women and children. In a nearby building, they found something so complicated Higginson could not understand it until it was explained to him. It was a machine so contrived that when someone was imprisoned in it, he could neither sit nor stand nor lie. Rather, he must support his body half-raised, a position scarcely endurable. Higginson leaned against the door to that jailhouse with unutterable loathing. He thought he was seasoned to the horrors of slavery, but the visible presence of such torture devices seemed it might choke him.

There were few colored people in this vicinity, and most they took with them. Only an old man and woman preferred to remain. All the white males they took as hostages to shield themselves from attacks as they proceeded down river. They knew their wives would send word to the Rebel forces. They informed the prisoners that they would be freed once the boats were out of danger.

They steamed one or two miles farther to the brickyard, which was unprotected. The men toiled for several hours loading the boat to the utmost with bricks for Fort Clinch. Higginson questioned the men at the factory and learned that the *Berosa* was at the head of the river, but it was in such disrepair that it was not seaworthy and would never make it out to sea. This proved to be true. When the attempt was made, it quickly floundered and sank, the crew barely escaping with their lives.

During the return trip, rebels on the bluffs fired on the boat, and the boat returned fire. Higginson ordered the men to stay below so as not to have unnecessary injuries or deaths. The men complained about this, as they wanted to stay on deck to return fire, but their muskets would have been useless. William stayed below deck with the others, and like them, he wished he could get involved in the action. The gunboat returned fire, scattering the rebels.

Though the expedition was small compared to the overall war itself, there was a great interest in it around the nation due to the experiment to employ black soldiers. So obvious were the troops' knowledge of the area and their enthusiasm for fighting the rebels that its successes undoubtedly found new confidence for using black soldiers in the war.

When the men settled down again in camp, the memory of the expedition was well-preserved by many legends of adventure growing vaster and more incredible as time wore on.

One time, just when ever'thing was a'goin' fine, a sad thing happened. My young mistis, de one named for her ma, ups and runs off with de son o' de Irish ditch digger and marries him. She wouldn't a-done it if dey'd a-let her marry de man she wanted. Dey didn't think he was good 'nough for her. So just to spite 'em she married de ditch digger's son. Old Miss wouldn't have nothing more to do with her, same as if she weren't her own child. But I'd go over to see her and carry milk and things out o' de garden.

—Prince Johnson, age–about 85 *(Voices from Slavery, p.190)*

Chapter 32

Sally

At sixteen, Sally had become a young woman, and she had her eye on the handsome new schoolteacher.

"My, you sure do look nice this morning. Is there some young man caught your eye?" her mother asked.

"Oh, Mother, I'm just trying to look nice. There aren't any boys around here I care for."

Robert Patton was twenty-one and had come to Florida for the excitement of exploring a new frontier. Like so many of the young men who came as teachers, the adventure of the Florida frontier called him. Teaching was a means to pay for it.

As the only teacher in the area, Robert had avoided conscription. This did not sit well with many people in the community. To make matters worse, his support for the South seemed flimsy at best. Robert walked a thin line so as not to offend those paying their children's tuition. Although he told everyone he'd grown up in Tennessee, in reality, he called Maine home. It was impossible to pin down his views regarding the war, slavery, or any of the other divisive issues. Robert could out-politic a politician. Truthfully, he abhorred slavery, only concealing his views out of necessity to earn a living and reside in peace.

Several of his female students expressed their enamored feelings for him, but no one as much as Sally.

The rain came hard and fast, inducing John to scamper up the steps to the front porch. He removed his hat and beat it against his thigh, shaking off loose water. He was enjoying surveying the lush green of the crops when the door opened behind him. Martha eased up, putting her arms around him. "The rain is beautiful, isn't it?"

"Yep," he said and wondered what she could be plotting.

She hugged his arm, resting her cheek against it. "We haven't talked about it because of Adam's death, but Sally turned sixteen a few months ago." She straightened, giving his arm a squeeze. "We never got to celebrate her birthday. Let's have a party, John. It's time for us to get together with our neighbors."

His discomfort with this discussion brought his hand back to rub his neck. "We're in the middle of a war. You think a party is a good idea right now?"

She hesitated only a second. "Yes. It's a very good idea. People are tired. They need a break. They need something to celebrate, and so do we. I think it's a really good idea."

The rain came harder now, making it impossible to see as far as the road. It had been six months since Jacob brought word of Adam's death.

Martha is right, John thought. *We all need a break from the stress of trying to get by. The mood's too somber. We need to get on with living our lives.*

"All right," he said. "A party it will be."

The party became the big event for the area. Word spread that all friends were welcome—friends meaning Southern sympathizers. They planned the party to take place in three weeks. The idea of a fun gathering appealed to many people. Their lives, difficult and monotonous, badly needed a change. The war had been dragging on—loved ones gone indefinitely or lost forever. Any excuse to set aside the war and its tragedies, if even for just a few hours, would do. Celebrating a young woman's coming of age made the event even more special.

John and Martha set the slaves to sprucing up the yard and buildings. John directed Roscoe to have tables built for guests to gather outside and to have a pit dug for the pig roast. Harriet and the women prepared the food. Everyone pitched in.

While the Higgins family anticipated the party with gusto, to the slaves it meant added work. Later, the party would be enjoyed by them as well. They, too, would take pleasure in the music and eat better than their usual fare. They didn't mind the extra work, for they liked and respected Sally.

The afternoon of the party arrived. Jacob and Silas tended to the pig roasting as neighbors straggled in, bringing their own favorite recipe. The food was laid out on the tables by the women, who made sure every detail was taken care of. Children played off to the side out of the way. The men gathered, watching the pig roast, as they enjoyed a drink and conferred about the war, their crops, and whatever else came to mind. The women talked of many of these same topics while helping with the meal preparation. Conspicuously absent were able-bodied men aged eighteen to forty-five. Present were young men with missing limbs and widowed women with fatherless children in tow, all reminders of the bloody war that seemed as though it would never end.

Todd Carpenter and his son, Pete, showed up, though not invited or welcome. They were never invited to functions, but with free food on hand, they always made an appearance. Todd guessed his age to be around sixty, though he didn't know for sure. His lean frame and bronzed skin resulted from a hard life of deprivation. His long, snow-white beard and small eyes gave him the appearance of a mythical troll. He always squinted, which made it impossible to see more than a sliver of his eyes. The rumor that he had an allergy to bathwater seemed well substantiated.

Pete, in his early thirties with a dark beard, looked to be a younger version of his father. Both men kept to themselves most of the time.

The Carpenter men lived in a run-down shack somewhere between town and the Higgins' place. Most people had no idea where they lived. They built their cabin far back in the woods, out of sight from the road, so most folks hadn't seen it and wouldn't have guessed it was there. Those who had seen it, often commented that a strong wind might level it. When Todd's wife died four years ago, the town's people thought she'd died from overwork. Todd and Pete were so lazy, the Confederate army didn't bother to recruit them, although both claimed to be proud supporters of the Southern cause. Their tough talk did not extend to actually doing anything to help.

When Pete spotted Sally, his eyes followed her from friend to friend and place to place. Todd moved alongside his son, tracking his gaze to Sally. Pete said, "Sure would be nice to have a woman like that around."

Todd sneered. "Yep, sure would."

John saw Todd and Pete and wished they weren't contaminating his festivities. While he didn't want to cause a ruckus by forcing them to leave, he was fearful they would offend guests with their body odor, or they just might walk off with whatever they could get their grubby little hands on.

Sally stood in a circle with three of her friends who chatted energetically. She was having a problem concentrating on the conversation. Her eyes darted around, always going back to the road. She anticipated the arrival of someone special. An hour after most guests had arrived, a lone figure appeared. Robert Patton. Upon seeing him, Sally clapped her hands and then blushed as she caught herself. She quickly left her friends and made her way to greet him.

John watched Robert ride in. He frowned and wondered who the hell had invited him. Then he saw Sally's enthusiastic greeting, and he knew Robert had come at her invitation. Robert, he believed, had no intention of staying at the school long. Most teachers moved on after a stay of one or two years—when they had tired of an area and sought further adventure elsewhere. John did not want any man breaking his daughter's heart, especially a Union man, if that's where his loyalties lay.

Sally grabbed Robert's hand to escort him to the refreshments, where he amply helped himself. A friendly sort who made conversation easily, he moved smoothly from the men's group and their conversation to the women's group, where he shamelessly charmed them all.

When most had finished eating, Andy Jefferson from the east side of town, stood and clapped his hands to get everyone's attention. Once quiet had settled over the group, except for the children playing off to the side, he announced that he had a Negro who could play the banjo better than any he had ever heard. He summoned a slight, brown-skinned youth who was holding a scruffy banjo that was probably older than the youth himself. If anyone had doubts about his skill, they were quickly erased. His music squelched serious conversation in favor of dancing and lighter talk. The tinny musical sounds created a merry atmosphere. The slaves joined in, dancing off to one side. The children, enthralled with the magical sounds, quit their play to listen and dance. At times, talented couples grabbed the limelight, as guests stopped to watch them perform.

Sally danced with Robert as much as the other young ladies allowed, daring to get as close to him as she could without alarming her father. Adoring his smell and the touch of their hands, she bristled when having to share him.

After several hours, the party wore down. One or two families at a time expressed thanks to John and Martha and well-wishes to Sally before taking their leave. Through all of this, John kept occupied watching Sally and Robert, as well as keeping his eye on Pete and Todd.

Before Robert left, Sally approached her mother. "Let's invite Robert over for dinner next week. Would that be all right with you?"

Martha, seeing such happiness in Sally's face, said, "Yes. He seems like a nice young man. Tell him Saturday evening."

Later that night, Martha sat in front of the mirror brushing her hair. In the reflection, she watched John climb into bed. "Sally is growing up. She invited her teacher to have dinner with us on Saturday. Perhaps you could finish up a little early so you can get ready for our guest. I think he—"

"What do you mean that teacher is coming here for dinner?" John interrupted. "I don't want my daughter seeing that man. I don't trust him."

"Why, John Higgins, I'm surprised at you. How can you say that? He really is refined, and Sally likes him."

"I don't care what kind of person he is or if she's madly in love with him, he's not the kind of person I want in this family. We don't know anything about him. He could be a Union man for all we know."

"John, it's too late now. He's been invited, and this is very important to Sally." Martha turned to face John directly. "I want you to be pleasant, and maybe you'll learn to like him," she said, holding her gaze before turning back to the mirror.

John rolled onto his side and muttered under his breath, "Women."

John fumed all the next day and into the evening.

After dinner he said to Martha, "That Robert is not so much a decent young man as he is a rascal. I kept my eye on him during Sally's party. I don't like the way he and Sally stayed so close. I have a good mind to pull her out of that school. Who knows what he's teaching those children."

"John, you're being unfair to him, and you don't even know him. You be mannerly to him when he comes for dinner. He's very special to Sally."

John decided he couldn't have Robert courting his daughter without knowing where he stood on the war. He determined he would find out after dinner and not let him weasel out of a straight answer.

The night of the dinner arrived. Sally thought it would never come. All day she had been making sure everything was perfect—in effect driving her mother and Harriet a little crazy.

John came in from work early to clean up and be nicely dressed when the guest arrived, as Martha requested. Robert arrived on time, and the meal went as planned. Robert complimented the dinner and his companions. If Sally could have planned everything right down to the conversation, it couldn't have gone more smoothly. But Sally didn't plan everything. When the after-dinner small talk began slowing down, John said to Robert, "Why don't we go out for some cool air and some manly conversation?"

Surprised, Sally said, "Papa, can't this wait till later? We aren't through visiting with Robert."

"No, Sally, it can't. We'll be back shortly. And Martha," he pointed his finger in her direction, "don't you say nothing. Right this way, Robert."

Robert stood and said, "Thank you both for a lovely dinner."

"Momma, what is Papa up to? He's not going to spoil everything is he?"

"I don't know what he's up to, dear, but I'm sure he won't spoil anything. You know he loves you and wants to see you happy." She patted Sally's hand. "Don't worry, they'll be back soon." But Martha, too, wondered. She knew her husband's ways all too well.

She walked to the floral arrangement and straightened the flowers to get her mind off John's "manly talk." Sally glanced at the door every few minutes, hoping to see the two men return having had a pleasant conversation. Time dragged on. Fifteen minutes seemed like an hour.

As the two men walked away from the house, John said, "Robert, Sally seems to like you. I'm sure you know I only want what's best for my daughter. So, I think it's time we had a man-to-man talk."

"That's fine, Mister Higgins."

"Good. I'll get right to the point. To be perfectly blunt with you, one of my main concerns is that I don't know which side of the war you're on. So, I want you to tell me, straight out, are you a Union man, or are you loyal to the Confederacy?"

"Well, Mister Higgins, you do get to the point, don't you?" Robert felt boxed in, but he had gotten out of boxes before. "To tell you the truth, Mister Higgins, the reason you haven't heard my opinion on this matter is that I try to stay neutral. After all, I teach children from different families, and some of them may be for the Union and others for the South. I try not to let politics interfere with my first love, which is teaching children."

"That won't do, Robert. I don't believe there is a man alive who can live in this country and not have an opinion about the war. If you won't give me your opinion, then I will have to make the assumption that you favor the Union."

Robert paused to think on his predicament. "So, if I don't tell you how I stand, then you assume, rightly or wrongly, that I am on the side of the Union?"

"That's right," said John.

Robert knew John had strong connections to the Confederacy. After all, he had lost a son fighting for the South, and he owned slaves. Finally, he said, "Mister Higgins, I'll have to think on how to answer your question. Please tell Sally and your lovely wife how much I enjoyed the meal and your company. Thank you for the invitation."

John watched him ride off. He knew if Robert had Southern sympathies, he would have said as much. He returned to the house, preparing how to explain Robert's departure to Sally and Martha, when a figure in the dark startled him.

"What do you want?" he said, figuring Harriet had nothing pleasing to say.

"Massa John, you gonna lose that girl sure enough."

"What are you talking about, Harriet?"

"These young girls like Sally in there, when they falls in love with a man, they don't quit him easy like. Them girls leaves their own family before they leaves the man they truly loves. Yes, sir, you gonna lose that girl of yours." She walked away, shaking her head.

Hell, what does she know? John walked to the house and went inside.

When Sally saw her father return without Robert, she ran at him. "Papa, where is Robert?" she asked, panic-stricken. "What have you done?"

"I didn't do anything. Robert and I had a chat, and he decided to leave."

"But Papa, what did you say to him?"

Martha added, "John, I hope you didn't offend that young man."

John could contain himself no longer. "Here's what happened. That young man is a Union sympathizer, and I won't have him in my house, eating my food or seeing my daughter! I am the man here, and you had better stop disrespecting my decisions. For God sakes, he's a Union man, and them sons a bitches killed my boy." John sizzled as he charged out of the house.

Sally's eyes narrowed. "Papa has run off the man I love. Robert had nothing to do with Adam's death." Seething, she demanded, "Momma, do something."

Martha hugged Sally. "After we've all calmed down, we can discuss Robert again. I know this is hard for you, dear, but your father has a point. And so do you."

Sally pushed out of her mother's arms and ran to her room, slamming the door shut. She threw herself on her bed and slammed her fists into the mattress until exhausted. She wanted to leave this house and never see her father again. She rolled over and lay on her bed, staring at the ceiling. She must think of a way to convince her father that Robert was right for her, and then convince Robert that she was right for him—in spite of her father.

As her emotions calmed, an idea emerged. She decided she would go see Robert tomorrow so she could have some time alone with him. She would smooth things over, and she and Robert could see each other as much as they wanted.

Sally clutched her pillow and buried her face in it. *Oh, Robert, I love you.* She rolled onto her back. *We'll get married, and Papa can like it or not.*

Robert returned to his one-room apartment attached to the back of the school. He didn't take his horse to the stable, where he boarded it. He entered his apartment and sat at his table, pondering. After some time, he rose and went to his desk. He took out a sheet of paper, his pen and ink, and began writing.

The morning after the disastrous dinner, Sally arose early and stole to the barn while her father and the slaves were occupied with their morning duties. She entered unnoticed, saddled her horse, and rode to town.

She arrived at the schoolhouse and slipped around back to Robert's quarters. She knocked on the door. No answer. Thinking he might be in the schoolhouse, she went to the front and raised her fist to knock when his note caught her eye. She pulled the note from the door.

> *There will be no school today.*
> *I have resigned my position as teacher.*
> *Signed, Robert Patton*

She placed a hand on the wall to steady herself. She read the note again in disbelief. She hoped he hadn't been gone long. She glanced to the west, thinking he might have gone to Tampa, or he might have gone south to Ft. Meade, or east to the coast. She didn't think he had gone north. He often talked of the adventure of trying new territories.

Seeing a lone individual in the road, she asked, "Have you seen the teacher, Robert, in the last few minutes?"

"No, I haven't," he replied.

"He left town today. Surely you saw which way he went."

"Like I said, I haven't seen him."

She didn't care what it took, she would do anything to find him. If she didn't make a decision soon, and the right one, she would lose him forever. Every second delayed, Robert traveled farther away. Her best chance, she thought, would be to ride south.

She pushed her horse hard, its hooves striking the earth with a swift, rhythmic pounding. She rode for hours. She finally stopped, her horse exhausted, having lost all hope of finding him. She stood tall in the saddle, closed her eyes, and, lifting her face to the sky, called his name with all her strength. "Robert, Robert!"

The realization that she had lost him overwhelmed her. She shook with sobs. She led her horse to the edge of the road, dismounted, and sat there alternately crying for her loss and cursing her father.

Having drained every tear from her body, Sally mounted her horse to return home. She traveled, oblivious to her surroundings. Several miles from home, she crossed paths with beady-eyed Pete Carpenter, who blocked her way.

"Miss Sally, what're you doing out here all by yourself?" asked Pete, with anticipation in his heart and an evil glint in his eye.

Sally, her stomach turning with disgust, said nothing. She gave her horse a nudge to move around Pete's horse. Pete quickly caught up to her, grabbing her horse's reins.

"Now just a minute here, missy. I was being nice to you, and here you go and treat me rude. Where's your fancy manners now? If you just give me some time, I'll grow on you."

He had a satisfied "look what I caught" grin on his face.

"You let go of me right now, Pete, you hear me! If my papa knew what you were up to, he would shoot you. Now let me go!" Sally struggled to get her horse loose from his grip.

"Your pa don't scare me none, Miss Sally. You might think you're too good for me, but you know what? You ain't. You ain't no better'n me. And someday, you'll find that out." His dirty, rough finger moved along the softness of her cheek. He laughed as he let go of the reins and gave her horse a slap.

Sally's hands shook as she drove her horse to a gallop. She dared not look back until she was close to home. She rubbed her hand across her cheek to rid herself of the feel of Pete's finger.

She rode directly to the barn. She didn't want to see anyone. She didn't want to answer questions. She wanted to be left alone. One thing she knew—this was her father's fault, and she hated him for it.

When she left the barn, she saw Harriet hanging clothes. She stopped, closed her eyes, and tried to breathe normal.

"Hi, Harriet, it sure is a hot day, isn't it?" she asked, trying to act casual, trying to hold her emotions inside, but knowing they might explode any minute.

Harriet, surprised, said, "Where you been, child?"

"I just went for a ride."

"Your parents been worried sick. They knows you don't just up and leave for no reason. Your papa been out looking for you. You best go let your momma know you is home."

Sally's grief burst forth. "Harriet, what am I going to do?"

"What's the matter, child?"

"What do you do when you love someone, really love someone, and they just leave you without even saying goodbye? Harriet, it's so unfair."

"Now, now, Miss Sally. I know it seem pretty awful right now, but it ain't all that bad. If some man up an' leaves you without even saying one word, then I say he not the kind of man you ought to be with no how. I do know one thing for sure. There will be plenty more men that love you 'cause you is a pretty girl and a good girl. Plenty more men gonna be looking after you."

"But I don't want some other man, Harriet. I want Robert."

Sally trudged slowly up the back steps and into the house. Her mother rose from her chair. "Sally! Thank God you're all right. Where have you been?"

Sally took a step towards her room and stopped. She lifted her gaze from the floor and turned to her mother. In a weakened voice she said, "Momma, I was worried about Robert, so I went to talk to him, but he wasn't there. Oh, Momma, he has left town."

"Sally, you went all the way into town by yourself? I hate to think what could have happened to you. Promise me you'll never do that again."

"Momma, weren't you even listening to what I said? Robert is gone! He's left! Can't anyone understand?"

"Sally, I am sorry he's gone, but you must not act like a child. Please, Sally, tell me you understand this. I don't want to lose you because you're chasing after some man."

"Oh, Momma." Sally ran to her room and threw herself onto her bed.

John returned from his search a few hours later. Martha told him Sally's story, which enraged him.

John barged into Sally's room. "I been lookin' all over creation for you, and you been out chasing after that damn Yankee! Don't you have any pride? Them Yankees are our enemy. They killed your brother, why in—"

"Stop it, Papa, stop it! I love him, and you ran him off."

"How could you love such a man? If he scared away so easy, he's not worthy to be my son-in-law. Better you marry a good Southern boy than any Yankee. Especially that schoolteacher."

"Is that what you want me to do? I should marry anyone who thinks like you whether I love him or not?"

"Yes, dammit!"

"I hate you! I hate you! I wish you weren't my papa," Sally yelled, pounding on her father's chest.

John grabbed her wrists, opened his mouth to speak, but decided it would fall on deaf ears. He stormed out of Sally's room.

Martha, overhearing, entered Sally's room. "When you're feeling better, you ought to let your father know you didn't mean what you said. He loves you and is just trying to do what he thinks is best."

Sally turned away from her mother and sat on the side of her bed, her hands folded in her lap.

"Could I be alone for a while, please, Momma?"

After her mother left her room, Sally sat for a while considering her options. In her disturbed state of mind, the options she considered were not good.

Well, Papa, you got rid of Robert, but this isn't over. I'm not your slave, and you can't tell me what to do or who to marry. Maybe I'll run away and marry some Yankee after all. You think any Southern boy is better than a Yankee. Maybe we'll find out if you really believe that. I'll show you, Papa, I'll show you.

CHAPTER 33

William

Jacksonville, Florida, on the St. Johns River, had been taken twice by the Union and evacuated twice, the last time in October of 1862. It was estimated that it would take 5,000 men to hold the city, and this number of men could not be spared. The present thought was to take it and hold it with less than 1,000 men. The belief was there were fewer Rebel troops in the area now, and the St. Mary's expedition showed the advantage of having colored troops with their local knowledge and their gaining the confidence of loyal blacks. Some thought the risk worthwhile to hold Florida and possibly bring it back into the Union.

Thus, Corporal Higginson's Regiment began preparing to leave their camp, possibly forever. The vast amount of baggage and no wharf meant that everything had to be loaded onto flatboats first, then transferred to their gunboats. It made for a tremendous job, but it was accomplished in 24 hours.

After stopping briefly at Fernandina, they reached the St. John's River. Admiral Dupont had furnished them a letter of introduction, so they were received well by Commander Duncan of the *Norwich*, and Lieutenant Watson, commanding officer of the *Uncas*, who were to escort them up the river. The rebels had repeatedly threatened to burn the town if attacked again, as they had at one time burned their mills and great hotel. The Union officers kept a wary eye in the direction of Jacksonville, looking for any telltale smoke.

The river was difficult to navigate, and at times the keel would drag on the river bottom, causing the boat to shudder. These were tense moments. The *Norwich* became hopelessly stranded a few miles from Jacksonville. Hopefully, the next tide would free her, but this left the *Uncas*, a small steamer, in poor condition to escort the black regiment alone. They had hoped to reach Jacksonville by daybreak, but the delays gave them several hours of fresh, early sunshine, which lit up the lovely shores—at times opening to an emerald meadow. Here and there they glided by the ruins of a sawmill burned by the rebels on the approach of a previous attack, but nothing else spoke of war, except perhaps the silence. The Florida men were wild with delight when they rounded the point and saw from afar its long streets, its brick warehouses, its white cottages, and its overshadowing trees, all peaceful and undisturbed by flames. There was a buzz of ecstasy.

Not knowing what lay behind the quiet buildings, they steamed ahead. Children played in the streets; some men, hands in pockets, looked out at the Union boats; and a few women came to their doors, shaded their eyes with their hands, and gazed listlessly at them. They grew nearer with breathless attention. The gunners were at their posts. It was eight o'clock. No sign of danger was seen, no rifle shot was heard, not a shell rose hissing in the air. Colonel Higginson's boat steamed out to an upper pier of the town; Colonel Montgomery, to a lower one. The boat-howitzers were run out to the wharves. The town was captured without a shot being fired. The surprise had been complete. Not a soul had dreamed the Union army was coming.

That night, everyone was anxious and tired. They were anticipating an attack by the rebels, but none came. The morning brought relief and a sense of possession. Jacksonville was now a U.S. post again, the only post on the mainland of the Department of the South. Before the war, it had around 3,000 inhabitants and a growing lumber trade. The mills had been burned, but the large warehouses and private dwellings were in good condition.

To hold this town with a small force of 900 men and to make forays up the river seemed impossible. Higginson had hoped to recruit black men, but there were none to be found, as all had been removed. Colonel Higginson had been reluctant to bring in white soldiers to mix with his black troops, but now he felt it necessary. He had been offered by Colonel Hawley, commander at Fernandina, four companies of men and a light battery in Fernandina and was now inclined to accept. Word was sent to Hawley that his offer would be welcome.

The men were set to work cutting down trees to barricade the main entrances to the town. And now the men were once again under a test as to their demeanor as victors. Here were 500 white citizens at the mercy of their former slaves. To some, it was a crowning humiliation, and they professed to be in constant fear. However, the wife of a Rebel captain said that it seemed pleasanter to have these men stationed here, whom they had known all their lives and who were generally of good character, than to have strangers.

The soldiers deserved their confidence, for there was hardly an exception to their good behavior. They felt their honor and dignity were concerned in the matter and took too much pride in being soldiers, to say nothing of their higher motives, to tarnish it with misdeeds.

Several of the men had seen their brothers hanged, and many others had private wrongs to avenge. One citizen was brought before the colonel, a small German grocer, and proclaimed by the escort with his highest compliment that this man had a "true colored-man heart." This man had been an object of suspicion by the whites in the community because he would loan money to black men and sell to them on credit.

Captain Perkins' company set up pickets most mornings on the main road leading north out of town. Every day, the rebels would come mounted and have skirmishes with the picket. Often, they would dismount and use a line of rundown cottages as shelter, where they fired upon the Union soldiers.

It was a cool, sunny morning when Perkins company lined up for their orders. "Men, I know you're as tired as I am at those damn rebels taking shelter behind those miserable shacks and taking shots at us. Well, today we're putting an end to it. We're going to burn the damn things down."

The men cheered at this news.

"I need five men—one for each cottage—to go inside and set it ablaze. We'll have everything you'll need to set a good, hot fire. The rest of us will stay at the picket line and make sure no rebels interfere. I'll choose the five men unless some of you want to volunteer."

It was no surprise to the captain when every man spoke up to volunteer. "We can't have everyone go up there. Someone has to stay back to keep the rebels away. So, I'll send William, Nathan, George, Jake, and Noah. Time for us to relieve the night picket. Let's go, men."

William went first, running from his company's shelter to the first house. He made sure the fire was going in several places before he dashed back. The house was mostly consumed by the time he returned to the Union picket. No shots were fired. Each man went one at a time, and each time, all went without incident.

The lack of shelter kept the fighting down but didn't end the fighting. The Union made daily reconnaissance missions into the countryside, which often led to an exchange of fire with the enemy.

On March 20, 1863, the white regiments arrived from Fernandina. The Sixth Regiment of Connecticut, and two days later, a part of the Eighth Maine arrived to reinforce the black regiment. Now it remained to be seen whether black and white troops could act in harmony together.

The white soldiers were able to move about without the hostile stares and the occasional ugly remarks aimed at the black soldiers. But the two groups worked well together, with no hostilities between them. On several occasions, William enjoyed talking with a couple of men from Maine who told him of life in the northern part of the country. William wondered how it could be possible to have such differences in the same country. But then, thinking back to Dr. Stone and his wife, he realized he'd had the good fortune to be witness to this difference.

The Union army in Jacksonville was safe now from an attack by a small force, and they hoped the South could not spare troops from Savannah or Charleston to mount a large attack. Colonel Higginson's main concern now was having black and white soldiers together. Any unfortunate incident would have terrible consequences on the national discussion of Negro enlistment and slavery.

On March 28, orders came for the black regiment to prepare to evacuate Jacksonville. With heavy hearts, the men made ready to leave to travel upriver. They expressed great disappointment at having to leave an adventurous life in enemy country, to their safe and familiar camp in South Carolina.

CHAPTER 34

Sally

The next day, Sally waited for the right moment. John had been up early and left with most of the workers. Martha had Sally help her with a few house chores and encouraged her to make up with her father. Sally smiled at her mother but said nothing.

When she thought the time right, Sally told her mother she wanted to go outside to help Harriet. Martha watched her speak with Harriet. Satisfied that Harriet would supervise her, Martha returned to her work.

But Sally had begun a sinister plan when she spoke to Harriet. "Momma wants me to give Papa a message, but I don't feel like talking to him. What do you think I should do, Harriet?"

"Well, you better do like your momma says. That's what families do."

Sally glanced back at the house to see whether her mother was spying on her. She noticed her standing briefly at the window and then leaving.

"I guess you're right, Harriet. I better get going."

She walked away, proud of her deception. She saddled her horse and rode off.

Well, Papa, now we'll see. When you come searching for me and find me with Pete, you'll realize how stupid it is to think that any

Southern boy will do. And when you see how desperate I am, you'll agree I should be with Robert.

Sally turned off the road onto a small path that led to Todd and Pete's place. But questions and conflicting emotions gave her second thoughts.

What if Papa doesn't come? Stop it. I'm being such a coward. I've come this far. I'm not going back home and letting him get away with ruining my life. This is a crazy and dangerous idea.

She moved slowly onto the narrow trail. After twenty yards, she stopped. Fear chilled her.

What if Papa can't find me? This is really stupid. I don't want to be here.

Sally laughed nervously. She turned her horse to leave the woods and came face to face with Pete.

"Hello, Miss Sally. I'm sure glad to see you. You're lookin' for me, I bet, ain't you?" Grinning, Pete pushed his hat back with his index finger, very satisfied with these circumstances.

"Uh, no, Pete. I was just curious about this path. But I have to be going now."

Pete positioned his horse to block her exit. "Now just hold on a minute. You don't come callin' on someone and then leave without talkin' to him. Come back here with me and be neighborly." Pete moved down the path, pulling Sally's horse behind him.

"Pete, stop. Let me go!" yelled Sally, struggling to get her reins back. "My papa is right behind me, and he'll shoot you for this."

"There ain't nobody behind you. I just want to be sociable. I don't get many visitors back here. If you'll come with me real quiet, we can talk an' you can go back home. But if you keep yellin' like that, I'll have to quiet you," he said, placing his hand on the handle of his gun.

Sally stopped yelling. She didn't trust him, but she knew he was capable of hurting her. She wanted to jump off her horse and run, but he could easily catch her, and that would only anger him further. She decided it might be best to humor him. After all, he'd let her go last time.

After zigzagging through the woods for twenty minutes, they arrived at his place. "Get down. We're home."

We're home?

Alarmed, frightened, and helpless, Sally knew if she dismounted, she would have no means of escape. "Let me go. You have no right to hold me here."

Pete grabbed her by the waist and dumped her to the ground.

"I only ask once. Next time, you best do as I say."

He tied both horses to a nearby post. Taking Sally by the arm, he escorted her into his ramshackle home. "Come in and sit a spell."

His one-room house smelled musty. Flies attacked rotting food left on the table. The sweaty stench of unwashed clothes and bodies hung in the air.

"Please, let me go. I promise I'll come back some other time, and we can get to know each other," Sally pleaded.

"Ain't no time better'n right now."

He pushed her roughly into a chair that creaked and swayed, sounding as though it might collapse under her sudden weight.

"Where's your pa?" asked Sally, fearing that both men might be home.

"Don't you worry none 'bout him. He's gone for quite a while. Don't rightly know when he might get back. Looks like it's gonna be just you and me. Kinda cozy, don't you think?"

Light slipped in from open space around the door, cracks in the walls, and one small window, but not enough to illuminate the room.

A table in need of repair and two rickety chairs stood in the middle of the room. Sally sat in one of them, calculating how to escape. Two bedrolls lay in separate corners, where, she guessed, Todd and Pete slept. Two rifles occupied a third corner.

Flies found their way to Sally's hair and arms. She swatted them away. "Don't you ever clean this place or take a bath?" Her outburst surprised her She didn't want to anger Pete.

Pete laughed. "When my ma was alive, we were better at those things. 'Course, she done all the cleaning. Our only water is a stream that runs north of here. So, we don't do much bathing or cleaning. But for you, I'll clean up."

"That would be nice, Pete. Why don't you get cleaned up, and I'll wait for you here."

"I got a better idea. How 'bout we both go down to the creek an' get a bath. Yes'm, that's a great idea."

"Pete, I don—" Before she could finish her sentence, Pete rose and said, "Get up, Sally, let's go to the creek."

They walked along a narrow path through dense woods, Sally in front. Pete shoved Sally when she slowed too much for his liking. The creek measured thirty feet across and flowed gently through the pines and oaks that thrived in the area. Smaller trees competed for sunlight, bending and stretching to touch the sky. Pine needles covered the creek's sandy banks.

"Please, Pete, don't make me do this."

"Do what, Miss Sally? I'm just lookin' after your health. You shouldn't be walking around in wet clothes."

"But, Pete, my clothes aren't wet."

Pete shoved her into the creek. "They are now."

He jumped in with her. "Yahoo!" He shouted and splashed like a kid. He drew near to Sally and grabbed the front of her dress, ripping it open. Sally's fear dissolved into fury. Any hope that she could talk her way out of this mess vanished with Pete's violence. She knew she must fight. She went for his eyes, but he reacted, knocking her hands away. Before she could strike again, he hit her hard in the chest, knocking the breath out of her. She fell back into the hip-high water. Having taken in a mouthful of water, she coughed, trying to get control of herself. Pete took her by the arm, straightened her, then slapped her head with his open hand. She fell again, her head under water. He held her under for what seemed like forever; she expected he would drown her. Finally, he took her by one arm, roughly pulling her from the water, and shoved her onto the bank. Choking, she struggled to breathe.

Finally able to talk, her eyes riveted on Pete. "If you touch me, my papa will kill you."

"Like I said, I ain't afraid of your pa. I enjoy a little fight in my women, so you go right on. That suits me just fine."

Sally's eyes narrowed as he closed in on her. She kicked at him, hitting his thigh. He laughed and jumped on her, pinning her arms to the ground.

"I had my eye on you for a long time."

Sally never stopped struggling, but he had too much strength. Her mournful cry pierced the stillness but went unheard.

When Pete finished, Sally felt disgusted with herself for her reckless stupidity. Sore and bleeding, she hated herself.

Upon their return to the hovel, Sally vomited. She wanted to rid herself of the feel of Pete on her. She lingered at the door, resisting entry as though to do so would seal her fate. He shoved her. She stumbled in, and the confinement of the four walls cut off any hope of her returning home.

No man would want me now. Not Robert, not any man.

She felt revulsion. The disgusting feel of him, his grunts in her ear, his spittle on her face, his scratching beard, his stench. She wanted to die, ah, yes, sweet, welcome death.

"Harriet, have you seen Sally?" Martha asked.

"No, Mrs. Higgins, I ain't seen her since she rode off to give your message to the massa."

"What are you talking about, Harriet?"

"Why, she came out here this mornin' an' said you sent her to give a message to the massa. Then she got her horse an' rode off."

"Harriet, I never did no such thing. She's run off again. Come to the barn with me quickly and help me saddle a horse!"

When John saw Martha approaching, he dropped his work and ran to her. "What's the matter?"

"Sally has run away," she said, her voice cracking. "She left on horseback after telling Harriet some crazy lie about my sending her here to you. I haven't seen her since this morning. What are we going to do?"

John had Jacob take Martha home in the buckboard. He took Hector with him in search of Sally. He spoke with everyone they encountered. They called on every house in the area, but no one had seen her. They searched until darkness forced them to quit.

That night, Harriet called all the slaves together to pray for Sally's safe return. She hoped there might be strength in numbers.

At dawn, John and Hector renewed their search, this time going all the way to Ft. Meade, thirty miles to the south. During the next few days, they covered every road, every house, but no one had seen her. John wondered if she had met up with Robert, and they had run off together. They eventually came to that dreadful point in their search—they had no place left to look.

"I'm going into town now. Be back late. I'm goin' to tell you one more time just so you don't forget. If you leave, if you ain't here when I get back, I'll kill your family an' then I'll bring you back here."

Did he really leave this time?

Once before, he had said he was going to town. Instead, he hid outside to see what she would do. When she left the hut, he jumped her, throwing her to the ground, kicking her. He could be faking again, waiting down the path ready to ambush her. Even if he had left, Sally wouldn't leave for fear of what he would do to her family.

Since her arrival, Sally had been forced to cook meals, do chores, gather firewood, and chase down chickens to kill for dinner. Food had become scarce. He would have to bring more in, but maybe he wouldn't—not right away. He might eat while he was out, making

Sally go hungry for a few days to remind her that she depended on him for survival.

She moved slowly, in part from lack of nutrition, in part from the soreness of her body and limbs where Pete had hit her repeatedly. He intended to keep it that way. Fear kept her obedient. She thought of shooting him when he slept, but what if she couldn't do it? She had never killed anyone. If she failed, he would hurt her badly, maybe kill her. Besides, he slept with his pistol and the two rifles beside him, between him and the wall. She would have to reach over him to get a weapon. What if he only pretended to be sleeping?

He told her Todd had been arrested for stealing cattle and wouldn't be home anytime soon.

Sally peeked outside. Something moved in the bushes off to the left. *Pete?* She quickly shut the door. She would have cried, but she stuffed the tears back. She crouched behind the door, trembling.

A month later, Roscoe and Hector rode in the buckboard going to town on an errand. Hector saw a figure, a woman in the woods, gathering firewood. She wore a tattered dress. Her hair was a tangled mess. She needed a bath. There was something familiar about her.

"Roscoe, stop right here!" yelled Hector.

Roscoe hauled back on the reins. Hector jumped from the buckboard before it came to a full stop and ran towards the woman.

"Miss Sally! Miss Sally! Is that you?" Hector yelled.

Sally looked up with tired eyes and managed a weak smile at seeing her old friend. She felt ashamed that Hector was seeing her like this. Then panicked when she realized how close to the road she had wandered.

My family mustn't find out.

"Sally, how are you? Are you all right?" But he could see she wasn't. She had lost weight—lots of weight. He had never seen her so uncared for. As he moved closer, her faded bruises and fresh ones tore at his heart, and her lifeless eyes—he would not forget those. "What's happened to you?"

"I guess I have been better."

"We been looking everywhere for you. We can take you back now. Come with me and Roscoe an' we take you home."

"I can't, Hector. I live here now, with Pete."

"With Pete?" Hector hesitated before saying, "I don't think Pete be good for you, Miss Sally. We sure wish you would come back to Massa John's. We all misses you."

Sally refused to let herself cry. "I can't, Hector. You better go before Pete sees you. And Hector, don't tell anyone about seeing me. It would only upset my parents. And…and bad things could happen if they knew. Will you promise me?"

How could he not tell about finding Sally? *What bad things?* He stammered and finally said, "Yes'm." Hector stood before her, yearning to take her by the arm and walk her to the buckboard, get her to a safe place. He couldn't persuade himself to leave her.

"I think I'm going to have Pete's baby."

He nodded. "You ought to come on with us. Your momma can take care of you."

"Hector," she backed away, "tell no one. Promise me. He'll kill us all." She ran down the path, away from Hector.

Only after she disappeared from sight could he coax himself to leave. He walked slowly to the waiting buckboard whispering, "There ain't nothin' good about this. Nothin' at all."

When Hector returned to the buckboard, Roscoe asked, "Was that Miss Sally?"

Hector mumbled, "Guess I was wrong."

For two days, Hector struggled with telling or not.

He will kill us all.

In the end, he decided Sally's wellbeing mattered more than his promise to her or Pete's threat.

"Momma," he said, "I gots me a problem, an' I needs your help."

Though tired from a long day's work, she said, "Well, let's hear it. Maybe our two heads can figure it out."

Hector stood, fidgeting. "Roscoe an' me were going into town the other day, and I saw Miss Sally gathering firewood."

Harriet gasped, placing her hand to her chest. Her voice quivering, she said, "You what? Miss Sally? Where?" She fanned herself with her hand. "Lord have mercy."

"I spotted her on the side of the road near that old path leading to Pete and Todd's place. Momma, she living with Pete. She gonna have his baby."

"Oh Lord, no. That poor girl. An' her momma and daddy gonna be miserable hearing this news."

"Momma, she asked me to not say anything. She say her family in danger if they finds out."

Harriet remained silent, pensive. "Even so, they gots to be told. Every parent wants to know about their children. Wouldn't be right."

"I give her my word I wouldn't tell."

"Don't matter. You and me going over to the house."

Hector shared his story, and then he and his momma left.

Martha and John discussed their options.

"Thank God she's alive," said Martha. "I lay awake endless nights worrying about her."

"How in the hell did she get mixed up with that rat? They must of spotted her and forced her to their cabin. No wonder we couldn't find her. They're doing something to make her stay. She would never live with those low-life thieves unless they threatened her. I'm going to get her home. Even if she does have Pete's baby, she belongs here, not in their stinking hole."

"I want her home, John, but what would we do with that dreadful Pete and the baby?"

"Pete's not coming here. I'll see him dead first. We'll deal with the baby later. First, I want to get her home."

"Be careful." Martha hugged him. "You know those men can't be trusted. I would feel a lot better if you took Roscoe along."

"You're right. Those two would as soon shoot me in the back. I'll keep Roscoe out of sight with a rifle aimed at those rascals should they try anything."

John didn't want the neighbors involved if he could manage it. Better to avoid talk of this in the community. He still had hopes of her marrying into a proper family. Pete's baby complicated matters.

John and Roscoe arrived at the path. John made his way cautiously on horseback. Roscoe followed on foot, keeping out of sight. A small structure stood to the left of the path. It tilted to one side and had so much rotted wood he thought it uninhabitable and intended to keep going, but he saw Pete's horse, tied in a copsewood, swishing its tail. Sorrow for his daughter churned inside, along with hate for Todd and Pete.

Pete spotted John coming. He grabbed Sally by the arm. "I'll be standing right beside you out of his sight. Get rid of him, or I'll kill him."

John called out Sally's name. There was movement inside. Sally opened the door.

"Hello, Papa." Sally, stoically, fought back tears.

John's throat tightened on seeing her. He resisted his impulse to hold her—instead, he followed her lead. He took her all in—stringy haired, filthy, bruised. "Hello, sweetheart. We've been worried about you. How are you?" He asked this last question and immediately wished he hadn't. He stepped towards her, but she held her hand between them, keeping them apart.

He tried to notice her pregnancy but couldn't tell.

"I'm doing fine, Papa." But her voice cracked. Tears broke through, welled up.

"You don't look well. I want you to come home. Everything will be better there. Your mother and I want what's best for you. I don't know what that skunk Pete did to make you come here, but you don't have to stay. We love you. Please come home."

Sally forced herself to say, "Papa, this is my home now. This is where I live. I can't live with you and Momma anymore. Please don't try to talk me into leaving."

John didn't believe a word she said. She couldn't prefer this life. She couldn't love Pete or want to live in this filthy place.

"But, Sally…"

"Please, Papa, don't say anymore." She gave him a quick hug. "Give my love to Momma." She turned to go inside, but John grabbed her arm.

"I don't believe you want to live like this. Don't worry about Pete and Todd. I won't let them hurt you. You belong in your own home with your family."

Sally pulled her arm from John's grip. "Listen to me, Papa," she shouted. "This is where I want to be. Now GO! I don't want to see you again."

She ran inside, slamming the door. She held her breath, praying he would leave. Pete stood beside her, gun in hand. His eye caught hers for a second. She looked away, ashamed.

John stood at the door, stunned into silence. Sally's words had shocked and wounded him. He had come to save her, and she'd rebuked him. John left, confused and dejected.

What has happened to Sally? She's my flesh and blood.

As her father rode away, Sally held her face in her hands. She fought to control the scream welling up inside.

Pete put his hand on her head, brushing her hair back with his hand. "You done real good, sweetheart. Yep, you done real good."

Pete's touch, seeing her father, making him leave—all more than she could bear. Using the only avenue of escape left to her, her mind went blank, and she collapsed to the floor.

John rode back a diminished man, his head hanging, his heart rent. He needed to share this burden, to rid himself of this poison. Roscoe rode beside him, but he couldn't share his feelings with a slave.

Once home with Martha, John sighed, shaking his head. He conveyed everything, the words choking him.

When he finished, Martha eased herself into a chair, folding her hands in her lap. "We've lost our children. Every single one."

"She stayed there of her own free will. Riding back, I felt like I didn't ever want to see her again. If that's where she wants to be, then she's made her bed."

Panic rose in Martha. "You can't mean that." She spoke with such intensity, John could only walk away.

That night, when Harriet told Hector that Sally refused to come home, he said, "Sally real skinny when I saw her, Momma. She don't have much to eat. I got to help her."

"What can you do to help?"

"At times, there be food left over from the meals of Massa Higgins and his wife. Maybe you cook a bit more. What if you gives me that food, and I takes it to Sally?"

Harriet smiled. She touched Hector gently on his cheek. "You a kind young man. That good. I is very proud of you. But what about your work here? You won't have time for that. And you won't have no pass to get past them patrollers. You know they kills slaves that don't got no note. And what about that Pete? He be mean. He might kill you hisself just for being on his property." Harriet placed her hand on Hector's. "You is like your papa with that big heart of yours. I hopes you always keep it. But I don't want nothing happen to you on account of it."

"I know, Momma, but if I is careful, I can do it. Sally needs my help, and I know she'd help me. I can get her food two or three times a week. Sundays there won't be no trouble getting food to her. The patrollers will never see me in those thick woods. Most weeks I go by there with Roscoe to do some errands." Hector grasped his mother's hand. "Papa told me long time ago—it all right to be scared. It doing what is right when you scared, that's important."

Harriet's eyes watered on hearing her son's words, for they went to the heart of William. "I knows you is right, Hector. I will ask the missus about the food, and if she all right with it, I bring it to you, but you be careful. Maybe she give me a note for you, too."

On his first delivery, he stopped a safe distance from Pete's shack and hid behind a tree to make sure Pete had gone. When he felt it was safe, he approached the cabin and tried to get Sally's attention by whispering to her through the door. The first time Sally heard Hector's whispers, she feared she might be losing her mind.

Hector brought Sally food twice a week, the note Martha wrote him tucked safely in his pocket. Although grateful for the food, Sally wanted to minimize the risks Hector was taking.

They came up with a plan in which he would leave the food under a discarded crate hidden among palmettos some distance from the cabin. He carried it in a pot and each time would retrieve the empty one. He saw Sally rarely, usually when she was outside during his delivery.

When bored with his game of dominating Sally, Pete spent time in town gambling, drinking, stealing, whatever suited him. He came home late in the evening or early morning. Now and then, he would steal a chicken on the way home, or if feeling good after having won some money, he might buy something for Sally to eat. But this almost never happened. He didn't like the idea of Sally being pregnant. He didn't like the idea of a baby interfering with his fun or his sleep. But then again, maybe a baby would tie Sally to him permanently.

Nourished by the food Hector brought, Sally gained a little weight, though not so much as she had lost. Pete noticed she appeared better fed than she ought to. "Where you getting your food from?" he asked her one day.

"I just eat what you bring me, and what I can find in the woods."

"Well, I think you're lying to me, you little bitch," he said, thrusting his face inches from hers.

Sally flinched, her chin trembling. She knew better than to respond.

"If I catches some man bringing you food, I will kill him. You got that!"

"Nobody's bringing me nothing," she whimpered.

"You better hope there ain't for your sake and that baby of yours. Now I'm going to get me some sleep. Got a big night ahead of me."

While Pete slept, Sally mulled over her situation. She had to warn Hector, even though he might stop bringing her meals.

When Hector next spotted Sally, her pregnancy had begun to show. Alarmed that Pete might be around, he left without speaking to her. He realized she needed fresh milk for herself and later for the baby. He devised a strategy that would require courage and luck.

On the following Sunday, he marched to the big house. "Miss Martha," he said, his voice quivering, "I seen Miss Sally the other day, and she is sure enough with child. I suspects she could use some milk. I'd like permission to take her one of them cows we got out yonder."

Martha thought of Sally every day. How could she not help her precious daughter? Deep inside of her, yearnings of being a grandmother took root. She closed her eyes, and she could almost hear her grandbaby cry, could almost feel the softness of baby skin. She longed to see Sally, to be with her, to share with her the journey of growing a child and giving it birth.

"How did she look, Hector?" she asked.

"She didn't look too bad, ma'am. Except she been working mighty hard." He then added, "She and that new coming baby sure could use some milk, Miss Martha."

"Yes, Hector, take her a cow," she said. "Wait a moment. I'll give you a pass that says you have our permission to have the cow so no one will think you stole it."

Hector picked out the best cow he could find. He arrived at the path leading to Pete's place and turned in. His pace slowed when he saw Pete's horse tied to a tree by the house.

When Hector arrived, Pete came out to challenge him.

"What's this? A damn nigger and a cow. What the hell are you doing on my land? This better be good because I don't allow no niggers on my land." Pete drew his pistol.

"Massa Higgins done ask me to bring this cow as a gift to his daughter. He thinks she ought to have milk."

"Well ain't that sweet." Pete checked out the cow. "That's a mighty fine cow. It should bring a good price."

Hector said, "Yes, sir, I'm sure it will. Massa Higgins asked me to give you a message about that."

"And what would that be?"

"Well, sir, he say he want his daughter to have the milk from this cow for one year, and after that the cow is yours."

"Well, you tell your massa that I'll think about it. But nobody tells me what to do."

"Yes, sir, I'll tell him."

"Just a damn minute there, nigger," said Pete. He walked over and put the barrel of his pistol to Hector's head. "You the one bringing food to that woman in there?"

Hector felt the hard steel pressed against his skin. He knew Pete would not regret pulling the trigger.

"Why, no, sir. I hardly got enough food to feed myself."

"Listen good, nigger. If I ever sees you on my land again, I don't care if you're bringing a whole herd of goddam cows, I will kill you." Pete pulled back the hammer and said, "I'm going to count to three. You better be out of sight by then or you're dead. One—"

Hector ran for his life. He ran until he reached the road, Pete's laughter echoing in his head.

A few days later, John approached Hector. "I heard you took a cow to Sally the other day."

"Yes, sir, I did," said Hector, nervous that he hadn't spoken to the master about it.

John stared at Hector without speaking. Then, barely audible, he said, "Yeah. Well…" and walked away without finishing.

That night, he talked with Martha while she lay in bed. John stood by the window.

"Why do you suppose Hector took that cow to Sally?"

His question caught Martha by surprise. "What was that, dear?"

"That cow Hector took to Sally, why do you suppose he did that?"

Martha sat up. "Hector is a nice person. He was concerned about her."

"Well yes, but why? He could have got himself shot."

"What is it, dear? What's bothering you?"

He started to tell her but couldn't bring himself to say it. He thought of Lindi, and a surge of shame came over him. He started to say that if Hector could show compassion for a white person, if he would risk his life to help Sally, then did he have a soul? Was he as human as John was? And what about Otis and his family? Surely, they were not his equal. Or...? But John kept his thoughts to himself. Speaking them out loud would give them life.

CHAPTER 35
William

On April 1, 1863, the black regiment was recalled from Jacksonville. However, their disappointment was soon erased when they received word that their next order would send them out on picket at Port Royal Ferry.

This picket station was known as a military picnic by the soldiers stationed at Beaufort, South Carolina for it meant blackberries and oysters, flowery lanes instead of sandy trails, and a sort of guerilla existence instead of camp routine. For the black regiment especially, with their love of nature, it seemed like a festival. And the adventure would continue, for their picket stations would be on the Coosaw River right across from the enemy whose stations were on the other side of the Coosaw.

On the day of departure for Port Royal Ferry, the soldiers arose at daybreak and were ready to leave by sunrise, their tents struck and the wagons loaded. It was a seven-mile march to the picket station, and once they were underway, the men began the "route step," which allowed them to walk along with nothing being required except that they remain four abreast and no one lagging behind. Talking and singing were allowed, and this they took advantage of so that the stamping of feet and clanging of equipment could hardly be heard.

At plantation gates, colored people gathered to see them go by and greeted them with glad salutations. Pretty girls ogled and made eyes at half the young soldiers. All the while the singing rang out, first "John Brown," then "Marching Along," and "Hold Your Light on Canaan's Shore," and on and on.

Seeing these young girls made William think of Margaret, who would be the age of these girls and, were she here, might also have been greeting the soldiers.

Arriving at the station, the scene became busy and confused: unloading wagons, pitching tents, bringing water, cutting wood, and making fires. The regiment had an area of twelve square miles to maintain and keep safe out of Rebel hands. The region was a wild medley of cypress swamp, pine barrens, muddy creeks, and cultivated plantations—all crisscrossed with innumerable lanes and bridlepaths through which the regiment must travel day and night. The men were distributed at different pickets; their maintenance of this line was essential for the Union's ability to keep a foothold on the Sea Islands.

At the time of the regiment's first picket duty, there was concern that the Confederates would mount an attack to recapture the Sea Islands. The orders for the regiment were to watch the enemy closely, keep informed of his position and movements, attempt no advance, and if the enemy should try to advance, to delay them as much as possible and send instant notice to headquarters.

William and five other men—Wylie, Clinton, Henri, Ben, and Abram—were stationed at a picket a mile from their camp and on the river. Although the river was wide at this point, they could see the Rebel picket on the other side and had no doubt the rebels were watching them. They had a shift for twenty-four hours, and two each would take eight-hour shifts keeping watch.

The night was dark, with only a sliver of moon. Captain Perkins had left an hour ago, making his rounds of the picket stations. William and Clinton were on watch until midnight.

"Hey, William, you see that?"

"Seem like somethin' floating out in the river."

"Yeah. I think it coming our way."

"Hard to tell."

The other men, aroused from sleep, looked out over the water and agreed there was something floating nearby.

"Think maybe it them rebels comin' to fight?"

"Don't know, but if it is, we sure 'nuff give 'em one."

William said, "I'm going down. See if I can make contact." He moved quickly and settled in behind a large cypress. He called out, "State your name and password."

No answer.

He repeated this several times, all with the same result.

He fired a shot into the object, but even this did not bring a response.

He waited a few more minutes. The object bumped into the shore. William looked back at his picket companions. They were at the ready with their rifles aimed at the object.

William eased down to the edge of the river and found that the object was merely a clump of weeds and grass that had floated down the river and ended up here. The men had a good laugh and returned to their duties and sleep. The remainder of their duty passed uneventfully, the only company was each other, the bellowing bull frog, and the hooting owl.

Life back at the picket camp was routine, with reveille at six and breakfast at seven. Then mounted couriers would arrive from different directions with written reports of what happened during the night—a boat seen, a picket fired upon, a new battery constructed. These were sent to headquarters, and the couriers were given new orders and passwords and sent off.

They ate alligator and drum fish mostly. Large blackberries were in good supply. Sometimes eggs were available, and the bakery made a good bread. For vegetables, they suffered through very poor sweet potatoes. Beverages were vapid milk and delicious sugar cane syrup brought from Florida. They had visitors daily, and women were especially welcome. After dinner, their evenings were taken with dress parades and drilling.

Over time, William and the others realized it was unlikely the rebels were going to attack, but they continued to remain vigilant. Perhaps their worst enemies at this time were the sand-flies, whose tortuous bites and constant buzzing made their life miserable. At least on picket duty they could swat at them; while on dress parade and while drilling, they were at the flies' mercy.

It was still, however, important to know what the enemy was up to. Both sides would occasionally float down the river in a dugout during the dark of night to get a closer look and, perhaps, to overhear something useful.

Two months into their three-month tour at the picket station, it became William's turn to accompany a small crew on the water. Their instructions were to obtain all possible information about the enemy's position. They pushed off from shore with muffled oars, their eyes straining in the darkness to spot the enemy and their ears straining to listen for any suspicious sounds from shore. And every sound made by someone in the boat—a cough, a movement, a whisper—seemed as though it would arouse the enemy twenty miles away.

After several hours of drifting down the river and learning nothing of value, the men rowed back to shore and disembarked. On the walk back to camp, Captain Perkins commented that these excursions were a waste of time, as they never came up with any information that was of use.

"That true, Cap'n," said William, "but a boat ride better than sittin' in the picket all day."

"Yeah," said Nathan, "but it would be a heap better if one of you was a pretty woman."

To which they all had a hearty laugh.

Captain Perkins, making his rounds of the picket stations, approached the end of the causeway, their most important station. As he approached, he heard a tremendous snore, which caused him to become extremely angry. As he neared with wrath in his soul, William came out and implored him to be quiet. They suspected that a Rebel boat was in the vicinity, and they were trying to lure them onto shore. As it turned out, there were no rebels, and Captain Perkins' wrath melted away.

At times, the two sides exchanged prisoners. On these occasions, a truce was called, which allowed the two sides to meet peacefully to make the exchange. The truce did not sit well with the black troops because there was not a truce for them. In fact, should a black soldier or one of their officers be captured, they were to be given a felon's death according to orders from the Confederates. On this particular evening, an officer from the Confederacy came over to the Union side to retrieve several Southern women who had become intolerable. A Union officer met with him; they exchanged pleasantries as well as cigars before the Confederate officer and the ladies left to return to their side of the river.

As this exchange took place, it was towards the end of picket duty for Nathan and William. Nathan spotted the two men first. "Damn rebels ain't got no business comin' over here. This not how no war is fought."

"Sure would like to shoot that look off his face," William said, scowling.

"These truces just ain't right."

"Look at them. Saluting each other like they on the same side in this war. And giving each other a cigar like they best friends. Nothin' make me madder than seeing this truce."

"An' I tell you what—I sure glad to see them Rebel women go 'cause they be mean bitches. Should jus' put 'em in a boat and make them row across."

"Or make them swim across."

"That even better."

"Ain't no flag of truce for us."

"Nope. They catch one of us, we not gonna be no prisoner. Nope. We be dead."

CHAPTER 36

Hector

It was Sunday afternoon, and Hector was delivering Sally's food. He arrived at the designated spot where he was to lift out the pot that should now be empty, but it didn't feel empty. The food had not been touched.

He didn't see any sign of life—not Sally nor Pete. He crept forward to peer through a crack in the wall. The sight of Sally stunned him. She lay in a pool of blood around her midsection, her face bruised and swollen. *That bastard Pete.* Forgetting caution, Hector rushed in to give aid. He knelt beside Sally, touching her shoulder. She moaned.

"Sally, it's me, Hector."

Sally said, in a garbled voice, "Hector, get out! Pete's here."

Hector surveyed the room. He didn't see Pete. "I can't leave you like this, Miss Sally. I got to get you to the doctor."

"Well, I'll be damned. That same goddam nigger." Pete stood in the doorway, blocking any possible escape. "If I'd a knowed you was meeting a goddam nigger, I'd a killed you, bitch. Now I'm goin' to kill you both."

"Now look here, Mister Pete, I'm just here to help Miss Sally. I don't mean nothing. Why don't you let me get her some help?"

"Shut up! You ain't going nowhere. I got a idea. I'm gonna let you watch your bitch die. Then I'm goin' to kill you. Stand over there." He motioned with his pistol for Hector to move aside."

"Please, sir—"

"Shut up! Move back from her."

Hector took a step back.

"Any bitch of mine that lets a nigger help her don't deserve no bullet." He pointed his finger at Sally. "You let a goddam nigger on my land when I was gone. What else did you do with him? See what I do to nigger-loving sluts."

He worked himself into a frenzy. He holstered his pistol and picked up a chair. He neared Sally, raising the chair over his head. Too weak to defend herself, she closed her eyes and awaited the blow.

With the chair at its peak, Hector jumped between Sally and the chair, moving quickly to absorb the strike. His body smashed into Pete. The chair broke to pieces. Pete and Hector fell to the floor. As they struggled, Pete reached for his gun. He managed to pull it out. Hector grabbed the barrel as they both strained to gain control.

Pete, the experienced fighter, used his left hand to pound Hector in the head with crushing blows. Hector gripped Pete's left wrist, but he was growing weak. His grip on the gun barrel waned. Taking a chance, he let go of Pete's left wrist and lunged, grabbing the gun with both hands. Withstanding Pete's blows, he pushed the barrel towards Pete's head. Pete grabbed the gun, and they pushed against each other, grunting.

Hector managed to roll on top of Pete, slamming his knee into Pete's groin. The painful distraction allowed him to force the gun into Pete's face. Pete groaned. His eyes filled with fear. Hector slowly brought his hand back to the trigger and fired the gun. The bullet pierced Pete's head, killing him instantly.

On the verge of collapse, Hector went to Sally. He knelt beside her.

"Miss Sally, I'm going to make you comfortable and then go for help." He took a blanket from Pete's bedroll and placed it under her head.

"Hector," Sally whispered.

"What is it, Miss Sally?"

"Hide Pete's body," she warned.

He knew that would be smart. If he brought help, and they saw that he had killed a white man, even one as despicable as Pete, it's possible they would kill him.

Hector grabbed Pete's feet and dragged him out and into the bushes. He felt there was no time now to do a better job. He rushed back and placed a blanket over Sally. "I'll be back soon with help. Don't give up."

She raised her hand and touched his wounded face. "Thank you."

Hector mounted Pete's horse and rode for Higgins' farm. Though dangerous to travel the road, he had to get Sally help quickly. If caught, he feared he would be hung, and she would die.

A mile from the farm, Hector came upon two patrollers moving slowly, their backs to him. Surprising them would be his only chance. He pushed the horse into a gallop. Caught off guard, the two men took a moment to realize who had just rushed past them. They took off in pursuit.

Hector had a good start, but his horse was tiring. The patrollers, more experienced riders, drew closer. One of them drew his pistol and fired at Hector. Hector turned in at the Higgins' farm, where John and Martha stood talking in front of the house.

Hector jumped off. "Massa, it's Sally!"

The patrollers arrived, dismounting quickly. One of them grabbed Hector. The other hit him. John grabbed the one hitting and pushed him back.

"What the hell are you doing!" shouted John.

The one holding Hector said, "He went riding fast as blazes past us, so I know he's hiding something."

"Look!" said the other one, "he's got blood all over him. I bet he killed someone and stole his horse!"

"Now just hold on," said John. "Hector, what's going on?"

"Sally's hurt, Massa. I come as fast as I can to get some help. She bleeding real bad."

"John, we must help her. Get these dreadful men out of here, and let's go," said Martha, already running to the barn. "Jacob, Jacob, come fast. Get the buckboard ready. Hurry!"

The patrollers were confused. "Now just a minute—"

"Get off my property now!" John rushed to the barn. "Come on, Hector, show us where she is." Martha, already there, prodded Jacob to hurry with the buckboard.

Disgusted, the patrollers left.

Martha rushed into the shack ahead of John. "Sally," she screamed, upon seeing her daughter lying on the floor.

John knelt beside her, taking Sally's arm. He checked her wrist for a pulse. "She's barely alive."

Martha brushed the hair from her face. "Sally, we're going to get you to the doctor. We love you so much."

Sally's eyes remained closed. She didn't respond.

John said to Hector, "Help me lift her into the buckboard. Very gently, very gently."

Martha sat in the back of the buckboard cradling Sally's head in her lap. She spoke to Sally in soft, hushed tones, hoping for a response of any kind—a sound, eye movement—but none came. John drove as fast as he dared, but he knew the jarring was not good for her. John was terrified. If they lost her, how could they survive such a loss?

They arrived at the doctor's house after what seemed like forever. The doctor instructed them to bring Sally in and put her in the room for his more critical patients. She had bruises to the head, face, and abdomen. She'd lost the baby and a lot of blood, but the doctor thought she would live.

Sally remained at the doctor's house for three days. When her strength returned, she told her story. Pete had returned home drunk and enraged. She could do nothing to calm him. He cursed her for getting pregnant and beat her.

John declared, "I'm going to get that son-of-a-bitch and when I find him, I will kill him."

"No need to worry about that, Papa," Sally assured him. "Pete packed up his gear and left the area for good. He won't dare come back. I know that. Please don't go looking for him."

"All right, I'll stay with you as long as you need me, but I'm not forgetting about him."

"Papa," Sally said, looking up at John, "that day you came to get me, I'm sorry for what I said."

"That's all right," he said. He bent over and kissed her cheek.

"I just want you to know I had to say those things, or Pete would have killed us both."

John took Sally's hand. "Pete won't ever get you again. Don't worry no more about him."

For the next few days, John kept tabs on Pete's place to see if he had returned. On the fourth day, John smelled the stench of death. A short distance into the bushes, a cloud of flies reveled in chaotic commotion. In a palmetto thicket lay Pete's body. The body had dark bloodstains on its face and head. He recalled Hector's bloodstained shirt and surmised that some of the blood on his shirt belonged to Pete. Hector fought Pete to save Sally.

I'll be damned.

John went home and returned with a shovel to bury Pete's body. He then covered the grave with leaves and junk from the yard.

That night he talked with Martha. "I rode out to Pete's place today. I intended to kill him if I found him."

Martha took a breath; her hand rose to her mouth. Then, in a whisper, "What happened?"

"He was already dead. I think Hector killed him that night he found Sally."

Martha's eyes widened.

"I buried the body. Wouldn't want anyone to figure it out. Could be trouble for Hector."

Martha left her bed and went to John. "Poor Hector, what all he's been through."

"Yeah. I can't figure it out. It doesn't make sense. Why would he do that?"

"I don't know, but I am eternally grateful to him. He saved Sally's life."

That night, John sat in the rocker in his bedroom, his mind full of questions. Martha's steady breathing comforted him at first, but soon he no longer heard her. He remembered the black couple who had saved him and fed him while he regained strength. And now Hector. *Hector saved Sally's life. My Sally—the daughter of the man who almost killed his father. Why would he do that?* John considered these questions long into the night but found no satisfactory answer.

The next morning, a weary John put Roscoe in charge of the work details as he and Martha went into town to bring Sally home. Physically, Sally had pretty much mended enough to return home, but her spirits continued to sag. When they returned home, Sally went straight to bed.

"Give her a few days," said Martha. "She will heal."

"I sure hope so," said John, shaking his head.

John left the depressing state of affairs in his house to see how the work outside progressed. He walked along a path leading to an area being cleared by the slaves. As he approached, he heard them talking. He stopped to listen.

"Hey, bring that spade so I can dig these palmettos up."

"Katie's little one had a bad fever last night."

"Yeah, maybe so, but she better get herself out here before Massa come, or she be in a peck o' trouble."

"Let's get this brush cleared. Somebody give me a hand."

Cracking sticks and rustling leaves interrupted John's eavesdropping as someone approached from behind. Katie drew near, carrying one of her small children.

"Morning, Massa John," she said, her voice shaking. "My littlest one here is hot and not so well today. Thought I'd bring her with me to keep an eye out, make sure she be all right. Don't worry none. I'll get my work done just as fast, an' I promise I'll make up the work I missed."

John nodded. Then he reached out and touched the child. "She is hot," he said. "Wish Sarah were here to look after her."

It was an awkward moment for them both. He wondered about going easy on her.

Would the others still respect my authority? Will they still work as hard?

"Yes, sir," Katie said, walking around John into the work area. She laid her child down in the shade and said, "You get better, you hear?" She brushed her hand over the child's head and, after making her comfortable, joined the work crew.

Katie noticed a change in the massa. He seemed more understanding. Perhaps he was just reacting to all the problems with Sally. She had no doubt he would be back to his mean old self in no time.

As a matter of habit, John felt inclined to tell them to get working faster, but he saw they worked as hard as he could expect from anyone. Roscoe worked with a crew mending fences along John's east border. John decided to check on them and come back here later. *Let's see how they do without supervision.*

When he checked later that day, he was in for a surprise.

Well, I'll be damned.

They had done all he had asked and a bit more.

That night at the dinner table, Sally set her fork down and looked at her father. "Papa, I have a request."

"Of course, sweetheart, anything. What is it?"

"Well, Hector risked his life to feed me while I was at Pete's, and then he did it again when he found me…well, he found me like I was. What we owe him, or maybe I should say what I owe him, I can never repay. But you could do something that would repay him. I want you to free him. He deserves more than being a slave. Please, Papa, he—"

"Wait a minute, sweetheart, I can't just free him. Why that could cause all kinds of problems for us. And where would he go? I feel indebted to him, too, but…"

"No, Papa, please. You have to give him his freedom. You don't know how horrible it was to be with Pete. I might have killed myself if it weren't for Hector. His coming bringing me food, it was…was like my connection to you, to the outside world. He was so brave. Pete could have killed him…would have killed him if he had caught—"

"Listen, sweetheart, I know how brave he was, but I can't just—"

Sally, having lost none of her fiery spirit, picked up her plate and slammed it on the table. "Listen, Papa. Listen to me," she shouted. "I will not live here one day longer if I have to watch the person who saved my life live as a slave. If I have to pack my clothes and walk down that road to wherever it takes me, I will do that. This is not up for discussion." She rose quickly, her chair falling back, crashing onto the floor. She dashed into her room, slamming the door, leaving John and Martha speechless. After a few moments, John rose and walked outside.

That evening, John returned after mulling over and over again and again the demand Sally had made. Would she carry out her threat to leave—he had no doubt. She was as bullheaded as anyone he knew.

He slipped into their bedroom, where he found Martha getting ready to retire. She set her comb down and looked at him. "John, where on earth have you been?"

"Been out thinking. Couldn't sit still after what she said."

"I've been thinking about it, too. What do you plan to do?"

He closed his eyes briefly and sighed deeply. "Don't know. I don't know what to do."

"I'll tell you what I think." He was surprised by the hardness of her voice, the strength of it, like there was no compromise, no negotiating. "What I think, John, is that we had three beautiful children not too many months ago, and now we are down to one. Just one. I love Sally." He saw the tears well up in her eyes but heard the conviction in her voice stay strong. "John, listen to me. If Sally leaves, I will leave with her. She is what I am living for."

John stood in stunned silence. Then Martha asked, "Who is Lindi?"

John grabbed a chair to steady himself. "Where did you hear that name?"

"You've said her name in your sleep quite a few times since you returned. When you say Lindi, you seem troubled."

John looked away from Martha. "She was a slave we had when I was a kid. She was beautiful. I liked her. At the time, I thought I might have loved her. But I was just a kid. What did I know about love? She ran away. My father made me whip her. I've always regretted it. In the end, they killed her. She was a good woman."

"You were just a boy then. But now you are a man. Don't make a decision this time you will regret for the rest of your life."

The next morning, John called Hector aside. "Hector, I want you to know that I went to Pete's house the other day and saw Pete's body in the woods. I know that was his blood on you the day you rode in here. I know you killed Pete."

Hector feared this might happen. He had considered sneaking back at night to bury the body. But to do so was a huge risk. What if Todd showed up or Patrollers caught him? But doing nothing—that, too, could be dangerous. Now he wished he had buried Pete. He needed to defend himself, but how? He doubted words could save him. He had killed Pete to save a white girl. So what? It didn't matter. He wanted to flee. But where to?

"No need to explain," said John. "You saved Sally's life. You saved me the trouble of killing him myself. Didn't deserve to live, the way I see it. I buried the body and covered the grave so no one else need ever know. We owe you a great debt, Hector."

Did I hear right? This Massa Higgins buried the white man I killed?

"I'm just happy that Miss Sally is safe and back home," Hector said. His panic eased, but he wondered whether this was all just a trick. He wanted to see Higgins' face, to see if he had an evil smile… and a noose to slip around his neck.

"The misses and I talked over what we should do to repay you. Hector, we're giving you your freedom."

Freedom?

At first it didn't register, like words from a foreign language. He wanted to hear it again. He *needed* to hear it again. For a fraction of a second, he glanced directly at John.

Is he serious?

"We're giving you some land you can live on, and what you earn is yours. You saved Sally's life and risked your own. That's the least we can do for you."

Land? He's giving me land?

"I don't know what to say, Massa."

"Tomorrow, I'll give you a paper that'll state you're free, and I'll show you the land that'll be yours. I can't say enough how grateful we are." But in the back of his mind, John couldn't help but think, *Now we'll find out. Can someone of the African race be successful on his own?*

"Yes, sir. Thank you." Hector tried to make sense of the last few minutes. He'd heard his master's words, but he couldn't believe it, he couldn't feel it—not yet. These moments, when he became a free man, startled him. They would remain hazy in his memory. He dwelt on what freedom meant for him and his future. One clear obstacle dampened his joy—freedom loosened his chains, but still he remained a black man in a white man's world.

"Something the matter, Hector?" asked his mother. "You is acting mighty strange."

"Momma, look at me," said Hector.

"What you talking about, boy? I sees you."

"No, Momma, look at me real good. Do I look different?"

"You is talking crazy now. Of course, you looks just the same now as when you left this morning. Now cut out this here foolish talk, and let me get to my work."

"Momma, I is a free man. A free man, Momma."

"Now you listen to me, Hector," she said, glancing around. She grabbed Hector by his arms. "I done lost one good man 'cause of that kind of talk, and I ain't about to lose another. Please, Hector, please don't start nothing."

"Momma, you don't understand." He moved to Harriet and held her. He took her shoulders, keeping her at arm's length. "Massa done give me my freedom for saving Miss Sally. And he give me some land, too. It all true, Momma."

Harriet had difficulty taking in what she had just heard. "Massa truly give you freedom for helping that poor Miss Sally?"

"That's right, Momma. Now, look at me again, 'cause you is looking at a free man."

Jubilation filled Hector. He let out a cry of joy and danced around his mother. Harriet laughed heartily watching her grown son dance with abandonment.

Played out, Hector stopped and took his mother's hand. "Listen, Momma, I is a free man, and I got me some land. I'm gonna build a nice place for us to live. I'm gonna see if he let you come and live with me. Wouldn't that be good?"

"Yes, Hector, that would be real good. But don't get your hopes up too high, 'cause you know how Massa Higgins can be."

"All right. We'll see."

"Now we better get over to the barn to help with the last bits of work." Then she added, "Or maybe just me."

"I'm going with you," he said. "Don't nobody else know yet. Don't know what to say to everybody."

Harriet never believed that she or any of her children would ever be free. Now her son stood before her a free man. But she remained guarded, for being a free black man in a slave society could be dangerous. Harriet had no doubt that not all of Hector's future would be easy to bear. There would be jealous men, both black and white, and no doubt some of those men would try to force him back into slavery.

Just before the slaves completed their duties, John came into the barn. A hush came over everyone as he stood before them. "I got something I want to say. Hector saved my daughter's life. Most of you already know this. He risked his own life to do it. As a reward to Hector, I've decided to make him a free man. Now, that don't change nothin' for anybody else. I'm giving him some land he can work. The rest of you will need to work harder to make up for him." John left the barn full of doubts about his decisions.

Well, it's done now. Let's see what happens.

After John left, and all the tasks were finished, everyone congregated around Hector, talking about what being free meant and asking what he planned to do. Hector explained that he would be growing crops and building a home on the land Massa had given him.

They all wanted to help him build his cabin and, in fact, would do so every Sunday. When the talk slowed, someone started a song, and soon they all sang in celebration. The high spirits continued well into the night in spite of the prospect of an early start in the morning. They danced in honor of Hector, but they also danced for themselves. Freedom had now become a possibility.

"Hey, Hector, is you gonna buy some slaves now for yourself?"

"Maybe you buys me. Is you gonna be a mean massa?"

"Hector gonna have to wash that black off his skin and be like the white folks."

The teasing went back and forth for a short time, but after a while they all rejoiced for Hector, even as they yearned for freedom for themselves.

In the morning, Roscoe told Hector to report to the massa at the house. John met Hector as he approached the house.

"Morning, Hector."

"Morning, Massa."

"Hector, folks around here are going to ask for proof that you're free if they see you walking in town or along this road. This note I'm giving you states that I have given you your freedom. Carry it always, and show it to whoever asks for it." John read the note, then handed it to him. The paper read:

> "This former African slave, a dark-skinned Negro, of approximately six feet in height, weighing approximately 180 pounds, with no visible scars or marks, well spoken, and who answers to the name of Hector, is hereby on this 10th day of June of the year 1864 A.D. given his freedom by his owner John Higgins."
>
> Signed by John Higgins

Hector examined the note briefly, then folded it and stuck it in a pocket. He recognized the letters and many of the words, but he put it away quickly. "Thank you, sir." He tried hard to suppress a smile but found it was impossible.

"Let's go take a look at your land," said John. "I've staked out what I figure to be two acres. It's at the north end and sits on the road. There's plenty of trees to make a little cabin. And the land is good. I think you can make a decent garden with it."

John showed Hector the stakes he had placed to indicate his boundaries. Hector noted the tall pines that would become his very own cabin.

"You can borrow my tools and a mule until you're able to get your own."

"Thank you, sir. You're being very good to me."

"I'll be getting back now. You want a ride back, or you plan to stay here for a while?"

"I guess I'll be staying, if it's all the same to you, Massa."

"Don't reckon you need to call me 'master' anymore."

Though it seemed awkward to him, he replied, "Yes, sir, Mr. Higgins."

"You can stay with your mother until you finish building. And you're free to eat with the others until you get some crops in."

"Thank you, Mr. Higgins, sir."

Hector explored his land. The dirt belonged to him. The scrubs, the trees, palmettos, perhaps the birds, maybe even the sky—all his. How he wished his father could be here. He ran his hands along the rough bark of a pine. Plenty of straight, tall trees. And once he cleared the land, he would plant his own crops. *His* crops.

He thought of practical things, like where he would build, where he would plant, and how he would get Mr. Higgins to agree to let Momma come live with him. But his father stood uppermost in his mind. His father, who understood that the risks could never be too great a price for freedom.

Hector never again lived in the slave quarters. Until he completed his own place, he would sleep on his land under the stars. For his protection, he built his cabin well back from the road and left plenty of trees between the road and cabin.

Hector showed his freedom paper to his friends, even though they couldn't read it. Each one asked to hold it, as though it held some powerful magic. Silas handed the note back to Hector with this warning: "Be careful, Hector. Keep this note with you all the time. I heard of one freed man what was knocked over the head and his note burned. Then he taken somewhere else that he not knowed and sold. He never heard from again."

The next morning, Hector trapped a rabbit. He skinned it and roasted it over an open fire. He cured the skin and later cut it into a rectangle larger than the note. He folded the note into the skin to protect it from the weather. He hoped he would be wise enough to keep it safe.

Later that day, John considered Martha's words of the previous night. Her question triggered a flash of insight: the woman with the piercing eyes in his nightmare was Lindi. Why hadn't he understood that before now? And the monster? He shuddered, realizing he was his monster. He was filled with shame. He stood still, eyes closed, contemplating his years and how he had lived them.

CHAPTER 37

William

William and Nathan walked together towards the *John Adams*. They were about to board her to make another excursion up a river, this time to blow up a bridge supporting the Charleston and Savannah Railway.

"Let me ask you somethin', William. Is we in the navy or the army, 'cause it shore do seem like we on a boat lot more than marchin' around on land."

"You got that right, Nathan. But I thinks I like getting to these places more by boat than marching so far."

"I agree with that. Yessir, marchin' all up an' down this coast shore don't sound good to my feets."

"Yeah, and don't forget what Colonel Higginson said."

"What you thinking about?"

"He say we might be able to free a bunch of slaves since we going inland. That's where all the mens what owned them went when the Union come here."

"That right. Shore would be nice to free 'em. Ain't right, keeping slaves."

"Yeah, and maybe we get more recruits."

They would have to go up river thirty miles to reach the black population, and it would be necessary to navigate at night, as the smoke from the steamboat could be seen from a great distance. Also, they would need a full moon and a flood tide, as the river was often shallow, winding, and muddy.

"This won't be the first time we done this. We getting pretty good at it."

"That's right. We just show up when the sun come up and surprise 'em. They never even knowed we was coming."

Once all the men were aboard, Higginson laid out the approach. "We believe there are rice plantations about twenty miles from the coast still being worked by slaves. A battery is protecting the area from a place called Wiltown Bluffs. Also, they put obstacles of wooden pilings across the river.

"We'll take the *John Adams* and an armed ferry boat to Wiltown Bluff, silence the battery, and clear a way through the obstructions. Then I'll take a small group of you in two light-draft boats down the smaller stream about ten miles to the bridge and burn it. The *John Adams* will stay behind to keep the Wilmont battery from falling into enemy hands. Any questions?"

There being no questions, everyone settled in—the action would start soon enough.

They arrived at Wilmont Bluff at four in the morning. They fired their first shell into the battery. The battery returned fire very quickly, but after only three shells, fell silent. The crew aboard the *John Adams* couldn't tell why, nor could they see the battery due to the woods. The decision was made to land and investigate.

Higginson looked across the rice fields that lay beneath the bluffs and saw that the meadows had come alive with human heads. Along the paths, there was a file of men and women all on the run for the river.

The plantation owner had yelled at them, *"The Yankees are coming. Quick, run and hide in the woods, or they will grab you and sell you in Cuba."*

And run they did, right past the owner and to the boats.

Higginson went ashore with a boatload of troops. The astonished Negroes helped pull the boat ashore. They kept arriving, increasing the crowd, jostling, mutually clinging. Soon, they began coming from the houses also, with bundles on their heads. Old women, trotting on the narrow path, would kneel to pray then would suddenly spring up, urged by the accumulating procession behind. As they reached the boats, every human being grasped a hand of one of their rescuers and exclaimed, "Bless you, mas'r," and "Bless de Lord."

Women brought children on their shoulders, and little boys brought brothers on their backs. Yet Higginson and the other officers were a little impatient at all this piety, for they needed to learn how many soldiers were on the bluff and if they were still there. But the Negroes were too absorbed in their freedom to be of any help.

Captain Perkins recruited William, along with nineteen other soldiers, to take control of the bluff. They moved cautiously, but when they arrived found only a hastily abandoned camp amid scattered equipment and suggestions of a very unattractive breakfast. The bluff being abandoned allowed the crew to set about removing the wooden pilings blocking the river's passage. The work was hard and time consuming, so much so, that they saw their window of a surprise attack on the bridge slipping away.

All day the rebels fought occasional skirmishes with the men on shore while the Negroes ran to the river and were transported aboard the steamer. As ordered, the soldiers burned the rice houses but not the dwellings.

At last, a passage was cleared. The tide turned by noon, so they began ascending the river to the bridge, leaving the *John Adams* and a small group from the regiment to secure the bluff. But the tide remained too low, and after running aground several times, they had to turn back. They waited an hour and tried again. This time, they were able to continue along the river, giving them high hopes of achieving their goal. But it grew more difficult by the minute, and eventually, two miles from the bridge, Higginson's boat ran aground on a mud bank. He waved the other boat, a tug that moved on unhindered by the shallow water, to continue on and finish the job.

When the tug rounded a point, it became engaged with rebel batteries. Higginson could not help, nor could he see what was happening. The men tried moving from side to side to rock the boat to dislodge it. At last, the stern of the boat moved around, and the gunner reported that he could fire on the battery, but it would be necessary to shoot away the corner of the cabin. Higginson told him to fire away. Then they spotted the tug adrift, its engine disabled and their engineer killed. Finally, Higginson's boat got off the mud bar, but their engine, too, gave up. All they could do was to follow the others where the tide carried them.

Now a new danger faced them with a battery firing at them from a bluff they were approaching. Fortunately, they were in a boat with a thin hull, so the shells went through the boat and exploded in the water. The danger that a shell might hit the machinery or strike below the waterline never happened.

They later found that fifteen projectiles had gone through the boat, a few causing casualties that were instantly fatal. Higginson suddenly felt a blow to his side, having been grazed by a ball. It made his side black and blue and gave him the sensation of paralysis. He found it difficult to stand. Higginson put Captain Trowbridge in charge, and he, exhausted and in pain, sought rest.

Every corner of the boat was filled with bedding and bundles, along with the now freed men, women, and children. They were ill, or asleep, or talking among themselves, or singing or praying.

They encountered another battery on their return voyage, and the Quartermaster kept bringing Higginson news of what was happening. Finally, in the morning, they reached Beaufort after thirty-six hours of absence. At the wharf, the prisoners, the wounded, and the dead were dutifully attended. The black regiment returned to their camp to await their next orders.

CHAPTER 38

Sally

Sally recovered physically, but her spirits did not. She often stayed in bed, refusing food, bathing, and conversation. She reflected upon her ruined life. She found talking with her parents difficult. She could stand firm and be unyielding, as she did regarding freeing Hector, but by and large she was unhappy. Any future she had dreamed of, any hope to marry and have a family, seemed impossible now.

Sally sat on the back porch helping Harriet prepare vegetables for dinner when Harriet said to her, "I sometimes gets down, too. Just like you."

"I don't think anyone can get as low as I am."

"Oh Lord, yes, child. I've known sorrowful times." Harriet stopped, the knife in one hand, the half-peeled potato in the other. She gazed out into the back yard, seeing images of her past. "You not alone when it come to losing something important in life." She went back to peeling. "But when I'm sad, I just gets busy. I gets my mind off me. And you know what helps the most? When I gets busy helping someone else. That's when I really gets to feeling better."

The next evening, Sally walked along a familiar path where, in more innocent times, she had run and played carefree. Now she walked deliberately, absorbed in her thoughts. She walked past a group of slaves working in a field but did not respond to their greetings. She arrived at the lake, where she sat looking out over the water. High above, an eagle circled on outstretched wings searching for dinner. To her right, there was a timid deer, frozen in place. Her large, brown eyes fixed on Sally. Sally, preoccupied with ugly memories and destroyed dreams, questioned what possible meaning her life could have. The eagle circled lower and lower, then suddenly, swooping down, his talons brushed the water. When he flapped his wings and rose, the glint of a silver fish trapped in his claws reflected a burst of sunlight. Sally's chest heaved. She sighed and muttered, "How unlucky to be a fish, and how wretched to be me." Her eyes followed the hapless fish as the eagle rose and flew over the treetops out of sight.

Sally had seen enough. She brushed off her dress and headed back to the house. Along the way, she met Hector.

"Good morning, Miss Sally. Sure is good to see you out."

"Hello, Hector. I haven't really thanked you for saving me."

"Well, that's—"

"Oh, and I'm real happy about my father giving you your freedom and some land. You really deserve it."

"Thank you, Miss Sally."

She watched him walk away and muttered, "It would have been better if you had just let me die."

From a living room window, Martha watched Sally wander aimlessly. She said to John, "What are we going to do with her? She sulks around like her life's at its end."

Harriet stood outside washing clothes. A sharp pain made her wince. She wiped her soapy hands on her apron and reached around with her left hand to rub her back. She shook her head at the pile of dirty clothes yet to be washed and waved at seeing Sally. "Good morning, Miss Sally."

Absorbed in her thoughts, Sally paid no attention to Harriet.

Not to be so easily ignored, Harriet moved to stand in Sally's path with her hands on her hips. "Now listen here, young lady. I knows you been through some mighty rough times, but so has we all. I suspects it's about time for you to stop feeling sorry for yourself and get on with living 'cause you is just making life miserable for everyone." Harriet then brushed past Sally, returning to her wash.

Sally swirled to face Harriet, her hands clenched in fists. She raised her head skyward, where huge white clouds drifted by and in the distance, gray ones holding rain. A breeze kissed her face. Life seemed so hard. She held her arms tightly around herself to keep from falling apart. She walked a few steps to the edge of a thicket of pines.

Turning her head in Harriet's direction, her voice barely audible, she said, "I hate what I've done to my family, what I put Hector through. I don't deserve to be alive."

She started to leave when Harriet called out.

"Miss Sally."

Sally stopped but did not face Harriet.

Harriet called out again, "Miss Sally."

Sally walked listlessly to Harriet.

Harriet said, "We all loves you, Miss Sally. You done some foolish things, and some terrible things happen to you, but you is a strong woman."

She took Sally's face in her hands and said, "I loves you. You been good to me. You was good to my man, William, an' my boy, Hector. That take courage."

She put her arms around Sally, and Sally eagerly put her arms around Harriet. The two hearts bound to each other, beating each to its own rhythm, providing life to these two women whose circumstances were so different, yet they gave so much to each other.

Their embrace relaxed, and their eyes met. Sally said, "Everything is so hard."

"Well, you ain't got to let it be hard all by yourself."

A few days later, Harriet returned to her quarters, where an aroma instantly revealed how hungry she felt. On her table stood a pot she recognized from the big house kitchen. She lifted the cover. The smells filled her senses. She shook her head and smiled, knowing Sally had been making this dish in the kitchen and was the reason she kept shooing Harriet out. Beside the pot of chicken stew lay a loaf of fresh bread wrapped in a linen napkin.

Harriet sat at her table and said aloud, "Lord, child, you don't know how tired I am tonight. This going to taste mighty good."

The next morning, Harriet winked at Sally when she came into the kitchen and said, "Somebody around here is getting to be a mighty fine cook."

"Well, somebody around here deserves a good meal," said Sally, as she stepped over to give Harriet a big hug.

John hollered from the dining room, "Am I going to get any breakfast this morning?"

Harriet reluctantly released herself and finished up John's breakfast.

Sally quipped, "Some things never change."

Harriet observed her go out of the kitchen and heard her say, "Now Papa, I was talking with Harriet, so you will just have to be a little patient this morning."

Harriet chuckled. She hummed to herself. *It's going to be a good day.*

CHAPTER 39

Hector

Hector soon realized he would need money to purchase seed, tools, and other essentials. He considered all his options, finally deciding on one that seemed his only real possibility—though not something he felt safe about doing. He decided to ask John for a job. He approached John with caution.

"Good morning, Mr. Higgins. If you have just a moment, sir, I would like a word with you."

"All right, Hector, what's on your mind?"

"Well, Mister Higgins, sir, now that I owns land, I needs a way to make some money, especially as how I won't have any crops in for a while. I was thinking that maybe I could work for you for wages." Hector spoke calmly, hoping he appeared relaxed.

John didn't answer right away. He took his hat off, wiping his brow with his sleeve. After chewing over Hector's request, he said, "All right. I'll pay you wages. But just until your first crops come in."

Monday through Saturday, Hector worked for John. At the end of the day, and on Sundays, Hector cut trees and cleared land for crops. On most Sundays, the enslaved men spent some of their free time helping. They built his cabin in thirty days.

John kept a close eye on all that transpired. After a few weeks, he began to relax, as Hector's owning land and receiving wages didn't affect the slaves' work or attitude.

Several months after freeing Hector, John traveled into town for provisions. Two men approached him.

"John, we need to talk with you about that so-called free nigger you got livin' on your land."

"Make it quick, boys. I got lots to do."

"We don't like the idea of free niggers in these parts. It gets the others a bit agitated. Hell, they're already riled up over this damn war. We don't need something else to get 'em riled up even more."

John placed the bag of flour into the buckboard, then faced the two men.

"What's done is done, and I ain't undoing it. That boy earned his freedom, and he's not making trouble for anybody. I don't think you got anything to worry about from one free nigger. If you want to fret about something, this war should do it. If it keeps going the way it is, you won't have any slaves anyway. That'll give us all something to worry about."

The men left, scowling.

On his way home, John decided to tell Hector about the confrontation in town and warn him to be careful. He had been satisfied with the way Hector's freedom had worked out. Hector working alongside the slaves kept everyone peaceful. His slaves saw that even with freedom, they had to work, and Hector chose to work with John.

Hector's eyes snapped open, his sleep shattered by someone pounding on his door. John's warning leapt to his mind. He jumped out of bed and grabbed a thick piece of firewood to defend himself.

He shouted, "Who's out there?"

"Hector, it's me, Jackson. Let me in 'fore someone sees me."

Hector recognized the raspy voice of Jackson, a slave from down the road. He didn't know him very well. Aware this could be a trick, he tightened his grip on his weapon and cautiously raised the cross bar. The hinges creaked when he opened the door a crack. Jackson pushed his way in. He slammed the door shut behind him.

"What's took you so long? You want me to get caught?"

"Never know who be on the other side of the door."

"Listen, Hector, I'm running away. My master done sold my wife to a man in Georgia. I'm going there to be with her. Ain't right they sell a man's wife."

"So why you coming to see me?"

"You can write me a pass so I can get past them patrollers."

"Why you think I can write a pass?"

Jackson grinned. "You think you smart hiding that you can read. But I smart, too. One day, when you and Roscoe come to get them plows from my massa, I seen you looking at the paper on the chair. You didn't know I was there, but I seen you. I figger if you can read, you can write, too."

This could be a trap. It wouldn't be the first time a slave had laid a trap for another in order to get special favors for himself. He could lose everything he had, including his life. On the other hand, he believed in helping his friends. If he had been given the opportunity to read and write, then shouldn't he use it to help others? The answer wasn't clear.

"Jackson, would you betray me?"

"'Course not, Hector. I ain't that kind of man. You got to believe me. I just wants to be with my wife. And I'm going to, whether you gives me the paper or not. I just figures it'll be a whole lot easier with that paper."

Hector wasn't sure why, but he believed him. "I'll write you a note, but you gots to promise never to tell who give it to you."

"You got my word, Hector."

Dreadful images of hangings and beatings hung heavy in Hector's mind. "I need you to step outside. Go around back where you can't be seen if someone come riding down the road.

"Why you want me to go outside?"

"I just needs to protect myself as best I can, that's all."

With Jackson outside, Hector pulled a loose stone from his fireplace and withdrew a pencil and paper.

He sat at his table thinking how he might write a note giving Jackson safe passage all the way to Georgia. He decided to write a note giving him his freedom. He based the note on the one John had given him.

When he finished, he called Jackson back inside. "Please, in the name of God, if you get caught, don't tell it was me that give it to you."

"I done say I won't. I ain't gonna lie to you."

He sent Jackson away quickly. That night, Hector feared another knock, this one by men with a noose. When dawn came, he relaxed some. By now, Jackson should be far away.

The day passed slowly, every minute dragging on with possible discovery. By sundown, Hector believed he could stop worrying.

The following day, Hector was working in the barn when a buckboard pulled up to the big house. A rough looking white man drove the buckboard and another rode alongside. As they moved past the barn, Hector saw something in the buckboard covered with a canvas. John came outside and spoke with the two men. Hector couldn't hear what they said, but the tone led him to believe that the conversation was not friendly. The man riding the horse took a paper from his shirt pocket and showed it to John. John read it and shoved it back at the man. The three men went to the back of the buckboard, and the one with the paper lifted the canvas. Hector could make out the feet of a man. After another brief discussion, the men left. John looked toward the barn. He took his hat off and hit it against his leg exclaiming, "Damn, damn, damn!" and walked towards the barn.

"Hector!" he hollered, as he reached the barn door.

Trying to be composed, Hector responded, "Yes, sir, Mr. Higgins."

"Hector, those two men who were just here caught a nigger try-ing to run away, and he had a forged paper giving him freedom. Now how do you think he got such a paper?"

"I don't know, Mr. Higgins." Hector was annoyed that his voice trembled.

"I'll tell you how. You gave it to him, didn't you?" John said, scowling.

"Why, no, sir. You knows I can't read or write. How would I do such a thing?"

"Those two men claim that before he died, he told them you wrote the note. 'Course, I don't know whether to believe them or not. One of them is the one who came up to me in town a while back and complained about you being free. You're sure in a heap of hot water now. I'm sure we haven't heard the last of this. I hope you're tellin' me the truth."

"Yes, sir. I be telling the truth."

John looked into Hector's eyes. "You watch your step. Those two men are dangerous, and they don't like you being free."

Hector felt saddened about Jackson, but his own safety became his most immediate concern. He thought about the pen, paper, and speller hidden in his cabin. He had a strong urge to run home to get rid of them, but that would only raise suspicion.

Continuing his work in the barn, he ripped out the rotted boards. He wondered if he was somehow to blame for Jackson's death. Could he have written the wrong words? He knew his read-ing needed vast improvement. His writing needed even more. *Never again,* he vowed.

When he returned home, Hector removed the paper, pencil, and speller from the fireplace. They had all been gifts from Sally. To preserve them, he wrapped them in a leather hide and buried them in a corner of his garden. He had no plans to retrieve any of it for some time.

That night, and for a time after, he slept in the woods instead of inside. If a mob came for him, he wouldn't have a chance if caught in the cabin. But in the woods, he could slip away before they found him.

Two days later, in town buying supplies, John recognized the brown horse with black spots on its rump as belonging to one of the men complaining about Hector. The horse, tied to the post in front of the saloon, caused John to worry that the man might be drinking and getting worked up to do something about Hector.

He pulled the buckboard over and went in. The two men stood at the bar talking to four others. The taller of the two, Earl, saw John first. He nudged his partner and pointed in John's direction. All eyes turned to John.

"Well, well, if it isn't John Higgins hisself," said Earl. "And what do you have to say in defense of your nigger?"

"You still harping on that note?"

"That note could get a nigger killed," said a burly, squat man standing with the others.

"Listen, men. You know if I thought for one minute that any nigger on my place had written that note, I'd be with you. But I can honestly say that none of my workers can read or write, including Hector. I have never let them get anywhere close to a book or any kind of schooling. He couldn't have done it. Whatever that runaway told you, he must have said it to get you to stop beating him."

"That's a lie!" said Earl. The other man, Collin, nodded in agreement.

Earl began waving the note in the air and calling for others to join him in lynching Hector.

At this time, the sheriff, Robert Wilkinson, walked in. His booming voice penetrated every inch of the saloon. "Men, let me have your attention." He approached Earl and the group of men around him at the bar. "I understand that you two have been trying to get up a vigilante group to take the law into your own hands. Further, that you two are claiming that the dead man told you one of Higgins' slaves wrote him a note. That right so far?"

"That's right, Sheriff," said Earl. "'Cept it weren't a slave, it were that free nigger Higgins got." The other men nodded their heads.

"Now here's the problem I'm having," said the sheriff, turning his attention to the man with Earl. "Collin, I heard last night that you were in here drinking and you told several people that the dead nigger never said anything about who gave him the note. Now isn't that correct?"

"Um, well, Sheriff—" stuttered Collin, looking nervously over at Earl.

"Don't lie to me, Collin. I have several witnesses, so be careful what you say. Lie to me, I'll slap you in jail."

"Sheriff, it's like this. Higgins has got this nigger he freed. An' when we caught this other one with the note, Earl thought it would be the ideal way to get rid of the free nigger."

"Shut up, Collin! You ain't got to go an' tell everything! What's the matter with you?" shouted Earl.

The sheriff turned and addressed the small group, "Okay, men, this whole thing has been a lie. There is nothing here to get riled up about. So just go on about your day and forget this whole thing."

The men glared at Collin and Earl and went back to their drinking.

The sheriff turned to Collin and Earl. "Now if anything happens to that nigger of Higgins, I'll come hunting the two of you. It's best you forget this whole thing." He spoke to John. "You got anything to say about this?"

"No, Sheriff. I reckon it's all settled. Right, boys?"

Collin said, "Yeah. I'm done with it. It was a stupid idea anyway." He stepped to the bar and ordered a drink.

Earl grabbed his hat off the table and started to say something to Collin. The sheriff spoke first. "Just let it go, Earl. Why don't you go outside and cool off?"

John said, "Thanks for the help, Sheriff. It was beginning to turn ugly."

"I can't tell you how to run your business, but having a free nigger sure does stick in the craw of a lot of folks around here."

Back at his place, John approached Hector. "I think this whole business about you writing the note is settled. Apparently, you never were named as the one who wrote it. Even so, you best keep your eyes open. Some men don't like you being free, and they're liable to come after you."

"Yessir, Mr. Higgins. Thank you, sir."

After a month of sleeping in the woods, Hector returned to staying indoors. He debated going North, where he had heard all blacks were free, but he didn't want to leave his mother with no family. He changed his mind about her living with him. Freedom didn't come with safety.

CHAPTER 40
William

In June of 1864, the Regiment was ordered to Folly Island. They remained there and on Cole's Island until the siege of Charleston was finished. It took part in the battle of Holly Hill and in the capture of a fort on James' Island.

In February 1865, the Regiment was ordered to Charleston to do guard duty; in March, to Savannah; in June, to Hamburg and Aiken; and in September, to Charleston and its neighborhood.

Daily Chronicle

WAR COMES TO AN END!!

April 9, 1865
General Robert E. Lee surrenders to General Ulysses S. Grant at Appomattox Courthouse in Virginia. A costly four years, with 625,000 lives lost…

After the war, the commander of the First South Carolina Regiment (later changed to the Thirty-Third United States Colored

Troops) Colonel Higginson wrote the following: *We who served with the black troops have this peculiar satisfaction, that, whatever dignity or sacredness the memories of the war may have to others, they have more to us…. But the peculiar privilege of associating with an outcast race, of training it to defend its rights and to perform its duties, this was our special meed… We had touched the pivot of the war. Whether this vast and dusky mass should prove the weakness of the nation or its strength, must depend in great measure, we knew, upon our efforts. Till the blacks were armed, there was no guaranty of their freedom. It was their demeanor under arms that shamed the nation into recognizing them as men.*

𝔇𝔞𝔦𝔩𝔭 ℭ𝔥𝔯𝔬𝔫𝔦𝔠𝔩𝔢

President Lincoln Killed

April 15, 1865
President Lincoln was shot on April 14 while attending a play at Ford's Theatre. He died the following day. Vice President Andrew Johnson becomes president.

On February 9, 1866, the Regiment was mustered out of service after being detained beyond its three years, so great was the need for troops.

"Nathan, what you gonna do now that we is out of the army?"

"Don't know for sure. What I do know is that I'm gonna live in the North. Them peoples in the South ain't gonna treat us so good. Nope, don't believe they will. What about you, William?"

"Headin' to Florida. Gonna find my family, get us some land, work for ourselves. Shore will feel good."

"You crazy. Secesh ain't gonna sell you no land. You got money in your pocket, but you never have enough to buy you some land. Them secesh don't want our kind unless we slaves. You better be careful on them roads, too. You ain't no white man." Nathan reached over and grabbed William's arm. "Look at your skin. It be black as night. They see you ridin' a horse and carrying a rifle and pistol...what you think they gonna do? You think they gonna be happy to see you on a horse and with guns? Hell! They gonna kill you right off. You better get some sense in that head of yours."

The day before they were to be mustered out of the army, Captain Perkins called his company together. "Men, you've heard all the speeches of thanks and congratulations from officers higher up than me, but I want to add my compliments to you all. It has been my pleasure to serve with you. You're a fine bunch of men, and don't let anyone tell you different. Now, anyone have any comments or questions?"

Nathan spoke first. "Cap'n Perkins, you been a good captain to us an' the first white man ever treated me right. I'm headed to your state, Massachusetts, where I hope I never have to lay eyes on another secesh again long as I lives."

Several others spoke, and then William said, "Cap'n Perkins, I plan to go to Florida to find my family. I plan to buy a rifle and pistol and a horse. Nathan here think I be crazy."

Nathan jumped into the conversation. "He gonna get killed by them secesh ridin' around with guns. War be over, but them secesh ain't changin'. They only wants us for their slaves. They don't care 'bout nothin' else."

All eyes went to Captain Perkins, who paused to think for a few moments. "Nathan's got a point. South Carolina and probably other states are passing new laws to keep you in something like slavery. You have to have proof that you have a job or you could be arrested and then rented out to a white man. You would be required to work for him until you paid off what it cost him to rent you, plus pay for the food and place to stay while you worked for him. Of course, you might never earn enough to reimburse him, so you—"

"That just like slavery!" All the men yelled and talked at once. "That not right; seem like we didn't even win no war." "Better not try arrest me!"

When the men's voices calmed, Captain Perkins spoke again. "So the point is you all need to be careful travelling. We're in South Carolina now, so no matter where you're headed, you'll be in danger for some time. I think riding a horse is okay—I have seen a few black men on horseback—but carrying a gun openly is risky. Travelling in a group is a good idea, and there are plenty of groups on the roads. Keep your eyes and ears alert. If you see or hear a group coming toward you, jump in the woods and hide until you know if they are friendly.

"I know some of you will be looking to find family members. I have a couple of suggestions for you, and I'm sure you know that finding family members will be difficult. I'm not trying to discourage you, and I know how important it is. I admire you all for making this a priority. It's what I would do if I were in your shoes. I can think of two suggestions. If you have some idea what town they are in, put an ad in the newspaper. A lot of freed slaves are doing this, and many are attending schools set up by the Freedmen's Bureau. But I think it's a long shot. Do it anyway. It might pay off. The other suggestion is to go to the land office and look for anyone registering to homestead land with your family member's name. Even if it's just their first name. See what you can find. Most of you attended the chaplain's reading and writing classes, so hopefully you can read the names registered so long as the writing is clear. My last suggestion is to check with the Freedmen's Bureau—maybe they can help.

"If any of you are going south, let me know. We have a boat going to the St. Mary's area in two days. I'm sure you remember our little visit there a few years back. I'll try to get you on board. We also have a boat going north to Virginia. Let me know if you want to get on board that one. If there are no further questions, you're dismissed. I wish you all a safe journey."

Two days later, William boarded the steamer headed for St. Mary's. He was the only one of his company to go south. He was grateful for this boat ride—it would save him much time and travel and was, by far, safer. He had purchased a pistol, which he kept hidden under his shirt, and a rifle, which he hid in his bedroll. He would buy a horse the first chance he got. He settled in on the boat as it glided smoothly along.

It was a strange feeling, this being free, not belonging to John Higgins or to the army. It felt glorious…and frightening.

I am an American. I fought a war to be free, and we were victorious. And yet, I am a Negro. Hated by many in the South. Not free at all, according to the laws in the South Captain Perkins told us about. How can I be American and Negro? Am I free or not? What are my rights? Can I buy land?

He took a deep breath of the sea air and decided for himself. *I am free, and I am American.* He whispered to himself, "If anyone wants to take this from me, let them try.

His mind then shifted back to the first time he'd made this journey along with others in the black regiment. This time there was no anticipating a fight with the secesh, no war to fight. But perhaps travelling alone through the South would prove to be even more dangerous. Even so, at long last he had begun the search for his family.

CHAPTER 41

John

On May 25, 1865, a company of Union soldiers turned into the Higgins' farm. Every slave stopped work to admire and wonder at this group of all colored soldiers accompanied by a white company commander. A black corporal ordered them to halt when they reached the house. The noise of the advancing company brought Martha from the house. The corporal tipped his hat to her and asked that she ring the bell to summon everyone to the house. Offended at receiving orders from a black Union soldier, she did not comply. The soldier's eyes locked onto hers, something she had never experienced before, and she thought better of her refusal. She stepped to the bell and pulled the cord five times. Something about this colored soldier seemed familiar, but she couldn't determine why.

John came running to the house. "What the hell is going on?" He stopped short upon seeing Martha's worried look and a company of black Union soldiers.

When everyone had gathered, the black soldier giving orders dismounted and walked up the steps to the porch, ignoring John. He turned to face the others. At that moment, Jacob recognized him and yelled out, "Richard!" which brought immediate recognition from everyone else. Their friend, the runaway slave, had returned to them.

"It's good to see you again," he began, his voice solemn and formal. "We have come to tell you that the war has ended. On April 10, 1865, General Lee surrendered to General Grant. President Abraham Lincoln has declared that all slaves are free!" He then read the Emancipation Proclamation to them. "You is as free as any white man. You can choose to leave here or not. The choice is up to you. There are no more slaves."

When Richard came down from the porch, the now freedmen and women crowded around him talking and asking questions. After a few minutes of getting reacquainted, Richard said, "Got to say goodbye. We going farm to farm spreadin' the news."

After the troops left, the former slaves stood facing John and Martha. Neither former slaves nor former masters knew what to say to each other. Several minutes passed before John stepped forward. "I reckon you're free to go if you want. But you're welcome to stay here where you've got a roof over your head, and we'll feed you. You ain't got no place to go, so you might as well stay."

John took Martha's arm and led her into the house. Once inside, he collapsed in a chair. "Now what are we gonna do? If they leave us, we're done for. The crops will rot in the field."

"And those poor people?" said Martha. "They'll starve to death if they leave."

The former slaves gathered in the clearing in front of their shanties. They sat in a circle, some on the ground, others on tree stumps or rickety chairs.

"What we going do now?" asked Wiley.

"Me an' my family," said Silas, glancing at Katie, "we leaving. Going to find us a job working for wages. With all these men leaving their masters, there be plenty a work for us."

"You think Higgins give us wages if we stay?" asked Roscoe.

"Don't know," said Silas. "Don't much care either. Had me enough of Old Man Higgins. Got too many bad memories to hang around here." Many nodded their heads to this, and there were murmurs of "ain't that right."

Soon the mood turned festive, with singing and dancing into the night. John observed their celebration and thought, *This whole country's going to hell.*

In the morning, John stood in the door of his house watching large numbers of blacks travel up and down the road. The quarters remained quiet, abandoned, no sign of anyone. By this time, the fields usually bustled with workers. Not this morning. John walked to the quarters, peeked inside each cabin, and verified his fear.

He wondered had Hector gone with the others or stayed. He wanted to find out. He hoped Hector had stayed. He needed Hector. He didn't understand why, but Hector had become important to him. When he saw Hector and his mother working in their field, he waved, relieved.

John asked Hector to continue working at the farm. Hector agreed, but not before negotiating fewer working hours and a higher hourly wage. "I needs more time to tend my own farm," he told John. Over time, John hired other freedmen who had come by seeking work.

Change and uncertainty ruled the day.

Daily Chronicle

April 1866

Congress passes the Civil Rights Act

This Act establishes that all persons born in the United States to be citizens, "without distinction of race or color, or previous condition of slavery or involuntary servitude." President Johnson vetoed it, but the Congress overrode his veto. The states will need to ratify it.

Lots of niggers was kilt after freedom, 'cause the slaves in Harrison County turn loose right at freedom and them in Rusk County wasn't. But they hears about it and runs away to freedom in Harrison County and they owners have 'em bushwhacked, that shot down. You could see lots of niggers hangin' to trees in Sabine bottom right after freedom, 'cause they catch 'em swimmin' 'cross Sabine River and shoot 'em. They sure am goin' be lots of soul cry against 'em in Judgement!...

—Susan Merritt, age at interview, 87 (Voices from Slavery, p. 226)

I don't know what the ex-slaves expected, but I do know they didn't get anything. After the war we just wandered from place to place, working for food and a place to stay. Now and then we got a little money, but a very little. I only voted once in my life and that was when working for Mr. Gerhart. He was a real estate dealer and he taken me to the polls and showed me how to vote for a Republican president. It has been so long ago I don't even remember who the president was, but I do know he got elected. I think the time will soon be when people won't be looked on as regards to whether you are black or white, but all on the same equality. I may not live to see it but it is on the way. Many don't believe it, but I know it.

—Delicia Patterson, age at interview, 92
(Voices from Slavery, p. 241)

CHAPTER 42
William

𝔇𝔞𝔦𝔩𝔶 ℭ𝔥𝔯𝔬𝔫𝔦𝔠𝔩𝔢

May 3, 1866 Memphis, Tennessee
For three days, mobs of white men have attacked black neighborhoods, killing forty-six black residents and burning homes, churches, and schools. Two white men have been killed. What began as a confrontation between several black veterans and white police…

William disembarked from the boat and walked the short distance into the small town of St. Mary's. Some of the buildings had been repaired and rebuilt, but much of it remained destroyed, as it had been by the Union gunboats. Many of the buildings were either burned to the ground or in shambles, with their blackened walls and caved-in roofs testimony to the war. The residents, mostly white, eyed him suspiciously. There were a few black persons, and these were the people he approached to inquire about buying a horse. None of those he approached were able to help.

He walked down the main street through town and stopped when he noticed a black individual placing supplies into a buckboard. The man was better dressed than most, giving him the appearance of being successful. William approached him.

"Excuse me, mister."

The man turned and nodded.

"I got a long way to travel and looking for a horse to buy. Know anyone in this town with a horse to sell?"

"Don't know of anybody trying to sell one. But there is a white fella 'bout a mile down this road that got several horses. Might sell one if the price is right."

"Okay. Thanks, I'll go ask him."

"Where you headed, if you don't mind my snooping?"

"Headin' to Florida."

"I know Florida pretty well. Used to take my master there when he got too old to get there himself. What part you headin' to? Maybe I can give you a few pointers."

"Don't know exactly. My family was taken there. Just need to look 'til I find them.

"Well, I'll tell you this, Florida be a big place. You going to need a lot of luck to find them in your lifetime. Lemme ask you this, was your master a fisherman or a farmer?"

"He grew cotton."

"More likely you and your family grew his cotton. Here's my advice to you. You can take that road over there to Florida, and it would be quicker. But that road is along the coast. That's where fishermen live, but farmers live more inland where the soil is better. He most likely traveled the road that goes down the middle of the state. In that case, you might want to travel this road that heads west. In twenty miles or so, another road will cross it that goes north and south. That's where you go south, and it will take you through more of the farming land. It's up to you, of course."

"Mor'n likely I'll take your advice. But first I want to get me a horse. Much obliged for your information."

William was not able to strike a deal for a horse and began walking west looking for the road that would lead down the middle of Florida. In a few hours, he came to a road that had many foot travelers, mostly walking north.

He went south, at times encountering freedmen traveling north searching for relatives or hoping for a fresh start. William learned where the white farmers lived who gave food or provided work for food to passing freedmen. At times, to survive, they would steal fruit from a grove or vegetables from a garden. Some of the freedmen and women stopped to work on farms and ended up settling there.

The sun hung low in the sky. William hadn't seen anyone on the road for the past hour. A refreshing breeze blew over the land. Most every evening close to dusk, William considered finding a place to sleep, but usually he pushed himself onward knowing each step brought him closer to his family.

One evening, after many days of travel, William left the road to look for a place to bed down. A flickering light beyond a stand of trees caught his eye. He eased up to the light, which turned out to be a campsite occupied by a black man cooking a rabbit over a crackling fire.

Seeing no danger here, William stood in the open and hollered, "Hello!"

"Well, you sure am noisy. Come on and set down for a spell, or for the whole night if you wants," said the man with a smile. He was yellow-toned and commanding, though dressed in tattered clothes. His fire burned brightly, giving off a welcoming heat, and the aroma of cooked rabbit sizzling over the fire pulled William in.

"You go ahead and get yourself some of them vittles. Just help yourself. My name's Boots. What's yours?"

"Boots?" *Where'd he get that name?* mused William, when he noticed Boots' bare feet. The calluses and scars made it unlikely he had ever worn boots or shoes of any kind.

Boots told him that he'd come from a master who gave his workers a lot of freedom, more so than other enslavers in the area. When they finished their labor for him, they were allowed to work for other people and to keep any money they earned. He treated them so well that other enslavers refused to allow their workers to associate with them, fearing Boots and the others might give their slaves ideas of what could be.

Boots closed his eyes, and in a low, scratchy voice, told about taking bushels of corn to the still and trading for whiskey. But then he leaned in towards the fire, his voice harsh and his eyes narrowed. He told of his first master, who had been harsh and didn't treat his people well. "I learned about white mens and how they treats slaves by watching him. He think that we should like him and be happy he give us a place to live and food to eat while we working ourselves to de bone for him be rich. Never mind dat the shack he give us not fit for a mule, and the food he feed us not fit for a dog. He treat us proper long as we obey. But just disobey one time, and then you see de masters cruelty. Can't be our own man, not have our own thoughts, not want the same as he have. He go to church on Sunday an' talk about love and all that, but let one of us mess up, and all that talk gone. Don't think that preacher do him any good."

Then Boots became quiet. His face turned serious as he faced William. William looked into his old, bloodshot eyes.

"You going south?"

William nodded and then added, "To Florida."

Boots turned towards the fire. The light danced and gave his skin an amber glow so that he resembled the hot coals. "Lissen to me good now, 'cause this ain't no lie. My master's land weren't far from a swamp you going to pass. Be careful, 'cause that swamp got spirits livin' in it. I ain't never heard o' the spirits hurting no Negro. But them spirits calls white mens to go in the swamp, and they never comes out. They say when they calls you, you can't do nothing but go. What happen is that long time ago, some slaves meet by the swamp an' was fixing to kill their masters. The owners find out and ambush them. Killed most of them, but some escape into the swamp. Never did find them. Place been haunted ever since."

William found the old man's story strange and unlikely, but nevertheless he responded, "I'll be careful."

As the fire died and the flames turned to embers, the men grew weary and lay down for the night.

William lay there, tired as he was, thinking about seeing Harriet again after all these years. His mind wandered back to the day the massa put him and Harriet together and said they were man and wife. It wasn't the way he would have liked to get married. But he had noticed Harriet, and he liked her.

He remembered the ceremony where they jumped over a broom held about a foot off the ground while holding hands. And the vows they said to each other with the revised wording, "'til death or the white man do us part."

William thought of his first night with Harriet and how much he loved her. Lying together entangled in each other's arms had literally saved his life. Before that moment, he'd spent his time planning how he might escape, no matter the consequences if caught. After Harriet, he'd felt more satisfied—someone loved him and needed him. He pushed to the back of his mind that his master could take his wife if he wanted, or he could sell his children if he had a mind to.

William slept content with Harriet occupying his mind and the joy he would have when he found his family.

A day later, close to Florida, William passed a burned-down plantation house. Only a partial chimney stood to mark where the once-proud house had been. The remains of the plantation house, overgrown with flowering vines and small trees, would have been unrecognizable had it not been for the chimney. A mile farther down the road, he came to a swamp that stretched on for miles—a dense, dark, dreary place, teeming with life and sounds. He camped in a clearing next to the swamp, as winged bugs and bats, along with other night creatures, sprang to life.

William remained restless, unable to accept the comforts of sleep. Annoying mosquitoes buzzed him, but it was mostly the anticipation of being with his family and the anxiety of being able to locate them that kept him awake. That, and dark thoughts about Higgins.

The swamp made him uneasy. Nevertheless, he retrieved his pistol and stuck it in his belt, then stood and walked to the edge, where he sat on the rough trunk of a fallen tree. While observing the tangle of trees, vines, and dark shapes, his thoughts went to Boots' talk of ghosts. He closed his eyes, hoping the quiet would encourage drowsiness, when a splash caught his attention. He peered into the swamp but saw nothing out of the ordinary. But something stirred. He was sure of it. Probably an animal, he mused. More movement. Something came towards William. In the darkness, he made out a tall figure, more man than ghost.

William stood, then stepped back quickly. "You a ghost?" he called out.

"You alone?" it responded.

"Just me is all."

"No white mens?"

"No."

"You sure?"

"I'm sure."

"Then I ain't a ghost."

"What you doing in there?"

"I lives here."

"You lives in the swamp?"

"Now hold on a minute. I got me a few questions, too."

"Go ahead an' ask."

"Last few days I seen a bunch of black folks walking down this road without any white mens. Is all the whites gone?"

"Naw, they ain't gone, but the war's over, so now we's free."

"What war?"

"Don't you know? The war President Lincoln fought to free us slaves."

"You saying we is free?"

"Shore is. Now why don't you come on outta there so I can see you."

William waited while the man, creeping along, looking to his left and then his right, came towards him. Before stepping out, he peered up and down the road, checking and rechecking. He then asked again, "You sure there ain't no whites about to jump me soon's I steps out?"

"There ain't no white mens here."

The man could've been a ghost, or perhaps the devil, himself. His long, tangled beard and hair down well below his shoulders gave him a menacing appearance. He carried a gnarled walking stick as tall as himself. His tattered clothing hung loosely on his bony frame.

"I see why folks be afraid you is a ghost; you sure is a ugly sight."

"You'd be ugly, too, if all you ate is frogs and bugs."

"Maybe so."

"I seen you had a fire going earlier. Might we build up the fire and sit by it? I ain't felt the warmth of a fire since I been living in this swamp."

"Sure," said William. "Come on over. I'll get it going again." The coals were still hot, so it didn't take long before William had the fire going. "Why you live in swamp?" asked William.

The man held his palms out to the fire, embracing its warmth. "I didn't know how much I missed the heat from a fire. This heat going to chase out all the cold that got in my bones these long years. It sure feel good." He paused again, not taking his eyes from the fire. "It were a long, long time ago that me an' some other mens got together an' planned to kill our masters. They was some mean masters, they was. Beat us half to death just 'cause they likes to. Pleasures our women folk right there in front of us. Nothin' we could of done about it. If we say anything, they swing us from a tree.

So, we stand there an' watch, wantin' to kill them. Couldn't protect our own families. Lord, that make me feel 'shamed.

"So, we decided it time to kill them. But didn't happen. Somehow they got wind of it, an' they ambush us. Killed ever one, 'cept me. I took off runnin' into the swamp. Bullets flying ever which way. Hittin' trees an' everthin' but me. Dogs couldn't trail me in there. They can't sniff no water. So, I got clean away. Been livin' there ever since.

"I shore seen plenty. Seen peoples going up an' down this here road. White mens whippin' their slaves. Then the strangest thing. These past days, seen plenty black folk comin' and goin' without even one white master. An' now you tells me we is free."

"What's your name?" asked William.

"Just call me Rouse…that's all, just Rouse."

"Rouse, we is free. That the truth."

The men sat in silence.

"I knows what you mean 'bout wanting to kill your master. Too bad you didn't get to."

Rouse peered into William's eyes, then back at the fire. "Then what?" he asked. "No, I reckon it just as well we didn't kill them."

"Why you say that?"

"Oh, they deserve to die an' I wanted to. Many times. For long time, I planned to get revenge. But one day in the swamp, I realize if we kill them then more white mens come kill us, an' where it all end? When I seen all these black folks travelling up an' down, I figure maybe I was right all along."

"What you right about?"

"One day, I figure those white mens so bad, they gonna die or something bad gonna happen to them. Now I seen all those black folks by themselves, so I figure something bad done happen, an' they gone for good. Now you tells me this here Lincoln feller done whipped them in a war. I knowed it would happen."

"But white men still around. They not gone," said William. "They still treat us bad. My old massa still alive, I suppose. I hates him. When I lay eyes on him, I won't hold back."

Rouse nodded. "I spent long time hating in that swamp. After 'while, I think, hate start killing me. Couldn't sleep. Couldn't catch no food. Always feeling bad, never have no peace. So, I stop thinking about my mean massa."

"How you do that?" asked William.

"Thought about things around me, and tried to find the good that were there. Not saying it were easy. That swamp taught me a thing or two. Besides, long as I think about old master, he stuck in my head. Only way to be free of him was to think about what was around me. Frogs makes for better company than him, anyhow," he said, with a gentle laugh.

They talked into the night. When they finally lay down, William said, "Rouse, you're welcome to join me."

"That mighty kind of you." Rouse glanced back at the mystifying swamp. "Been there so long. Sure do feel strange sitting out here, talking with you." He nodded towards the swamp. "Maybe I'll sleep by this fire tonight and decide in the morning."

"Okay, Rouse. Good night."

The men lay down to sleep.

When William awoke, Rouse was gone.

CHAPTER 43

John

John was in town buying a few supplies when he noticed a crowd in front of the sheriff's office. As he got closer, he noticed around ten black men and women in chains standing on a platform. The sheriff stood next to one of the men taking bids on him. John stopped.

What the hell is going on?

He recognized Phil Sherman towards the back of the crowd. He approached him and tapped his arm.

"Hey, Phil. What's going on?"

"Ain't you heard? There's some new laws that if a nigger ain't working and don't got papers to prove if he is, he'll be arrested and sold—I mean *rented* to the highest bidder. He has to work for that person until he pays off what was paid for him. You oughta get some to work your land."

"Sounds mighty close to slavery to me."

"Better'n slavery. Cheaper. And you can charge 'em for food and rent, so they might never stop workin' for you."

Something inside of John churned awake.

"Hell, they just paying a few hundred dollars for a big strong male. And all the money goes to the sheriff's department. Might even cut down our taxes."

"Yeah, okay. Thanks, Phil." John rode home thinking about this new law. He figured that he could bring a greater profit with the "rented" criminals, could work them longer and just "pay" them with food and a place to sleep. He could have them sleep in the old slave cabins. When he arrived, he explained his plan to Martha, and she said, "It would be kind of like the old days. I think it would be wonderful, John."

John began renting black men and women slowly, as he began letting the workers he paid go. The rented men and women were angry, for they had done nothing wrong. They could be arrested while looking for a job. Or, if there existed a shortage of workers, made up charges often led to their arrest. Yet, for the most part, they remained compliant, for they had learned under the system of slavery what might happen if they stepped out of line.

"Just look at our crops, Rebecca. We got plenty for us and to sell, too."

"You done a wonderful job, Hector. My pa say you the best farmer in this area."

"Your pa a good man. And don't forget, you help me with these crops. Couldn't do it without you. My life be very lonely without you, Becca." Hector placed his arm around her shoulders as they admired their crops.

"I'm so happy to be your wife. We happy, ain't we, Hector?"

"Shore is. Ever since Momma die, I been needing someone like you."

"Know what? I'm gonna pick some corn and beans, tomatoes, some of just about everything and make us the best supper you ever had."

"Uh oh, look who comin' down the road. Can't be no good news when ole John Higgins come this way."

"Afternoon, Hector, Rebecca."

"Afternoon, Mr. Higgins," they responded together.

"You probably heard by now that a new law gives the sheriff the right to arrest any colored person that can't prove he or she is working. So, I brought you both a note that I hope will keep you safe."

"Thank you, sir, we appreciate it."

"Yes, we do," added Rebecca.

"Nice looking crop you folks have. How about bringing me by some tomatoes and corn when they're ready?"

"We'll do that, sir."

"Well, guess I'll be moving along. Oh, by the way, how's your pa, Rebecca?"

"He's about the same, Mr. Higgins. We're praying he'll be improving soon."

"Have you heard from Sally recently, Mr. Higgins?"

"Got a letter from her a few days ago. She's doing fine. Oh, almost forgot. She sent you a note also. Got it right here in my pocket." He handed the letter to Hector. Like for me to read it to you?

"Thank you, sir. We been going to that new school in town. I'd like to try reading it myself, but If I can't read a word or two, I'll be sure to call on you."

"Okay. Be sure to take those notes with you when you leave your place."

"Yes, sir. Thank you for stopping by."

"Let's go inside and read Sally's letter."

As they walked to their cabin, Rebecca said, "He wants to protect us, which I appreciate, but he takes other men from their homes just so he can have cheap labor. Don't he see the wrong in that?"

"I think he must. It's the greed. Making a few bucks off other men's backs. That's what it's all about."

She looked over at Hector and brushed her hand across his cheek. "We so lucky we have each other, ain't we."

"That we is, that we shore is." Hector thought back to their first meeting. It was close to a year ago, a chance meeting in town. Hector had been shopping for basic supplies at Robert's Hardware when Rebecca entered with her father. Her father had not been feeling well for the past few months. Now, he ordered several heavy sacks of feed. When he faltered carrying one of them, Hector had managed to grab his arm to keep him from falling. Hector then carried the bags out for him despite his protestations. But Rebecca persuaded her father that it was okay to accept the help of this man, and she thanked him. Hector asked if he could call on her on the pretext to check on her father. Her father started to protest—he didn't need someone to check on him—but when he saw the looks these two young people gave each other, he kept quiet.

They both sat as Hector unfolded the letter. He began to read.

Dear Hector,

I hope this letter finds you and Rebecca well.

I am living in the town of Beaufort, South Carolina, not far from where we lived years ago before moving to Florida. I work at a hospital for freedmen and women providing what help I can and learning a little each day about being a nurse.

I have a room in the home of a very nice family, and I am quite happy, though I do miss my family and friends and, of course, you. And, I must tell you that I miss your mother very much. You saved my physical body, and she saved my spirit. I am so sorry that she has passed. I think of her every day.

Take care of yourself. Say hi to Rebecca.

Your friend,
Sally

Daily Chronicle

July 30, New Orleans, Louisiana
A peaceful demonstration of mostly black freedmen was set upon by a mob of white rioters, many of whom had been soldiers of the recently defeated Confederate States of America, leading to a full-scale massacre…

CHAPTER 44

William

A few days later, William arrived in Florida. Towards late afternoon, he approached a farm. The modest house stood in amongst a smattering of pines. He stopped and observed a man enjoying the afternoon breeze. Two small, frisky children played a game nearby. Their play stopped when William walked towards the man. As William approached, they ran behind a tree, where they remained curious and vigilant.

William tipped his hat in greeting. "I be looking for my family. They was living with a white family by the name of Higgins. You ever heard of that family?"

"Ain't never heard of any Higgins around here. Don't you know what town they lives in?"

A woman, perhaps his daughter, came out from the house wiping her hands on her dress. The two small children ran to her and peeked out from behind the safety of her skirt.

"Nope, sure don't know that. Just knows they is somewhere in Florida."

"Well, this here is a small town, and we would know them if they lives here. The next town be about twenty or maybe thirty miles from here."

William expressed his appreciation and moved on. As he neared towns, he would turn from the main road into the safety and seclusion of the forest. He checked for patrollers. He felt powerless without a pass, though he knew these no longer existed.

How strange this Freedom. He still must hide, take care not to offend a white, still live on the edge. Backs of buildings, visible through the trees, were for now the best route a lone black man could manage.

This scenario repeated with every small community he passed through. He could always find a black family willing to feed him. Though they never asked, he always gave them something to pay for his food and their generosity.

After two days, he came to the larger town of Lake City. He needed a different strategy here. He would stay for several days to investigate the wider area. He slept in the woods, moving to a new location each day.

The next decent-sized city he came to, Gainesville, was the largest so far. More blacks than whites lived in Gainesville. Numerous plantations throughout the area provided work. A company of United States Colored Troops, commanded by a white officer, were stationed here to keep the peace. Although William followed the same pattern as before, in Lake City, he felt safer here and spent more time in town.

A freedman named Andrew Thompson had come to town with murder on his mind. Andrew Thompson had just arrived in Gainesville, having traveled from Georgia. He came in search of his former master who, eight months earlier, had raped Andrew's wife and sent Andrew, who had become moody and uncooperative, to his Georgia plantation. Now Andrew had a gun and intended to get revenge.

Andrew knew his old master's habits: every Friday evening around six o'clock, he frequented his favorite saloon. Andrew waited nearby. Shortly after six, when his target showed up, dozens of people milled about the area. Andrew didn't want witnesses, so he would wait until his former master exited the saloon. Hours later, when the man left the saloon, Andrew stepped in front of him, blocking his progress.

"Well, old Massa, now you gonna pay for what you done to my misses," he shouted, as he pulled the trigger.

Andrew escaped by running down an alley. Several women and an elderly couple saw what happened. Like feathers in a brisk wind, word quickly spread that a Negro had shot a prominent plantation owner.

By chance, William turned a corner only a few blocks from the crowd gathering around the dead man. Someone spotted him and called out, "There he goes!" That person drew his gun and fired at William. Surprised, but quick to act, William spun around and fled. A group of men pursued him.

William had initially put some distance between himself and the group chasing him. But now they gained on him. The open streets of the town provided no cover for William; how long before a bullet hit its mark? Seeking to shield himself as much as possible, William turned down a side street leading into the woods. He entered where the earth lay flat, but shortly the terrain sloped treacherously, the low ground damp with rotted leaves and slick clay. A fallen tree lay across his path. He leapt over it easily, but when he came down on the other side, disaster struck. He slipped on the slick ground and fell hard on his side. He panicked, struggling to get up, but had difficulty making traction with the ground. By the time he managed to get upright, William's pursuers had surrounded him with guns drawn.

"Let's hang him now an' get it over with," said one of the men.

"Ain't no trees around here that'll hold 'em," said another.

"What you want to hang me for?" asked William.

"Shut up," a man said, as he pushed into William.

Then the colored troops with their white lieutenant rode up. "What's going on here?" said the lieutenant.

"Ain't none of your concern," said one of the men.

"Yeah, take your nigger Yankees back up north where they belong. We'll take care of our own business."

The lieutenant gave a nod to one of his men and then said, "You weren't doing such a good job of taking care. That's why we're here. There won't be no lynching without a trial."

The soldiers had fanned out, surrounding the lynch mob. Each soldier had his rifle ready.

"He don't need no trial," said one. "We all seen him shoot a white fella in cold blood in broad daylight. And that calls for a lynching."

"He killed a white man," shouted another. "We're making sure he don't do it again. You soldier boys go on home; we got this under control."

"Troops," said the man in charge, "each of you pick out one man as your target. If he fails to do as I say, shoot him."

"You can't do that," a man uttered, but his voice wavered, and every man there knew he could.

"Now, put your guns away."

After a brief hesitation, they complied.

"Who saw this man kill that fella in town?"

Silence. Finally, the self-appointed spokesperson said, "Someone in town saw it and pointed him out. We was just chasin' him down when he run away. That in itself proves he's guilty."

"What do you have to say for yourself?" he asked William.

"I didn't kill nobody. I was just walking through town when someone shot at me. So, I ran."

"All right, let's head back into town and see if we can straighten this out," said the officer. "You men from town walk along in front. Sergeant, you walk alongside the accused."

When they arrived back in town, twenty or so men and women stood near the victim lying in the street. The sheriff talked with them, trying to find out who saw what. Everyone stopped to stare at the procession of townsmen and troops coming towards them.

The officer dismounted and asked, "What have you learned, Sheriff?"

He nodded in the direction of a man lying in the street. "We got a man shot down by a black feller. This the one that did it?" he asked.

"Don't know yet," he answered. Then the officer hollered, "Anybody see who shot this man?" He scanned the crowd. No one spoke up. "Anyone at all see what happened here?"

He scanned the crowd again, making eye contact with many. Then, a woman standing in the back said, "I saw what happened." The officer pushed his way through the crowd. The sheriff followed.

The woman, with a reputation for being outspoken, was known in town as Miss Beatrice. She had moved to Gainesville ten years ago with her son, where they had purchased a small tract of land. She claimed her husband had been killed in an Indian raid years before. They had eked out a meager living, as did many. Then her son had been killed in the war.

"Tell me what you saw, Miss Beatrice." He hoped to get the truth from her and thought being friendly might help. She blamed the Union army for killing her son, and she despised all Negroes. He wondered how accurate a report she would give.

"I don't like blacks any better'n I like your army." She held eye contact with the officer to make sure her point hit him. "But I ain't stooped yet to being a liar. So, you can believe me or not, I don't much care. I was standing over there," she said, pointing to the general store, located across from the bar. "I seen that dead man come out and some damn nigger run in front of him and said something and then shot him outright."

"Can you describe the Negro?"

"He were short, shorter than you, 'bout as short as ole Tank over there." This brought laughter from the crowd. "He was round, too. Heavy. But not as heavy as Tank."

"Sergeant," hollered the officer, "bring the prisoner over here."

William walked in front of the sergeant to face Miss Beatrice.

"Now, Miss Beatrice, is this the man you saw do the shooting?"

"I done told you, the man I saw was short and round. This man's taller than most and not round atall. 'Course he ain't the one."

The officer faced the crowd. "Did anyone else see anything?" No one responded. Turning to the sheriff, he said, "Sheriff, are you satisfied that this isn't the man?"

"Yeah, I reckon he ain't the one."

"Everyone listen to me. This man does not fit the description. We are looking for a shorter, heavier black man who may be the killer. Do not take the law into your own hands. If you see someone fitting this description, let me or one of my men know."

The sheriff took care of the body, and the crowd began to disperse.

"Thank you, Captain," William said. "Sure glad you showed up when you did."

The captain looked at William. "I'm Captain Stanton. You almost got yourself killed. You from around here?"

"Not from around here. I'm lookin' for my family. I'm trying to find a white man name of Higgins. He was the one had us before we freed."

"You're not very popular right now. Lots of folks are disappointed they didn't get to see a lynching. How about coming over to my office for a word in private." Stanton led William down the street to an office with a sign on the door reading "Freedmen's Bureau." He led him into a small room with a desk and chair, but not much else.

Facing William, he said, "What's your name?"

"William Stone, sir."

Well, Mr. Stone, I'm going to hazard a guess and say that you were in the army not too long ago."

"Yes, sir. How'd you know?"

"It seemed pretty clear to me when I first laid eyes on you. The way you carried yourself. Then you knew by my insignia that I'm a captain. It all just sort of fit together. What outfit you fight with?"

"First South Carolina, sir."

"First South Carolina? You don't say. Well, I'll be goddamned. Old Colonel Tom Higginson's command. He's from Massachusetts same as me; we were practically neighbors. You men did a hell of a job."

"Thank you, sir."

"Can you keep a secret, Mr. Stone?"

"Yes, sir, don't reckon I got anybody to tell it to even if I wanted to."

The captain laughed. "That makes me feel much better." He walked around to his desk and pulled out a bottle of bourbon. "I'd like to drink a toast to you and your regiment." He handed William a glass and poured them both two fingers worth.

"I ain't never had none of this to drink."

"In that case, I suggest you go slow. Let's drink to you, William Stone, and all the men you fought with. Thanks to the likes of you, we have won this war and have made all men and women and children free at long last. My god, why did it take us so long? Now we have to do the hard part—convincing these Southern men and women to accept you as equals."

"Yes, sir."

"So, where are you headed to?"

"Looking for my family. Don't know where they are, just have to keep lookin'. Pretty sure they still in Florida somewhere. My old master brought them down here before the war."

The captain looked serious for a few moments. "Tell you what. How about we go over to the land office and see if your master might have a homestead somewhere in the Gainesville region? If so, he would be registered. That would make it much easier for you to at least contact him. Can't say if your family is still with him or not, but it would be a start."

Yes, sir, I would be much obliged if we could do that."

The land office was five doors down from the captain's office. A little bell tinkled when the door opened. The man behind the desk stood and nodded at the captain. "What can I do for you?"

"Like to know if anybody name of Higgins has homesteaded land in this region."

The man looked at William and back at Captain Stanton. "This army business or personal, 'cause we don't give out any information just for personal reasons." He looked hard again at William.

"I'm askin,' so it's official army business."

The man hesitated briefly, then sighed deeply. "Look, I can't help every damn nigger that wants to find someone. I run this office by myself. I'd be swamped."

The captain leaned in closer to the man. "Army business. And I don't see no line out your door."

The man walked to a file cabinet, shaking his head and mumbling to himself. He opened the second drawer. "Let's see…Hampton, Harris, Harrison, Henson, Higgins. Here it is. John Higgins. Bought some land in Hillsborough County that is now Polk County. Near a town called Shallow Lake. It's south of here, looks like about a three-day ride."

"Thanks, Eaton. That wasn't so hard now, was it?"

The man scowled as he shoved the drawer shut.

"Come with me, Mr. Stone. I got something I want to show you." As the two walked back to the captain's office he said, "I don't know how you stay so calm when these people are disrespectful towards you."

"Lots of practice."

"Yes, I guess you're right."

They turned down an alley, which came out behind the office, and continued walking until they came to a corral. "See them three horses on the far end over there? I don't need them. We arrested some men a while back who were calling on black folks and stealing whatever they had of value. The judge turned their horses over to me to sell and give the money to the folks they stole from. I can sell you one, and you'll get to your family a lot quicker. What do you say?"

I could sure use a horse. Been trying to buy one every place I go, but no one's selling to me. I'll take the best one you got."

"That'd be the brown there on the left with the two white front legs."

"You've been very helpful, Captain. I do appreciate it."

"There's one more thing I can do. I'll have some of my men escort you out of town and ride with you for a few miles to make sure you're safe enough. From there, you're on your own."

CHAPTER 45

William

William's anticipation grew as he rode south. To be with his family again would fill an emptiness he had felt since that day years ago when he regained consciousness in the Stones' basement. His happiness was dampened by his also growing closer to the moment he would face Higgins.

On his third day from Gainesville, he came upon a mature couple—the man working in his garden, a woman, perhaps his wife, sewing on the porch.

The farmer looked up at William and smiled. William forced a return smile.

"You look like you could use a good meal there, young fella," the man said.

"Yes, sir, that sounds mighty good." William hadn't taken the time to eat this morning, but now his hunger made him regret having been in such a hurry.

"Well, come in, and we'll fix you up something," he said, waving his arm for William to come in to the yard. "Hey, Ma, can you take a break from your sewing to fix this man up something to eat?"

William entered the yard. The man took a chair off the porch and put it in the yard for William.

"Yep, I seen many a poor Negro traveling this road. Though you're the first one I seen with a horse. Seems like ever since the slaves been freed, they been more of you folks going hungry than before. Now mind you, I wasn't for slavery, but it sure has been hard on you Negroes, just turning you loose. Seems a shame, all those people, little children, no place to go, no place to call home."

During slavery, William had never dared look a white man in the eye and speak the truth. Not until Dr. Stone and then the army. And now?

"Freedom is better than slavery. As slaves, we had rundown shacks to lay in after workin' all day for someone else, but never called it home. These freedmen you see walking down the road, they's searchin' for a place to call home. Don't need to feel no sorrow for them. They a heap stronger than they looks."

"I suppose you're right. Looks like the missus has got your meal."

His wife, a kindly looking woman with gray hair worn in a bun, came down the steps carrying a plate of cornbread and potatoes with both hands and walking so as not to spill a morsel.

"Now you enjoy this," she said, patting William on the shoulder.

"Thank ya, ma'am."

William's hunger and desire to continue his search led him to devour the food in large bites. "Thank you for the meal," he said. "I have some money to pay for the food, if you tell me how much."

The man laughed aloud. "Well, I'll be. You the first one come by here with money, at least that we know of." He shook his head, smiling. "No need to pay us. We're happy to do it."

"Then I best get going. Looking for the town of Shallow Lake. You folks know how much farther?"

"Why, you're about there," said the man. "Just another ten miles or so straight ahead."

"I'm looking for my family." William's voice quivered. "They come here with John Higgins. Has you ever heard of him?" He held his breath.

"Yes, of course we have. They live just down the road from us."

Just down the road. So, this would be the day.

The words stunned William, turning his dreams into hard reality.

What will I find when I get there? And how will it end?

"You say they lives just down this road?"

"They live two farms down going toward town."

"No, dear. It would be the third farm now that the nice young black man has his cabin on this road."

"That's right, my dear. Thank you. It would be the third house; my wife is quite correct." He laughed at his mistake.

William's chest pounded—possibly only a few miles separated him from Harriet, Margaret, and Hector. And from Higgins.

William stopped in front of the cabin set back in the pines described by the older couple as belonging to the young black man.

Perhaps they'll know where my family is.

As he approached the door, he heard talking behind the cabin.

"Hey, Rebecca, can you give me a hand?"

Though he hadn't heard him speak in years, William swore the voice belonged to Hector. He stood still to hear more. But only silence followed. He ran to the back of the cabin. There, in a field, stood two figures. Hector, now a young man, admiring his future harvest, and a young woman standing at his side. William froze, paralyzed by emotion. Then, in a flash, he ran, shouting his son's name.

Hector stopped talking to Rebecca. He turned. A man ran towards them, his arms outstretched.

Hector yelled, "Papa," and ran to his father.

They embraced, crying and laughing. This moment seemed like a miracle. It was all William had dreamed it would be. Holding Hector in his arms and hearing the sound of his voice made William feel whole again.

Wanting Harriet and Margaret to join them, William called out for them.

"Papa, they cannot hear you. Momma died some time back."

"No! Harriet died? What happened?"

"She was living here with me. We were working planting our crops when suddenly she fell to the ground. I ran to her, but I think she was dead before I reached her. I am sorry, Papa."

"I wanted so much to see her again. I can't believe she died. All the dreams I had for us."

"Papa, she is buried by those trees over there."

"And what about Margaret?"

"I am so sorry to tell you so much bad news. When we first arrived here, Margaret was stolen from us. We never found her. I have put information about her in the newspaper but have not heard anything."

"Margaret has been gone all these years?"

Rebecca came up beside Hector, taking his hand in hers.

"Papa?"

"Yes, Hector?"

"I am sorry to have to do this with so much sad news, but I don't know how else to do it. There is some good news to report also. I would like for you to meet Rebecca, my wife."

William looked into Rebecca's face and smiled. He felt joy for this young couple when a moment ago he thought he might never again feel such gladness. "Your wife? How wonderful. I be happy for you." He embraced Rebecca and then Hector.

Hector placed his hand on his father's shoulder. "Come with me. I'll walk you over to Momma's grave. When you're ready, we can go inside where we can sit an' talk."

William kneeled beside Harriet's grave. He saw that Hector had carved a wood headstone with Harriet's name and date of death. He breathed deeply and then spoke. "Harriet. My sweet Harriet. I had such dreams for us. I wanted us to all go live up North where we could be a real family. No one telling us what to do. We could be real parents, be in charge of our children. You was a good wife and mother." He reached over and laid his hand on her grave. "I wish I could have got here while you was alive."

When he was done, he and Hector sat together and spoke of the years they had been separated. William told of his adventures with Itch and Dr. and Mrs. Stone, his time in the army, and his travels to Florida.

"Life is dangerous here, Papa. Fighting still goes on between some of the white families. Lot of people be leaving 'cause there isn't money. Most of the freed people already left. It's not good."

"But you would be so proud of Hector." Rebecca set a plate of cornbread and molasses before them. "This is Hector's own land that Mr. Higgins gave him, and he has the best crops in the area. You'll see." She smiled at Hector.

"Higgins gave you land?"

"Yes. I saved Sally's life. He gave it to thank me. I work for Higgins during the week. He pays me, not much, but we can use the money."

William stood and walked to the fireplace, where he ran his hand over the stone. "This place real cozy, Hector. You done real good for yourself and your momma." He remained silent for a moment. Then, hoping to unravel the puzzle of what to do about Higgins, he asked, "You think Higgins' changed? Or he still mean as ever?"

Two weeks later, in town picking up supplies, John encountered his neighbor. "Did that tall colored fella ever find you, John?" asked Martin.

"No, I don't recall seeing anyone like that. Was he looking for work?"

"Don't think so. Said he was lookin' for his family."

"That's odd. What did he look like?"

"Well, like I said, he was a big fella. Dark skin. He seemed nice enough. Sound like someone you know?"

"I'm not sure. Maybe. Maybe. We'll see," said John.

On his return trip from town, John wondered if William had found him.

If it is William, does he want revenge? How the hell did he find us?

John agonized all day that William lurked close by. Noises startled him. He imagined William waiting in ambush. He became obsessed.

When early morning light filtered in through the curtains, he arose from his bed and walked in his bare feet to the window. The sun burned brightly through the trees, sending shafts of light, awakening the land.

I can't go on like this. I'm gonna have to go to Hector's place an' see for myself.

When John arrived at Hector's place, he dismounted and called out, "Hector, you in there? I need to talk."

No one responded. He walked to the side of the house, where he spotted Hector and a man working alongside him. He recognized William at once.

I'll be damned. I have to hand it to him. Finding us way down here must've took one hell of an effort.

He gathered his rifle and walked towards them. As he walked past the cabin, Rebecca saw him at the open window. She called out, "Hello, Mr. Higgins. What brings you here today?"

"Never you mind. You just go on about your business."

Rebecca became uneasy and went to the back door to watch. She called out, and both men turned towards her. William knew he would come face to face with John eventually, but this unexpected visit caught him by surprise. He felt his old anger rising. He noticed John carrying a rifle and wished he had his.

"Good morning, Mr. Higgins," Hector called out.

John stopped about twenty feet from the two men. He held his rifle loosely at his side but could bring it up quickly if need be. He didn't respond to Hector's greeting.

"William, I understand you were looking for me. Well, here I am. Now what do you want?" He spoke in a menacing tone, which didn't go unnoticed by either man, though it surprised Hector.

"Well, that ain't quite right, Mr. Higgins. I came looking for my family, and I done found them."

"You got anything to say to me?"

The words, "You will know what to do" played over and over in William's mind. He remembered Itch's counsel and the many hours he had spent in quiet contemplation focusing on this very moment. He wanted to be open to receiving a sign, a clue as to what he should do, but nothing came to him.

Back at the cabin, Rebecca's concern grew as she watched the confrontation. She picked up William's rifle and walked to the door, determined that John would not take any of her family from her.

Hector stepped closer to his father and put his hand on William's shoulder. "Ain't no problem here, Mr. Higgins," he said. His eyes met William's, and in that moment, William knew what he would say.

Looking at John, William felt vulnerable. John could take everything from him again. William's anger rushed back. He may not have a gun, but now he wasn't helpless, as he had been before. Now he wanted to hurt John. He wanted to make John feel pain. He pulled his shirt off and turned his back to John. "This is what you did to me. You had no right. You took my family from me. No man should do that to another."

John's grip tightened on his rifle. He raised the barrel.

William closed his eyes to control himself. Words came to him from deep inside his being. "I am a man, just like you. We are all men."

William glanced at Hector. He peered into his strong, dark eyes. He remembered Itch's words one night long ago:

Our difficult times help make us who we are; we become stronger because of them.

William's pulse slowed, and his mind calmed. "I am not your enemy, Mr. Higgins."

"And just how am I supposed to know that?"

"If you look at me like one man to another, you would know. Touch my hand, and you would know we both made of skin and bone. We both be men who want to make a good life for ourselves and our families We all the same, some just got different color skin is all."

Perhaps he saw something in William for the first time, or perhaps something William said struck a chord with him. John dropped the barrel of his rifle. Hector and William relaxed. Rebecca, standing in the backdoor, lowered William's rifle.

"Mr. Higgins, you can see plain that I ain't got no gun. I don't got no plans to get revenge on you; I just come to live out my days in peace with my family."

After an uneasy silence, John said, "Guess I was wrong. I have learned those things that you said. Or maybe I should say that I'm still learning. I'm beginning to see that we are all men and very much alike. Though some are better than others, I reckon. Hector risked his life to rescue Sally. That was…well, let's just say it made me think. And it changed me. A man named Otis probably saved my life. He didn't have to, of course. But he did. And I'll never forget Harriet. She was good to Sally. Helped her get back to her feisty self. I've had plenty of good people around me."

The two men stood eye-to-eye. Then John said, "I'm sorry that Harriet wasn't here when you returned. She would have been happy to see you… Well, I should go."

He walked back to his horse. Memories swirled in his mind—Hector risking his life to help Sally, Hector able to run his farm without a white man's help, colored folks going to schools and hungry to learn, and, of course, Lindi…so many things turned out different from what he'd expected. He mounted his horse only to stop for the moment to gaze over Hector's farm.

Damn fine farm. I did the right thing giving him this land.

William walked up to Rebecca with a wry grin and said, "What you gonna do with that rifle? You likely to hit Hector or me as hit ol' Higgins."

She smiled back. "Us women gotta protect our men. That's for sure."

"You a lucky man, Hector, got yourself a strong woman."

"I been knowing that, Papa."

After being with Hector and Rebecca for a few months, William approached them.

"I needs to talk with you."

"Sure, Papa."

"You knows I loves you both, an' I thanks you for lettin' me stay here. But I gots to move on. Can't stay in the South no more. Just can't. Too many ways they can hurt you. They got laws to keep us like slaves. Want to go north, maybe Canada. Someplace where I be respected. No danger of being arrested or killed by hateful white men. Place where I can work for pay. I knows you gots this land here, but I hopes you would go with me.

Hector and Rebecca looked at each other. Hector spoke first.

"Papa, we loves you, too. I be sorry to see you leave. But we not able to go with you. It not just our land. Rebecca got her papa here who be sick, and we can't leave him alone."

"And papa, I loves you, too," Rebecca said. "I wish you would stay, but I understands you wants to leave. Hector has worked hard on his land. And this our home. I going to miss you."

William saw that Hector had his own life now, and it was good. William was content. Hector gave William the address of a local church where he could keep in touch with an occasional letter. Once William settled down, he would do the same for Hector.

Several days later, William set out for Canada. He stayed with groups heading north whenever possible. When he rode alone, he stayed mostly off the road, riding through the woods to avoid trouble.

He spent much of his travelling time remembering Harriet and his children. The time Hector and Margaret were born and Harriet being so careful taking them out to the fields with her and laying them down on the ground so she could pick as much of her quota as possible. William did his share and much of hers as well, working faster to make up the difference.

He remembered the days when he and Itch had their long talks, often turning to what William would do when he confronted John. William closed his eyes, and he could see Itch's strong face, his piercing look as he spoke. Itch had told him on one such occasion, *"Many times, difficulties bring out good qualities in us that we didn't know were there. And if you live life fully, those difficulties just might bring out the hero that lives in you."*

William shook his head and cracked a smile. *Itch was quite a talker.*

William continued his journey, moving cautiously through Kentucky and crossing the Ohio River into Cincinnati. Here, he rode proudly along one of the main streets, feeling very relieved to have crossed into the northern states and now very close to Canada.

While riding, a window display caught his eye. He had difficulty believing what he was seeing. It seemed totally foreign to him. He dismounted, walked up to the window, and, with his nose almost touching the glass, stared at the photographs. Before him were the photos of handsome black men and beautiful black women dressed in the finest clothes he had ever seen. He was amazed and proud. He stood there for a time, not wanting to lose those images, wanting to remember such fine black people. He was seeing proof that he was as good and as lovely as anyone.

He was so engrossed in the photographs that it took him some time to notice a slight tug on his pant leg and a tiny voice trying to get his attention. "Hey, mister."

He looked down to find a small boy of perhaps five or six years looking up. William crouched to speak to the child eye to eye, when he heard a mother's voice calling.

"Benjamin, come here right now and leave that man alone." She scooped Ben into her arms. "I'm very sorry. I hope he wasn't bothering you." She wore an apron, her hair tied up in a bun and a smudge of flour on one cheek.

"No, ma'am, he wasn't bothering me none. Fact is, he kinda reminds me of my own son quite some years ago."

"Oh, well Ben's daddy went off to war and hasn't returned. We are so worried. Ben asks every man he sees if he's his father."

"Yes'm, I knows that must be hard on him and you, too. I was in the army, so I understand how easy it could be to lose your family."

Her eyes widened. "Do you think you might know him? His name was Henry Roberts. He was—"

"No, ma'am, I wouldn't of known him. I was stationed in the South in South Carolina. If he joined from Ohio, he would be stationed farther north."

Her shoulders sagged. Well, I best be going. I'm one of the cooks at the café. Seems like every time I get busy little Ben here takes off to find his daddy."

Goodbye, ma'am, and you, too, Ben."

Ben waved goodbye, then buried his face in his mother's shoulder.

William watched them leave for a few seconds before he noticed a man standing in the door of the photography studio watching him. William nodded a greeting.

The man, as tall as William but thinner and older with graying hair, reached out his hand to shake William's and said, "I'm Jim Boll. This is my photography shop. I see you met Kathryn and Ben. A real fine family. I noticed you admiring my portraits earlier."

"Yes, sir, I never have seen such fancy colored people before. Real nice photographs."

"I wasn't trying to listen in on you, but I heard you say that you were in the army during the war."

"Yes, sir. The first black regiment of South Carolina."

"Well then, you're a hero."

"Don't know about a hero. Just doing what I had to do."

"You're a hero all right, to me and all us black folks. You risked your life to get us free. That's a hero."

William smiled. "Thank you. We did what any of us would like to have done."

"I'd like to take your photograph, if you would allow me."

"Me? Thank you, but I don't have no fancy clothes like those folks."

"You were in the army. That makes you special. And I have a Union uniform that might fit you. How about giving it a try? I'll take several and give you one."

William had his photograph made, and it was displayed with the "fancy colored people" he so admired. After the photos were made, the two men sat talking for a long time. Finally, Jim Boll made William an offer—he wanted to make one last trip to the mountains to capture their majesty, but he was getting too old to trudge around the mountains with so much equipment. He offered to hire William to go with him, for pay of course, and as an extra bonus, he would teach William the trade as much as he could during the month or so they travelled. William accepted his offer.

During their travels, William learned to love the mountains and the scenic views of forests and rivers. He took to the intricate process of photography and felt an awakening—zeal and an exhilaration of spirit for the beauty he was able to create through photography.

Five Years Later

"Well, look at you, Ben. You sure do look handsome."

"Tell William thank you," said Kathryn.

"Thank you, Mr. Stone."

"Are you two ready to have your picture taken? You'll be my first customers."

"Sure is nice of you to offer to do this, William. And congratulations on buying the studio."

"Mr. Boll has been mighty good to me. Sure glad I ran into him that day I met you and Ben. Fact is, you two were the first people I met here, so it only right you be the first two I photograph.

"So, Ben, how 'bout you sit right here."

"Mr. Stone, how come you got such a big smile on your face?"

"Ben, you shouldn't ask such personal questions."

"Oh, it's all right, Kathryn. I don't mind."

"See, it's okay, Momma."

Kathryn shook her head and smiled.

"It's like this, Ben. I come here a few years back headin' to Canada. Didn't really know where I might end up. Then I met Mr. Boll, and he needed help with his business, so I began helping and learning the trade. Now he done sold it to me. So now I got a studio, and I got two good friends."

"That's me and Momma, right?"

"That's right. It seems to me that now I also got a place to call home. Somethin' what I never had before."

"We're glad you're here, William. Aren't we, Ben?"

"Yeah, we are."

"Me, too," said William. "Me, too."

Billy's Story
(John's older brother)

1832

Billy rode into town feeling good. His father had given him a Francotte pinfire revolver for his birthday, and he rode high in the saddle with it strapped to his side. He tied his horse outside the saloon and strode in, trying his best to look at ease.

"Give me a whiskey, Arne," said Billy, loud enough for everyone in the saloon to hear. He slapped his coin onto the bar.

Arne glanced around. "Where's your pa, Billy?"

Billy lowered his voice. "Today I turned sixteen. My pa let me come in on my own."

Arne gave Billy a big, toothy grin. "Hey everybody, Billy here turned sixteen today. First one's on the house, Billy." He poured a shot glass half full of the colorless liquid.

A tough-looking man in need of a bath, not someone Billy was familiar with, stood at the end of the bar. "Careful, kid. Drinkin' this here rotgut'll kill you before you set the glass down."

Arne lifted the bottle. "Shut up, Jackson. Billy, this here is the best damn whiskey within a hundred miles."

Someone at a table behind Billy spoke up. "Might be worth the trip."

Even Arne laughed at that.

Billy chugged the liquid like he had seen other men do. His face burned red. He let out a whistle, then sucked in a long, hard breath.

Arne leaned in and whispered, "Go easy, Billy. This stuff takes some getting used to."

Billy stood at the bar staring at his second drink when Lars Tomlinson sauntered in—the eighteen-year-old only son of the wealthiest man around and a fierce competitor who hated Billy.

When he spotted Billy, he strolled over to him. "Aren't you a bit young to be hanging out in here?"

"Nope." The bartender spoke quickly to ward off trouble. "Billy turned sixteen today."

Lars glared at Billy for a few tense seconds before saying, "Congratulations. Let me buy you a drink."

Arne relaxed a bit. Later he would recall the two seemed to get along better than they ever had.

For the next hour or so, Lars treated Billy as a good friend. They laughed together. Lars slapped Billy on the back and bought him more drinks than Billy could handle. Billy, his stomach a raging storm and his brain a confused, swirling tornado of wreckage, had succumbed to the best damn whiskey in a hundred miles.

Lars leaned over, whispered in Billy's ear, and soon after they left together. Billy's old enemy, now new-found friend, couldn't be chummier. Billy mounted his horse against serious protest from his body. His hope for what the future held outweighed his body's complaints.

Billy, more drunk than smart, asked again in his slurred voice, "Lars, tell me who these young ladies are that we're going to meet."

"Ah, don't worry Billy ol' buddy. I assure you that you will be extremely pleased."

Billy decided against any further talk. Keeping his mouth closed and his brain silent seemed to him a wise decision. They rode mostly in silence over the next several miles. Lars made an attempt now and then at conversation, but Billy could only muster a grunt or two in reply.

Five miles from town, Billy leapt from his horse and puked violently. Lars laughed. "C'mon, follow me." He turned his horse into the woods. Billy reluctantly climbed back on and followed.

The trees, plentiful and dense, often surrounded by bushy undergrowth, shot up to the sky, each struggling for a bit of sunlight. The two youths weaved to the right, then to the left and then back right searching for a way deeper into the forest.

A hundred yards in, at a small clearing and out of sight of the road, Lars said, "This is the spot." He dismounted.

Billy looked around. "The girls are meeting us here?"

"Hop down, and I'll show you."

Billy thought he heard the insolent voice of the old Lars in this last comment. It had a touch of contempt in it. But he dismounted. What else could he do?

"Guess what, there are no girls." Lars punched Billy in the gut, sending him sprawling to the ground.

Billy fought to breathe. A burning bile rose from his stomach; he forced it back down. He kept his eye on Lars. He should have known Lars planned to hurt him. What a fool he had been to trust him.

"Think you're tough with your fancy revolver?"

Billy fought to get control of his reactions as he struggled to get past the grogginess brought on by the whiskey.

"You made a fool of me for the last time."

"What are you talking about? I never did nothing like that."

Lars went to his saddlebag and pulled out a pistol.

Starring at the barrel of a pistol caused Billy's heart to pound faster. His mind cleared, and he became more alert. He stood facing Lars.

"You're the great Billy Higgins. You know everything, and you're better than everyone." Lars had no reason to hurry. He wanted to see fear in Billy's eyes.

Billy knew he didn't have a chance. In his weakened state, he couldn't fight anyone, much less Lars with a pistol. If he went for his revolver, he would be shot before he could pull it from his holster.

Lars pulled the trigger, but his gun misfired, giving Billy the chance he needed to draw his gun. Now Lars' eyes grew large and fearful as Billy drew and fired. The bullet struck Lars in the chest, knocking him to the ground. Blood seeped from his wound and soaked his shirt. Billy stood motionless, still holding his gun, looking down at Lars. He dropped his gun and fell to his knees, shaking uncontrollably. "I've killed him."

Billy stared at the motionless Lars. His mind was now sharp, the danger of his situation becoming clear. He had killed the only son and the pride and joy of the wealthiest man in the area.

Thomlinson was pretty much in charge around here. The town had no sheriff, and the judge came to town once every two months. By the time the judge got here, Billy knew beyond a doubt he would be hanged whether Lars had been killed in self-defense or not. His only chance to live would be to run as far away from here as possible. Quickly. No time for family goodbyes. Just leave.

He removed the saddle from Lars' horse and brought the extra horse along for most of the night. He rode south. He took the horse into the woods and slapped its flank, sending him deeper. He hoped this might confuse anyone who tried to follow.

He rode by moonlight through the night with no idea where the road led him. By daybreak, both he and his horse sagged from exhaustion. Hot sun beat down on him. He longed for water. His tongue swelled and grew sticky. He left the road to search for a shady resting place and water.

For the next few days he followed a stream, living off the land. He trapped small animals, mostly rabbits and squirrels, with snares built from rope and sticks. When the stream turned east, he found the road again and rode hard south. Billy rode through South Carolina, Georgia, and into Florida, where good fortune would smile upon him.

He had been riding for half a day when he spotted a small cabin sitting a good fifty yards off the road, surrounded by a cultivated field. *Here's as good a place as any.* He followed the trail leading to the cabin and stopped. Without dismounting he shouted, "Hello, the cabin."

The door opened a crack. Billy glimpsed someone, possibly a woman, peering at him through the crack. Then the door closed.

"I don't mean you no harm, ma'am," he shouted. A sound to his left alerted him.

A man carrying a rifle came from around the house. "How can I help you, mister?"

"Didn't mean to frighten nobody. Just saw your cabin and thought maybe I could do a few days' work. Just pay me with food and a place to bunk."

"Know anything about farming?"

"Been farming all my life."

"Where you come from?" asked the man.

Billy sensed the man's suspicion. He knew he would get asked this question sooner or later. "Virginia. Striking out on my own. I was raised on a farm. Been growing things since I can remember."

"Why'd you leave your home? Folks must be worried."

"My parents died in a fire. Cabin burned to the ground. I had no reason to stay after that."

The man studied Billy for a moment. "I could use some help around here. Get off your horse, and I'll show you around." The man stuck out his hand. "Name's Craig Larranger."

Billy shook his hand. "Dusty."

"Sorry 'bout your folks. Everybody down here is from somewhere else. But you've come to the right place. Florida is where fortunes are made."

Billy, or Dusty as he now called himself, worked three years for Craig before setting out on his own. He traveled south to Gainesville. Here, he met Santiago.

Many considered Santiago one of the fiercest warriors of Jorge Biassou in Saint Domingue. Those who knew him admired his strong sense of justice. In 1796, Biassou, his family, and twenty-five of his followers—including Santiago—were exiled to St. Augustine, located in the Spanish territory of Florida.

Santiago brought with him his wife—a beautiful French woman who happened to be white. At his wife's pleadings, he left Biassou's army. They moved farther south and inland, where they purchased a small ranch and settled down with hopes to begin a family. Over the next twenty-five years, Santiago and his family prospered.

Then, in 1821, the bottom fell out.

Spain, no longer able to protect Florida, ceded it to the United States. Shortly after this, fearing the coming of a brutal slavery system, Jorge Biassou and his men left for Cuba. Santiago sent his wife to Cuba, but he was determined to stay and defend his ranch.

His son came to persuade his father to leave for Cuba with the others. Santiago's response was this: "I cannot ask my family to stay, but I will not give up my home without a struggle. No, *more* than a struggle. I will not give it up without a terrible war. If they take my land, they will pay a terrible price."

After much talk and persuasion, Santiago agreed to remain behind to sell their land. Once sold, he would join the family immediately in Cuba. After his dear Claudette and their children and their children's families left for Cuba, Santiago advertised the land for sale. The one thing they had not considered—there was no one to buy their land. Many of the Spanish and free blacks left Florida. The whites would not buy it, for they knew the new government would confiscate it and sell it at a fraction of what Santiago wanted for it.

Six months later, Santiago's fate would be set by five men who rode at a slow pace towards his ranch. The two men with suits and bowties appeared to be relaxed and talked too much. The other three spoke little, their faces tense.

One of the bowties said to the other, "There is no way we can allow Santiago to keep his property. He would have every slave in the area revolting if he had his way."

"He's mean all right," said the other bowtie. Got quite a reputation as a fighter. I don't want any of you men to get sloppy and think this is just any nigger we're facing here. If he gives us any trouble, any trouble at all, jest shoot him. You hear me? Just shoot him dead. Ain't nobody going to care."

"Now look here, Mr. Peacock. Ain't nobody going to do any shooting unless I say so. I'm still the sheriff, and I aim to uphold the law."

"Yeah, Sheriff? Well, don't forget who's paying your trip out here and for your deputies here. And besides, this here Santiago has done broke the law. You know it's against the law for blacks to have white women. I heard he's got himself a white woman from France or someplace like that. Anyway, shouldn't have any property anyhow. There's laws about that now, and this Santiago's got too much property. Might be better dead anyhow. He's likely to make trouble after we kick him off his land."

"I'll take care of him, Mr. Peacock. Don't you worry," said the sheriff, but he knew Peacock might be right. Santiago had the reputation for being a very tough and skilled fighter. The sheriff didn't expect this to be easy.

The men rode on in silence. The sheriff stopped them a mile from Santiago's ranch to give his deputies instructions. "Now listen. Santiago is a soldier, and he's been in plenty of battles from what I heard. He's not going to be afraid of the five of us. When we approach his place, I want us to spread out so we're not so much of an easy target. No shooting unless he goes for his gun first. If you're going to shoot, shoot to kill him, or he'll sure get one or two of us. Everybody understand?"

As they came into view of Santiago's ranch, they saw him working in his field. He stopped his work as they approached and picked up his rifle.

"Just take it easy, boys," the sheriff whispered to the others, "and start spreading out."

"Now lissen here, nig—"

"Peacock, shut the hell up!" shouted the sheriff. "I'll handle this." He glared at Peacock before turning his attention to Santiago. "Santiago, this isn't easy for me to tell you, but I don't have any choice."

"We all have choices, Sheriff. Be a man and do what's in your heart."

Peacock sneered at this black man talking to white men with such disrespect.

"Santiago, there are different laws here now. People here have a different way of life than what you're used to. You've broken some laws, and now we have to take your property. Blacks aren't allowed property no more anyhow. It's just a matter of time before you and all of the blacks in this area will have to give up their land. Santiago, there's another ship leaving for Cuba in a few weeks. You might be better off if you take it and join your family in Cuba."

"Tell me, Sheriff, what kind of law would take away a man's land from him? Land he has worked for over twenty years to make it into a home and to make it profitable for his family? What kind of law would take away a man's home where his children were born and raised? What kind of law would take from one man and give to another just on the basis of the color of his skin?"

"Now listen here, you uppity nigger," Peacock spluttered. He had never had anyone talk to him like this, especially a black man. "It's the way things was meant to be. This is God's law that you was meant to serve us whites. You are inferior to us and always will be. You can't do the great things the white man has done. Don't ever talk to me like that again, or you'll be swinging from that tree over there."

The sheriff became tense. He expected the worst. But Santiago surprised him. "Sheriff, mind if I get a few things and pack them in my buckboard? Then I'll be leaving this land to the great white men."

"Go ahead, but I'll have my deputies go in with you. Don't try anything."

"Don't worry, I'll be leaving."

As Santiago walked to his house with a deputy on either side, Peacock said to the sheriff, "See there, Sheriff, you just have to know how to talk to his kind. Once I put him in his place, he was as docile and obedient as a lamb."

"Don't count on it, Peacock," said the sheriff, baffled by Santiago's reaction.

In thirty minutes, Santiago and the deputies walked out of the house, Santiago with his arms full of personal belongings wrapped in sheets. He put them in his buckboard, hitched it up, and rode off without saying a word. The sheriff watched him leave, hoping he would take the next boat to Cuba.

Peacock and the other bowtie entered the house to look at their new property. This, the third property they had confiscated in the last two months, would bring them far more than the other two.

The sheriff continued to keep an eye on the departing Santiago. His curiosity piqued when Santiago drove his buckboard off the road and made a turn towards the rocky terrain at the bottom of a hill. Santiago jumped from the buckboard and walked towards the rocks. Then he bent over and fiddled with something behind the rocks. Suddenly, it became very clear to the sheriff. He turned to sound the alarm to those inside. His warning never made it past his lips as the house, barn, the bowties, and the three lawmen exploded into thousands and thousands of pieces.

For a time, Santiago stood by the rocks surveying the rubble that had once been the home he had built for his family. He had mixed feelings about what he had done. Not for the five men, who would have robbed him of his home. But for the house he'd loved so much. Full of warm memories, it seemed alive, a part of the family. But he had sworn no white man would ever live in his house, especially if taken from him by force. He knew that someday, after the Americans took over Florida, they would come for his land and home. Now, as he stood there, he felt sadness for his loss, and he felt hate for these Americans who had caused it.

Santiago had kept one promise, but now he would have to break a greater promise—one he had made to his beloved wife, Claudette. Having killed five white men, every lawman in Florida would be looking for him. To buy passage on a ship to Cuba would be too risky. He was essentially a prisoner in Florida, far away from his beloved family, whom he would never see again.

He headed towards the Indian lands, for this is where he would make his new home.

1833

Dusty rode into Gainesville feeling good about himself and his future. He had heard the land had good soil for crops and plenty of good pasture land. He pulled up to the local land office.

"Well, mister, we got a good deal on about 100 acres a day's ride south of here. It's good land, and it's pretty cheap."

"If it's good land, why is it so cheap?"

"You ever heard of Sant—"

"What he means to say," interrupted another man who appeared to be in charge, "is that people around here are superstitious. You aren't superstitious, are you?" asked the man.

"Well, no, I guess not," said Dusty.

"Good. Why don't you go out and take a look at this property? I'll give you a map, and when you come back in a few days, we'll talk price."

Dusty arrived as the sun fell below the treetops. He surveyed the grounds and saw that portions of it had been cleared at one time. You could see for miles, the flat land interrupted by a coppice here and there of tall, straight pines mingled with wide, sturdy oaks. The purple sky grew darker, and his spirits grew lighter. *Perfect.*

Dusty knelt to inspect the soil. The soil slipped through his fingers, triggering memories of conversations he'd had with his father not too many years ago. The memories stirred his emotions, causing his heart to ache for his family. The soil on this new land was rich—good for producing what he needed to eat—and the pastureland was plentiful. He decided to camp overnight and return in the morning.

In the morning, Dusty shot two rabbits and built a fire to cook them. He was relaxing, thoughts of his new life going through his mind, when he caught sight of movement. Someone was hiding in the woods about fifty yards to his left.

Dusty slowly stood and walked off in the opposite direction of the person hiding. He went into the woods, and when he thought he could no longer be seen, he dashed towards the person hiding.

As he approached that area, he glanced in the direction of the fire and saw someone creeping towards it. He suspected there may be more than one person. He decided to sit tight and observe.

When the person reached Dusty's camp, he quickly glanced around, then snatched a roasting rabbit from the fire and bolted back to his hiding place. But this time, he ran straight towards Dusty.

When he reached the edge of the woods, Dusty stepped out from behind a tree and smacked the man with a powerful blow to his face. The man went down hard and lay still for a moment. Then he screamed, "Please don't kill me! Please don't kill me! I just wanted something to eat! Please!"

"Shut up!" said Dusty. "I ain't goin' to kill you, though I should you being nothing more than a low-down thief."

As he lay there, the man showed that he was more hungry than scared, for he brought the rabbit to his mouth and bit off a large chunk.

"Who are you anyhow?" asked Dusty, "and what are you doing out here?"

"My name's Ed. I live out here."

"You live on this land? I was told it was for sale."

"No, I live out here, anywhere, everywhere. Just goes wherever. Don't got a home or people. Haven't had much luck trapping animals lately, so your rabbit smell got the better of me. Guess the animals all got wise to my traps. Don't own a rifle to shoot nothing."

"I see. What can you tell me about some superstition causing folks to be afraid to buy this land?"

"That weren't no superstition," said Ed. "That was Santiago. An' people around here got good reason to be afraid of him."

"What are you talking about?"

"Santiago had himself a big house and ranch right here on this very spot. After the government took over this territory, they tried to run ol' Santiago off. But he wasn't going nowhere without a fight. No, sir. He blowed up his house and barn and all the men what come to run him off. Now everyone's afraid to buy this here place, what used to be his. They's afraid they's goin' to get blowed up, too."

"So that's what they were talking about. Where is this Santiago now?"

"Don't know. Don't nobody know. Nobody seen him for a year or more. Spect he's with the Indians, makin' raids on white folks. They say he hates us with a passion. Say, you ain't thinkin' of buying this property, are you?"

"Yeah, yeah, I reckon I am. And I'll bet they would give me a pretty good deal for this piece of land everyone's afraid to buy."

Dusty ended up with Santiago's land. And he got it for a good price.

When he returned to the ranch, Ed was still hanging around.

Dusty kept Ed on even though he never trusted him completely. He never could shake the memory of that first meeting when Ed stole his rabbit dinner. And Ed had a bossy streak in him that Dusty resented coming from his hired hand. Yet Dusty did appreciate his help and company. In two years' time, they built a small cabin, a barn, a smokehouse, and grew their own food.

The land could support much more cattle than Dusty had been able to purchase. One hot summer day, he traveled to Gainesville hoping to find a sympathetic banker. He rode all morning and into midafternoon. The blistering heat scorched man and horse, forcing Dusty to seek water. He turned into the woods and headed for a lake located about a half-mile from the road. There, he dismounted where man and horse rested and drank of the warm, clear water.

He walked to a shaded spot to rest a few moments when he spotted three Indians watching him from forty yards away. He stopped and stared back. One Indian tapped his horse. Uneasiness crept over Dusty. This Indian, whose black skin caused him to stand out from the others, had dark, intense eyes. Dusty searched his mind but couldn't recall any problems between whites and Indians.

The Indian stopped thirty feet away. When he spoke, Dusty understood. *Santiago.* "You're living on my land, Americano," said the stranger.

"You must be Santiago," said Dusty, trying hard to hide his nerves.

"I swore no Americano ladron would ever live on my land. An' now there is you. You are not welcome on my property. I will give you three days to get off. If you are not off, you will wish you were."

"I am not a thief. I paid for the ranch, and I plan to stay there." He wondered whether his bravado might get him killed.

"Three days," said Santiago. He turned his horse and galloped away with the others.

"Well," Dusty whispered to himself, "I'll be damned if anyone's goin' to run me off my land." He mounted his horse and rode to Gainesville, determined to get his loan.

Though not successful in getting his loan, over the next forty years, he and Ed managed to add to the ranch and make it profitable. They even added a few slaves—all the while waging their private war with Santiago. Santiago shot at the two white men often. Once he nicked Dusty's arm. Twice he burned down their barn. Their feud became legend in the area. The *Gainesville Chronicle* printed a story every time one of them fired a shot at the other. Of course, the *Chronicle* wasn't beyond embellishing the story, which added to the excitement. Once, when Santiago fired one shot at Dusty then rode off, the *Chronicle* printed a story of a ferocious gun battle lasting several hours. They had to print a second edition.

On July 23, 1860, while rounding up cattle, Dusty clutched his chest as a piercing pain gripped him. He slumped over but managed to stay on his horse and ride him to the cabin, where Ed helped him down. Within the hour, the pain had subsided, but Dusty saw it as a warning. For all these many years, he had never forgotten his family. He yearned to see them, tell them his story of what happened that terrible day, and show them what he had accomplished in Florida. And he hoped to leave the ranch to family. Most of all, he wanted to make peace with whatever family he had left before he died. One evening, he sat by the light of a kerosene lamp and wrote a letter to his brother.

A few days after sending the letter, he rode out to inspect the farthest reaches of his ranch. It was a typical hot, muggy day. No one had heard or seen Santiago for the past six months, so Dusty kept a wary eye, but relaxed more than usual. While sitting by a stream, his mind lost on questions of how his brother would react to his letter, a voice that he knew at once startled him back to reality.

"Hello, Dusty."

Dusty responded without even turning around. "Hello, Santiago."

"I've been watching and waiting for several days for you to leave the cabin. This will be the last time that we will meet. I've been doing mucho thinking lately. I'm growing old, and soon will not be able to fight as I once did. I swore once that no Americano would live in my house. And no one has. But you live on my land. You, my enemy, have been a good enemy. I have not been able to kill you. But today, I vowed one of us must die. I do not wish to die knowing you remain on my land. So now we fight to the death. What do you think about that, eh, my good enemy?"

Dusty stood slowly and faced Santiago. He did look old. Dusty also knew that he meant everything he'd said, but he hoped he could talk him out of a fight to the death. He wanted more than anything to live to receive a response from his brother.

"Look, Santiago, we're both too old to be fighting anymore. How about we call a truce and forget this fighting? I'll even give you a piece of land to put a home on, and we can live out our days in peace. What do you say?"

Santiago snorted at Dusty. "What! You would give me back a piece of my own land! You would throw crumbs at me when it is you and your people who have stolen my life and my land from me? For this you will die, damn you!" As he said this, Santiago drew a knife and hurled it at Dusty. Dusty drew his gun and shot Santiago in the chest just as the knife sliced deep into his stomach.

Dusty fell backwards into the stream. His blood turned the water into swirling pools of red. He feared he would pass out. Dusty lay on his side, then steeled himself for the intense pain he knew would come as he gripped the knife with both hands. He yanked hard. Close to passing out, he pressed his hands against the cut to stem the flow of blood. Slowly and with great difficulty, he tore his shirt to press against the wound. He crawled to the edge of the stream and could go no more. His abdomen felt like it might explode. He knew he was going to die.

When Dusty woke, he marveled at being in his own bed, though his blurred vision kept him from seeing anything very clearly. But he recognized the general shapes of things and the familiar smells and colors. He remembered his encounter with Santiago. But he mostly dwelled on the incredible pain in his abdomen. Every movement, every twitch, felt as though the knife remained in him and had been twisted.

At some point Ed walked in. "Hey, Dusty, you're awake. How you feeling? Not too good I bet."

Too weak to respond, Dusty tried to make sense of Ed's ramblings. Dusty eventually lost consciousness again.

The next day, Dusty awoke with a bit more coherence. Ed related how Dusty's horse had returned without him, so he'd retraced the horse's tracks where he found Dusty unconscious. He brought him back to the cabin and treated his wound as best he could. He suspected that Santiago had done this, but there was no sign of Santiago.

"Listen Ed, I'm going to die, and I know it. I have a brother in South Carolina. I want you to write him a letter. Tell him I'm dying and offer him to come and take over this ranch if he wants."

Surprised to learn that Dusty had family, Ed turned bitter towards his old companion. He didn't like the idea that Dusty would offer the ranch to his brother, especially since Ed had been here all these years and had been the one to help build the ranch. Ed recalled all the work he had put into the buildings and the land—there had been nothing when he started out. He had put in forty years—that's a big chunk of time, that's a man's whole life. Ed never wrote the letter. Dusty died three days later.

Three months later, John Higgins sold his plantation and started out on his long trek south to be with his brother.

Itch's Story

Near the West Coast of Africa, 1821

Today, Intikuma celebrated his seventeenth year, for seventeen years ago his song came into his mother's mind and heart. His mother, Tandi, had gone to a quiet place by the great river that flowed near their village. Here, she sat under her favorite shade tree, as all the young women of her village did when they desired to bear a child, and waited. She was listening for her unborn child's song to come to her from the music of the flowing river. This strong, nourishing river would tell her of her child.

Tandi was taller than most of the women in her village. Her high cheekbones and soft eyes accentuated her beauty. Whenever she walked through the village, her figure tall and graceful, others would smile on her with respect. She had earned their respect, not as the daughter of a village leader, and not as the widow of another leader, but rather because of the courage and grace she so often displayed. Now, she watched proudly as her son went through a ritual that would alter his life forever.

Today, Intikuma was about to undergo one of the most difficult rituals known to his people. As the ceremony progressed, Tandi's mind wandered back to that day when her son was first thought of....

She sat, eyes focused on the surging waters, prayed quietly to the spirit of the earth, and meditated, feeling the union of herself with all creation. After a period of time, a song formed in her mind. It started with an awareness of a pattern in the sounds of the wind as it blew through the grasses and trees, and of the babbling waters stroking half-hidden rocks and cuddling the shore. Tandi's heart beat faster as her unborn child's song came to her, a spirit whispering the words in her ear, pressing them to her heart. She sat straight to be more alert—closed her eyes to avoid distractions, wanting to suck it all in. By the time the sun burned high in the sky and the warm breeze swayed the tall grasses like the breath of a ghost, her child's song had come to her.

She knew her child would be a boy, and his name would be Intikuma. With the song complete, she continued to sit for a while, a faint smile on her lips. She sang the song aloud to hear it and know that it was real.

Intikuma, of great courage
Whose soul soars with the great birds of the mountains
Intikuma shall lead his people
Intikuma will show his people the way
Intikuma will not be defeated
With gentleness and kindness, he will lead the way

She was pleased with the song, for it told of a brave and kind person who would be a leader of her people—just as her husband, Ndoda, had been, and his father before him. Intikuma was the name of a mythical character in many of the village tales. He was wise and clever, always defeating his opponents.

When Tandi returned to her hut, she entered slowly, sat across from Ndoda without speaking to him, although she thought she might burst with news of their child's song. Though he saw Tandi sit opposite him and knew by her squirming she had news, he continued the delicate work of shaping a spearhead for tomorrow's hunt. She watched his firm muscles work the stone. She loved his piercing dark eyes. Finally, he stopped, smiled at her, looked into the deep brown of her eyes, and knew.

"Teach me our child's song," he said.

As she sang to him, her voice filled him with love for her, and his heart swelled with pride. When she finished, they gave thanks to the Spirit of all Creation.

"It is a good song," he said. "Our son will be a leader for all our village."

"Yes," she replied, locking her gaze onto Ndoda's shining face. The River of Life coursed through her veins, and The Wind that Touches All Living Things caressed her. She laid her head on Ndoda's chest, his beating heart encircling her, enveloping her very being.

During the night, they made love to conceive their child. They sang his song to invite Intikuma into their world.

Nine months later, the time arrived.

"It is time! It is time!" shouted Mawranda, the midwife, calling her assistants. Mawranda spoke with authority when it came to delivering a baby.

"You must wait outside now," she insisted, shoving Ndoda out of the hut.

After a short wait, there came the sound Ndoda had longed to hear—the wailing of a newborn. The sound of new life filled Ndoda with joy. He rushed into the hut, where he found Intikuma lovingly wrapped in Tandi's arms.

As a child, Intikuma's winning smile and playful ways won him friends and admirers throughout the village. Intikuma grew into a strong young man, and he showed great ability at hunting and other skills the men of the village needed to learn for survival. He developed into a model for the youth and showed great promise as a leader of his people.

In time, all of the villagers knew Intikuma's song, just as they knew the song of every village member. So, as a child, when he hurt himself, they sang his song to comfort him; when he proved to be the fastest, and when he tracked and killed a wildebeest, which fed the entire village, they sang his song to praise him.

With great joy, Tandi remembered the early years of her beloved son, especially now, as she proudly watched him prepare to go through the apprentice ritual. If he passed, he would become the apprentice to her father, the Sangoma, the spiritual leader of her people.

As the first part of his ceremony came to a close, Intikuma sat facing the fire, eyes closed, preparing himself for what lay ahead. All the villagers joined in Intikuma's song as a tribute to him and to give him their love and support. Intikuma opened his eyes and faced the villagers. The time had arrived for him to depart. For a moment, his eyes met his mother's eyes, and they silently communicated their love. Then, without a word, raising his arm in tribute to the village, he moved silently into the jungle.

Intikuma's task was to complete a seven-day spirit journey. During this time, he must remain in a location selected by his grandfather, where he would put his grandfather's teachings to test by communing with the spirit world. The spirits would either speak with Intikuma and give their blessing for him to be the apprentice to the Sangoma, or they would remain silent, indicating he was not ready.

He felt the earth beneath his feet as he walked to his destination. Although night had shrouded the jungle in blackness, he walked with confidence. He walked in *his* forest. He knew every tree and every obstacle along the way. He heard the chirps and the roars, the skirmishes of the hunters, and he knew them all. He loved this forest; he called it home.

He had named some of the trees—those great giants that revealed qualities he admired. The Ndoda tree, struck by lightning years ago, a survivor with a long black scar down one side. A casual observer might look at the tree and consider it ugly, with its scarred trunk. Intikuma saw a sign of strength and determination. He named the tree Ndoda, out of respect for and to remember his father. Whenever he walked past, he thanked it for teaching him about strength and about sharing. It had grown taller than the other trees in the forest, and many birds, monkeys, and other animals depended on its leaves and branches for shelter and food. The tree had great strength and generosity, just like his father. Sadness entered his spirit when he remembered the night his father had been killed by two lions while hunting. That night, and for many days and nights, the village mourned.

At times, Intikuma dreamed of the Ndoda tree. In his dream, the branches of the Ndoda tree touched all of creation, and he could see how everything connected. He saw how clouds brought rain, which nourished the plants and trees, which brought food and provided weapons to hunt. These same plants and trees provided sustenance to the animals they hunted. His grandfather said this dream was a gift to him, and he should remember it always.

"Hello, my good friend," he said to the tree as he passed by on the way to his destination.

The sliver of yellow moon that hung in the sky did nothing to light the path, but still it was a friend coming along. Intikuma made his way comfortably through the woods—every root he stepped on, every rock, every bush and tree his map, giving his exact location in the forest.

The cool night air blew gently across his body. Occasionally, a monkey called out, or a bird chattered. Intikuma felt confident. *The earth is good to us.*

He arrived at the sacred place of his Spirit Union, a small clearing in a copse of baobab trees. He could hear the river, not thirty yards away. Here, he first gave thanks to the Earth for guiding him, and then to the moon for its company, and to the villagers for send-ing him here under their protection. He removed sacred objects from his pouch to prepare for his Spirit Quest. In the East corner of the clearing, he placed the Sangoma pipe and a secret mixture of herbs prepared by the Sangoma himself. This he would smoke on his fourth day to help him communicate with the spirits. On the West corner, he placed bark he'd cut from the baobab trees to be burned on his first night. The aroma would cause him to dream of his ancestors, whose wisdom might enter Intikuma if found worthy. In the North corner, he laid a small bowl of blue powder and a large blue topaz gemstone—so deep blue and yet clear, smooth as the skin of a child, it is said to be a piece of the sky left over from creation. On his second day, he must mix the powder to make paint for his face and meditate with the sky-stone to become one with the sky and all the stars. In the South corner, he placed the whitest feathers from the great white bird of the river. On his third day, he would tie the feathers so they covered his head and then sit in tall grass by the river until the birds spoke with him. Thus would all the creatures of the forest know him.

Intikuma was not to leave the area while on his Spirit Quest. He had a few berries and dried meats, barely enough to sustain him for the duration of his spiritual journey, and water he could drink from the river. This Quest would teach him sacrifice and compassion. He would come to know hunger and thirst. He would learn that he could endure hardships. Even more than this, however, as his physical body weakened, the spirit world would open to him; he would begin to have visions and visits from his spirit ancestors.

For the first three days, Intikuma did as he had been taught. And on his first day, he did dream of his ancestors; and on his second day, he did feel a special union with the sky. On his third day, the great white birds did approach him, and he listened. He remained quiet in the sacred ground, spending his time focusing on the gifts of the Earth and of his village. He recalled the stories of the wise leaders of his tribe's past, and he called on them to teach him of the things they knew. Even though he experienced hunger and thirst, he rationed his food so he would have enough to last to the end.

Into his fourth day, Intikuma began to hallucinate. He had tried to stay awake day and night, though he would doze briefly and awaken with a start, feeling ashamed that he had drifted off to sleep. During the heat of the afternoon, while in a semi-conscious state, he heard strange voices. At first, he thought the spirits spoke with him, but he couldn't understand the language. As the voices grew nearer, he also sensed an unfamiliar smell—a smell of evil.

Intikuma struggled to rally his body to fight off the evil, but before he could do so, the evil force grabbed him and dragged him away. Rough hands held his arms, and a hard object clamped his legs. Through his blurred vision, he saw people with skin the color of clouds. Were the spirits angry with him?

When Intikuma came to, he lay on the ground surrounded by others—men, women, and children from different villages, all tied to each other with a heavy chain. The people with skin-like-clouds guarded them and beat them. Intikuma could understand no one.

Using gestures, Intikuma learned that no one knew where they were going. These men had powerful magic that could kill a man with a loud noise. Surely the Sangoma would come soon with men from his village to rescue him.

After days of walking chained to four men from other villages, they arrived at the shore of a great body of water. There, Intikuma saw a great vessel afloat on the water. He had never seen anything so huge that could stay afloat. The men who had captured him must have special powers. They must have great Tagati, or Black Magic. But they were not good spirits, for they treated others with cruelty.

Intikuma studied his captors, for he had never seen men such as these—light skin, hair growing past their shoulders, and some with hair hanging down from their face. *How strange is their dress,* he thought. Clothing covered their legs and torsos, and they wore covering on their feet. They carried long knives made of something harder than stone, which glistened in the sunlight. Strangest of all to Intikuma was their behavior. They had no compassion, no caring for their captives, or, for that matter, for each other. *These men seem to have no spirit, or perhaps their spirit is dead,* he thought.

The men guarding Intikuma and the others made them sit in the hot sand. They were fed very little, and even then, the food was barely edible. They were given water too rarely. His leg had become sore and was bleeding where the leg iron had rubbed it, and now an ugly blister oozing puss caused him to limp.

Intikuma watched as several of the light-skinned men rowed a smaller boat to the shore. They forced small groups of villagers into the boat and rowed them to the big ship. He watched as they climbed rope ladders onto the ship, and soon they disappeared from sight. Long after the sun had reached its highest point, Intikuma's turn had come. He stood and moved quickly, for he had seen what punishment happened to those who moved too slowly.

He and the three chained to him, along with others, were crowded into a boat. The small boat bobbed in the water, making Intikuma's head spin. Intikuma had heard of this large body of water. Several villagers had journeyed here and returned to tell about it. He knew you could not drink the water and that strange fish lived in this water. He thought again of his family and how worried they must be. He wondered whether he would ever see them again. He had great concern for his mother. Who would look after her with him gone? He must do something to get back home, but he felt powerless against the Tagati of these strange men.

As the small boat heaved and bobbed its way to the large ship, Intikuma looked back at the land he so loved. His eye followed the sandy beach up to the thick forests, and, rising above the treetops, two beautiful, snow-capped mountain peaks—a sight he would carry in his memory always.

They arrived at the big vessel and were made to climb rope ladders to get onto the ship. Once on the vessel, they were shoved down a door in the floor and down a ladder. They descended into the dark for a long way before coming to a large room already half-filled with other African men chained to the wall and packed very close together—so close that no one could move without the person next to him having to move to accommodate the new position.

The room stank of feces and vomit and sweat and urine. The smell alone made some vomit. And, perhaps thankfully, they had little in their stomachs to vomit. Very small amounts of light filtered down from above. Voices of many men mingled together, speaking different languages, and while Intikuma could not understand them, he heard their fear and dismay and hopelessness. As each prisoner arrived at the spot where they would remain for the next three to four months, their ankles were unshackled one at a time and then shackled to the wall.

The incessant motion of the vessel made Intikuma nauseated. He could hold it no longer, and he vomited on himself and others nearby. He felt bad about this, for he did not wish to offend the people around him. But he could not even apologize to them.

As he lay in the darkness on the hard floor, Intikuma sought to understand what was happening to him. He recalled hearing stories about the occasional disappearance of a villager, but there was always a reasonable explanation.

Long after the room was crammed full with men, noise and confusion sounded from above, and the vessel sailed out to sea. Intikuma could not tell how long he had been on the ship—perhaps three days, if the number of times the faint light from above came and went could be any indication. Once a day, two of the light-skinned men came into the room with buckets of water, which they used to splash the slaves and the deck around them, but this had little effect on the stink of human waste.

Once they put to sea, twenty captives at a time were taken to the main deck for fifteen minutes of exercise each day. The crew made them walk about or, if they craved entertainment, made them dance. The slaves received meager food once or, rarely, twice a day. Tasteless slop dropped on the deck in front of them eased some of their hunger pangs. Many of the captives died on the voyage. The lack of respect the light-skinned men had for the dead surprised Intikuma. The men dragged dead prisoners to the main deck and threw them overboard. Intikuma mourned for these dead and their families, who would never see them again or know that they had come to rest in this great body of water. At times, he could hear the screams of women and children, and he thought of his own mother and the grief she must be suffering.

The voyage grew longer and longer. It seemed that it would never end. He thought maybe the voyage would not end until they had all died. He decided that he, too, must die. To end his suffering, Intikuma stopped eating. Within a couple of days, he became semi-conscious. He felt someone kick him in the side and heard a low moan. Was the moan his? He couldn't tell.

"This one's about ready for heavin' over the side," said one of the crew. "Let's give 'im another day, I say," said the other. Intikuma heard the voices, which sounded very far away.

Sometime later, Intikuma heard another, more familiar voice, this one closer and more distinct. It called his name. He stared at a man from his village standing before him. Intikuma knew him at once.

"Father, how is it that you are here?" he asked.

"I am always with you, Intikuma." How good to hear his father's voice, and how good to hear his own language.

"Father, take me away from here, or have I already died? Is that how we are together now?"

"No, Intikuma, you have not died. I have come to tell you that you must live."

"But Father, I cannot bear this suffering any longer. I believe this voyage will go on until we are all dead."

"This voyage will go on longer, and many more will suffer and die, but it will come to an end. I have come to tell you that you must do what you can to live."

"But Father, why would I live in such a terrible place with such terrible beasts in control of us?"

"Are you not of the Earth? Did the Earth bring you to your mother and me just for you to perish in an unknown place before you have finished what you were born to do?"

"But Father, I do not know what I am to do. Here, I can do nothing."

"You will learn."

"I do not know if I can finish what I am meant to do."

"Intikuma, only you can complete your task. It is important that you do this. It will not be easy, but it must be done. Many people will suffer if you do not live."

"But Father, how can I do anything when these evil beasts have me chained and allow me no freedom?"

"These are mere men, Intikuma. But yes, they are evil. You are good. You must be stronger than them."

"But how can I be stronger than them?"

"Intikuma, do you not remember Ndoda, your tree of great strength and generosity?"

"Yes, Father."

"Your tree continued to live even though it was marked by fire from the sky. Ndoda continued to give what it could, even though it was damaged and had less to give. Ndoda lives day by day. Get through one day at a time. Your journey across this great water will end. Remember your song. It will help you to discover your purpose and thus find your strength."

"I will try, father."

He looked at Intikuma for a few moments and then said, "I must go now."

Intikuma pleaded, "Please do not leave me, Father." But he spoke in vain.

He thought deeply about what had transpired between him and his father. He realized this visit was a gift of life.

Footsteps. Voices. Intikuma brought his awareness back to his chains and the suffering around him. The crew, working their way through the tangle of human cargo, slopped down the meal. The crewmembers looked at Intikuma scornfully and asked, "Well, you going to eat today, you ungrateful black bastard?"

Intikuma did not understand the words of these men, but he heard their hatred. In obedience to his vision rather than to the demand of the men, he slowly picked up a handful of slop and put it to his mouth. He had been reminded that he belonged to this Earth and had a reason for being. He thought of his family and his village. He remembered his song and began to sing it softly. As he sang, his song seemed to mock him, for bound in chains, far from his people, how could he possibly lead when he had no control over his own life? He decided that for now, he must endure this voyage as well as he could.

By mid-morning, an alarmed Tandi stared down the path hoping to see her son return from his spirit quest. He should have returned shortly after the sun peeked over the horizon. Tandi went to her father, asking, "Father, it is now well past when Intikuma should have returned. Should we not send a runner to find him?" Tandi remembered well when her husband did not return from his hunt. This felt much the same to her.

"We will give him until the sun touches the top of the sky. If he has not returned by then, we will send a runner. We must have faith in him, my child. We mustn't act too quickly."

"Yes, Father," said a nervous Tandi.

She returned to her hut to await her son.

At the appointed time, the Sangoma sent a runner. He reported back the missing Intikuma and the many footprints around the sacred area. A group of the village's best warriors followed the footprints, finally sighting the kidnappers and their cargo at the beach, where they watched from the jungle as the kidnappers loaded their human captives. The men of the village, greatly outnumbered and in awe of the strange men's Tagati, could only watch. They searched from a distance for Intikuma among those sitting on the beach, but they did not see him. With great sorrow, they left to return to their village.

Tandi could not bear the news of her son. There had been rumors of such things happening, but Tandi could not believe she had lost her husband and now also her son. She fell to her knees and wept. Other women came to her and helped her into her hut. There, she grieved all day and night.

At dawn, she arose and went out to sit under the tree where she had first heard the song of her son. She quietly and tearfully sang his song. For three days and three nights she remained by the tree in deep mourning. She asked the gods to give her understanding of what had happened and why. She implored them to intercede and return her beloved son to her.

On the fourth day, she went to her father and spoke with him. "Father, my chest feels like it is broken. Air does not want to come into my body. My legs are heavy. My spirit has been taken from me." Tandi thought that she could not survive her grief. Her anguish never seemed to ease.

The great Sangoma stood in the doorway of his daughter's hut, watching her sit so still, her eyes downcast. He remembered her as a little girl, so full of life, running through the village, how she loved to play tricks and how she would laugh. He could hear her laughter, the laughter of a little girl enjoying life so much. He wanted to help her, but he felt powerless.

Then, from somewhere inside of him, came Intikuma's song. He began singing it, softly. Tears welled in his eyes for his grandson. Tandi looked up at her father as he sang so beautifully. When he finished the song, he knelt down and held his daughter as she wept quietly. He held her for a very long time.

Intikuma and his fellow prisoners were aboard the Spanish schooner *San Jose* under Capitan Villar y Aprisa and headed for

Amelia Island, located just off the northern coast of Florida. Although the United States of America had outlawed the further importation of slaves in 1808, Amelia Island and the city of Fernandina had become bustling slave centers. Between 1808 and 1860, according to estimates, more than 250,000 slaves were illegally imported—many of them came through Amelia Island.

Intikuma made it safely to Amelia Island after five long, difficult months at sea. Promptly their captors cleaned them up, fed them enough to make them look healthy, and sold them to the highest bidder. Of the 190 slaves originally aboard the *San Jose,* sixty-four men, women, and children died before reaching Amelia Island. Thirty-seven sold at a discount due to their weakened condition. None would ever see their families again.

Jeremiah Walden, a ruthless slave owner with a large cotton plantation in Kentucky, purchased Intikuma and fourteen others. They stayed overnight in a camp and left the next morning for the long trek to Walden's plantation.

"Le's go," shouted Jeremiah's foreman, cracking his whip near the heads of the newly purchased slaves.

As they walked, Intikuma's thoughts jumped from fear of what the future might hold to remembering his family. In spite of his chains and the fearsome snapping whip, he felt grateful to be on land and off the stinking ship of misery and death. This new land amazed Intikuma—so many light-skinned men riding atop strange, four-legged animals. And the huge huts they lived in. He wondered at the large number of trees it must take to build such things. And he marveled at the large clearings with row after row of plants that were all alike—and why do people bend over these plants? These things and many others filled his mind.

After many long days of hard walking, the exhausted captives arrived at the plantation. They had marched in single file, each one chained to the one behind and to the one in front. As they entered the plantation grounds, Intikuma saw many Africans bending over and picking something white from a plant. None looked up, so intent were they on their work.

A tough, surly white man shoved Intikuma and the two men chained to him into the hastily built shack.

Later, a man brought three bowls and placed a dipper of runny porridge, not much better than the ship's slop, into each bowl. The men gobbled it up. One of the enslaved spoke. The other said something in response, and both men attempted a conversation, struggling to grasp the meaning of the other's words. Their dialects were similar, but Intikuma could only grasp the meaning of an occasional word.

"All right, all you niggers get out here," someone yelled.

The three men did not understand the command, but they knew they had best look out the door to see what was going on. The fourteen newly enslaved gathered outside, where they were assigned a task and a more experienced slave to teach them their duties. Intikuma was assigned to work in the fields. It was tedious, back-breaking work. He soon learned why so many people bent over the cotton plants. At the end of the day, the enslaved men and women lined up to have their pickings weighed. Those not meeting their quota were whipped and made to work on Sunday, their day off.

Over time, using gestures and single words, the men learned to communicate and to respond to commands.

Intikuma often thought of his homeland and family and sang his song to remind himself of the promise of his future.

One early morning, as Intikuma and his two cabinmates neared the barn to claim a bag to fill with cotton, they heard a thump and someone call for help. Intikuma rushed into the barn, Martin and Tom right behind him. There lay Jeremiah Walden, flat on his back. He had fallen from the loft onto the floor below. His arm was twisted at an odd angle, and a heavy bale lay on top of him.

The three enslaved men stared at their feared and hated owner. Then, Intikuma took action. He rushed to lift the heavy bale, moving it to the side.

To Martin, he shouted, "Go an' get some help!"

As groups of slaves rushed to the barn to retrieve a bag, they all stopped, staring quietly at their feared master lying dazed on the floor.

"The rest of you grab your bags an' head out to the fields," said Intikuma. The crowd did as he said—not because he had any control over them, but because they knew he was right. No matter about Massa Walden, they were going to be held accountable for their quota come the end of the day.

In spite of his predicament, Jeremiah Walden took notice of the young Intikuma. He was young and strong and had a way with people. Maybe this young slave's talents were being wasted in the fields. He would think carefully about how best to use this young African.

A few days later, the overseer approached Intikuma. "Hey, you, Inti. Come with me."

"Yes, sir," answered Intikuma, his nerves set on edge. Since the barn incident, Intikuma had worried he had been too aggressive, acting like a white man in charge. Intikuma walked behind the overseer as they headed towards the barn. There, old Amos, the slave in charge of the horses and the livery, brushed a horse.

"Go on up there an' talk to ole Amos," said the overseer before he walked off.

When Intikuma reached Amos, he stopped and waited. After a few seconds, Amos laid down his brush. "Well, boy, it appears you going ta be workin' with me from now on. Don't know why. I don't need no help. Been doin' this for a long time an' doin' it all by myself. But de massa is de massa, so you an' me is working together. Now listen here. You best do just as I tells you, or else we both get a bad whippin'—then it's back to the fields. I don't think I could handle that. Probably kill me. So, you gonna do like I tells you. Got that?" grumbled Amos.

"Yes, sir, Mister Amos. I understands you real well. And I promises you I will do just as you says."

"All right then, here, take this brush to this horse an' do it just like I tells you."

"Yes, sir, Mister Amos," said Intikuma with a smile. Working with these beautiful animals was much better than the backbreaking fieldwork.

Over the next few months, Intikuma learned well.

Often, at night, Intikuma would sneak out of his shack while everyone else slept. He would creep into the woods, where he sat quietly meditating and trying to communicate with his mother and father and the Sangoma.

For six months now, Amos and Intikuma had worked together, and during that time they had become trusted friends. One day, Amos approached Intikuma.

"Hey, Inti, I want to talk with you 'bout something, but you got to promise you won't tell no one, an' you got to keep your voice low. You got that?"

"Why sure, Amos. What you so serious about?"

"Now, listen here, you promise to keep this a secret?"

"Sure, Amos."

"Before I come to this here place," Amos stopped and looked around, "I was taught some reading. Now you can't go telling that to no one else. They's liable to kill me if anyone finds out. But if you wants, I can teach you. But you can't ever let on. You understand me?"

"But Amos, what the use of learning that? 'Specially if it could be bad for me?"

"I'll tell you why. 'Cause it's learning that you're going to need some day. We ain't gonna be slaves forever. An' when we is free, you going to need to read so you can know what's going on. Don't you see these white men with their newspaper and reading the words on things?"

"You really think we gonna be free someday, Amos?"

"It going to happen. You mark my word! But for now, do you want to learn to read or don't you? An' you better hurry up your answer before the massa come back."

"I don't know, Amos. What if I'm not smart enough to learn it?"

Amos moved closer to Intikuma's face. "Now you listen to me. You an' every man here is smart as any white man. 'Course we can't let on that we is. But don't you worry none. You is plenty smart enough."

Intikuma thought for a few moments. "Maybe I'll try it an' see what happens."

Amos looked into Intikuma's eyes. "That's good enough fer now. You be careful that you don't let anyone see you, you understands?"

"I understands, Amos."

Amos glanced around. "Now I'm going to draw the first letter in the sand. It's called an 'A.' Now you make one."

Intikuma put his finger in the sand and formed an "A."

"That's good," said Amos. "Now we wipe it out, so no one see it. Tomorrow, we learn another."

And so his lessons continued for several months. At every opportunity Intikuma looked at writing—feed bags, newspapers left around, everything, and each day he learned a little more.

"Inti, you a smart fella. You learning to read good as me," whispered Amos with a smile. "You jus' be careful no whites ever see you doing that, you hear me?"

"Thanks, Amos. I understands."

In two years' time, Intikuma had developed a reputation as being excellent with animals, especially horses. Amos had slowed down considerably. More and more, the master looked to Intikuma to work with the horses.

"Hey, Inti, get over here," yelled Jeremiah.

"Yes, sir, Massa," said Inti, sprinting to his master.

"Tomorrow, I'm going to Ohio to pick up some horses, and you're goin' with me. Be ready to go first thing in the morning."

"Yes, sir, Massa."

A knot grew in the pit of his stomach. He had never traveled with the master before. Intikuma rose from his straw mattress long before he needed. With time to spare, he hitched a horse to the buckboard. He would be ready when the master arrived.

At daybreak, Jeremiah arrived. "Good. You're ready to go. I like that Inti. Remember, always be prompt."

"Yes, sir." He would not forget. Intikuma breathed a bit easier as he tapped the horse and the two men set out for Ohio. Intikuma drove the buckboard with the supplies, and Jeremiah rode horseback.

In a small town several miles beyond the Ohio border, they stopped to replenish their supplies. Inti loaded the supplies while Jeremiah paid the clerk. Left by himself, Inti studied with fascination the writing on the bag of flour. He read all of the words until he got stuck on a large word he had never seen before. He stopped loading for a moment and put his finger on the word, trying to sound out each letter as he had been taught.

At this moment, Jeremiah walked up. "What the hell is this? You learning how to read? Well, ain't no nigger belonging to me going to be readin', no sir."

Intikuma took a step back, not knowing what to expect.

Jeremiah took out his knife, and before Intikuma could react, he grabbed Intikuma's forefinger and sliced it off with one swift motion.

Intikuma panicked. He screamed, grabbed the stub of his finger, and ran.

"Come back here!" yelled Jeremiah. He took off in pursuit of the bleeding Intikuma.

Intikuma glanced back at his master, causing him to bump into a man, which sent them sprawled out in the middle of the road.

Jeremiah grabbed Intikuma by the shirt. "Now you goddam nig—"

"Hold on, mister. This boy is hurt, and before you take him anywhere, I'm going to have a look."

"The hell you are," bellowed Jeremiah. "He's going with me."

The shorter man grabbed Jeremiah's hand, which was holding Intikuma, and said, "The boy is bleeding. I'm a doctor. I intend to look at him before he goes anywhere."

Jeremiah, surprised by the strength of the stranger's grip, refused to allow some stranger dictate to him how to treat his slaves. Jeremiah pushed Intikuma to the side and reached for his pistol. But before he could draw it, someone from behind grabbed his shoulder.

"Best you leave that pistol where it is, mister."

Jeremiah turned enough to see that the man speaking was a big man, maybe six feet, three or four inches. He had a day's growth of beard, and his eyes, fixed on Jeremiah, stopped him cold. Then Jeremiah noticed his badge.

"You the sheriff?"

"That's right. And folks around here wouldn't take too kindly to your shooting the only doctor in these parts. Not sure I could protect you if you did the good doctor any harm. Not sure I'd want to either."

"This here is my slave. I want to take him and leave. That ain't against the law, is it?"

"Tell you what, mister. How 'bout the doctor here take a look at your slave, fix him up so's he's good as new, and then you can be on your way."

Jeremiah didn't like any of this, but he didn't have much choice. "All right, but I'm not letting this slave out of my sight."

"You can wait outside my office right over there. Your being in the room would make us both uncomfortable. Your slave isn't going anywhere," said the doctor.

Jeremiah glared at the doctor and then at the sheriff.

"Now don't worry none, mister. Your slave will be safe with the doctor," reassured the sheriff.

Jeremiah paced back and forth in front of the office for what seemed like a long time—too long just to sew a finger. Finally, he could wait no longer. He rapped hard on the office door three times. No answer. He rapped again. Still no answer.

"That's odd," said the sheriff.

The sheriff pushed the door open. Jeremiah stormed in. The doctor lay sprawled on the floor, unconscious. No slave. The back window open.

The sheriff helped the doctor up. "What happened, Doc?"

The doctor had blood covering the back of his head. A bloody wooden mallet had been dropped on the floor by the open window.

"I'm not quite sure," he said with a grimace. "I turned my back for an instant to get a bandage, and that's all I remember."

"And you let my slave get away!" shouted Jeremiah, pointing his finger at the doctor.

"Look, mister, I'm really sorry about your slave. If you hurry, you can probably still catch him."

Jeremiah stuck his head out the window. Four footprints led directly away from the office. He ran to the store to get his horse and rode off in the direction of the tracks.

After Jeremiah was well on his way, the sheriff turned to the doctor. "You okay, Tom?"

"I'm fine." He grabbed a rag and dipped it in a bucket of water. He wiped the blood off his head. "The boy had plenty of blood to spare."

They nodded knowingly at each other.

After the sheriff had left and darkness settled in, Doc Stone lowered the shades and locked the door. He pulled the table and rug from the wall, revealing a trap door. He opened the door and, taking a candle, climbed down into the concealed basement. There sat Intikuma, huddled in a dark corner, his cut finger stub bandaged.

"How are you doing?" asked the doctor.

"I'm all right," responded Intikuma nervously, not sure whether he should trust this stranger.

"I'm sorry to keep you in the dark for so long, but it's best we make sure the man you're with is really gone."

"I understand. I'm all right. The dark doesn't bother me."

"Good. I'm going to close the door again. I'll leave you this candle if you want it. I'll return in about an hour with some food. Don't worry, you'll be safe here."

There was a quality about the doctor that Intikuma recognized as compassion, and he believed the doctor would be good to his word.

"I'll be here."

When the doctor left, Intikuma closed his eyes and focused his mind. He needed a long conversation with the people he loved.

As he had done for slaves so many times in the past, Dr. Stone made arrangements to send Intikuma to Canada. There, he spent the next two years learning blacksmithing and living a quiet life. He grew big and strong and confident. He befriended local Indians, who taught him wilderness survival skills.

Intikuma sat very still, oblivious to the cool night air. The moonless night was black as coal. Only the red embers of the dying fire had yet to succumb. A vision came to him of his people. Suddenly, the vision switched to Doctor Stone, who called to him. Intikuma struggled to understand this vision, but it made no sense.

Several days later, the vision came to him again, even more strongly. He lived comfortably in Canada, and safe. He had no desire to return to America, where the risk of being taken back into slavery was great. Yet he wondered what this vision meant. He asked this question many times, but no answer came.

"Well, Catherine, I guess that about does it," said Dr. Stone. He stepped back to look at the wagonload of furniture and belongings they had piled high.

"This will be quite an adventure," Catherine said. She gave her husband a warm hug.

"I'll hook the horses up, and we'll be on our way."

"We're sure going to miss you around here," said the sheriff.

The small group of men and women standing around to see them off nodded in agreement.

"I sure wish you would change your mind. I don't like the danger you're putting yourself into there in the South. You'll be right in the middle of some of the worst slaving there is."

"You just stop that worrying," said Catherine. She patted the sheriff on the arm. "We can take care of ourselves, and we have faith the Lord will provide."

As Dr. Stone brought the horses around, someone called out, "Can I give you a hand with that?"

The voice sounded vaguely familiar, but he couldn't place it. He turned towards the voice, and there stood a large, muscular black man grinning down at him. A memory stirred to life. The black man held up his right hand, which was missing a finger.

The doctor shouted, "Intikuma," and hurried to embrace him. "How have you been? It's great to see you."

"I'm well," said Intikuma, returning the hug. "It's good to see you and Mrs. Stone again. And the sheriff. Hello, Sheriff."

When Intikuma learned the doctor and his wife were about to leave for South Carolina, he said, "Well, Doctor Stone, I'll be going with you."

"No, no, no!" exclaimed the doctor. "It's way too dangerous for you to go. Catherine and I can do this quite well by ourselves. But thank you for the offer."

"It's really not an offer, Doc. I'm here because I'm supposed to go with you."

"Well now, Doc," the sheriff spoke up, "you did say the Lord will provide. It looks like He just did."

After a few more minutes of persuasion, Doctor Tom Stone, his wife Catherine, and their good friend Intikuma were off for South Carolina. Intikuma would pretend to be the Stone's slave, as this would offer him some protection from being taken into slavery by others.

After the War, Itch Returns Home to Africa

Itch said farewell to Dr. and Mrs. Stone, then began his trek to Charleston, South Carolina. There, he planned to seek a job working on board a ship headed for any port in an African nation. Any ship would do. By now, his mother and the Sangoma must surely be dead. But to see childhood friends now grown, the Ndoda tree, and his old village—what pleasure this thought brought him.

But the port of Charleston, once the bustling center of the colony Charles Towne, lay in shambles, devastated by the war. Mines awaited their prey throughout the harbor, ready to blow a hole in their hulls, sending them to join their many sister ships resting on the sandy bottom. Perhaps it didn't matter that much—the South was bankrupt. It had little to export, and no one had money to import. So many men had been killed, few were able or willing to leave their families for months or years to go to sea. Most preferred to stay home to rebuild their farms.

Itch walked the cobblestone streets of Charleston's port disheartened at the ships so few in number and the lack of activity. He kept his Colt .44-caliber pistol tucked in his belt hidden by his shirt and carried his rifle as inconspicuously as possible. He stopped in front of a shop with a weathered sign above the door: Transatlantic Freight Co. Jos and Son Proprietors. He dusted himself off, pushed the door open, and stepped inside. The elderly man behind the counter glared at Itch, his eyes bouncing from the Springfield rifle Itch carried to his face and back again.

"What you doin' with a rifle? You steal that?"

Itch, accustomed to such comments, decided to get right to his purpose. "Just looking to work my way across the ocean. Any ships leaving soon for Africa, or Europe?"

The man behind the desk pushed his wire framed glasses higher onto his nose and snorted. "Anything to get rid of one more darkie. Try the *High Spirits*. Supposed to leave for Spain in a few days if enough cargo comes in to make it worth their while. Down that way 'bout a hundred yards."

Itch searched along the waterfront until he came to a three-masted ship with *High Spirits* painted on the hull in large white letters. He walked closer to the ship but stopped before climbing the plank leading to the main deck. The slapping of water against the ship, the occasional cry of a gull, and the nearness of this behemoth with all its sounds and smells, suffocated him with past memories. He closed his eyes.

A ship carried me here a prisoner. Now it will carry me home a free man.

He breathed slowly, felt his muscles relax. He waited a few more seconds before he walked up the plank to the deck of the ship, where two scruffy men were involved in a heated conversation. One wore a hat and a jacket, both with gold decorations on them. They both stopped talking when Itch approached.

"Excuse me," interrupted Itch, "I'd like to speak to the captain."

The shorter of the two, the one wearing the hat and jacket, said, "And what would ye be wantin' with the captain?"

"What I have to say is for the captain only."

"Well, you're speakin' to 'im. Now what is it ye want? We ain't got all day."

"I'm looking for work on a ship going across the Atlantic, and I hear you're looking for men to work on your ship."

The other one spoke up quickly. "We ain't lookin' for none of your kind to work this here ship. Now be off wit' ya."

The captain quickly intervened. "I still be's the captain of this ship, an' I'll be the one decides who works here." He studied Itch for a second. "Have ye had any experience working on a ship?"

"If you're looking for a man with a strong back and strong arms that can do what you ask of him, then I'm the best man you'll find.

The color of my skin doesn't matter to the ship. I can learn as fast as any man."

"If ye works as well as ye speaks, you'll be a fine worker. All right, I'll take ye. But if ye don't pull your weight, I'll have ye thrown in the brig for the rest of the voyage. We'll be leaving in two days, be on board at sunrise." He pointed to Itch's rifle. "If you bring that on board, you'll have to check it with the first mate here, and it'll be locked up. No crew member carries a firearm unless I says so."

"I'll be here, Captain, thank you." As Itch left, he heard the other man complaining.

"Cap'n, if ya don' mind me sayin' so, this man will be trouble. The rest o' the crew ain't gonna like it, no sir, they ain't going ta like this one bit."

"Well, let me tell you how it is," said the captain, staring the first mate in the eye. "We're lucky to have this trip comin' up. Most ships are just sitting, going nowhere. My job is to deliver the cargo to Portugal, and that's what I aim to do. None of us gets paid until it gets there. You're the first mate. I don't want nothing happening to that man because we need him. And I don't want any fights on board. I'll hold you responsible, and you'll end up in the brig along with whoever does the fighting. Now see to it preparations for sailing in two days are moving along."

"Ay, Captain," the first mate said, scowling. He stormed off, glaring towards the shore, watching Itch walk along the cobblestone street.

This nigger ain't going to make it to Portugal. I'll see to it.

Two days later, Itch reported for duty along with thirty-two others. When Itch came aboard, the other crewmembers stopped and stared. "What's he doing here?" said one. Others nodded with the same question on their minds.

"Take a good look, mates!" shouted the first mate. "Ye better get used to 'im 'cause we're all sailing across the wide seas together."

Amidst the angry grumbling and whispering, one said, "It's bad luck having a black on board. Everyone knows that."

"Don't worry," said another. "He ain't gonna last more'n one day."

The first mate walked up and down the line of men. "If there's any trouble, ye'll be spending the trip in the brig unless ye wants to swim home. Any man got a problem wit' that, tell me now."

"I ain't havin' him sleep with me. He's liable to slit my throat in the middle of my dreams," said one.

"Don't worry," said Itch. "I'm not going down below. I'll sleep up here on the main deck where the air is fresh and I can see the stars."

"Now that's settled," said the first mate, "let's get down to business. We're headin' to Cuba. Bringin' on sugar, tobacco, an' rum, then takin' it to Portugal. We got a long journey, so let's get this ship underway."

The other men, all experienced seamen, went to work. The first mate motioned to Itch. "Come with me." Itch followed him to the bow of the ship.

"Hey, Slim. This here is workin' wit ye. Make 'im earn 'is keep." He laughed as he walked away.

That first night, deep below the main deck, the first mate gathered a few trusted men around him. There in the pale light of a lantern barely lighting the walls of the musty room, the men put their heads together. "The captain's gonna get me ass if he gets hurt, so we got to treat him right for now," said the first mate. "But once we gets to Cuba an' he's off this ship, I don't care what happens to him. So, for now take it easy."

"Aye," said one. "In Cuba, he's ours." The others nodded in agreement.

The passage to Cuba went smoothly. A bit of rough weather accompanied by high seas as the ship sailed into the Straits of Florida concerned Itch, but the experienced crew kept the ship on course.

High Spirits sailed into the port of Havana on a beautiful sunny day. Itch admired the forts, two stone-walled giants on the rocky coast, greeting their entry into the bay. Slim, in an unusual moment of friendliness, said, "That's El Moro on the left, and that other one's La Cabana. Quite a sight, eh?" Both men returned to work without another word passing between them.

The captain gave the word that all the crew, except a necessary few, were allowed to go ashore for one overnight but must return the next day by 0800 hours to help load the ship's cargo and be off before nightfall.

The first mate and his five recruits followed Itch, who decided to explore Havana on his own. The six men stayed well back from Itch, talking, laughing, and acting much like any group of sailors. Although still a slave country, Cuba had many free blacks. Seeing so many walking the streets pleased Itch.

Itch entered a small restaurant and took a seat near a window. He ordered food and coffee. At the far end of the restaurant stood a bar. There, drinking at the bar, were five black men in a uniform he had never seen before. They had a different look about them than other black men he had seen thus far in Cuba. They spoke a language that was not Spanish but had a familiar rhythm. Their mannerisms captured his attention—how they used their hands when talking and the motion of their bodies. Intrigued, he decided to find out where they had come from.

"Excuse me, do you speak English?" he asked.

The men looked at him and then one said, "Only if you're referring to the King's English."

Grateful for this small bit of luck, Itch smiled. "Who are you? Where are you from?"

The man closest to him said, "We come from South Africa. We have sailed here to pick up rum and cigars and other such wonderful delicacies that we will never have the privilege of buying when we return."

Itch spent a long time talking with these men. They were sailors aboard a ship that had sailed from South Africa and was to return the following day. The ship had white officers and a black crew. The officers treated the crew well.

The six men outside waiting for the opportune time to jump Itch were getting restless. Their shore time was being squandered. One of the men suggested they go inside, ask him to join them outside for a few minutes, and take care of him in the woods so as not to attract attention. Agreed on this plan, they entered the restaurant, but they stopped when they saw him with a group of black men.

One of them said, "Hey Itch, come 'ere a minute, will you? We want to have a word with you."

Itch said, "You can have your word with me right here."

The men looked at each other. "Well, all right then, if you insist." They each pulled out a knife or a club and started towards him. They expected to see the other blacks run, but they pulled out their own knives. Itch reached for the gun hidden under his shirt, but before he could pull it out, the lady behind the bar ducked down and came back up with a shotgun. She pointed it at the advancing men.

"You stop or I shoot," she said, in her most menacing voice. The men stopped. "No more fight in here. You want fight, go out. You," she raised the shotgun to her shoulder and pointed it directly at the first mate, "get out now or you die."

The men scowled. "We'll get you. The first time you go to sleep, you're a dead man," said one of them.

After the men left, a sailor from South Africa said, "It sounds like your ship's not a healthy place for you. How about joining us? We're going where you want to go. I feel sure the captain will agree."

"Let's give it a try," said Itch.

Itch sailed to Africa aboard a ship with fellow Africans. Ramine, a friend Itch made on board the ship, taught Itch much about sailing, and the two often worked side by side. Ramine was a fisherman whose boat had been destroyed in a fierce storm that lashed the

South African coast a year ago. Ramine had worked on board various ships to earn money to replace his boat and equipment.

As they talked, and Itch got to know him, he felt trust and empathy for his new friend. He sensed Ramine was a man of good character and decided it would be fitting to make a deal with him—one that would be mutually beneficial. It would mean spending the money Dr. Stone had given him, but what better way to spend it than to find his home. A few days later, after thinking it through, Itch approached Ramine. "I've been thinking of a way we can help each other when we get to South Africa."

"If there is any way I can be of help to you, my friend, please tell me."

"You need a boat, and I need someone to take me up the coast of Africa so I can find my homeland. I have some money that I will gladly give to you to help you buy your boat. In return, you and I will sail up the coast of Africa. When I see what I am looking for, I will leave, and you will have your boat. What do you think, my friend?"

"That sounds like a fine arrangement to me. But let me think on it overnight and give you an answer in a few days."

"That would be wise," said Itch.

In two days, Ramine approached Itch. "I have given careful thinking to your plan, and I accept. It will be a pleasure to help you find your home."

In spite of the difficult work and being at sea for a long period of time, Itch found the remainder of the voyage very pleasant.

The ship pulled into the harbor at Capetown. Itch and Ramine received their pay and went ashore. Ramine, not married, stayed in a small shack behind his sister's home, which she shared with her husband and their three children. He invited Itch to stay with him, but Itch preferred to sleep outside where he could see the sky over the African land.

Ramine's family joyously celebrated Ramine's return and with great kindness made Itch welcome. Though poor, they willingly shared with the stranger Ramine had brought home. Itch, careful not to eat much, always bought food at the market for the family.

The next day after their arrival, Itch and Ramine looked for a boat. They stopped first to meet with Ramine's friend, Mick, who built boats. Ramine explained to him what he wanted. Mick replied that he could make him one, but it would take at least three to five months. Neither Ramine nor Itch wanted to wait that long. Mick suggested they walk the beach. He didn't know of anyone who wanted to sell their boat, but getting the word out sometimes brought positive results.

Ramine knew most of the fishermen, and he was aware that they would all be out fishing this time of the morning.

Itch said, "We've nothing better to do, let's follow Mick's advice."

As they walked, they talked to everyone they met, letting them know they were in the market for a fishing boat.

Finally, on the fifth day, Itch and Ramine received word that someone had a boat for sale about a mile north on the beach. The next morning, they rose early and went to find the person with the boat. After inquiring at several places, they came upon a very modest hut. Inside lived an older woman and her husband, who rested on a straw mat.

After proper introductions, Ramine inquired about the boat. The older man had been in the boat fishing, when he slipped, knocking his head very hard on the side of the boat. He lay unconscious for a while, and when he regained consciousness, his left side remained very weak. He had great difficulty getting the boat back to shore. He and his wife decided he could no longer manage the boat.

"Well then, my friend, what will you do? How will you eat?' asked Ramine.

"We hope to get some money for the boat," replied his wife. "After that money is gone, who knows?"

"Have you no family?" inquired Ramine.

"We have but one son, and he has no interest in fishing. He heard rumors that there are great riches to be found elsewhere. He left a long time ago, and we have not heard from him since."

"Has he gone in search of diamonds?" asked Ramine.

"Yes, it shames me to say it. It is as though he wants to be like the white men. Having great wealth, he believes, would bring him importance," said the woman.

"Is your boat seaworthy?" Ramine asked the man.

"Yes, it is a good boat. It always gets me to the good fishing spots and brings me back safely. Even now, when I could barely move, it brought me back. Go see if it is what you want. It is out there. Look, you can see it from here," he said, pointing to the boat.

Ramine stood and turned to see the boat. "Yes, it looks like a good boat. Come, Itch, let's take a look."

The boat, though old, was in good shape. Two men could handle it easily, but one experienced person could manage it as well. It had a mast and sail, or it could be rowed if there were no wind. They decided to buy it, as it suited their purposes perfectly and would be a good boat for Ramine to operate alone after Itch found what he'd come in search of.

They returned to the old couple and said they would buy it. Ramine asked the man how much he would like for it. When he told the amount, Ramine offered him more.

"You are very kind to us old people," said the old man. "Of course, we will accept your offer. You are a tough negotiator." They all laughed.

They paid the couple in cash, and Ramine said that he would ask his sister to look in on them occasionally to make sure they were well.

"Thank you for your kindness," said the woman. The man, smiling, nodded in agreement.

"Well, my friend, you did not say much. Are you in agreement with the purchase of the boat?" Ramine said to Itch.

"I figured I would let you work it out with him since I don't know the customs here. And, yes, I am in complete agreement."

They sailed the boat down the coast and beached it closer to where Ramine lived. That night, they talked of their trip. The next day, they began making preparations for their cruise up the coast of Africa.

They would start north up the coast in two days. They planned to always stay within sight of shore and would stop at night. This way, Itch would see every bit of the coast. If he missed even a small amount, he might miss the two mountains that would tell him he was near home. They would fish for their meals and eat fruit and nuts from the shore when they stopped.

On their fourth day out, huge black clouds covered the blue sky and erased the sun. The breeze that filled their sail grew to a blustery gale, whipping the water into a frenzy. The two men dropped the sail and struggled to get their boat to the beach. The boat now seemed very small, riding up giant waves and then down again. Finally, after an hour of thrashing about and great effort, they managed to get ashore. As they pulled the boat onto the sand, a driving rain hit them like steel balls being fired from a celestial cannon. They pulled the boat well up the beach, tied it to a tree, then sought high ground. With the temperature dropping, the shore shrouded in darkness, they fought against the wind and stinging sand to move farther inland. Fifty yards from shore, the two men huddled under a tree in awe and amazement at the strength of the storm.

After some time, sounds of splashing and "thuds" came from the area of the shore. Ramine leaned to Itch and yelled, "We better move back even more."

With great difficulty, they crawled farther inland. The howling wind made their every move difficult. Branches and other flying objects smashed into them. Exhausted, they stopped after going a short distance.

Several hours later, the wind died, and the rain drizzled. The clouds no longer covered the sky. Itch and Ramine, grateful to see the stars, could do nothing until daylight, and so they slept as best they could until morning.

At first light, they walked towards the shore to locate their boat and assess the damages. When they saw trees ripped down or broken in half, they became fearful their boat had been destroyed.

Then Itch pointed in the sand ahead. "Look! There!" At first, Ramine didn't see it. Then he saw the outline of the boat in the sand and, miraculously, the mast sticking out from the sand.

They hurried to the boat and knelt beside it. First, they removed sand around the outline to verify it remained in one piece. Then they began scooping out the top layer of sand with their hands. They soon realized how painstakingly slow this would be. They looked around for a scoop of some kind but found nothing. But, as Itch said, "We have nothing else to do and plenty of time." Digging out the boat wasn't their biggest problem, however. Once they had the sand out of the boat, how would they get it past the tangle of trees and back to the water?

After a few hours of scooping sand, they heard laughter and an unknown language as a group of men walked towards them. They soon found themselves surrounded by a small party of African men wearing colorful clothing. They stood observing and discussing the task at hand.

Itch and Ramine waited, not knowing what to expect. One of the men, dressed more colorfully and ornately than the others, approached the two men. The others followed. He said a few words in his language, then patted Ramine and Itch on the back.

Ramine said, "I'll try to communicate." He pointed to the boat, the ocean, then the sky. He made noises like the wind while moving his hand along like a boat on the water.

The well-dressed African smiled and nodded his head. He spoke to one of the men. The man ran off.

The leader motioned for them to sit. They all sat in a circle. One of the men opened a pouch and handed Itch an item, then motioned for him to eat it.

"Best you accept it and pretend to enjoy it, whether or not you really do. Don't want to take any chance of offending them," said Ramine.

Itch took the food and nodded with a smile, trying to show his appreciation. He bit into it, and he did not know where the strength came from to smile and swallow what tasted very much like rotten meat. He passed it over to Ramine, who did the same.

Through signs and gestures, they succeeded in communicating. In spite of the language difficulty, Itch felt a contentment he hadn't known since his abduction. Sitting with men he considered his brothers, who lived much as his village did, brought a rush of lost memories and feelings. His powerful father; his kind, doting mother; the mysterious Sangoma; his village people coming together; the trees he had named—ah…how he had missed this life stolen from him.

Itch had just commented to Ramine that they should return to their sand scooping when chanting could be heard in the distance. The chanting came closer and closer. Before long, twenty warriors appeared, chanting as they ran. The leader spoke to his men, directing them to the boat and fallen trees. The warriors at once busied themselves with clearing the trees to make a path to the shore. Others used large shells to scoop sand from the boat. By the end of the day, the path had been cleared, and the boat rested on the beach.

The leader invited Itch and Ramine to the village for the night. A feast, prepared in honor of the two strangers, tasted much better than the earlier morsel. By the end of the festivities, the two men were exhausted. The leader offered a hut to them, where they slept soundly.

In the morning, Itch and Ramine left their new friends. The entire village followed them to watch the launching of their boat. Itch smiled when he heard his friends on shore cheer and shout at the raising of the sail and it filling with the morning breeze. As the boat moved faster and faster, the children ran along the shore trying to keep up. Both men waved goodbye as they left the village behind.

Seven, eight, nine, ten days later, and still no mountain peaks. Itch became discouraged. He began to have doubts. Had they passed the mountain peaks, and he had missed them? Perhaps he had been helping Ramine when they sailed past, not noticing the two peaks. Perhaps this whole idea was not a good one. When they stopped that night, he asked Ramine what he thought.

"Listen, my friend, you must follow what is in your heart. That you must always do. And when you do, it seems that often doors are opened that we would never have thought possible. Each day brings new possibilities."

He knew Ramine spoke the truth, but his doubts lingered. They continued day after day after day.

"There is a nice beach to rest for the night," said Ramine, pointing to a stretch of white sand.

Itch studied the beach. A glimmer of recognition.

"Go past the beach," said Itch, his pulse quickening.

When they sailed past the beach, two mountain peaks came into view.

At once, Ramine shouted, "Look! Look! Is that them? Those the ones?"

"Yes. Yes. At last! We made it. I can't believe it."

With renewed energy, they brought the boat to shore. The men hugged. Itch whispered, "Thank you, Ramine. Thank you."

They talked for a long time. Ramine told of his dream to return to life as a fisherman, and Itch spoke of the friends and life he hoped to find at his village.

Late into the night, Ramine said, "Itch, my good friend, when you go on this, the last leg of your journey, you do not know what you will find. I will stay here for seven days. If you do not return, I will know you have found what you have come looking for. If it is not there, know you will have a ride back with me, or anywhere this little boat can take us. Mishe ke sumo, my good friend—may you have happiness and love."

"You are a great friend," said Itch.

Then both men lay down to sleep, hopeful about what tomorrow might bring.

At dawn, the men woke and fished for their breakfast. After eating, Itch and Ramine said their parting words, and Itch set off for his village. He remembered the walk from this beach to his sacred place taking about two days. Then, he'd walked with chains. Possibly now, he could make the journey in one day or a day and a half.

After the first day of walking, doubts and confusion entered his mind. What if he was going in the wrong direction? Nothing looked familiar. He believed if he kept in this direction, he would run into his old friend, the river. From there he would know his way. That night, he built a fire. To calm his spirit, he sat quietly, stilling his mind and listening. He sat for several hours, getting in touch with his inner self and listening for its wisdom.

In the morning, he felt composed and confident. At midday, he heard the rushing of the river, his river, and hurried to find it. He followed the river east. After walking for an hour, he spotted his old friend, the Ndoda tree, tall and sprawling, there to guide him after all these years. He went to the tree, running his hand along the rough, familiar bark. "Hello, my old friend. I, Intikuma, have come home."

He sprinted the short distance to his village, but to his disappointment, it appeared abandoned. The huts lay in ruins. There was no one about. Once, great ceremonies had echoed through the jungle. Now, this area had become overgrown with brush and trees.

He found the spot where he'd lived with his mother. Their hut had fallen into ruin. He sifted through the debris, hoping to find a trinket, some keepsake of his mother's memory. Nothing. Intikuma scouted the area looking for signs of life or clues as to what happened. Nothing. Thankfully, no signs pointed to kidnappings or war. Perhaps they had decided to move.

It rained. At first, it was a gentle rain. Then, it became harder. Intikuma took shelter under the Ndoda tree. "After all these years, you still give shelter." He touched the long black scar on the tree.

Though grateful for finding this friend, he yearned to know about his people.

All of this, and nothing, he thought. Tears welled up in his eyes. *Where could my people be?*

"What should I do, oh great and wise Ndoda?"

As he drifted off, a dream came to him. He was teaching other Africans to read and write. He did this in English in a small classroom in America. He sensed this was a great thing. He awoke and thought about the dream for a long time. There came a voice, his mother's voice, as though she stood next to him. So real, Intikuma looked for her. "You shall be a leader of your people, my son."

How good to hear her voice. She spoke these very words to him many years ago. He knew what must be done. Her voice confirmed it.

He said goodbye to the Ndoda tree. When he arrived at the beach, Ramine was there. Their return to Capetown was not so eventful as their trip north along the African coast. For this, they were grateful.

Itch returned to America, where he set up a small schoolhouse in Ohio, not far from Dr. and Mrs. Stone. Here, he taught adults and children alike how to read, write, do math, and how to survive in a hostile culture. He taught them how to live a life full of meaning and purpose. He taught his students to follow their hearts.

Three years after Itch opened his school, Dr. Stone died peacefully. Several months after the doctor died, his wife came to teach at Intikuma's school.

Margaret's Story

Dat just nearly broke my old mammy's and pappy's heart, to have me took away off from them, but they couldn't say nothing, and I had to go along with Miss Mary back to Texas. When we got away from the big house, I just cried and cried until I couldn't hardly see, my eyes was so swole up, but Miss Mary said she gwine to be good to me.
　　—Mary Lindsay, age 91 *(Voices from Slavery, p. 208)*

The two men rode hard, not knowing how long the slave woman would keep silent. One of them carried Margaret seated in front of him. They rode east a couple of miles and continued on for a hundred yards past a crossroad running north and south. Here, they rode into the woods for another fifty yards before backtracking to the southern road, where they continued on to Ft. Meade.

They arrived in Ft. Meade that afternoon and went straight to the slave auction to be held that day. They approached James Burke, the man who ran the auction, and after a bit of negotiating, Margaret was sold for $200.

"Easy money," said one, as they walked away.

Burke shoved the frightened Margaret into the stockade with twenty-five other slaves. He pointed out the pump and instructed her to clean herself. The stockade—nothing more than a high wooden fence fifty feet long on each side with a dirt floor and one opening leading into the offices of the slave traders—held the slaves to be auctioned.

A deep gloom came over Margaret. She observed each of the poor souls locked in confinement with her. A few raised their heads at the commotion of Margaret's entrance, but most continued in their own despair, heads down, lost in thoughts of separation from loved ones and the changes that lie ahead. This place seemed bereft of hope.

"Hey, chil', come on over here." The voice had a touch of kindness in it. Margaret's eyes followed the direction the voice had come from. On a rickety old crate sat a thin woman with strong eyes waving her hand for Margaret to join her. Margaret inched along towards her, head down, frightened, but hopeful she would be a friend.

"My name's Fanny. What's yours?"

Margaret spoke her name, her face pointing at her feet.

"Now you goin' hafta speak better'n dat so's I can hear ya." Her reassuring smile and voice encouraged Margaret to speak up.

"Ah'm Margaret, ma'am."

Fanny lowered her voice so only Margaret could hear. "Now lissen here, Margaret. You ain't the furst and won't be the last young black chillun been snatched from they momma an' sold in dese here slave markets. You gonna have ta be brave an' do like the white man says, or else he likely to whip you good 'til you bleedin' and hurts all over. An' when you gets big enuf, it best you runs away up north where black folks kin be free. Dat's whut Ah'm gonner do the furst chance Ah gets. Now you be brave, you hear me? Be proud o' yo'self 'cause you is God's chil' jus like any white. You unnerstan' me?"

Margaret nodded.

A rough-looking white man came near the two huddled together. "You, and the kid, git out there on the stage and stand straight, come on move out."

"Come on," said Fanny, being brave for the child. They followed the man out of the stockade to the stage. Fanny held Margaret's hand as they stepped up on the stage in front of the crowd of men waiting to bid on them.

The auctioneer told Fanny to take her blouse off. He pointed out that she had no scar tissue from lash marks, indicating she could be counted on to be obedient. He started her bidding at a higher price.

Fanny sold first, and then another young woman who seemed lifeless. Margaret sold next. A well-dressed young man purchased her. He paid for her and called for her to come with him, but she couldn't move. Her little body shook. She could think of nothing else but her mother. She wanted to cry. She forced herself not to.

The man came to her. "Don't be silly now. Come along." He put his hand on her back and gave her a push in the direction she needed to walk. She stumbled, caught herself, then walked with great anxiety a step behind her new master.

As they walked out of the crowd, the man said, "What's your name?"

"Margaret, sir."

"Well, Margaret, you'll be living with my wife and I now. My wife is named Miss Lizzy, and I am Mister Isaac. You will be the servant to my wife and will do her bidding. Have you lived in a white man's house before?"

"I worked in my master's house, but never lived there."

"Well, good. You will still have to learn to do things our way. I hope you are a fast learner. What do you know how to do?"

"I work mostly cleaning an' helping in the kitchen."

"It sounds like you are used to good hard work and have some basic knowledge of cooking. That's fine. Yes, I believe you will do just fine. But if you don't do as you are told, or if you don't learn fast enough, we will sell you at the next auction. The next person who buys you might not be as nice to you as my wife and I, so it would make sense for you to always be obedient and to do the best you can. Is that clear?"

"Yes, sir."

"Here we are. Go out back to the well and get yourself cleaned up before coming in the house. I'll lay some clean clothes on the back stoop for you to put on. They're from the girl we had previously. She was a bit larger than you, but I believe they will fit well enough."

A white fence ran along the front, and the yard seemed like a painting filled with color. Margaret didn't know the names of any of the flowers except the roses lined along the porch. She liked the house immediately.

Margaret followed the path leading to the back, where a well-tended garden greeted her. She wondered what had happened to the previous girl. She found a bucket of water by the pump. She took her dress off and used the dip to pour the cold water on herself and her hand to rub the dirt off. When she felt clean, she looked toward the house for her new clothes. She jumped, startled to see the man standing there on the stoop watching her. Embarrassed, she covered herself with her hands, though they didn't seem enough.

"Here are your clothes," he said. "Put them on and come inside."

The dress reached to the ground and hung baggy on her lean body. The sleeves covered her fingers but could be rolled up easily enough. The smooth cloth felt soft against her skin. The light blue color was to her liking. She spun around in it several times, causing the bottom to flare out. This was by far the newest and prettiest dress she had ever worn.

She opened the door and went inside to discover what this new life might have in store for her.

"Margaret, come over here so I can see you better. Don't be shy." Lizzy had blonde hair pinned in a bun and wore a pretty lavender dress with lace around the neck. She had a round face, a friendly smile, and a pleasant voice.

Margaret walked to her slowly, keeping her eyes on the floor.

"My land, we're going to have to fix that dress on you, Margaret. It's way too big. Do you know how to sew?"

"No, Mistress," said Margaret in a low voice.

"Don't be shy. We'll get that out of you in a short while. Before long you will feel right at home. One of your first lessons will be sewing. But for now, let me show you your room."

My room? Inside this house?

Margaret thought back to the days of living with her family in the cramped quarters of one room, but at least she lived with her family—people she knew and loved.

They walked to the back of the house through a dining area and a kitchen, to a small hallway, then into a room off the hall. The small room had a window, and when Margaret entered, her hands flew to her mouth. Her eyes grew big, and before she could catch herself, she exclaimed, "A real bed!"

Lizzy smiled and walked to the bed. "This will be your bed, Margaret. Do you know how to make a bed?"

"No, Miss Lizzy." Margaret began to worry that she would have to make beds like that one, and she didn't think she could make anything so big.

"Well, tomorrow, after we have breakfast, I'll show you how. You will be responsible to make both yours and the bed that my husband and I sleep in. You have a lot to learn, young Margaret."

A sense of relief swept over Margaret when she realized she didn't have to actually make a bed, but rather make it look nice after sleeping in it. That first night, she slept on top of the covers, not wanting to disturb the bed.

Over the months, Margaret learned many new things about caring for a house and became quite capable of completing the chores Lizzy assigned her. She cleaned the house, washed the dishes and clothes, set the table, began her sewing lessons, and assisted with cooking. For now, Margaret found life interesting with Lizzy and Isaac, yet she often thought of her parents and Hector and longed to see them and hold them close. At times, Fanny's words crept into her memory, and she wondered about going north and what freedom would truly be like.

Their conversations usually remained light and fun. Lizzy and Isaac loved each other very much, and it showed. At dinner, he would often tease her, and she would laugh and look at him with flirtatious eyes. Dinner often ended with Isaac dismissing Margaret and their going into their bedroom behind a closed door with much giggling and noise.

Margaret learned details about Lizzy and Isaac as she went about her work in their home. They had been married close to a year. Lizzy had a miscarriage shortly after they married and had a difficult time recovering emotionally. She so wanted a child of her own. She remained in a deep depression for several months, but her own strength and Isaac's charming ways gradually brought her to find happiness once again.

They had moved to Ft. Meade from New Orleans. Isaac was the only child of wealthy parents and received a stipend each month. His parents were deceased.

Lizzy never spoke of having other family. She would occasionally go into moods of depression and would stay in her room much of the day. However, more often than not, her days were happy, and she enjoyed life with Isaac.

The good times did not last. Tension erupted between Isaac and Lizzy. While Lizzy and Isaac ate their meals, Margaret stood nearby to wait on them. One dinner conversation in particular caught Margaret by surprise.

"Isaac, please, I'm begging you. Do not leave me. How will I survive without you?"

"My darling, you know I love you with all my being." He leaned forward and took her hand. "But duty to my country calls. All of my friends have gone. They will think me a coward if I stay here and live in comfort while they fight. Please understand."

"Would you place your friends over your love for me, Isaac? I am your wife. I need you."

"I swear I will write to you every chance I get. I will return to you as soon as the war is finished. I want to stay, dear Lizzy, but my duty demands I go. The choice is not mine to make."

"But it is yours to make. This damn war is not your responsibility. You swore an oath to me, your wife."

"You are not a child. Other husbands leave their wives to fight in this war and survive just fine. Grow up, Lizzy. You are a grown woman, for God's sake."

Lizzy stared fiercely at him for a few seconds, her chest heaving, then hurled her water glass at him before stomping off to their bedroom and slamming the door. For several days after the dinner argument, tension remained between Lizzy and Isaac. Their table conversation was no longer light, but stressful and strained. Isaac often stormed from the house rather than argue with Lizzy or deal with her bouts of depression.

One morning, Margaret stood over the washtub scrubbing clothes when she heard shouting coming from inside the house. She finished the wash and hung the clothes to dry. When she came into the house, she found Lizzy sobbing.

"Oh, Margaret, come here." She put her arms around Margaret and said, "Mister Isaac has gone off to war. He may never come back to me, Margaret. Now it's just you and me."

Margaret didn't know what to think. She had never had a white person hold her or show emotions to her like they were friends. She managed to say, "I'm sure Master Isaac come back to you, Miss Lizzy."

"I don't know if he will. He could get killed, or he could just decide not to come back. I fear that I have helped to drive him away with my sharp tongue and damned depression. Oh, Margaret, what are we going to do without my rock, my Isaac?"

"Everything going be all right, Miss Lizzy."

"You know, Margaret, you are right. Us girls will have to learn to get along without any men around. We are strong." Lizzy patted Margaret on the shoulder and then rose from her chair and went into her room.

With Isaac gone, the house became more somber—there was no laughter or animated conversation. Lizzy said very little. She didn't teach Margaret anything new. She spent most of her time in her room or going for walks in town. Margaret was often left alone to do her chores, after which she sat idle.

At first, letters came from Isaac every two or three months. They boosted Lizzy's spirits, and she read them to Margaret with great joy. His optimism always shined through, and he professed his love for Lizzy in every letter. She especially remembered and reread and reread his first letter:

My Darling Lizzy,

How I miss you. Especially in the evenings and nights, when I am so used to holding you in my arms. I trust you are well. Please know that I hated with all my heart to leave you, but I felt that I had no choice if I were ever able to hold my head high again in the presence of my countrymen.

I hope that Margaret is working out well for you. Be stern with her, and she will obey you and take care of the drudgery of daily work.

Life here is not so bad. We have had one battle and really got the Yankee bastards (please excuse my language, but that is just what they are) on the run. They have no stomach for a good fight and run at the first shot being fired. When we charge them with the rebel yell, it makes their hair turn white and they can stand no more of it and turn tail and run away as fast as they can. The men I am with are some of the meanest and toughest fighters I have ever seen. Nothing can or ever will defeat them. So you see, have no fear for me.

I really believe this will be a short war, and I should be home within a few months. When I arrive, I shall sweep you up in my arms, and we shall be together forever more. Perhaps we can take that trip we have been talking about for so long.

Know that I love you more than ever and think of you every moment we are apart.

I shall write again soon, but for now I must prepare to march on to our next camp.

With all my love,
Your adoring husband Isaac

Lizzy and Margaret did get along well. Lizzy began inviting Margaret to join in her walks to town and, at times, they would picnic at a nearby lake. Lizzy had Margaret walk beside her when they were out, and she talked to her as though she were an equal. The exception happened when some bit of drudgery needed done. On these occasions, Lizzy ordered Margaret about, and Margaret did all the labor.

Lizzy frequently bought material to make clothes and often purchased extra to make a dress or bonnet for Margaret. They sat in the house in the evenings sewing together.

On their walks to town, Margaret waited for Lizzy outside of the store. Here she met a young man named Marcus—the tall, lanky slave of a plantation owner named O'Reilly. A warm, comfortable glow always spread over her when she saw him.

O'Reilly frequented the saloon, and he always brought Marcus along. His plantation had a white overseer and thirty slaves working his crops of cotton and corn. While O'Reilly enjoyed a few drinks, Marcus had nothing to do but hang out on the street looking after his master's buckboard and horse—a rather boring task. Marcus had time to chat with the other slaves when the opportunity arose. The opportunity arose with Margaret several times a week.

Over time, they became well acquainted. Margaret liked Marcus. He was funny and always treated her like she was somebody. Marcus' smooth, friendly manner gave him a knack for making friends easily.

"Hi, Marcus," said Margaret, as she approached him on one occasion while with Lizzy in town.

He turned and said, "Oh, hello, Margaret. My you shore looks pretty all dressed up in dat blue dress. Did you make dat?"

"Yes, I did make it, with just a little help from Miss Lizzy."

"Well now, you shore do got a whole bunch o' talent fer makin' dem pretty dresses."

"Thank you, Marcus." Margaret stared at the ground, embarrassed with all his praise.

Marcus turned back around and leaned against the post.

"Something the matter, Marcus?"

"Well, I guess tain't nuthin' de matter dat ain't always de matter," said Marcus, with an uncharacteristic sadness.

"Did something happen, Marcus? You can tell me."

Marcus moved off the post and peered around. Seeing no one nearby, he stepped closer to Margaret. "Now, Margaret," he said, leaning closer to her, "you gots to swear to me dat you won't tell no one, no one atall 'bout whut I is goin' to tell you."

Margaret had never seen Marcus so serious, and it scared her. Her heart beat faster, and she feared whatever he might say to her.

"I just ain't happy being no slave. I ain't. Don't know what I kin do 'bout it just yet, but I shore ain't happy. I was just thinkin', here I is a sittin' here waitin' for Master O'Reilly to finish his drink, a man no better than me, an I gots to sit here an' wait for him. Now that ain't right. Ah could be goin' 'bout my business, makin' a livin' somewheres, havin' me a wife an' some childrens, but no, I gots to set here an' wait for him. It just ain't right, no sir, it ain't."

Margaret stared at him. She had never heard him talk like this. She wanted to say something, but she couldn't think of anything.

Her mind flashed back to the day she had been sold and the words of freedom Fanny had said to her.

Before she could respond, Lizzy called her. "Bye, Marcus," she said, as she rushed to meet Lizzy.

"I declare, Margaret, you talk to that boy entirely too much. You be careful of what he wants. Young boys his age have only one thing on their minds when it comes to young girls."

"Yes, Miss Lizzy." But she knew she would be seeing him again.

One of Lizzy's best friends was Belle. Sophisticated, opinionated, and popular about town, Belle saw herself as a mentor to Lizzy, and Lizzy valued Belle's opinions. On a later visit to town, Lizzy sensed tension between her and Belle. "Belle, honey, why do you give me such a look?"

Belle leaned towards Lizzy and lowered her voice. "It's your Negro. Quite frankly, the whole town is talking about how you two seem like friends. You dress her so well that when you visit here, my Negroes start talking. It causes such a problem for me. I was just looking at my Negroes admiring Margaret's dress, and I know they will be resentful when you leave. She is your slave, after all. If you want my advice, you should treat her like one."

Lizzy straightened her back. Thank you so much for your advice." She stood. "Well, it has been lovely, now I must be going."

On the walk home Margaret asked, "Is something the matter, Miss Lizzy?"

Lizzy stopped abruptly. "No. Just leave me be." Then she stormed off ahead of Margaret.

Isaac's letters stopped coming. It had been three months since the last one. She had moments of panic each day that passed without a letter. Her nights became restless fits and worries. She walked to town to check the post every day. Other families who had lost a loved one in the war were given notification of their death. But Lizzy heard nothing. In her uncertainty, she clung ever tighter to Margaret.

The army office in town had no news of Isaac. The officer in charge promised to look into the matter but never found any information to help her. She returned several times, becoming more demanding each time, until finally the officer in charge refused to see her.

One morning, Margaret awoke to a wet, sticky sensation inside her upper legs. She ran her fingers along the wetness and saw that she had lost blood. Embarrassed and nervous about making a mess with the sheets and bed that Lizzy and Isaac had given her to use, she quietly carried her sheets and clothes outside to wash.

While frantically scrubbing, she didn't notice Lizzy standing at the back door. After watching Margaret for several minutes, Lizzy walked out to her.

Margaret froze immediately. "Oh, Miss Lizzy, I am so sorry I done got these pretty sheets all dirty. I promise I'll get them clean if I has to scrub them all day long. Please don't be mad at me, Miss Lizzy."

"Don't be silly, Margaret. This means you've become a young woman. When you finish washing those sheets come inside. I have a nice surprise for you."

Margaret hung the freshly cleaned sheets out to dry and went inside, where Lizzy sat in the parlor waiting for her.

"Come here, Margaret. I hadn't even noticed how you are growing up. You are filling out nicely. Open your blouse and let's look at your breasts."

Margaret obediently, though slowly, unbuttoned her blouse and let it hang open.

"There now, let's see what's happening to you." Lizzy pulled open her blouse. "Why Margaret, I do believe it is time for you to have some underwear. This afternoon, you and I will do some shopping."

They walked down the main street together, Margaret step by step with Lizzy. Lizzy entered the clothing store. As usual, Margaret stopped at the door. Lizzy motioned for Margaret to come in. Margaret stepped inside.

As she followed Lizzy, she tried to ignore the unwelcome stares of other customers. Lizzy couldn't be bothered. She hummed as she moved about the store. Eventually, a customer said in a very huffy voice, "Why don't you have your nigger wait outside like everyone else?" Lizzy raised her eyebrows, smiled, and continued shopping.

When Lizzy paid for her purchases, the clerk said, "Miss Lizzy, we would appreciate it if you could keep your Negro outside so as not to offend our other customers."

Lizzy's smile seemed cemented to her face. She didn't respond to the clerk but rather strutted out the door, grinning and humming.

Margaret soon wore her first pair of underclothes.

Two months passed, and Lizzy still heard nothing from or about Isaac. Other families in the area had a letter or, in some cases, an official come tell them their loved one had been killed or captured. But nothing about Isaac.

One evening, when Margaret served dinner, Lizzy said, "Bring yourself a plate and sit with me. I'm so tired of eating alone."

Margaret froze briefly, stunned by Lizzy's request. "You want me to eat with you here at the table, Miss Lizzy?"

"Yes, Margaret. Bring yourself a plate and serve yourself, and we'll have a nice conversation. It's so good to have someone to talk with."

"Yes'm."

"I can't stop worrying about Isaac. I miss him so. I remember a beautiful warm day in April a few years ago he invited me to go with him to a…"

As each lonely day dawdled by, Lizzy came to confide more and more in Margaret. She told her how she'd met Isaac, and how he had wooed her. She spoke about his mannerisms, which she loved, her dreams from the night before, and all manner of things that caused Margaret to squirm in her chair.

The morning rain had cooled the stifling hot air. Still, the afternoon seemed unusually mild for the middle of June. Margaret stood outside the General Goods Store waiting for Lizzy to finish shopping. Margaret had a secret that made her smile on the inside and feel that she was as good as the white women who passed her by without seeing her. She wore underwear. How did she ever get along before without undergarments?

Her reverie ended when Marcus' voice broke in. He spoke to her in his usual manner, then his voice dropped very low. "Margaret, can you keep a secret?"

"Sure I can, Marcus. You can tell me anything, anything at all, an' I'll not tell nobody."

"Not even Miss Lizzy, not nobody. You swears?"

"O' course. You can trust me, Marcus."

He took her arm and pulled her away from the store. "Listen, if you tells anybody, you would get me killed. You understan' that?"

"What you goin' to do, Marcus?" she said in a whisper.

"Me an' some boys, we goin' to run away from this place. We gonna be free up in the north. We ain't goin' be slaves no more for nobody. You hears that, Margaret, free men at last."

"Marcus…"

"Come with us, Margaret. You could be free, too. Then who know what could happen. Maybe you an' me, we settles down and has us a family. Who knows what could happen. What you say, Margaret? Come with us."

Margaret tried to appear calm, but her insides trembled. Her voice shaky, she said, "No, I couldn't leave Miss Lizzy. I think she needs me until her husband come home."

"You a fool, Margaret? You a slave. You don't mean nothin' to her. She could get rid of you and buy another girl an' think nothin' of it."

"No, it really isn't like that between us."

"You really don't understan', do you? Look, Margaret, maybe you think you have it good living in the house with a white lady an' all. But when it come down to it, you is jus like a piece o' furniture or somethin' like that to her. She don't care about you an' would toss you out an' think nothin' of it."

"Oh, Marcus, I don't think so. She confides in me, and we have long talks."

"You got a lot to learn. Here, take this to remember me an' what I'm tellin' you." He held out his hand.

"How pretty. Did you carve it?"

"Sure did. Jus' for you."

She fixed her eyes on Marcus. "Thank you."

"It's a lion that live in Africa. It love freedom. When you look at it, think of me an' think of living in freedom. One day, you have to choose living with Miss Lizzy or your own freedom."

Margaret slipped the carving in her pocket. "Be careful," she whispered and turned to wait for Miss Lizzy. She didn't want to think of such things.

They hadn't been to town in two weeks, so Lizzy and Margaret set out for a day of shopping. Halfway to town, they noticed a terrible smell, and as they continued, they heard the flies buzzing and saw black vultures circling overhead. A short distance later, they made out the figures of five slaves hanging from the branches of a large tree. They had been badly beaten. The two women crossed over to the other side of the street and covered their noses. Margaret reached in her pocket to feel the carved figure. An emptiness overcame her.

Although sickened by the sight of the men hanging, she couldn't take her eyes away. Marcus. The others. "This not right," she said. "Those men should be alive." She heard Miss Lizzy's voice—it seemed far away.

"Margaret, these men were runaways. This is what happens to runaways. Someone had bought them and fed and cared for them, and they ran away. They needed to be taught a lesson so that others don't do the same. I know it is an ugly scene, Margaret, but you should look at it and learn from it, because the same thing could happen to you if you tried to run away. Think of it as a good lesson for all slaves. Now, come on, let's walk faster. I can't stand the smell."

An explosion of fear slashed through Margaret. Poor Marcus. Lizzy's impatience to get on with her walk, her cold indifference to the five young men whose lives had been cut short. Now she understood. She was a slave, nothing more. For the first time since she'd joined Lizzy and Isaac, she felt alone and afraid. She understood that Lizzy befriended her only as long as Lizzy needed her. And at any moment, Lizzy could change what she wanted.

On their walk into town, Margaret remained silent, her mind burdened with the sight of those five dead men. She remembered her own father being beaten and left to those cruel brothers. How could she have forgotten that? She had a better understanding of what others had told her about freedom. And she wondered whether Lizzy would beat her and hang her if she ran away.

From that day, Margaret tried to keep more distance between her and Lizzy, but the more she pulled back, the more Lizzy pulled Margaret to her. Over time, Lizzy developed a ritualistic lifestyle that sustained her. Each afternoon she closed herself in her bedroom. Sometimes Margaret could hear her crying, sometimes talking to her absent Isaac. When she came out, she was always composed and had Margaret serve tea and join her in small talk. Margaret felt ill at ease pretending to be friends. Often, while they chatted, the image of the hanging would pop into Margaret's mind, forcing her to cringe, forcing her to listen to Lizzy's idle chatter, and to work harder at pretending to be friends.

Lizzy gradually stopped socializing with the townspeople. When speaking with them, she did so in a curt manner. The townspeople, at first sympathetic with Lizzy, began to shun her.

One hot, dusty day while Lizzy and Margaret shopped in town, a group of soldiers rode into town. Lizzy recognized one of the men and ran to him, calling his name.

Removing his hat, he said, "Afternoon, Miss Lizzy. How are you?"

"Why I'm just fine, thank you for asking. Robert, has there been any word of Isaac at all?"

Robert's face fell. He stuttered and finally composed himself. "Miss Lizzy, Isaac was killed over a year ago. Didn't you never get a letter or somebody tell you?"

Lizzy raised her hand to her mouth. "No," she cried. Her legs gave way, and she would have collapsed onto the dusty road had Robert not caught her. He helped her to a sheltered area in front of Rosa's Fine Clothing store and set her on a bench put there for passersby.

"Not Isaac, my beautiful Isaac." She covered her face with her hands and cried.

Robert sat beside her, and when her crying subsided, he told her how sorry he was and how brave Isaac had been. After a few minutes, she composed herself and thanked Robert for his kindness. She assured him she would be fine, essentially dismissing him.

Margaret stood dutifully by watching the scene unfold. When Lizzie beckoned her to come sit beside her, Margaret came and sat and believed anew that Lizzie needed her now more than ever.

From this day forward, Lizzy's life changed, and so, of course, did Margaret's.

Shunned by the townspeople, her husband dead and having no other family, Lizzy clung desperately to Margaret. Perhaps Margaret meant more than companionship; she needed Margaret in order to survive.

"Margaret, come here please," Lizzy said. "I'm going to teach you something that is illegal, and we might both be punished if anyone finds out. Can you keep a secret?"

"Yes, ma'am," said Margaret.

"I'm going to teach you to read and write. People around here won't like that, but that's okay. We won't tell them. But if they should find out, if they should see you read something or write, they might whip you or punish you severely in some other way. Do you understand?"

"Yes, ma'am." Always curious about newspapers and the strange symbols she saw on posters, Margaret was excited and afraid.

"Very well then. We'll start tomorrow. Today, we're going into town. We'll need supplies if I'm going to teach you to read and write."

While Lizzy shopped, Joseph approached Margaret on the sidewalk.

"Hi ya doin', Margaret?" asked Joseph, his eyes cast down. Joseph, shy around females, had a reputation for speaking his mind. He had been chosen by O'Reilly to replace Marcus on his town trips.

"Hi, Joseph," She didn't look directly in his face but rather looked out of the corner of her eye, checking to see that Miss Lizzy wasn't watching her. She liked Joseph. Always polite, ears that stuck out a bit, but he had a nice face. In the middle of their chat, Lizzy came out of the store. She glared at Margaret, eyes flashing, and said in her most demanding voice, "Margaret, stop that this instant. And you, boy, you leave my Margaret alone. I don't want you to ever talk to her again. DO YOU UNDERSTAND ME?"

"Yes'm," said Joseph, his eyes cast down.

"Good, get away from here. Come, Margaret." She pulled Margaret along by her sleeve.

Lizzy hustled along with a stern face and said nothing for the entire first half of their trek home. Then she stopped and faced Margaret. "From now on, Margaret, you are to speak to no one. Do you understand? Furthermore, I just might not be so kind as to let you walk into town with me in the future. Is that clear?"

Margaret, feeling that she was suffocating, said, "Yes, Miss Lizzy." When they resumed, she reached into her pocket and held tight the carving Marcus had given her.

As Lizzy became more unpredictable and demanding, Margaret feared for her own safety. Should she run away? Would they hang her if she tried?

The next day, they went into town again. Margaret saw Joseph with O'Reilly's horse and buggy. She quickly looked away, though she wished with all her heart to walk up to him and engage in a friendly conversation.

Lizzy stopped at the door to the hardware store. She stared hard at Margaret. "Wait here. Remember our little talk yesterday."

"Yes, ma'am."

When she came out of the store a few minutes later, she said with a wry smile, "Well, I guess that will take care of my concerns."

"Ma'am?" said Margaret.

"Never you mind. We all do what we must."

Later that afternoon, a man came to Lizzy's house with lumber and carpenter tools. First, he boarded up Margaret's window, and then he installed a lock on her door that could only be opened from the outside.

After he left, Lizzy called Margaret. "I have made some modifications to your room for your own good. I know I can't always keep these little nigger boys from talking to you, and I know their hormones are doing whatever hormones do. You are getting to be a pretty young lady, and I don't want those boys talking you into something that could get you into trouble. So, this is the surest way of keeping you pure and sweet."

Lizzy smiled at Margaret and put her hand on her shoulder. "You know I only do these things because I care for you. I hope you appreciate me."

From that day on, Lizzy always locked Margaret in her room at night and during the day when she didn't take her to town.

This isn't to say all of Margaret's days were difficult. She progressed very nicely with her reading and writing. Some days, Lizzy spent several hours reading to Margaret. The stories transported Margaret to places she had never dreamed of before. She loved to listen to the adventures and romantic relationships as they developed in the novels. A thirst grew in her to see the world as a free person. She hated the hours of confinement in her room.

Margaret endured the dark nights locked in her room by remembering the prayers and talk of survival she'd heard in South Carolina. She remembered the stories her parents told her at bedtime. She tried to remember the faces of her family and their voices, but they were beginning to fade.

Lizzy always had a small glass of wine with dinner, but now she drank more heavily. It happened slowly. At first, she had Margaret pour her a drink with dinner. Then she had a drink before dinner and again at bedtime. Now, she locked Margaret in her room and had a few more drinks. Sometimes she awoke late the next morning on the couch.

Margaret noticed a pattern to her drinking. She would have too much wine two or sometimes three nights in a row and then resolve not to drink anymore. She sometimes made comments to herself about the evils of drinking too much. But always, by the fourth night, she tipped a glass of wine. Margaret increasingly worried about Lizzy. And about her own safety. Often, after a few drinks, Lizzy talked nonsense. Sometimes she talked angry, then laughed. Her walking became wobbly and difficult.

One day, after Lizzy asked Margaret to pour her a drink, Margaret responded, "Please, Miss Lizzy, don't drink tonight."

"How dare you." Lizzy slammed her hand on the table. "What right do you have to tell me what I can do?" She leaned into Margaret. "No right. That's what. My friends warned me I was too nice to you." She screamed, "Pour me a goddamn glass of wine."

Margaret hurried to pour wine into her glass.

After her third glass, she demanded another.

Margaret poured a little wine into her glass.

Lizzy peered into the glass. "That's not enough to wet my withel. My whitel." Lizzy laughed hysterically.

Margaret poured a bit more, then retreated to a corner where she sat quietly wishing to become invisible for the rest of the evening, fearful of what might come.

"Margaret." Lizzy's eyes were half shut as she swayed on the couch. "I wet you go mogur frenador." She fixed her eyes on Margaret, who hadn't moved.

Margaret had no idea what Lizzy wanted her to do. Lizzy waved her hand at Margaret. "Now! Do it now." She set her head back, resting on the couch, and closed her eyes.

"Yes, Miss Lizzy." Margaret hurried into the kitchen. She glanced around hoping to find something, some kind of clue to help her understand what Lizzy wanted. She stood quietly, shivering with fear. In a few seconds, she heard Lizzy rise from the couch jangling her keys.

"C'mon, Marg'et."

Margaret went into her room. Lizzy closed her into darkness. The lock clicked. Margaret heard Lizzy fall to the floor. "Miss Lizzy. Miss Lizzy, you all right?" She knew, just as in previous nights, there would be no answer.

Lizzy missed the company of men and of Isaac in particular. However, with the war, every eligible man anywhere near her age lived and marched on the battlefields, all in the name of duty and glory. When soldiers came to town, she struck up conversations with them, but so far, no luck in persuading one of them to join her for a steaming hot home-cooked dinner and whatever else might be on her mind. It's not that many men didn't want to take advantage of her offer, it's that they were just passing through and in town for only a few minutes. After a while, Lizzy's desperate state and feeble attempts to find a man became widespread gossip among the soldiers and townspeople. The women of town scorned her.

One evening, feeling more depressed than usual, and working on her fourth glass of wine, she went to her room and opened the trunk where she kept Isaac's belongings. She found what she had been looking for—an object wrapped in a red bandana. It felt heavy in her hand. Her heart beat faster as she contemplated what she might do. She peeled back each layer of cloth until Isaac's pistol lay before her. She ran her fingers over the ridges. She felt the cold, lifeless steel in her fingertips. The gun had a powerful effect on her. At times it made her feel strong, almost omnipotent. But at other times, she felt vulnerable and insecure.

Isaac had taught her how to use the pistol. The curve of the handle, the brilliant silver of the metal, how beautiful. It possessed such power, such danger. Somewhere, in the deep recesses of her mind, a thought formed that this pistol could be her final salvation.

That night, she slept with the pistol cradled to her chest. She slept soundly, comfortably.

Over the next few weeks, she vacillated. She would put the pistol away in the trunk one day. A few days later, she'd retrieve it, fondle it, touch it, feel safe with it.

Margaret trembled in her dark, gloomy room, assailed by the screams penetrating her walls. She heard Lizzy talk to herself as she wandered about the house.

Is she losing her mind?

What if Lizzy dies while I'm locked in my room? Who'll come get me out?

Margaret immersed herself in her reading and writing classes with Lizzy. She learned quickly, and this inspired Lizzy to continue her teaching, even pushing Margaret to learn faster. But the unspoken tension between the two was always present.

On good days, when Margaret finished her after-dinner chores, she stayed up later, visiting with Lizzy or practicing her reading. But when Lizzy locked her in her room immediately after chores, Margaret knew she would head straight for the wine and shortly the crazy talk and screams would begin. Margaret trembled as Lizzy led her to her room. Lately, Lizzy laughed as much as she talked. The laughter frightened Margaret more than the crazy talk.

One day, while she cleaned the house, Margaret slipped a candle and matches in her apron pocket and took them to her room, where she hid them under her mattress. That night, after Lizzy's talking and laughing quieted, Margaret lit the candle. The light comforted her. With the candle beside her, Margaret sat on the floor, back against the wall, arms wrapped around her legs, and chin resting on her knees. She thought of her family. She remembered her mother's kindness and the days when her mother lifted her and carried her after working in the fields all day. She remembered Hector and their games and talks. Mostly she remembered her father, big and strong and proud. What had become of them all? "Tell me a story, Papa," she whispered.

"Which story you wants, little girl?" he would ask.

"Tell me about the time Grandma had no more fear."

"Why I do believes that is your favorite story," he would say. "Well, it happened like this. A long, long time ago…"

Margaret's boldness grew. She always made sure she had a candle and matches at night. Now she pilfered a book, always sure to return it in the morning. She entertained herself by practicing her reading and writing by candlelight. When she came across a word she didn't know, she sounded it out or figured its meaning from the rest of the sentence. She practiced writing the sentences she read by writing on the floor with her finger.

To help her feel closer to her family, Margaret wrote them letters. She kept up a make-believe correspondence with them, which sustained her through these hard times.

Margaret gathered wood for the stove from the rear of the house. Lizzy was relaxing on the front porch reading when she heard a commotion down the street. She stood and shaded her eyes to check on the noise. A large group of slaves walked along the street. Lizzy's first thought was it must be a slave rebellion, one of the greatest fears during the war. But that couldn't be. White men stood nearby talking but not concerned.

The crowd walked down the street towards Lizzy's house. She resisted the urge to dash inside where she felt safe. Her curiosity got the better of her. Lizzy left the security of her front porch and went to her front gate. As the group approached, she called out, "What has happened? Why have you left your masters?"

The crowd laughed. "We ain't got no mo' massas ceptin' ourself," shouted someone. "De war is all over. We is free as you is," shouted another. They all laughed and playfully continued down the street.

Lizzy stood in shock, soaking it all in. Her pulse raced faster. *Margaret! Can't let her leave.*

Lizzy rushed inside. "Margaret! Margaret, come quickly!"

Margaret rushed to her. "Yes, Miss Lizzy, I'm coming."

Lizzy sprinted through the house, almost colliding with Margaret, who rushed in through the back door.

"Come quickly, Margaret. You must get in your room. Quickly now," Lizzy said breathlessly.

"What is the matter, Miss Lizzy?"

"There is danger, Margaret. That is all I can say now." She hurriedly pushed Margaret into her room and locked the door.

That night, Lizzy sat with Isaac's gun in her hand. No one, no one would take Margaret from her. Meanwhile, Margaret sat in her darkened room.

What danger? What's gonna happen to me?

Morning came. Shards of light streaked through spaces in the boarded window. Sounds of those passing along in the street made their way into Margaret's isolated room. But there was not a sound in the house. By the middle of the afternoon, Margaret felt the pangs of hunger and thirst.

Did something happen to Miss Lizzy? Am I stuck in this room forever? Margaret rapped on the door, soft at first and then harder. "Miss Lizzie. Miss Lizzie, are you there? Miss Lizzie? Is anyone out there?"

Lizzie was there, curled up in a chair, gun in hand, very much afraid of what her future might hold. Later that afternoon came a knock at the front door. Lizzy did not answer it. A voice called out, "Miss Lizzy? Margaret? Is anyone home?"

Lizzy peered through a window and saw that slave fellow who had talked to Margaret in town. Here he was, no doubt, thinking he could take her away. Lizzy was having none of this. "Go away! You have no business here! Get off my property right now!" she shouted.

"Ah'm jest wantin' to speak wit' Margaret for a moment," he responded.

Lizzy heard enough. She raised the gun, cocked the hammer. She walked towards the door, her feet heavy, her movements unsteady. She opened her door, pointed the gun at Joseph's head, and said, "She left. Now get out of here, or so help me God, I will kill you."

Joseph, wide-eyed, hands raised, backed off the porch. "Yes'm Ah'm goin' as fast as Ah can."

But Joseph didn't believe Margaret had left. He stayed close by, waiting for his chance to find out for sure. For two days Joseph watched. No one had left the house, and there had been no sign of Margaret. He didn't dare go to the front door again, not with that crazy white woman with the gun. Joseph decided that tonight, he would scout around the outside of the house. He would have to be quiet. He knew if that woman saw him, she would shoot him.

Joseph waited patiently, trying not to raise suspicion. He moved around, talked to other freedmen and women when they passed by, but always kept his eye on the house. At last darkness overtook light. He waited another hour for the streets to clear.

With the street empty, he quickly ducked around to the side of the house. No light or sound came from the house. He thought it strange that the lady would be in there but did not light any candles.

Joseph moved to the window towards the back of the house. The window had been boarded up.

Why would the lady board up a window? he thought. *Is she hiding something? Or is it to keep Margaret from escaping?*

Joseph had to find out.

To hell with the lady with the gun.

Ready to run at the first sign of danger, he rapped on the window, at first lightly and then a bit harder.

Margaret lay on her bed in a weakened state. Earlier that day, she'd panicked. She'd tried calling out with her parched throat for Lizzy. She'd banged on the door. No one answered. The stench of her chamber pot no longer bothered her. Margaret believed she was going to die.

At first, the rapping seemed a dream. Then she heard it again, louder. A distinct rapping. Perhaps Lizzy knocked on her door and would open it any moment to let her out. She waited, but nothing happened. Then more rapping.

How strange, it seems to be coming from my window.

With difficulty, she sat up. "Is someone there?" she said, her voice soft, weakened from her dry throat. She waited. No response. She tried to clear her throat but couldn't.

She moved in slow motion towards the window. She knocked on the window. "Anyone there?" Perhaps her imagination played with her.

Joseph knocked four times, the last louder than he'd intended. No response, so he moved to the corner of the house and peered into the backyard. He was studying the backyard and the layout of the back of the house when he heard a faint knock coming from the boarded window. He paused before rushing to it—what if it were a trap? The woman could be waiting with a gun ready to shoot.

Joseph eased back to the window. He stood to the side of the window, knocked, and jerked his hand back in case she started shooting. He heard someone speak in a faint voice.

Margaret, hopeful that she might be saved, said in her raspy voice, "Who is there?" After what seemed like a long time, she heard a voice. A man's voice.

"Margaret, that you?"

She pressed herself against the window. "Help me."

"Margaret, is that you?" he asked.

"Yes," she said, wondering who would know her name.

"I'm here to help you," he said. "Where is Miss Lizzy?"

"I don't know. I'm locked in my room."

"You gonna be all right. Don't worry."

She heard movement outside. "Don't leave me. Please, don't leave me."

"Lissen to me. I gots to get a crowbar an' a hammer to get these boards off your window. I won't be gone long, you just gots to wait a bit longer. When I comes back, I'm gonna get you free. You gotta believe me, Margaret. I be right back."

Lizzy slept on the floor, her gun in hand. Something, intuition or the whispering in Margaret's room, woke her. She glanced around. Though weakened from too much drink and too little food, she moved cautiously from room to room. Then, from the corner of her eye, she caught a glimpse of a young black man running through her yard.

Margaret!

Someone had come for Margaret. She braced herself along the wall as she made her way to Margaret's room. *Good, the lock is in place.* She went into the next room, where she had a clear view of the hall and, through the window, a view outside of Margaret's room. She sat in the dark and waited.

Joseph had at times worked as an assistant to the blacksmith for his master. The blacksmith lived next door to his shop.

The blacksmith, Ken Rawlings—a large, muscular, gentle man with a full beard, in contrast to the thinning hair on the top of his head—had always treated Joseph fairly. Joseph worked hard, and Ken respected that quality in any man, black or white.

Joseph arrived at the house winded and nervous. Even though the two of them respected each other, for a black person to come knocking on the door of a white person after dark, especially to ask a personal favor, was not common. Joseph knocked anyway.

Ken answered the door. "Joseph. What brings you out this time of night?"

"Good evening, Mr. Rawlings. Ah'm sorry to be botherin' you this time o' night, but Ah gots a problem an' Ah was hopin' to borry your crowbar and a hammer."

"Well of course you can. Is there something I can help you with?"

"Oh no, suh. Ah kin take care o' it jest fine on muh own. But thank you anyhow."

"All right. You know where the lantern is. Take what you need." Ken paused a moment and then said, "Joseph, are you sure everything is all right? You seem worried about something."

"Oh no, suh, everythin' is fine. Thank you, suh. Ah'll bring it back shortly."

Joseph found what he was looking for. He wrapped them in a tarp so as not to arouse suspicion and rushed to get back to Margaret.

Margaret sat on the floor below her window. The man outside, whoever he was, had not responded to her for a long time. He was gone, and with him any hope of rescue. Perhaps it was all her imagination. No one was coming to save her. She cried softly.

Joseph ducked into the yard and made his way to the back of the house. When he reached Margaret's window, he rapped on the boards. "Margaret, Ah'm gonna take these here boards off your window and then you gots to climb out and we gots to run like the devil."

Margaret immediately stopped crying. "All right." She forced herself up from the floor and whispered, "I'm not sure I can run very fast, but I'll do the best I can."

Lizzy heard the knocking and the muffled voices.

Someone's outside. How did I miss seeing him…must have dosed off.

She rose from her perch and went to the door, pressing her ear against it. More whispering. She reached into her pocket for the key, but her pocket was empty. Where had she left it? In her dark house, she would never be able to find it. Lighting a candle was out of the question. Lizzie's determination to keep Margaret strengthened her. She snuck out the front door and peered around the corner. She saw the man prying the boards off.

In the room, Margaret watched a board come off. She felt stronger, and hope began to return. Another board fell to the ground, and Margaret recognized Joseph. Her hands flew to her mouth. "Joseph. You came for me."

He pried off a third board, making enough space for Margaret to climb out. But before she could get out, she saw Lizzy come behind Joseph and put her gun to his head. "NO!" she screamed.

Joseph turned around. "Oh, no." He backed up to the house, his hands raised.

"How dare you try to steal my Margaret."

"In case you haven't heard yet, ma'am, de war is over, an' Margaret don' no longer belong to nobody. Just like the rest of us. We ain't slaves no more."

Infuriated, Lizzy screamed, "Stop! Don't you say that! Margaret is mine and always will be. You can't take her." She thrust the gun in Joseph's face. Joseph closed his eyes.

"Lizzy, don't shoot him," said the man standing behind her. Joseph at once recognized the voice of Ken. He opened his eyes.

"Who are you?" asked Lizzy.

"You know me, Lizzy. I'm Ken, the blacksmith. We've talked many times when you've been in town."

"Why are you here? This is no business of yours."

"I came for my friend, Joseph," he replied. He moved closer to her as they talked.

"Well, your no-good nigger friend is trying to steal from me the only person I got in the whole world," said Lizzy, her voice shaking.

Ken stood next to Lizzy. He grabbed her hand and pointed the gun towards the sky.

"What are you doing?" demanded Lizzy.

"Lizzy, you don't want to hurt anyone. Margaret is a free woman now. She should be allowed to go if she wants."

Tears filled Lizzy's eyes. She stared at Margaret. "No! It's not right!" she yelled, as she jerked her hand, trying to free herself from Ken's iron grasp. She could not budge her hand. She hit him with her other hand but did not faze him. He grabbed that hand as well. Lizzy finally gave in and released her gun. She sighed, and it seemed her life went out of her. She slumped to the ground. Barely audible, Lizzy said, "You want to leave me, don't you, Margaret? After all I have done for you, you're going to leave me, aren't you?"

"Yes, Miss Lizzy," said Margaret, in her raspy voice. In spite of her poor treatment, Margaret's heart went out to her. "You gonna be all right, Miss Lizzy."

"Get out. Get out now."

Ken said, "I'll get Lizzy inside. You two get going."

Joseph helped Margaret out the window. "Thanks, Ken. You saved my life."

Margaret was too weak to walk. Joseph cradled her in his arms and carried her to his mother's shack. His mother had stayed on with her former masters, living in her old slave quarters and working in their house. "I'm too old to be going on the road," she had said. "And besides, if I don't like it here, I can always leave." She chuckled at this thought.

With proper food and care, Margaret regained her strength within a few days. She remained in that cabin, enjoying her freedom and the good companionship. A month after he had rescued Margaret, Joseph announced he had heard of good opportunities for work in Jacksonville, and he had decided to move there. He asked Margaret to go with him. They married a week later in a simple ceremony and left the next day for Jacksonville. Ken, his best man, gave him a few blacksmithing tools.

As they walked out of town, they encountered Lizzy on her way to town. She stopped to stare at them as they approached. Margaret tried not to make eye contact but rather kept walking. But as she passed Lizzy, she had a change of heart. She stopped and faced Lizzy.

For a brief moment, their eyes met. Margaret said, "Goodbye, Miss Lizzy." She and Joseph continued their long trek to Jacksonville.

In Jacksonville, Joseph found a job as a blacksmith's assistant. Margaret did wash and house cleaning for several families. The blacksmith owned a small shack, which he rented to Joseph and Margaret. They lived in this shack, their first home together, for a year. Then they rented a nicer house. Their first child was born six months later.

Margaret gave birth to eight children. Two died in childbirth, but the other six brought Joseph and Margaret great joy. Every night, Margaret told her children stories about their grandparents and the stories she'd heard from her parents. Through her stories, her children came to know and love William and Harriet and Hector.

"Tell us a story, Momma."

"What story you want to hear?"

"The one about when Great-grandma wasn't afraid no more."

"Why, I do believe that is your favorite story. Okay. Once, a long, long time ago…"

Author's Note

rmy Life In A Black Regiment, Thomas Higginson, Enhanced
Media, 2017, First published in 1869

This wonderful and informative book was written by Colonel
Thomas Higginson, the commander of the First South Carolina
Regiment. All chapters relating to the actions of this regiment are
based on his recounting in this volume.

After the war, the commander of the First South Carolina
Regiment (later changed to the Thirty-Third United States Colored
Troops) Colonel Higginson wrote: We who served with the black
troops have this peculiar satisfaction, that, whatever dignity or
sacredness the memories of the war may have to others, they have
more to us...But the peculiar privilege of associating with an outcast race, of training it to defend its rights and to perform its duties,
this was our special meed...We had touched the pivot of the war.
Whether this vast and dusky mass should prove the weakness of
the nation or its strength, must depend in great measure, we knew,
upon our efforts. Till the blacks were armed, there was no guaranty
of their freedom. It was their demeanor under arms that shamed the
nation into recognizing them as men.

The "Planter," a new side-wheel steamer became famous when
it was taken from the Confederate navy on May 12, 1862 and given
to the Union navy by the enslaved Robert Small. His daring escape

earned freedom for himself and the other fifteen men, women, and children on board. (See page 199.)

All of the speeches given by black troops in their training camp were taken from *Army Life In A Black Regiment.*

Quotes of formerly enslaved persons are from: *Voices from Slavery 100 Authentic Slave Narratives* edited by Norman R. Yetman, Dover Publications, Inc., Mineola, New York

An important book of quotes from formerly enslaved people which help us to understand the reality of their lives when enslaved. This is especially important in this time when some are attempting to whitewash the truth of slavery.

The Hidden Wound, Wendell Berry, Counterpoint Press, Berkely, CA

This important little book was written in 1968 and still has meaning for us today. Mr. Berry, a white man, has revealed to us a very personal description of his thoughts and feelings regarding racism and our treatment of people of color in this country.

The hospital where Sally worked: Throughout the Civil War, the Sea Islands were a base of operations for the Union. This was one area where the Union had complete control. As a result, hospitals were established to treat the Union wounded. At least fifteen of the abandoned mansions in Beaufort were converted into hospitals. Initially, hospitals served both black and white, but as more black regiments were formed it became necessary to have segregated hospitals.

Sally wasn't the only one to come to Beaufort to treat the wounded. Many young women from New England came who were enthusiastic to contribute in the war effort. The first general hospital for black soldiers was established in Beaufort on the 12th of April, 1863.

From "Women History Sites."

The photographer Jim Boll was inspired by black photographer James Presley Ball (1825-May 4, 1904) who had a studio and gallery in Cincinnati, Ohio. He was a photographer, abolitionist, and businessman. He used his photography to help expose the atrocities of slavery. Known as one of the finest photographers, he photographed Frederick Douglass, and travelled to Europe where he photographed Queen Victoria and Charles Dickens.

From Jeff Suess of the Cincinnati Enquirer.

Charles Warren, January 2024

Acknowledgements

Judy Kahler of Kahler Media Group, read a very early draft of my novel back in 2005. The novel has taken many twists and turns since that time, but her feedback was valuable in helping me to arrive at where it is today.

Dr. Mike Denham, history professor at Florida Southern College, read an early draft and was helpful in correcting some historical inaccuracies and provided other valuable feedback.

Jean Reynolds, retired professor of English at Polk Community College, renown Shaw scholar, and author of numerous books very generously agreed to read the manuscript and provided me with invaluable suggestions. She spent many hours editing and helping me to understand her recommendations. I appreciate that, along with her suggestions, she always had time to write some encouraging words.

Richard Wilder, President Buffalo Soldiers Florida read the latest draft and offered his encouragement and a number of helpful suggestions. I am grateful that he took the time from his busy life to assist me in this endeavor.

Janet Durden, a friend and skillful builder of websites and marketing took me on as a project and taught me much even as I struggled through the intricacies of the digital and social media world. I am indebted to her knowledge and patience.

Bernie Warren, my lovely and always supporting wife who encourages me and pushes me on to greater heights. Ever so patient, she has read my books more times than anyone should have to and always makes them better with her suggestions.

Maria Gallo, a friend who, in spite of being very busy, thankfully read my manuscript and pointed out glaring errors as well as smaller ones. I am very grateful for her critical eye.

Stephanee Killen, my editor. There were several scenes in the book which I felt uncomfortable with and was unsure of how the characters should respond. Stephanee's comments were always insightful and helpful in resolving the issues at hand. I am impressed with Stephanee's work and appreciate her being quick to respond to my questions.

Pat Smithfield and Clifton Lewis, two friends who were willing to give me some of their valuable time to help me think through difficult character dialog.

I have been extremely fortunate to have such intelligent friends, family, and professionals be so generous with their time. Thank you all.

About the Author

Chuck Warren was born and raised in Jacksonville, Florida when segregation was in full swing. Prior to leaving home at seventeen to attend college, he had no opportunity to meet or interact with people of color, except for one. This was a young black woman who did ironing once every few weeks for his mother when he was a child. In the fifties, when many in the black population protested in the streets for better opportunities, it was an eye-opening moment for him as it burst his naïve bubble that had him believing "equal but separate" was preferred by everyone. Little did he know there was nothing equal about our society in terms of opportunities and resources.

After leaving home he had the opportunity to meet and befriend a number of black persons at his places of work and socially. As he got to know black individuals, he saw them as honest, hardworking, competent members of society, not the bumbling, lazy individuals often portrayed in the entertainment industry. He became aware that business and job opportunities were not available to the black population as they were to the white population. The same was true of housing, education, and other resources that facilitate success and enjoyment. This book was written to honor the history and struggle of persons of color.